To ANICE!
NICE TO MEET YOU!
ENJOY!

Meter of Corruption

A Novel By
Wolf Schimanski

ISBN: 1493741675
ISBN 13: 9781493741670

Library of Congress Control Number: 2013920773
CreateSpace Independent Publishing Platform
North Charleston, South Carolina

Dedications;

To Terri my love, wife, mother, grandmother, editor and bass player. You do it all! To Sandra my terrific daughter, your inspiration and courage motivate me. To my son in law, Richard whose name inspired the nemesis in this novel. To Wild T Toney Springer and his Spirit band for giving us all access to such terrific live music. To all the readers of my first novel who could not wait for the follow-up and to those who will discover my second one, thank you! Again to Images Inter Alia in Perth ON for your assistance with the cover art and of course the fine team at Createspace for making my dreams a reality.

Wolf Schimanski

Reviews of Wolf Schimanski's first novel, "Meter of Deception"

I found "Meter of Deception" to be a fast moving thriller with many twists and turns. The story kept my attention and I found the use of Toronto landmarks and areas quite relatable since I grew up there. I could see this book becoming a great movie!

Ted Yates, Author of the "60's, 70's and 80"s music books"

A real thriller that makes you want to turn the pages faster and faster. Once you start reading this book you won't want to stop until reaching the climax. An excellent read !

John Peaker, Author of "The Wayward Life and Times of a Dipsy Doodle Dandy" and "The Call Wizard".

Hope you set aside a copy of the new one for me, the first book was amazing!

Tammy C.

Along with exotic locations, mysterious and sexy characters with incredible action made this book really enjoyable. I cannot wait for the follow up book!

Therese S.

Chapter 1

Mabel Murtens was excited and apprehensive at the same time. Mabel and her husband Joseph of almost 50 years were frugal and worked hard all their lives to secure a significant nest egg but like so many others in this fragile economy were just not happy with their substantial portfolios performance.

Neither of them had investment experience and had blindly handed over their hard earned monies to their bank via a slick talking Investment Representative whom they were referred to. After years and years of investing, their portfolio was dwindling even below their original deposit and that was grave cause for concern especially since they were now retired from running their modest but successful neighborhood Variety Store business.

As they were self-employed most of their lives, they had no pension plans besides the meager offerings of Canadian pension and old age supplements aside from the money they socked away and received from the sale of their business. The elderly couple was dependent on their fixed income their investments yielded which was in dire jeopardy because their portfolio was way too aggressive for their risk tolerance as well as loaded with poorly performing Equity Funds.

After repeatedly complaining about their situation, today was the day when the bank was sending over a specialist to review their portfolio and hopefully make some much needed adjustments.

Mabel and Joseph had just finished their traditional afternoon coffee and cookies when the intercom to their two bedroom apartment in a fairly decent area of East Toronto buzzed.

"Who is it?" asked Joseph while blowing his nose; he seemed to always be stuffed up these days.

"Your banking rep, I am expected," came the answer.

Joseph buzzed him in while Mabel heated up another cup of coffee for their guest.

After hearing a loud rap on their door, Joseph opened the door to a small, weasely looking man in a black business suit with slicked back hair, a pasty complexion along with sharp looking ferret like teeth.

"Jimmy Rudiger at your service, I am here to make your day!"

Joseph and Mabel looked at each other but being polite showed the weird looking character now in their home where to hang his coat and then to have a seat at the table.

The specialist ignored the elderly couple totally, threw his coat in a corner, left his wet shoes on and lit a cigarette before plunking himself down on the living room easy chair.

"Ah, this is a non smoking apartment. If you need to smoke please go out on the balcony. My wife and I both have asthma and are extremely allergic to cigarette smoke," said Joseph with a concerned look on his face.

Jimmy ignored the request by flicking ashes onto their nice carpet and asking for a beer.

"Young man, you are being awfully rude, we are going to have to ask you to leave immediately and rest assured the bank will hear about this as soon as we can give them a call," admonished Mabel looking very forceful for someone in her mid seventies.

"Sit down and quit flapping your gums, chances are that's all you have left at your age anyway," instructed Jimmy with a dangerous look on his rat like face.

"And bring me that effen beer now or there will be hell to pay," added their downright rude and nasty guest.

Joseph was so shocked he did what he was told while Mabel ran to get the beer.

"Now that's better," said Jimmy after which he took a long pull of the bottle, sucked back another long drag from his cigarette which he blew in the direction of the now visibly upset elderly couple.

"Here is what's going to happen, I'm going to talk and you are going to listen unless you both want to become fish food for that pretty little aquarium you have there. Do I make myself clear?" snarled Jimmy while starting to brandish a formidable knife he produced from his jacket pocket.

"You can't speak to us like that. Leave now or we will call the police," stuttered Joseph getting very red in the face and all of a sudden clutching his chest.

"Joseph, your blood pressure and bad heart!" screamed Mabel.

"Please sit down and I will get you your medicine."

"You better do what your old biddy wife says or else!" instructed their weasely unwelcomed house guest after downing the beer in another large gulp and pointing for another.

After Joseph sat and was given a glass of water with a small white pill, their now very intimidating house guest continued, "I have some documents for you to sign. I am going to explain very little to you except that you are now an ex customer of your current financial institution who were doing nothing for you anyway. After you sign, you will be customers of FinCo and we will take care of your financial affairs from here. Your annuity will be transferred to us as well and we will pay you out the same amount monthly that you are receiving now, lucky you. The funds from the recent sale of your business will also be transferred along with all your other assets, with me so far?"

The elderly couple just looked at each other now visibly shaken and just nodded.

"Good, you are getting with the program which means you'll be around to feed your fish until hubby's ticker fails which will be sooner than later if you give me any grief. Part of the package will be a 1 million dollar insurance policy on each of you with the beneficiaries being a charity very near and dear to our corporate heart. How do you like me so far?"

"Your silence says it all, so let's get busy and start signing. If you contact anyone at all about this such as your pretty little daughter and her family, the police or anybody else, your daughter, grandson and her husband will be eliminated and then we'll come after one of you. Neither one of you want to spend the last years of your life alone. Nod if you understand?"

The elderly couple was still so much in shock all they could do is nod.

It took about half an hour and all the documents were signed. Jimmy gave them a copy of all the forms including some that stated that Joseph and Mabel had done this of their own free will and were not coerced in any way and understood what they had agreed upon.

"Pleasure doing business with you both, here is a FinCo calendar for the both of you and remember what I said. You, your family and friends as of this moment are all under surveillance and we will know immediately if you have talked to anyone about this. Don't get up, I'll just let myself out," and with a swish of his topcoat and a last annoying flick of ashes, Jimmy Rudiger scurried off.

Mabel and Joseph Murtens just sat on the couch holding hands and both looking ghostly pale. They looked at each other and almost simultaneously said, "What in heaven's name are we going to do?"

There was no comparison whatsoever between Heaven and FinCo, that much was already very painfully apparent.

Chapter 2

Angel rolled out of bed around eight thirty a.m. on a glorious winter Saturday morning. Jon-Erik was still sleeping; most likely still dreaming of the crazy sex they had last night. Even though the couple were now almost five years past the insane events that transpired in Toronto that brought deception, murder and extortion to light as well as being hunted by a psychotic Ninja and vicious Drug Kingpin from Argentina, they were still just as crazy about each other if not more so.

They finally had recovered sufficiently and got their personal lives back to normal to celebrate their engagement last night by staying in and ordering their favorite thin crust Pizza as well as downing a magnum of expensive Mumms champagne and ravaging each other the whole night. Jon-Erik and Angel just could not get enough of each other and waited this long until they were both sure their lives were once again on the right track before finally making this commitment to each other.

Jon-Erik had since left the employment of Triple Tech Corporation mainly due to the fact this Company seemed to be in the business of regularly laying off hundreds of highly skilled and productive workers and then hiring new less experienced employees for far less compensation and benefits.

Triple Tech's clients, as a result, got the short end of the stick with hugely decreased service levels because of the large scale downsizings. For the most part, their clients remained with the company due to the huge penalties levied for breach of contract and the higher amount of money other companies charged for similar services.

As a result, the higher level executives that instigated these questionable initiatives looked like geniuses (rather than the dream stealers and family life disrupters that they really were) to their shareholders operating the businesses more efficiently with less overhead. No one knew who was next and Jon-Erik was not going to stick around to find out whether he was part of the next round of cuts especially since his best friend Joey offered him a full partnership into the family furniture business which was flourishing with the addition of more brand names and show room space in the last few years.

Angel and Tina (Joey's lady and Angels best friend) wanting more flexibility in their careers, sold their Boutique in Woodbridge for a good profit and then after a lot of research decided that Productivity Consulting would be lucrative as well as exciting and the two beautiful ladies promptly went into partnership for this challenging new venture.

They decided on a crash online business course that they graduated from within a year's time and then hung out their shingle and A & T Productivity Consulting was born. Tina had suggested T & A and the ladies had a good laugh over that one. A website was set up showing professional photos of the two partners in business attire sitting at their computers, indicating they were both recent BA's in business (wasn't everyone these days?) graduates and were ready to help businesses streamline their operations to become more efficient.

The fact that they were experienced successful business owners in the past helped their credibility as well and some of their old customers provided excellent recommendations.

At first, they got nothing but a few annoying calls from horny businessmen who wanted to meet them in the Entertainment District for a few cocktails and hopefully much more afterwards. The ladies politely declined indicating they were a legitimate business and not an escort service, Angel having to get tough with one so called Day Trader who would not take no for an answer. After indicating he should discuss it more with her fiancée who was a defensive tackle for the Toronto Argonauts and weighed close to 300 pounds, she never heard from him again.

The ladies went to networking meetings in the city as well as in Brampton and Mississauga to exchange business cards and establish new contacts but the only two things that happened were more propositions for sex under the guise of dinner and drinks as well as being constantly barraged with the businesses that the other networkers represented. A waste of time all the way around they thought but felt kind of obligated to continue going especially in the light of the ridiculous annual fees that they had to pay to be part of these groups.

Since nothing was really panning out for them, Angel suggested making some appointments with recruiters who specialized in placing consultants. This was another exercise in futility as these Head Hunters had to answer to so called Account Managers who actually represented the clients that Angel and Tina actually never got to see. What a convoluted system that was; it was a wonder that anyone actually got hired anywhere through this process.

The next step was targeting companies and businesses that hired consultants on a regular basis and calling and asking for an appointment to discuss their current needs and how A & T Productivity Consulting could address their requirements. This line of pursuit worked a bit better as they actually got in front of some hiring directors and managers. Unfortunately for the job seekers, these businesses were all in a process of hiring freezes, downsizing and outsourcing and a good pitch by the ladies on the fact that they could find efficiencies without impacting current staff fell on deaf ears.

These executives seemed to prescribe to only one theory similar to what was going on at Triple Tech, the company Jon-Erik recently left. Trimming and cutting was the way to go without any regard whatsoever on the impact to their hard working employees who found themselves without pay raises for years while the cost of living was creeping steadily upward. What could be worse would be a paltry severance package and the prospect of trying to find a similar position in a nasty and unforgiving economy. Did they not teach them anything else in their expensive MBA programs, the ladies wondered?

After about 6 months of coming up short in their efforts, Angel and Tina were getting concerned as they were now using up funds they had put away from the sale of their business and Jon-Erik and Joey had to carry the brunt of their finances which was difficult since each couple had purchased a home close to each other in the beautiful lakeside neighborhood of Port Credit. Even though the homes were modest bungalows, the area was extremely desirable with the lake, shops, pubs and all amenities in the vicinity similar to the Beaches area in Toronto without the Boardwalk where Jon-Erik had his apartment a few years ago.

This brought the price of homes way up and the couples were stretching their dollars thin trying to handle their mortgages and expenses; one thought was to rent a room out in each home but right now they all valued their privacy too much. Something had to break for them and neither of them had any idea how true that statement would become….and soon.

Chapter 3

FinCo appeared almost out of nowhere, becoming a publicly traded company with a modest per share price of the Toronto Stock Exchange (TSX). But quickly the company became a mover and shaker in the Financial Services Industry consistently expanding their client base. While paying out ever increasing dividends to their shareholders who were initially their own employees and had a more than vested interest as well, increased their market value in leaps and bounds garnering growing interest and participation from other astute investors.

Richard T. Rasmussin was the Chairman, CEO, President and basically Mr. Everything for FinCo. Richard was tall with perpetually tanned skin, longish styled black hair, extremely fit, fast moving and fast talking. When he entered a room he immediately took command and there were no doubts as to who was in charge. He had an official looking MBA (Master of

Business Administration) from the prestigious Harvard School of Business out of Boston which no one dared to challenge and the very rare Chartered Strategic Wealth Professional Designation on the wall behind his desk along with a number of plaques and other awards.

FinCo and Richard were joined at the hip and together quickly rose from obscurity to one of the key players in Finances in the whole province of Ontario, no simple task considering the sizable competition.

Richard had surrounded himself with an extremely capable and well trained staff who executed Richard's motto "*New Business New Business and More New Business*" to the tee. Banks, Trust and Insurance Companies as well as independent Brokerages were losing high net worth clients of all ages to FinCo in record numbers and although there were a few accusations of luring clients under false pretenses, all the I's were always dotted and the T's were crossed. Richard ran a tight ship indeed.

Richard's staff was the brightest and the best talent in the industry, at least on paper. If one really took a close look they would find that these FinCo employees were a bit different than others in their field; very well dressed, trim with a hungry look in their eyes, almost wolfish you could say.

He did not have VP's, directors and managers like other similar organizations, just a close circle consisting of admins who looked after his advisors, advertisers and clerical staff. Christine Hertzog was Richard's personal assistant who was young, strikingly beautiful and no one got to see him unless they went through Christine which was virtually impossible.

Elmo Entwhistle, another key member of that elite group, who was impeccably dressed with well-defined muscles under his designer suit, had cold beady eyes that went along with his bald head. The last member of the elite team, Jimmy Rudiger, had a ferret like appearance and his demeanor was in stark contrast to the other admins. Everyone at FinCo kept a weathered eye on him as there was something noticeably dangerous and sinister about him.

Another work week had begun and Richard had texted his admins the night before to be at a very important meeting at 8 am Monday morning. They were all there at ten minutes before 8, coffee made and their blackberries in ready mode knowing full well not to piss off their boss. Those who did quickly disappeared not to be seen or heard of again.

After a quick rundown on how the company was doing and some future projections, Richard T. got right to the point. "We need to look at how we do things and do them more cost and process effective. With me so far?"

"I do not want to let staff go unless it is absolutely necessary. Unless they are visibly underperforming, I just want to optimize what we are doing today and do it more cost effectively and efficiently," he added looking at each person in the room in turn.

"Any ideas?"

"Make sense boss, who do we need to kill?" offered Jimmy with his rat like teeth gleaming.

"We're not there yet but hold that thought my weasely friend," replied Richard sporting a wicked looking grin of his own.

"How about we bring in a consultant to have a look at our internal processes to review and make suggestions to optimize?" suggested Christine Hertzog.

"And blow more money with negligible returns?" huffed Elmo Entwhistle.

"Hang on a minute. Christine may have something there. Consultants are tax write- offs anyway and it would show corporate good will to re-examine and streamline our operation. Christine, run with this but I make the final decision. And the rest of you, get the staff moving, acquisitions, acquisitions and more acquisitions is what we are after and you know the deal, failure is not an option," instructed Richard with a wave of his hand indicating the meeting was over.

Christine immediately returned to her office and told her staff to narrow it down to the top 5 most interesting Process Improvement Consultants out there and then schedule interviews starting tomorrow.

Results quickly showed that most of the established Consultants had just started or were in the midst of contracts so the choices quickly narrowed down to three that were currently available and had impressive credentials. The first two were older guys whose resumes claimed they had worked and done wonders for IBM, RIM, Microsoft and even the Canadian branch of the Trump organization. The third was an upstart group called A & T Consulting consisting of two good and professional looking ladies eager to prove themselves with their first large assignment.

The two older guys were quickly interviewed and dismissed as they looked and acted more like

Vacuum Cleaner salesmen and research and background checks showed they had padded their resumes significantly to match their large stomachs. So the call quickly went out to A & T Consulting, requesting their presence the next day for a personal interview at FinCo Financial.

Chapter 4

Angel and Tina jumped around like giddy school girls after they received the call and contacted Jon-Erik and Joey who were still at work in the Furniture shop to tell them the exciting news. The guys were very happy for them but Jon-Erik suggested they should check this company out because in his experience, those who are most knowledgeable about a hiring company have an edge on those who do not.

Angel thanked Jon-Erik and told him a bottle of French Champagne would be chilling in the fridge for him tonight along with a smoking hot Angel in a steaming whirlpool tub. Jon-Erik could not wait to get home and Joey also echoed that thought wondering what Tina had in mind for him.

"Jeez, we only have till tomorrow to get ready for the interview. What do we do?" asked Tina mostly depending on Angel to make any of the tougher decisions. Tina was a great sidekick and was very quick and reliable but it was mostly up to Angel to set the direction. That's most likely why their relationship as best friends and business partners worked so well.

"Internet, silly. It should have all the info we need," replied Angel while booting up her laptop. The FinCo.com website was found very quickly giving information as to what their company mission statement was, whom they were affiliated with, where they were located, etc. etc. As fat as clients went, the ladies did not expect to find specific information about the people FinCo dealt with due to confidentiality requirements.

They did, however, find ample testimonials from various seemingly very happy customers raving about how the values of their portfolios increased substantially, how the service was superior to other organizations as well as the fact they can now sleep well at night and do not care what the volatile Stock Market is doing; in short that they were well taken care of.

And these glowing endorsements were notarized by obviously untraceable handles such as; *John T, Mandy J, Vito C, Colton B and Trinity H* amongst many others.

"I guess people with designer names have designer portfolios," chucked Tina.

"Yes, it's now fashionable to name your children unique names. Remember Moon Unit Zappa and Chastity *now Chas* Bono? I can't help thinking these kids must have had a tough time of it with those names regardless of how much money their parents had," reflected Angel.

"Our first boy will be named Jon and if it's a girl Sandra. Jon-Erik and I want them to grow up as normal as possible in this weird world we live in. Ah, who I am to talk, with me being called Angel?"

"You could always go back to Clarisse your real name but somehow Angel suits you better. You'll always be an Angel to all of us," said Tina seeing a happy smile coming from her best friend and partner.

"Okay, so we know FinCo has come from relative obscurity to become the financial giant it is today, their motto is expansion and superior service and results and their president and CEO is someone name Richard T. Rasmussin. Let's see what we can find out about Richard," said Angel while typing his name into the Google search engine.

Nothing besides what they already knew about Richard showed up. The ladies tried Facebook and Twitter and a few other search engines and found nothing else at all on this senior executive which they both found very strange. Normally you can follow a history of the movers and shakers of fortune 500 companies but as far as Richard T. Rasmussin went….nothing.

"Let's try just Rasmussin," suggested Tina

Some sort of US government public opinion polls as well as some businesses and individuals with different first names popped up but nothing relating back to Richard T.

"Well, it looks like this individual values his privacy. Don't we all?" surmised Angel.

"Yes but we need to be careful here just the same. I'm kind of getting that spooky feeling back I have not had now for a few years since the Ninja incident," said Tina while hugging herself as if it was cold.

"I hear you, it's probably nothing but if we have learned anything it's that nothing is as it seems. Something none of us should forget after what we went through," said Angel looking a bit pensive herself.

"Well, when in doubt, a glass of white wine along with some cheese and crackers always works for me. I'll have them ready in a jiffy," replied Tina before heading to the kitchen.

What a sweetheart thought Angel to herself but continued to click the mouse and keyboard keys trying to find anything else about Richard T. Rasmussin or his company FinCo. But a wine break was always welcome.

Chapter 5

Jon-Erik and Joey had just helped one of the floor staff receive and put away a new shipment of Lazy Boy couches and chairs which would replace the current floor models as soon as they were sold. This was one of the fastest moving and most popular brands they retailed and the guys themselves used this furniture at their own homes... at a substantial discount of course.

It was now late afternoon and since it was a weekday, the two friends began to prepare the store for closing and were thinking of what their super hot fiancées had in store for them. Their thoughts were interrupted by a character right out of the movie *Sin City with Bruce Willis, Mickey Rourke and that super hot actress Jessica Alba* standing in front of them whom neither had noticed coming into their store, but that could be blamed on their pre-occupied thoughts... or maybe not?

"Can we help you, we are just in the process of closing but are always glad to help a new customer," said Joey not remembering that he had ever seen this individual before.

The guy standing in front of them was about 5 foot 8, looked to weigh around 260 pounds with solid muscle under his light designer suit and topcoat. He wore a stylish hat with a feather in it covering his bald pate under which sat two sinister looking beady eyes, a bulbous slightly red and veined nose topped off with a small scary looking mouth with large protruding teeth.

Jon-Erik stood by watching and decided to let Joey handle this since it was his family business but he was there to back his best friend and partner up if required.

"Elmo Entwhistle at your service," said their hulky visitor extending his ham hock fist and clamping Joey's hand in his.

Joey had to use every ounce of his strength and willpower to stop himself from screaming as this muscle bound idiot almost crushed the life out of his poor hand. Joey broke into a cold sweat, finally extracted what was left of his hand, shook it to try to get some feeling back and replied," Quite a grip you have there Elmo. You obviously did not read the sign on the door where you came in that plainly stated *No Peddlers, Agents or Solicitors allowed on these Premises. No Exceptions!*"

"Oh yeah, I read it but since I am neither of them I ignored it and came right in. I'd just like to have a little chat and make you a proposition that you just can't ignore or refuse," replied the thuggish character looking extremely pleased with his answer.

"Okay, fun is fun fella, but my partner and I are extremely busy and although you may have something interesting to discuss, we have no time to hear it right now. Give us a call and make an appointment and we'll see if we can fit you in sometime down the road," said Joey pointing to the door.

"You and that surfer dude behind you are going to kick me out of here? I think not," answered Elmo now looking very menacing.

What happened next really surprised Jon-Erik as Joey got right into the face of this hood and stated in no uncertain terms that the Agricola family had connections that their uninvited guest would not be interested in getting involved with if you got his drift and that he should leave now while he still could and that the business was also well connected with the local police.

"You guys are a riot and really think you are tough. No problem, I'll leave but you can bet your next delivery when I do come back, and I will, you will listen to what I have to say or be very very sorry. That is not a threat, it's a promise."

"I have left my card; call me if you change your mind in the meantime. It will avoid a lot of problems," added Elmo before tipping his hat and quietly leaving the store.

"Can you believe the gall of this guy?" exclaimed Joey while looking at the card.

Elmo Entwhistle Financial Consultant with a cell number is all the card had on it. No company name or address or anything else to check back on.

"That was super weird. If I did not know better, I would think this guy was trying to muscle in on our business. He obviously does not know or care about how well your family is connected in the circles around Woodbridge," indicated Jon-Erik with a worried look on his face.

"Don't worry buddy, I'll have cousin Guido check this guy out so we know what we are dealing with if he ever shows up again. I doubt he will though, we stood up to him pretty well," replied Joey.

"Maybe we should give Rollie a call to be on the safe side. He is in a private practice now and may want a break from finding rich old ladies' lost designer poodles or chasing down cheating spouses," chortled Jon-Erik.

"Sounds like a plan, my family won't be as nice, give him a call. We haven't touched base for a while anyway, always great to get together with Rollie," replied Joey.

Jon-Erik picked up the counter phone and dialed and the call was picked up on the fourth ring.

"Sampson Investigations, Rollie speaking."

"Rollie, this is Jon-Erik. How are things in the private dick business?"

"Well, it's taking some time to get established but I keep busy enough. How are things going with the four of you, staying out of trouble?" asked the still portly and now slightly graying former police now private Detective.

"Interesting you should ask that, things have been well and quiet for some time until just a few minutes ago. We'd like to talk to you in person if possible. Do you have time to stop by our place tonight? It's been a while anyway and we have some Heineken's in the fridge," said Jon-Erik.

"Twist my arm, why don't you, Okay, how does around nine sound? I have a few things to wrap up first," Rollie replied.

"Great we'll see you then and fill you in," said Jon-Erik ending the conversation and then making a quick call to Angel to let her know Rollie, Joey and Tina were coming by tonight.

"Jeez, Tina and I have a busy day tomorrow with that important interview at FinCo but it is in the early afternoon so there's always time for friends. Tina and I will have some snacks ready. Anything you want to share with me as to why Rollie is coming by tonight?" asked Angel with a bit of a suspicious tone in her voice.

"Joey and I will get into it tonight after Rollie shows up. We were sort of threatened by a muscle bound oaf who came into the store wanting us to listen to his pitch. When we told him we were not interested, he tried to intimidate us with coming back and things would not go as nice. Don't worry, we're fine, we got rid of him and hope he does not come back if he knows what's good for him, but it doesn't hurt to talk to Rollie and we have not seen him in a while anyway so it's good to catch up," answered Jon-Erik as he knew he could not keep anything from Angel.

"You guys be careful and see you soon," Angel replied in a worried tone Jon-Erik had not heard in some time. Those winds of change were at it again.

After Joey and Jon-Erik had completed their store closing procedures and locked up, they went out to Joey's late modeled Chevy Impala sedan to notice the front end seemed a lot lower than the back end.

Sure enough when they entered the car and turned the ignition on, the front tire sensor indicated that both front tires were flatter than pancakes.

"Shit, I can't even use the spare since its both front tires that are down. Oh well, we're going to have to use the truck and get my car fixed in the morning. I wonder if that Entwhistle character had anything to do with this." Joey snarled.

"No way of knowing but I do believe in coincidence and your tires were fine before that character showed up," replied Jon-Erik while having a closer look at the tires and seeing noticeable slash marks on the sides of both tires.

"Either him or some punk kids had fun at our expense. If it was him, he is sending us a clear message and trying to piss us off," offered Joey.

"Well he has succeeded, let's see what Rollie has to say," said Jon-Erik while Joey checked out the truck. After giving the thumbs up sign, they both jumped in and headed towards the 407 which they took to Mississauga Rd. and then south to the Lakeshore not taking any notice of the dark panel van that followed a safe distance behind.

Chapter 6

It was like a homecoming of sorts. First Tina showed up at Jon-Erik and Angel's with Mindy in tow and the ladies got busy in the kitchen putting some frozen bits and bites in the oven which of course Mindy, the large Kangal dog that Joey and Tina had permanently borrowed from Joey's cousin Guido, had to sample as well.

In no time flat Jon-Erik and Joey came through the door with Joey looking noticeably more pissed off than Jon-Erik since after all his car had been vandalized. Jon-Erik was about six foot tall with longish blond hair, piercing blue eyes, perpetually tanned skin, with a great physique dressed in a pair of well fitted Parasuco jeans, a ROCK ON Tee shirt and Ski Jacket.

Joey was slightly smaller with short cut jet black hair, fast moving brown eyes, a wiry but strong frame and wore his customary leather jacket and cowboy boots regardless of the weather. Mindy was at her full adult weight of 125 pounds, the males becoming much larger and heavier and was a terrific companion and guard dog as the breed tends to be. She was a real deterrent to anyone wishing Tina or Joey any harm as she proved in the bizarre events of a number of years ago.

Jon-Erik and Joey each gave a kiss to Angel and Tina, respectively and went to wash up and then sat down to have a well-deserved Heineken and relay the events of earlier that evening at the furniture store.

"Weird story. We have been living typically normal for the past number of years and then something like this happens out of the blue?" observed Angel.

"Be careful of your temper Joey. We have been talking of starting a family and I couldn't bear it if something happened to you," added Tina.

"No worries my beauties. That's why we called Rollie in to get his input. He'll know what to do otherwise we turn things over to Joey's family and we'd all rather avoid that if you know what I mean," Jon-Erik said with a chuckle.

"Maybe if we would have gotten my family involved a number of years ago, we would have all been better off," Joey replied looking pensive.

"Or maybe not," said Tina causing everyone to laugh and making everyone feel much better.

In no time flat a knock on the door brought Mindy to full attention but she did not growl but wagged her tail happily. Private Detective Rolland "Rollie" Sampson was at the door. Jon-Erik opened the door and let the stocky and graying smaller man in but there was no mistaking that Rollie was not one to mess with by his firm handshake and steely demeanor.

The group happily chatted for a few minutes, catching up on things over Heinekens and all sorts of scrumptious hors d'oeuvres which everyone enjoyed as it was getting late and no one had had dinner yet.

"So you guys had mentioned something happened at the furniture store earlier this evening?" asked Rollie.

Joey recapped the story again for everyone and everyone including Rollie just sat quietly sipping on their beer, munching on an occasional snack and listening intently, when all hell broke loose.

The front window of Jon-Erik and Angel's home which faced the street made a cracking noise which caused Rollie to react instantaneously and push Tina down, a bullet hole lodged in the couch where she sat a micro second before.

"Everyone down now!" screamed Rollie as everyone hit the carpet at the same time and more bullet holes replaced where the group of friends had just sat. Joey covered Mindy's body trying to keep her down but she freed herself and sprang at the door growling furiously.

As quickly as the trouble started it ended; nothing but silence once again. Rollie flew to the door as fast as his little legs could carry him, opened the door and shoulder-rolled onto the front lawn coming up in shooting stance with his 22 revolver ready to blast but all he saw was the tail end of a dark van peeling around the corner.

The rest of the shocked group, including the dog, now stood outside looking at a cold and still night as if nothing had happened.

Rollie got on the phone immediately and called the main switchboard of the Police Precinct where he used to work and asked to page a Detective Cragan that he knew just before he resigned his post there. Within five minutes his cell phone rang and Rollie explained the situation to the officer on the other end of the call. Cragan indicated he was off duty but would radio the call in and meet them within half an hour at Jon-Erik's.

Rollie explained it was best to file a police report but he would be glad to handle this case privately and work co-operatively with the police. Within no time at all Detective Cragan, a tall man with a sharp nose and features arrived along with a squad car with two more officers from the station.

Rollie did most of the talking. The group of friends answered questions when asked.

"You were all very fortunate this evening and lucky Rollie was with you," said Detective Cragan.

"As I understand it Rollie will provide you private support but I'll remind you to share all information with us and take no un-necessary risks. We will send a patrol car to check on the furniture store a few times a day. We will also send over a police artist tomorrow so we can get an idea of what this guy Entwhistle looks like but his name is most likely an alias," Cragan added.

"Thanks and much appreciated. Have a good rest of the evening and be assured you will hear from me if something else develops," said Rollie shaking Cragan and the other officer's hand.

"No hero stuff, Rollie, we have heard of your reputation," said Cragan before getting back in his car and driving off, the squad car right behind him.

"Can Cragan be trusted?" asked Angel.

"No idea. As far as I know, all the corruption from years ago has been rooted out but there are new people in charge now and I know very little about them. Cragan was someone I worked with briefly who seemed like a stand-up guy but you never know where one's bread is buttered," Rollie answered.

Chapter 7

A sleek black late modeled limousine with tinted windows and fully bullet proof windows was cruising through the now almost deserted streets of Toronto. The late night partiers had almost all disappeared getting ready for another boring day at the office so they could do it all over again the next night. It was eerily quiet as the limo pulled onto the Bridle Path entering one of, if not, the most prestigious residential area in the whole city.

The homes were ultra large, lavishly designed, sitting on huge lots with tennis courts, pools, immaculately landscaped although the grounds were very seldom utilized in the winter. These homes were also empty as most of the owners had headed south to the Hamptons, South Beach Miami and in some cases their own piece of paradise on some secluded and highly exclusive Caribbean Island to wait out the winter; yachting, attending black tie events and supporting their favorite charities and philanthropic events for those much needed tax write offs to offset their strategically understated incomes.

The inhabitants of number 77, however, had unfortunately for them, not gone south as yet needing to wrap up some business transactions before jumping on their private plane and heading down to their secluded villa in Belize Central America to restore their pale bodies and dark souls.

Irving Morgenstein was an investment banker who had, in his later years, gone into private practice and craftily bilked his unfortunate clients out of millions of dollars. He had done it in such a subtle way that most of them still did not know what was going on. Most of the losses they incurred were blamed on the declining economy and fickle stock market. Their portfolios were so large but as long as they received their dividends faithfully, a few hundred thousand were hard to track.

That money added up and made Irving the self-made man he was today and his wife Ida, well, he only kept her around for appearances. His tastes were more of the underage girl or boy variety, not surprisingly. The problem was that Irving and Ida were approached by FinCo to reallocate their ill-gotten gains under their management and had flatly refused indicating they were just fine the way they were.

Most acquisitions like these were done by Richard T. Rasmussin's henchmen but this one was special and Richard decided to handle it personally. After all, what type of example would he set if he could not walk the talk himself and once in a while a little field work was just what the doctor ordered.

The limo ran silent as a ghost pulled up to the front gate of the Morgenstein home just after 3:00 am. The window rolled down and a thin laser beam sliced through the crisp snowy air pointing straight at its target, the security lock on the gate. Normally the gate could only be opened via remote or from within the house but this sophisticated laser device mimicked either and opened the gate silently.

Richard was all dressed in black from head to toe and equipped with special grip gloves and runners. He had a belt strapped under his ultra-light but warm black jacket containing a pistol with silencer, a rope with grappling hook and a few other ice pick like utensils. You could never be prepared enough according to Richard's estimation.

He walked right through the now open gate which closed immediately after he came through it. The house's exterior was all in white looking very low and sleek architecturally from the street. The main entrance was at the back of the lavish home, all the better for Richard as he would not be seen and he very much doubted anyone would pay attention to a black limo parked in front of the entrance at this time of night. Even the business owners and high priced executives, who lived in this neighborhood and who had not escaped for the winter, would not be getting up for at least another hour to start another day in the pursuit of becoming even richer, something he could very well identify with.

Richard knew this home would have the highest priced and most sophisticated security system money could buy but he also knew there was always a way around everything. No security cameras on the grounds that he could see, they must trust their house security greatly. Their mistake.

After he made his way to the back entrance, he noticed another structure that looked like a guest house about 200 yards behind the main house. Most likely the servant's quarters where the servants, chances were, would be fast asleep.

Richard planned to leave them that way unless they happened to get in his way but the lights were all out in the servant's quarters, luckily for them.

He went around to one side of the house that had a huge white brick chimney snaking up to the top of the roof, expertly swung the rope whose hook caught the wide opening and held fast. Richard was up on the roof in no time flat blending right in with the shingles. The chimney opening was large enough at the top and it took a few seconds to dislodge the cap and flash a thin but effective flashlight beam down the chute.

It looked as if the chimney had not been used for some time, *no little rich kids for Santa to visit,* Richard chuckled and the hole looked plenty large enough to lower himself down. He quickly re-secured the rope hook and scampered down the dusty opening until he hit the bottom. The fireplace was wide open not even having the traditional grille to deal with, all the better for him knowing full well that the security system would not encompass the chimney, as after all, who besides Santa would ever try a stunt like this?

Richard was silent as a ghost as he crept around the large home, no indication dogs or other guards were on the premises. This was a huge bungalow like structure and the bedrooms were adjacent to the huge living, dining room and kitchen separated by a long hallway.

His keen hearing picked up snoring from the second bedroom and more quiet breathing from the bedroom across the hall as well. *Irving is in the large bedroom and the Missus must be in the one across the hall* ascertained Richard.

He silently opened the door to Ida's bedroom as she slept peacefully curled up to one side with a black night mask covering her eyes. *The better for her not see what was going to happen next.* The jab of the needle that injected air into the main vein in her neck was so quick and painless the poor unfortunate socialite never felt the air bubble that entered her blood stream killing her instantly once it hit her heart.

Richard quickly checked her vitals, felt no pulse and heard no breathing and knew Ida would no longer be a problem. Onward and upward.

He opened the door to Irving's bedroom just as silently, slipped ultra-strong twist ties around his hands and feet and a piece of duct tape on his mouth. Chances are no one would hear him screaming but why take the chance?

The trussed up chubby older man woke up sputtering and straining against his bonds to no avail.

"Hello Irving, hell of a way to wake up?"

"Haruuumph," is all Irving could muster in response.

"Here is the way we are going to do this, I talk, you don't. Understand?"

"Uhhhhhhhhnnnnnn," was all that came back.

"Nod if you understand," directed Richard.

Irving nodded with his eyes looking huge from sheer terror.

"Good. First smart thing you have done since you refused to do business with us but we are giving you one more chance to make amends. With me so far?" asked Richard.

All the trussed up captive could do was once again nod and grunt quietly under his gag.

"Excellent and I just happen to have the paperwork with me to rectify your earlier misjudgment." Richard pulled out a plastic enclosed folder from beneath his black jacket.

"Very simple, you either sign where the X's are and stay alive or you don't sign and you don't live. Still with me?" Richard probed.

Irving Morgenstein nodded and started making guttural noises to indicate he wanted to have the tape on his mouth removed so he could talk.

Richard got the message but indicated that if he tried to scream, he would be killed immediately reinforced by the silenced revolver now in his hand. Again Irving nodded and Richard removed the tape taking some of Irving's facial hair with it.

"Could I have a glass of water?" Irving gasped.

"Who do you think I am, your butler who is hopefully for his own good still asleep next door? Get on with it, I am on a tight schedule," replied Richard looking annoyed under his dark cap and sunglasses.

"I do not sign anything without my lawyer present and he is out of town on business. Now untie me and we'll forget this whole thing. I have friends in high places and you would not want to get to know them," sputtered the tied up financier.

"Wrong answer and your time is up. You win some and you lose some but I win more than I lose," answered Richard while restoring the tape to Irving's mouth.

He quickly placed the silenced revolver to the helpless man's temple and fired two quick bursts into his brain killing him instantly. He then removed the tape from the deceased's mouth and wiped it down with a wet cloth from the lavish ensuite bathroom.

Next he removed the ties from his hands and feet rubbing them to remove any sign the dead man had been restrained in any way. He had left no fingerprints since he wore gloves, so nothing to wipe down. He pocketed the ties and tape and left the bedroom as quietly and quickly as he entered and checked his watch. 3:45 am. Okay, he had a few minutes left before his time was up to leave, not wanting to have to kill the servants, but he would do what had to be done.

A quick check on Irving's private study and sure enough, the safe was behind an oil painting of Whistler's Mother, undoubtedly a copy since the original was locked away in some Parisian Museum to his recollection.

Richard quickly attached a small package to the safe, lit the small fuse and after a muffled poof, opened the safe and quickly looked through the contents. Inventory revealed wills, a number of sizeable security certificates which were useless to him since they were in either Irving or his wife's name, a few expensive Tag Heuer and Rolex watches and at least half a million dollars all conveniently in twenty dollar donations which would be virtually untraceable.

Richard pulled out a satchel out of his pocket quickly placed the watches and cash into it, sealed it and strapped it on his back and then closed the safe and put the painting back in place. *He may as well make it look like a professional robbery; the police will never figure this one out as he will leave no trace behind. And why not come away with something, a bit more cash and jewelry is always welcome* he thought to himself as silently pulling himself back up the chimney, reattached the rope to the outside of the house and slithered quietly back down the side and then retrieving the rope and hook.

Final time check, 3:57 am. He was cutting it close. He looked over at the servants' quarters, still no sign of life but he knew there would be soon. Last step was to retrace his steps back to the gate backwards while erasing his tracks with a pine branch he snapped off from the underbrush of a large tree beside the house.

Once he was back to the gate, he opened it again with his laser pointer, seeing it close behind him once he cleared. Next he got into the limo and drove it away from the gate, parking it on the street after having a quick look around. *No movement yet in the pitch black night.*

He went back out and removed all footprints and tire tracks from the still light falling snow with the pine branch, jumped back in his limo and drove slowly out of the affluent area. He did not accomplish what he wanted but he made the best of it. This was just another night for Richard T. Rasmussin, unfortunately the last night for the Morgensteins.

Chapter 8

The Morgenstein's butler, maid and cook arose around 4:30 am the next morning and were at their posts as usual by 5:00 am sharp with a fresh copy of the Globe and Star papers for Irving and Ida, respectively. The cook began to get the customary breakfast of perfectly timed soft boiled eggs, freshly baked bagels and lox along with freshly squeezed orange juice and Columbian coffee, most likely ground by Juan Baldez himself, knowing these two wealthy perfectionists.

The butler set the lavish breakfast table that was so long he wondered how the two millionaires could actually converse with each other. *Maybe they use their Iphones,* he chuckled to himself.

The maid stood by ready to change sheets, make up beds and thoroughly clean the bedrooms once the master and mistress arose and come down for breakfast which was on the clock, 6:00 am sharp.

Except for this morning, as it was now 6:15 am and still not a sign of them arriving for their usual breakfast. William the butler was dispatched upstairs to let the obviously sleeping-in couple know that their breakfast, even under the heated plates, were getting cold. He quietly knocked on Irving's bedroom door, no answer. He repeated the knock, this time a little more forcefully, still nothing.

After he called out to his employer and still heard nothing, he knocked again and then entered the bedroom. It looked as if Irving was sleeping in his king size memory foam poster bed until the butler came closer and noticed all the red around the pillow area.

"My God!" exclaimed William knowing enough not to touch anything and ran screaming out of the room.

"Call 911, it looks like Mr. Morgenstein has been seriously hurt or could be dead!" screamed the upset servant.

"Mary, go up and check on Mrs. Morgenstein, she has not come out of her room either and do not touch anything in the room, this place may become a crime scene."

Mary the maid told Otis the Cook what was going on, called 911 while running upstairs to Ida's bedroom. After repeatedly knocking on the door and getting no answer while speaking to the dispatcher on her cell, she entered the bedroom and saw Ida Morgenstein laying there not moving with no obvious signs of trauma.

The 911 dispatcher asked the now very distraught maid to check for a pulse. There was none. The dispatcher said that police and ambulance were on their way and that the servants should remain on site until they were interviewed by police.

The three shocked servants sat together in the spacious living room too distraught to say anything when they heard the scream of sirens, saw the pulsing colored lights from the police cruisers and even the piercing wail of a fire engine.

What happened next was like a blur. Three burly fireman burst in and after being reassured by William there was no smoke or fire on the premises, the firemen took a backseat to the swarm of plain clothes and uniformed officers now flocking the premises.

The two plainclothes officers who looked like detectives ran upstairs and quickly ascertained they were in a crime scene after seeing the very shot and dead Irving Morgenstein.

Instructions were shouted out to lock down the scene and no one was to leave the building besides the firemen who were no longer needed. Another officer called for the forensics team to be dispatched immediately while the ambulance attendants verified that both Morgensteins were dead, Irving by gunshot wounds to the head, Ida by unknown causes. The coroner was also on route to examine each body to try to make a determination of cause of death. In the meantime, the crime scene techs arrived and began their investigations to find and bag as much evidence as they could come up with.

For now, Otis the cook, Mary the maid and William the butler were separately interviewed and asked to step through the events of the early morning as they saw it. Their stories matched almost description to description, the detectives had no choice to release them and indicating that they needed to gather their things and leave the property immediately under the watchful eye of two uniformed officers and not to leave town as they would certainly be called back for additional questioning.

The crime scene investigators went through the place for hours and came up with nothing concrete other than the two elderly residents were killed and nothing substantial on Ida until the detailed autopsy was performed tomorrow. There was no motive so far and nothing looked disturbed first glance but possibly the Morgensteins had a safe but that had not been ascertained as yet. However this was done, it was done extremely professional, maybe even a mob hit. The research, paperwork and media scrutiny on this one would be huge and would be a night-mare for the already under resourced Toronto Police Department. A tough day for all involved, especially Irving and Ida.

Chapter 9

After Rollie Sampson and the stunned group of four had finished with the police, Jon-Erik and Angel decided to bed down in Joey and Tina's guest bedroom just in case their unknown assailants had any more surprises up their sleeves for the rest of the evening.

The police agreed to send a patrol around every hour or so but the group was taking no chances since the assailants obviously knew where Jon-Erik and Angel lived. Rollie got clearance from detective Cragan that he could open his own investigation as long as he kept the police in the loop and Rollie had every intention to begin in the morning after some much needed rest.

The tired team of four finally made it to Joey and Tina's house a few streets away after making sure they were not followed having become good at covering their tracks after what happened to them in the past.

"Well here we go again. Five years in peace and now this!" shouted out Tina once they had settled down for a nightcap.

"This for sure has something to do with that muscle bound oaf that came to see us the other day at the furniture store," added Joey

"We have learned a lot from what we went through and we'll be fine if we stick together," said Jon-Erik, his beach boy good looks turning grim and hardened.

"Right now, let's turn in. It is almost 3 am, Tina and I have an important interview with FinCo tomorrow afternoon and you two have a furniture business to run. Come on lover boy and I'll show you my special tuck-in technique," said Angel huskily.

Jon-Erik was up the stairs before she could finish her sentence but he was not the only one. As Angel and Jon-Erik closed the door to their room and fell onto the bed, a dark and menacing shape began to materialize right beside the window. Angel instinctively pushed Jon-Erik right off the bed to the floor and screamed at him, "Stay there and do not move!"

She then quietly sat on the bed cross legged in the Lotus position with her eyes focused on the spot where now a large all in black dressed man stood with his huge arms folded across his chest. He wore a black cap, had piercing almost yellow translucent eyes, a broad nose with a pearly white set of teeth, a gold cap on a large tooth setting a sinister contrast.

"It has been a while and you have been well," spoke the executioner slowly with his thick Russian accent. "And you have learned and become a better martial artist and person since we last met."

Jon-Erik knew not to move a muscle but was ready to spring in defense of the love of his life if needed.

"Tell your lover there he has nothing to fear from me unless he moves in any way against me," growled the Ninja as if sensing Jon-Erik's thoughts. Perhaps he was.

"Honey, please stay there and do not move," implored Angel.

Jon-Erik complied and listened from his spot on the floor. Wise decision.

"So, it looks as if once again the four of you and that pudgy little detective friend of yours have run into a problem. The good news is, you do not have me pursuing you. The bad news is, those after you now are professional and absolutely ruthless, "said the monster.

"Do you know who they are?" asked Angel with a very even tone.

"No, but I will make it my mission to find out and when I do, things will not go well for them. I have been plying my trade abroad but have always vowed to keep you safe and just like I served my master Boris and avenged his death, I never break a vow.

This you know."

"Yes, and I suppose there is nothing I can do to change your mind?" said Angel.

"You suppose correctly. I will be watching to ensure no further harm comes to you and your friends and be happy that large dog downstairs is sleeping. I do not wish to harm it but will if I have to as you also know. Until we meet again."

And with a swishing sound and a flip of the open bedroom window curtain, the apparition disappeared. Angel told Jon-Erik to come out, everything was safe once again.

"He's back," whispered Jon-Erik holding Angel as tight as he could.

"Even though he was away, I do not ever think he was far. Sometimes, I would get that funny feeling I was being watched but never saw anything. I'm sure it was him," replied Angel while snuggling herself tighter against Jon-Erik.

"Let's talk about this further tomorrow. Right now, I want to do nothing else but make love to the woman of my life and dreams," answered Jon-Erik quietly.

"Oh, don't worry, you will be," whispered Angel with her lips on top of his, her tongue running circles around his mouth. With her left hand she found his hardness and guided it gently into the now very moist center of her being; the two forgetting their troubles for the next hour while melting into each other deeper and deeper until finally sleep overtook them both.

Chapter 10

The next morning, Jon-Erik and Joey took off early back to the furniture store to have Joey's car repaired and open the business, keeping a wary eye out for unwanted followers. Angel and Tina slept in and then took Mindy out for a jog along the lakeshore. It was a cold, crisp sunny day and the ladies and the large dog enjoyed the exercise.

After the run, Angel headed back to her home to shower and get accessorized for the big interview in the city at 2 pm this afternoon. Tina did the same and would pop over as soon as she was ready so they could take Angel's new Chevrolet Cruze jet black roadster into the city. Angel took a look around outside as she dead bolted her front door shut seeing nothing suspicious but sensing the Shadow was close by and thinking to herself that this was not a bad thing. Anyone that ever crossed Mikhail always got the short end of the stick or any other pointed object for that matter.

Tina was at the door a scant hour later looking fabulous in a beige jacket, white blouse, a subtle gold necklace with a matching beige skirt bordering on exciting. Her dark hair was pulled tight to her head accentuated by a long, lustrous ponytail. High, sexy winter boots completed the killer ensemble.

"Wow, you look good enough to eat," purred Angel getting a sexy kiss from her BFF as a thank you.

Angel's long beautiful blond hair was straightened and her makeup was subtle but very enticing showcasing her large cat like greenish blue eyes. A made to measure black pantsuit along with light green high heels finished her stunning look.

"I'd rather have a few glasses of wine and explore our options, but duty calls," whispered Angel huskily and then returned the favor with a deep kiss of her own.

"Rain check for sure, maybe a night when the guys are working late and you know what happens when they do get home" said Tina using all her willpower not to jump Angel right there but they had run out of time.

"We'd have the time of our lives," replied Angel while opening the car door for Tina.

They pulled out of the driveway and were on the QEW headed east into the city in a matter of moments. The traffic was still fairly light at this time of day but the two gorgeous girls hoped the interview would not last longer than one hour because traffic would become nasty after 3pm sharp on a working day in Toronto and getting back out of the city would be a real chore.

"Well, if the interview is longer, we'll just stay down there, find a cozy place, have a couple of glasses of wine and a bite to eat and cuddle. Once the traffic dies down, we'll be home in no time and all warmed up for the guys," suggested Angel.

"Guess what, it's a date. We haven't been downtown for a while and the guys will understand," replied Tina rubbing the inside of Angel's leg suggestively.

"God, if you keep that up I'll have to buy new panties before our interview and we have no time for that but we'll definitely do the downtown thing afterwards."

The restaurant at the top of the TD Tower had a great view of the city and some secluded intimate bench seats. "Either way this interview goes, we celebrate," replied Angel got off the Gardiner Expressway and headed up Spadina Avenue, then turned right at King Street, pulling her car into an underground parking lot close to King and Bay.

Angel punched the green button to print a parking ticket and opened the gate to the parking area which undoubtedly would cost a fortune but Canoe was within walking distance so at least it would be somewhat worth it to park there.

A parking spot close to a street level entrance was open and the ladies pulled right in. *Most likely some executive, who had a heavy afternoon date before he went home to his wife and two and one half kids, vacated that spot* chuckled the ladies to themselves while locking the car up and heading up to the street.

They crossed at the lights and headed right into the stately BMO Tower, FinCo being located on the 42nd floor. They checked the time, 1:50 pm; just enough time to check their look, have a quick washroom break and announce themselves at reception. They quickly strode through the stately building lobby, found the bank of elevators that serviced the 42nd floor and pushed the up button. The elevator, wouldn't you know it, came up from the parking area occupied with 3 staunch looking banking types that pushed the buttons for various floors before the 42nd. These guys tried their best not to be conspicuous but were ogling the ladies like there was no tomorrow.

In turn, the ladies decided to leave them with a lasting memory and gave each other a hot kiss knowing they could touch up when they reached their destination, confident that these guys would have other things besides banking on their mind once they got back to their offices.

They reached their floor, got off and headed directly to the washroom to touch up and then came out announcing themselves to the equally gorgeous receptionist who sat behind an official looking counter with FinCo engrained in it.

"Have a seat ladies, Christine will be with you in a few minutes. Coffee, Tea or Soft drinks?" asked the red haired receptionist.

"Sure, a couple of diet Pepsi's would be fine," replied Tina. *A glass of Pinot Grigio would be better but that's not in the cards*, the ladies thought to themselves.

The receptionist poured two tiny cans of diet Pepsi into two plastic cups filled with ice and gave one to each lady. After a few minutes the receptionist indicated that Christine Hertzog was ready to see them in the boardroom and for them to take their drinks and belongings and follow her.

She opened the doors to a spacious oak furnished room with a large table, chairs, video screen and breathtaking view of the eastern part of the city including the lakeshore.

Angel and Tina picked two seats where they could enjoy the spectacular view, Angel getting their documents ready for the interview. After a few short minutes, a stunningly beautiful young woman dressed impeccably in a fashionable pin stripe pantsuit with large gold hoop earrings, short spiked blonde streaked pixie type hair and an even golden tan made Angel and Tina almost do a double take. This was going to be a very interesting afternoon, a hot day in the middle of winter.

Chapter 11

Mikhail was on the prowl in the Toronto area once again. After the events of a number of years ago bringing down that scum sucking drug lord Miguel Alvarez and his organization, he kept a low profile for a while and healed his wounds. He then went back to the trade he knew and hired himself out to individuals that had a use and could afford his special brand of talent.

His work took him to various US cities such as New York, Chicago, Boston and even Los Angeles which he had a real distaste for because of the pretentious and superficial lifestyle people led there. They all acted like gangsters and actors; everyone was a big shot in L.A. so at least they thought. The people who hired him to guard their interests or bodies could also have an occasional threat to their business or well being eliminated, were discreet and paid well and that was all the Assassin cared about.

The Monster was a legend that was a whisper in the wind and he very rarely ever worked for anyone a second time since his time with Boris Brotzky. The greedy Strip Club owner had been eliminated by his own organization for being too money-grubbing and hands on. Mikhail was untraceable as he changed his cars and living quarters more than some people changed their underwear unfortunately and only ever dealt in cash which he always had plenty of. His most recent assignment was the disbanding of a vicious east L.A gang that was starting to muscle in on an established territory run by an old Chicago style hood who had prostitution, drug trafficking, arms dealing and other not so niceties all sown up in his territory but was starting to feel the heat from this rival gang who were beginning to put a dent into his business. As a result, the streets were being littered with bodies and bullets.

The Police were frustrated; people were afraid to come out of their homes, and the addicts and johns were upset because of delays in obtaining their products or services. Mikhail was never contacted. He always made the first contact to offer his services. There were never any face to face meetings as the Ninja eliminated most people he ever met face to face, that was, always his policy. Exceptions were, Angel, her friends and that pesky Detective Rollie Sampson, as he had taken a sort of liking to this tough and determined group; as much liking as the Monster could stomach at any rate.

He would contact the key decision maker or money man and leave instructions where to drop off the money, usually in a forested area in the outskirts where Mikhail had the advantage. He always asked for full payment up front as his work was legendary and he never failed once he was on the job and everyone agreed to his terms as their lives were on the line if they didn't.

Only one foolish company executive who wanted a rival eliminated decided to change the rules and only half the agreed upon sum was delivered. Bad mistake as the delivery team was never seen or heard from again. The executive's corpse was anchored in about 400 feet of murky Atlantic Ocean, feeding the marine life there. Of course, Mikhail pocketed all the money agreed upon and one lucky competitor lived to cheat another day.

The last L.A. job was handled in his usual quick and efficient style when the young, tattooed, spaced out on PCP and Heroin gang leader thought he was having a hallucination. He had just injected himself and his Latina main squeeze with a speedball and was pushing her head down to service him, saw a dark and menacing shape materialize right beside the bed he and his girl were about to bring back to life.

"What da fock, madre de dios," exclaimed the drugged out punk pushing his dazed girlfriend off him. "How did you get in here, puta?" he screamed while reaching under the mattress for his trusty revolver. He never got the chance as Mikhail grabbed his wrist with lightning speed, twisted and heard the crackly crunch of snapping bone.

The hapless gangster tried to use his good hand to pull a nasty looking hunting knife from his belt which was embedded in his left eye socket for his trouble. Not wanting to prolong the agony, Mikhail delivered a lightning fast and powerful chop to the throat killing the gang leader instantaneously.

The scared to death girl lay beside the bed begging for her life in Spanish but Mikhail had long since disappeared as fast as he came. The new Mikhail; as the old one would have killed the unfortunate girl just for fun. He had changed. Next he paid a visit to the gang's hangout and rather unceremoniously made his entrance flying right through a side window into the middle of the group of gang members just dividing up their latest ill-gotten gains.

Everyone scattered in all directions with the two largest hoods lying dead in the middle of the floor, their necks snapped like twigs. A couple of the more enterprising bad guys tried to pull weapons; one was stuffed down his throat and the other into his more private orifice for their troubles. The rest just sat there stunned, not believing their eyes as to what occurred.

"Your leader is dead, your operation has ended. Anyone who continues in this business will suffer the most painful of deaths. Is that understood?" hissed the killer.

The rest of the motley crew just shook their heads dumfounded when just to emphasize, a shuriken was hurled with lightning speed embedding itself into the brain of another gang member trying to make for the door.

"Understood?" snarled the monster.

The few in the room left alive just nodded watching the apparition put all the weapons, drugs and money on the table into a satchel and then disappearing in a black haze right in front of their eyes.

The job was done; the ones who lived decided to go back to pimping individually or working at the local carwash. They did not sign on for something like this and Mikhail was on his way back to Canada in his new tinted Range Rover, which he would trade in as soon as he was across the border.

Mikhail was one of, if not the deadliest killer for hire on the planet today. He came from the tough streets of Russia, was an expert in most of the major martial arts systems such as Tae Kwon Do, Karate, Mui-tai and even the mysterious Russian ROSS system as well as the forbidden art of Ninjitzu. No one that he had ever encountered could stand against him; those who tried were no longer on this planet. He had disposed of his instructor in Russia to prove he was ready for his life for hire. Only Angel and her crew had survived multiple encounters with him, his only explanation was pure luck which he now respected.

The monster was now in reconnaissance mode and on the trail of those that had threatened Angel and her friends. He was always true to his word but even he had no idea where this trail would lead him. Let the chips fall as they may.

Chapter 12

Christine Hertzog made herself comfortable in a seat across the board room table from Angel and Tina, licked her ample glossy lips and crossed her legs. To counter, Angel and Tina took a sip of their diet pop and trying to show proper protocol, waited for Christine to start the conversation. This took a little longer than expected causing the ladies to shuffle around looking a tad uncomfortable, exactly what Christine wanted.

Finally having achieved what she was after which was exerting her authority, she began by saying, "I'm Christine, not Chris or Chrissie. With me so far?"

Neither Angel nor Tina recalled calling her anything else but her full name and not even that as yet, just looked at each other and nodded.

"Good, the strong, silent types. I like that. So what makes you two think you have the skills and the intestinal fortitude to win a contract with FinCo?" asked Christine with a nasty smirk on her pretty mouth.

Angel was very quickly tiring of this game, patted Tina on the leg which meant *Leave this with me.*

Well, if we did not have the skills you were look-ing for, you wouldn't have called us in for an inter-view," replied Angel returning a quite serious look of her own which a lot of women and men alike shrunk away from when they were facing her in a sparring ring or in an actual confrontation.

"Excellent response, I see you are not easily intim-idated. How about your quiet sidekick there?" probed Christine Hertzog.

"I am her business partner and totally agree with her answer," said Tina with a more serious look on her own.

"Okay, let's cut to the chase. What can you do to streamline our business practices and optimize our processes," asked Christine.

Angel produced some Gant, SWOT (Strengths, Weaknesses, Opportunities and Threats charts as well as a couple of pages of a Microsoft Project break-down of a previous project they had worked on and indicated," Please see for yourself. In this particular scenario, we were able to add half a million dollars to this company's bottom line without having to let any staff go." said Angel confidently.

"Yes and most of it was accomplished by elimi-nating duplication as well as cross-training current staff giving them additional challenges and making them more valuable employees. So no new hires were required and there was always someone around who could cover for someone that was away on business or absent," added Tina.

Christine studied the information briefly before replying," Very simple, direct and impressive, just what we are looking for."

Before I leave and have you speak with our President, I am very interested in hearing about your martial arts training. Angel, I see you are a 3rd Degree Tae-Kwon-Do black belt as well as a master instructor in Kick Boxing. Tina, what is your background?"

"I'm a student of Angel's as well as being her business partner and best friend. I am testing for my red belt in Tae-Kwon-Do next month but Angel is in a class all of her own," replied Tina very modestly.

"Well, I am also quite accomplished in the self-defense arts and would surprise the both of you. Hopefully, we get the chance to find out at some point soon. Please wait here, our President and CEO Richard Rasmussin will be with you shortly. Thank you ladies, I appreciate your time," and with a swish of her skirt she was out the door.

"What the hell just happened in here, she was trying to intimidate us wasn't she?" whispered Tina.

"You think? It didn't work on my part, I'd love to have a chance at her anywhere, anytime," said Angel.

To the complete surprise and shock, the door opened with Christine now in a jet black outfit complete with black belt and 4 white stripes designating 4th degree master. She flipped Angel and Tina a similar white outfit, one with a black belt for Angel and a blue belt for Tina.

"The change rooms are just outside beside the washrooms and our Do-Jang is down the hall. Let's see if you can back up what you say or you can just turn around and leave now, your choice. Oh, it will be just the three of us in there; Richard is only interested in the outcome. Tina, since you are a much lower rank, you can sit this one out.

Angel, are you in or are you out?" asked Christine.

"Just give me 3 minutes and we'll be there. Never had to fight during a job interview before but there's always a first time," replied Angel now looking extremely determined and grim. That look was not lost on Christine.

Tina was shocked by what was developing here but knew her best friend too well. She would never back down from a challenge like this. Tina entered the spacious gym facility and sat down with her back against the far wall. The place was fully matted, and had all sorts of training equipment in it including punching bags, treadmills, exercise bikes, pads. It was fully equipped. There were obviously a number of employees that were into martial arts and training and that was very interesting but Tina was still concerned for her friend.

Angel came in decked out in full headgear and gloves and sat down in the middle of the room. Christine Hertzog entered the room immediately after, bowed to Angel and went into fighting stance. *No warm-ups, no problem* thought Angel. *Let's see what this bitch has.* The two women circled each other warily looking for an opening and suddenly with lighting speed Christine went into a series of incredibly quick punches, blocks and kicks. Angel had never seen anything like it and was clipped by a few of the unorthodox moves.

She shook her head to clear it as she could hear bells ringing after that onslaught and did as she was taught to do; back off and regroup. Her attacker did not stop however and came after her with a whirlwind of punches and kicks even more aggressively than the first time. But now Angel used a technique she was taught years ago which was to focus and concentrate until she saw her opponents movements come at her much slower than they were actually coming and as a result she was able to duck under all that flurry of motion and deliver an uppercut that lifted Christine right off the ground and sent her flying a good distance before she landed flat on her back.

She was up in a split second and came at Angel even faster and harder who, unfortunately for Christine, was now somewhat warmed up. She blocked the onslaught or at least most of it and came in with an attack of her own, throwing some hard punches to the body and head. As only Angel could do, she unleashed a high turning kick from her hip which landed squarely on Christine's unprotected jaw and that ended the sparring match for Ms. Hertzog as she dropped like a stone… out cold.

Tina ran to get some water and Angel squatted down, removed her opponents head gear and massaged her face and neck to get her back into a conscious state. After about 30 seconds or so, Christine sat up, rubbed her sore jaw, took a sip of water from Tina and said, "Very impressive. You really are the real deal. Never been knocked down, never mind knocked out before and I have sparred many women and also men with very high skill sets. Get changed and Richard will speak with both of you in the boardroom."

And with that, Christine left the two still stunned ladies in the Do-Jang.

"What kind of techniques was she using? Never saw anything like that before, you were amazing. I have the best friend, partner and instructor I could ever have," said Tina hugging Angel passionately.

"I've never been exposed to anything like it either but it looks like something I saw in a movie years ago, something called Kenpo Karate where they use a series of lightning fast continuous movements to overwhelm their opponents. Thankfully, I was able to focus and slow her movements down and duck inside of them. Hopefully, I did not hurt her too bad but she got me going and I actually enjoyed it. You only get better facing various opponents although I never thought this would happen during a job interview," replied Angel.

"So what now? Should we continue with this madness or go snuggle at Canoe?" asked Tina.

"Come with me while I change and try to get myself looking corporate again. I'm almost thinking we should do exactly what you said and call it a day, this is too crazy but I'm also curious what type of individual this Richard Rasmussin is that runs a company like this. So let's meet this guy and see what he has to say and then it's off to the TD Tower for a few drinks and appetizers before we go home to the guys for the main course," said Angel huskily.

"Fine with me. Your call. You know I am always up for an adventure," said Tina.

About 15 minutes later, Angel and Tina emerged from the change room looking even hotter than they did before the altercation. Nothing like a bit of exercise to get the blood flowing. They re-entered the board room and found two Espresso coffees waiting for them which were very strong but tasty. *What next?* The two gorgeous applicants thought to themselves.

Chapter 13

Next came suddenly through the boardroom door. He was tall, lean and moved with a fluidity and confidence that was immediately apparent. Richard T. Rasmussin was impeccably dressed in a charcoal grey 3 piece suit, expertly shined shoes with long but stylish black hair, and a dark tan and jet black eyes that seemed to look right through Angel and Tina.

He came to each of them, shook their hand with just the right amount of pressure and then sat down at the head of the table.

"So I'm Richard and this is my company. I apologize for the unorthodox interviewing methods of my admin Christine but she could not resist mixing in a bit of fun into the interview process. Unfortunately, she is still nursing her sore jaw. That was quite a shot you gave her. Impeccable technique."

"Tina and I are still a little bit taken back by what has occurred but I take my martial arts very seriously and my instincts just took over," said Angel.

"Our company prides itself on how fit the employees are here and we like to let off some steam once in a while. A lot of our workers here are proficient in various self-defense techniques, some even quite deadly. I saw your sparring match, my compliments as Christine is one of our best. But she obviously has more work to do, that has become apparent."

"But let's talk further about you two and whether you are the right fit for some contract work with us. You definitely are. I am very impressed with both of your credentials as well as your fighting skills, Angel. We are prepared to offer you a six month contract worth 250 K. Half up front and the rest paid out on completion with proof that you can save us substantial monies in operational stream lining and process improvement, fair enough?"

Angel and Tina looked at each other and Tina answered," We would be proud to work for FinCo and rest assured we will have a number of valid recommendations for you."

"So if we are to understand things correctly, we receive 125K up front regardless of our findings?" asked Angel.

Absolutely, can't have you working here for nothing and I am confident you will fulfill your obligations and then some. We would like you both to begin Monday morning and Angel, be prepared to share some of your fighting skill expertise with our employees. That's part of the deal. Are you in or are you out?" asked Richard leaning back in his chair.

"We are excited to join FinCo and also work with your employees. Your company obviously uses out of the box techniques to motivate your workers which is commendable," replied Angel.

"Terrific, welcome aboard. I will leave you now but report to me and me alone although Christine will be my liaison once she recovers sufficiently. Someone will come in and work with you to sign a few documents and issue you your access badges and upfront payment. See you at 9 sharp Monday morning at which time you will be issued side by side desks and computers," and Richard left the room, the door shutting almost silently.

Next, an elderly lady who looked more the administrative type came in and explained the paperwork briefly, showed them where to sign and initial, produced a check for the agreed upon amount made out to A & T Consulting as well as floor access badges for each of them. After everything was completed, the lady escorted them back out to the elevators.

Angel and Tina could hardly contain their excitement hugging each other and jumping around once they got back outside on the street. Angel pulled her cell and called Jon-Erik and told him the news and what happened.

"You had to spar with someone and now you have a check for 125K?" he replied incredulously.

"Yes baby and we are going to celebrate tonight when you and Joey get home. In the meantime, Tina and I are going for a couple of cocktails and a nibble since we are downtown here already but should be back by the time you get home. See you soon," replied Angel.

"You too hon and congratulations to both of you. Can't wait to get all the details and get my arms around you," said Jon-Erik

"Me too... and a lot more... and Tina said for Joey to get prepared for a hot evening. Don't work too hard, signing off for now."

The two beautiful women headed off arm in arm to the Toronto Dominion Centre and the Canoe Restaurant. They had a date with some drinks, appetizers and cuddling in a dark corner that was long overdue and then a wild night with their sexy fiancées. Could it get any better? But things were not always as they seem. Angel and Tina knew that as well... but that thought at least for the rest of today and the evening was completely forgotten.

Chapter 14

Richard T. Rasmussin was a boardroom psychopath of the very worst degree. He operated without empathy, devoid of feelings and used and manipulated people and situations for his own gains. What turned him on was wealth, more wealth, power and domination. He was pleasant enough in his day to day dealings with his staff, was active in social circles, donated generously to a few chosen high profile charities that in turn supported and bolstered FinCo.

Richard in reality could not give a damn about these charities or the stuffed shirts and phony social-ite types that administered them. He had no loyalty or caring about his own company and staff or any-one else he dealt with but would carry on the sham as long as it benefited him.

This Angel he had just hired intrigued him how-ever. Drop dead gorgeous, one of the best martial artists he had seen in some time and seemed to know her business as well. Her friend Tina did not interest him much except for possible leverage as they came as a pair. Being the psychopath he was, his mind was always planning, plotting and scheming and he had already decided he was going to have this Angel.

Not for any length of time as he got tired of everyone quickly and relationships were nothing that interested him, but he was going to submit her, humble her and then get rid of her, one way or the other. He closed his eyes and thought of this Angel while a gorgeous young Asian girl named Miko was playing an intricate tune on his organ.

"Faster, harder," instructed the CEO as the poor girl was having trouble containing him.

After ravaging the unfortunate girl for another hour, he got tired of her and told her to wash up and get out of his upscale, classy TO condo overlooking the waterfront. It was lavishly decorated and had all the electronics and gadgets money could buy to impress no one but himself and he had quick access to everything this city had to offer including sports, theatre, nightlife and anything else someone like him would require having almost unlimited means to obtain them.

He poured himself a shot of Chivas on the rocks settled back on his custom designed doe skin sectional couch when his secure phone rang.

Richard answered on the second call and effortlessly switched to fluent Russian. The conversation was short and to the point. The caller asked brief poignant questions and received answers in kind.

"Business good?" asked the deep voice on the phone in Russian.

"Yes, you do not read the Canadian papers in the old Country?" replied Richard.

"Being rude is not good for health," said the voice.

"Understood." *He may have to go over there and kick some ass at some point* Richard thought to himself these guys were no light weights, even for him.

"We are ready to ship more cash. Can you handle it?"

"Always. It's easy to overstate our generous client's contributions," answered Richard.

"Good. Business is good here but the Russian police and Interpol are always just one step behind. A shipment is on its way to your loading docks, customary packaging and caution apply," and with that the phone went dead.

I'll play ball with them for now but they are in store for a few surprises down the road vowed Richard before he put on his jacket, grabbed his keys and headed out to one of the discreet After Hours Clubs he frequented. A few vodkas and some sexy young female company always helped him clear his head and the night was still young. Sleep was something he just had no time for.

Chapter 15

Angel and Tina got home from their intimate night at Canoe and their more than weird interview with a happy little buzz on, Tina more than Angel as she was the passenger. They had really caused a stir in the upscale downtown eatery with a number of propositions from older executives and young stock traders that frequented the establishment but were too pre-occupied with their drinks, the delicious appetizers and themselves to give much notice.

At around 9:30 pm the ladies decided they were feeling good enough to devour their fiancées and asked for a doggie bag for the rest of the food that they were too occupied to eat, wanting to surprise their hard working lovers with some haute cuisine as well as their hot bodies. It was an expensive night but they had an officially endorsed check for 125K in Angel's purse.

What's a few hundred dollars, the ladies giggled to themselves but still winced after paying the ridiculous parking fee and pulling onto Bay St. and smoothly merging onto the Gardiner Expressway, destination—home.

While Angel drove, Tina called Joey and told him they expected two showered and horny studs waiting for them and they would be home in around twenty minutes with appetizers in tow as well.

Joey got right on the phone to Jon-Erik and told them the girls would be home shortly. They would be ready for some good loving and some good food.

Jon-Erik could not jump into the shower fast enough, towel dry his hair and comb it back, splash on some of Angel's favorite aftershave and put out some mango rum punches which the girls loved. Joey was at the door in no time flat and a few short minutes later two gorgeous, tipsy ladies came through the door looking sensational. They were even more so, after they dropped their clothes off, and walked over to their fiancées who were too speechless to say anything.

What happened next would have made a terrific film for one of the many adult pay per view channels but this evening was truly for the two couples who finally came up for air later to sip on their drinks and munch on a few tasty tidbits.

In the meantime, things were developing that if known would have surely put a dent into the lovers' celebrations but for the rest of the night they were safe with the eyes of the night shadow not far away to ensure they remained that way.

Mikhail so far had run up against a blank wall with his more than discreet inquiries and probing. Anyone that ever had any dealings with the Shape Shifter and lived to tell about it erased anything about him out of their minds, computers, rolodexes, etc. if they wanted to keep breathing the air on this earth.

It bothered him that he had found out nothing so far about these people who went around intimidating people in the guise of helping them with their finances. But it did not deter him and he continued with his underground queries, as he knew that if you turned over enough stones something would pop up.

So he kept himself busy by exercising his body, doing long runs along the Lakeshore and practicing his deadly arts in his lair in one of the many seedy motels in that area. In close proximity to where Angel was living. All the better to keep an eye on her and see what developed as something always did sooner or later, patience was one of his less lethal virtues.

His surveillance was done out of his two year old Ford F10 pickup that he had traded his Range Rover in for when he returned to Canada. The vehicle was jet black with no discernable markings and the cab was fully tinted so you could only see out but no one was able to see in.

To stretch his legs, he took to the backyards and fences in the neighborhood and quickly got to know every inch of the area including all trees, bushes, garage roofs and cubbyholes. Since it was winter, most of the trees did not provide him with the usual cover but he had no issues with melting into a fir or pine tree if required. If there was snow, he always retraced and eradicated his tracks if new snow did not do that for him.

The only problems were neighborhood dogs but most were kept in doors in the cold winter nights. For Mikhail, the Toronto weather was balmy compared to the cruel and biting cold of his native Russia so he felt very comfortable operating here in weather that most escaped to avoid. Normally, the Monster was paid extremely well for his particular set of skills but this one was a freebee, he had given his word and that meant more to him than anything, even money.

Chapter 16

Since it was now the weekend, Angel and Tina spent the morning cleaning up their respective homes while Jon-Erik and Joey were back at the furniture store since Saturday was a working day and they had just launched a big new sale, 40% off of any purchase over a thousand dollars plus a no name brand 32" LCD TV thrown in for good measure.

The trick was that the furniture was already marked up by a whole bunch so these sales just brought them a more subdued profit but what they lacked they would made up in sheer sales volume. The TV's were a dime a dozen these days as most people were going for the 50" to 60" inch and above models that still cost a pretty penny but no one would refuse a free TV even if they did only last for a year at the most. In general, living in a disposable society, no one really cared.

Jon-Erik and Joey were walking a little gingerly after last evening's incredible sexcapades; the ladies almost insatiable, which was great last night but the guys were both hurting units the day after, especially when they had to work. And they were not as young as they used to be but still gave it the old high school try. *Nothing that a few beers and sports on TV would not cure this evening but since the ladies now had real money to spend, the evening's plans were dining, a movie and dancing the night away.*

No thought given to the fact that they had to work all day but they could sleep in on Sunday since the furniture store was only open in the afternoon and Joey's cousin Guido and his wife took that shift most weekends to give Joey and Jon-Erik a much deserved rest.

The sale was now in full swing and stock and TV's were moving quickly, most of the stuff was taken right there and then, as most of the customers had large SUV's with fold down seats or even pick-up trucks that could hold couches, chairs, etc. as long as they were tied off properly. For those who did not, Joey and Jon-Erik would be busy with deliveries during the week when things slowed down.

With Angel and Tina's sudden success, the guys all but forgot about the threatening visit, the slashed tires and the shot out window, which their insurance had already replaced. Everything seemed to be going extremely well in the last few days. The ladies had a decadent night planned at Club Wicked in town, as this was a place where they could really shed their inhibitions for a night and eat a good steak dinner at the same time, according to Tina.

Jon-Erik and Joey were just as happy staying home and watching the latest UFC pay per view and having a few rum and diets with beer chasers. They had not been out together for quite a while, the ladies were treating and that was fine with them as they both tried to take as little profit out of the business as possible and re-invest the money to grow the business.

6:00 pm could not come fast enough for them and after their normal store closing and money securing processes, they left the store at just before seven, jumped into Jon-Erik's yellow Vette and cruised down the 427 to the QEW and home. Just before the QEW west on ramp, however, they noticed flashing lights in their rearview.

"Cripes, how fast were you going?" asked Joey.

"Wasn't even paying attention," replied Jon-Erik looking visibly upset while pulling over to the far right. When things were too good to be true they usually weren't and this seemed to be one of those times.

The O.P.P. cruiser pulled in behind them but no one got out of the car pissing the guys off even more as they wanted to get home, have a shower and hopefully a quickie not necessarily in that order before they left for the city.

Finally, a large officer as wide as he was tall, the guys had no idea how he got in and out of his cruiser, waddled over to them and motioned for them to roll down their window.

"Evening officer, what seems to be the problem?" asked Jon-Erik as politely as he could under the circumstances.

"License, insurance and registration," was the almost snarky reply.

Jon-Erik dug out his papers and handed them over to the large mit.

"Can I ask what this is regarding?" said Jon-Erik trying not to sound as annoyed as he really was.

"You yuppies in your Corvettes, you guys think you own the road. These cars should be stored for the winter but you can obviously afford the high priced winter tires for this vehicle. How fast do you think you were going?" came the reply.

"I wasn't paying attention, we were chatting and anxious to get home," answered Jon-Erik.

"Anything to drink tonight?" said the officer while sniffing into the car.

"No sir," replied Jon-Erik. "We were saving that for tonight."

"You have the choice to take a breathalyzer test right here at road side or be taken to headquarters. Your choice."

"I told you I have had nothing alcoholic to drink, we were working all day," said Jon-Erik raising his voice. Not a good tactic to take.

"Sir, we are partners in a furniture business and have been extremely busy with a huge sale all day. We have had no time or even thought to drink," added Joey sounding upset as well.

"Will you take the test or we go to the precinct, I won't ask again," said the huge officer very authoritatively.

"Fine, whatever you wish," said Jon-Erik getting out of his car and heading towards the officers cruiser. He could not believe what happened next when his legs were kicked out from under him and he was quickly and expertly handcuffed and pushed into the passenger seat of the cruiser.

"What the hell?" screamed Jon-Erik.

"What do you think you're doing?" yelled Joey now getting out of the Corvette.

"Get back in the car and shut your mouth or I will arrest you for obstruction of justice. Do I make myself clear?" growled the portly cop.

Joey reluctantly complied but was fuming. He pulled out his cell and called Rollie.

"Hi Joey," answered Rollie on the third ring.

"Listen, we seem to have run into a problem," and Joey quickly relayed the situation.

Rollie listened and then responded, "Do everything the officer tells you to do. Do not act rude or upset. Hopefully, this will be resolved when he finds out that Jon-Erik has not been drinking. He will most likely get a ticket though, looks like this cop means business. Remember, I have no more police jurisdiction, especially with the O.P.P. Be calm." instructed Rollie before hanging up.

As Jon-Erik blew repeatedly into the breathalyzer unit following the instructions of the policeman, the beefy cop looked at the results, put away the machine, instructed Jon-Erik to turn around and removed his handcuffs.

"Sorry about that, just procedure especially for someone recently involved in a shooting," said the cop. "I had to make sure you were no threat and this was the easiest way to do it. Hope you understand, no hard feelings," said the officer returning the papers back to Jon-Erik.

"Fine, by all means contact detective Cragan. Here is his card. He will tell you that me and my friends were victims not the perpetrators," said Jon-Erik.

"No need. I have all the information I require. Sorry for the bother and here is something to remember me by," handing Jon-Erik a nice juicy speeding ticket.

"You were doing 135 in a 100 zone. Not the smartest thing to do on our highways. Also, not very bright not to do business when offered. Three strikes and you are out." the burly cop added before turning around, squeezing himself back into his cruiser and driving off.

Jon-Erik just shook his head, went back to the car, put on his seatbelt and eased it back into traffic and exited west to the QEW. No easy feat in this traffic, even on a Saturday. The interrogation had taken over half an hour and it was past eight when they finally got to their homes. On the way home it hit him as to what this cop actually told him. He was too stunned to even say anything to Joey until he got to Joey's house to drop him off.

As Joey got out of the Corvette, Jon-Erik stopped him cold.

"That cop threatened me and it did not even register at first."

"What? I thought he was nice at the end and just wrote you a ticket," said Joey.

"He was and did but it's what he said at the end that's throwing me for a real loop!"

"Well, what did he say?" Joey prodded.

"Something about not doing business and three strikes and you're out," answered Jon-Erik looking extremely confused.

"I don't get it. Let's look at the ticket to see who this clown was," suggested Joey.

"Me neither," offered Jon-Erik before unfolding the ticket and passing it to Joey.

Joey examined the ticket carefully before indicating that it in fact was a hundred dollar speeding ticket but was written out on a generic receipt rather than an official O.P.P ticket book and wasn't signed.

"What the hell just happened?" the guys asked each other simultaneously but then decided to each go their own way and then meet back up at Joey's after everyone was cleaned up. They still had to relay everything to Angel and Tina and this could and most likely would put a damper on their evening plans. They could always hope for miracles.

Chapter 17

Private detective Rollie Sampson was getting nowhere fast. He had his nose to the ground from many years on the police force, had a lot of contacts and someone always knew something about something. In this case, however, it was nothing but stone silence; no indication of any kind of extortion deals going down or any type of shakedowns for that matter.

The mob was known to operate in this manner but mostly they had gone mainstream and used much more sophisticated methods and if there was any resistance, chances were the resisters were pushing up daisies somewhere and unable to tell the tale.

But the fact that nothing was coming up at all had Rollie concerned even more that something much bigger was going on here and Jon-Erik and Joey had been lucky so far. Given what had happened five years ago, you would think their luck had run out so

Rollie knew he was on a short timeline and had to come up with something.

The only thing he could think of to do was to stake out the furniture store in hopes that this Elmo character would come back for another try and then it hit him, *why not help things along a bit?* But he had to check with the guys first and it was Saturday night. But Rollie was not one to let things slide so he dialed Jon-Erik's cell.

Angel answered on the third ring and after exchanging pleasantries told Rollie Jon-Erik was in the shower and they had been planning to go out to celebrate their new contract. But Jon-Erik would call him back as soon as he was finished.

"Who was that hon?" asked Jon-Erik opening the door to a still steaming bathroom.

"Rollie. Can you call him back as soon as you are dry?" Angel replied.

"For sure, how did he know I need to speak with him?" said Jon-Erik with a worried tone in his voice which Angel picked up on immediately.

"What's happened?" asked Angel.

"Hang tight, you can listen in when I speak with Rollie. I did not want to worry you and get the days dust off me before I get into this," said Jon-Erik coming out with a towel wrapped around his lean waist and his long hair still dripping water.

He selected the last number that called him and pressed the dial key. Rollie answered almost immediately and Jon-Erik began to relay what had happened to him and Joey after they had called Rollie earlier for advice.

Angel sat quietly trying to take in what Jon-Erik had just said but it was easy to see she was concerned to say the least.

"I don't know what to tell you as I have never heard of anything like this in my career. These guys must have tremendous clout to be able to pull something like this off. Are you all still planning to go out tonight?"

Jon-Erik looked at Angel who answered," We've always survived adversity together. We'll be together and we'll be careful. We can talk to the police tomorrow but we deserve this celebration tonight."

"Okay, be careful and call me if anything comes up. I'm going to give detective Cragan a call and let him know what happened. We need to stay on top of this. I am also going to try to set a trap for this Elmo Entwhistle and get him to come back to the furniture store next week. I'll let you know more tomorrow," indicated Rollie before hanging up.

Jon-Erik and Angel discussed it further but decided they would not be intimidated and all four deserved this. They were going partying and would deal with everything else tomorrow as Monday was Angel and Tina's first day on the job.

When the big stretch limo pulled up in front of their door just after eight, Jon-Erik could not believe his eyes.

"What the!" was all he could get out before Angel grabbed him from behind and gave him a sexy lick on his neck which almost caused him to grab her and take her upstairs in spite of the huge surprise.

"Grab a change of undies and your toothbrush. This is going to be the night of all nights. I have my stuff all ready and Tina and Joey are already one drink ahead of us. Hurry it up, hot stuff!" coaxed Angel looking super-hot in a tight pair of designer jeans, a white silk blouse and a faux fur jacket.

A scant five minutes later Jon-Erik and Angel jumped into the Stretch joining Joey and Tina who had already uncorked a bottle of Mumms and were drinking out of each other's glasses.

The Limo pulled out of their residential area and headed onto the QEW heading west. "Are we going where I think we are going?" asked Jon-Erik finding it hard to talk with Angel all over him.

"Where do you think we are going?" answered Tina between caressing Joey causing him to feel like a pole-vaulter.

"Casino Niagara?" guessed Jon-Erik with Angel beginning to explore his body all over in between sips of the delicious champagne.

"You're too smart for your own britches. If you do not watch it, you won't have them on for long," purred Angel feeding some more champagne to the love of her life.

The rest of the trip was all about the two couples and how much in love they were and the guys had to use incredible restrain otherwise the ride could have turned into something uncensored.

The Limo arrived at the Fallsview Hotel and Casino with the passengers more than slightly inebriated and horny as hell. Since they hardly had any luggage besides a night bag each, the driver told them to have a great time and he would be there to pick them up tomorrow afternoon.

Angel checked them into a luxury suite overlooking the falls in all their winter glory and all their jaws dropped when they saw the beautifully decorated room including fully stocked fridge, snacks, two huge king size beds along with a huge hot tub right in the center of the room with a terrific view of the lightshow that was Niagara in the winter.

But no rest for the wicked, the couples did not even have time for a quickie as Ringo Starr and his All Star Band consisting of some of the greatest musicians from years past were on stage in fifteen minutes and the group barely had time to freshen up; good thing the concert hall was just a short walk away from the elevators.

Jon-Erik and Joey were totally floored by what their ladies had planned and everything was already paid for so all they had to do was enjoy. The concert was terrific; they were still too young to remember the Beatle hysteria but really appreciated the great music Ringo and his band put out there.

A scant two hours later, they were all back in their suite cracking another bottle of bubbly, Angel and Jon-Erik getting funky in the hot tub while Tina and Joey jumped right into their king size posturepedic bed and proceeded to set the comfortable coils to singing a tune of their own.

After they had relieved some of their pent up sexual tension, Angel announced it was time to get down to the Casino and win back some of the money the ladies spent on this incredible night.

The couples managed to clean themselves up somewhat after their romps and walked hand in hand down to the Casino where the atmosphere was truly electric. The place was packed to the rafters with every type of people you could imagine from young to old, frumpy to fashionable and everything in between. It took them well over half an hour to find a couple of side by side slot machines that were just abandoned so they each took turns playing the 25 cent one armed bandits.

Angel and Tina had set out a two hundred dollar limit for each and they had all agreed to stop once that was exceeded. Tina and Joey were out in about half an hour, the greedy machine sucking up their money like a starved calf on its mother.

Angel was out shortly after but Jon-Erik was on a roll, actually up over two hundred from his initial investment when the machine he was playing burst out into a ton of noise and flashing lights. He had hit the mini-jackpot and had collared an additional five hundred dollars.

After Jon-Erik cashed in his winnings the happy couples went off to the lounge for some more drinks and celebration. Tina excused herself indicating she had to pee like a racehorse, Joey escorting her visiting to adjacent facilities leaving Angel and Jon-Erik doing sneaky and possibly questionable things to each other in a dark corner of the lounge.

Joey finished his business, washed his hands and went out to wait for Tina who was really taking her time. When she did not come out after over 5 minutes later, Joey became concerned and yelled into the woman's facilities, "Come on baby, lot's more partying to do!"

The answer came back," Hold on lover, be right there," and two blitzed blondes staggered out holding each other up and giggling. But no Tina.

"Come on honey, are you okay in there?" shouted out Joey hearing no answer but the flush of a toilet.

Not feeling brave enough to go in there after her, he ran back to the lounge to alert Angel and Jon-Erik who pried themselves away from each other and the three headed back to the women's washroom as fast as they could, sending Angel in after Tina.

"Tina, it's Angel. Are you in here?" shouted Angel.

"No Tina but I'll party with you," slurred a tall red head coming out of one of the stalls coming up to Angel trying to lay a sloppy kiss on her. Angel quickly side stepped the drunken women and started to check out all the other washroom stalls. No Tina.

"Shit, this is not funny!" yelled Angel heading back out to the two waiting now very concerned looking guys. "She's not in there!"

"Maybe she decided to go for a walk and see the sites?" suggested Jon-Erik.

"We doubt that," said Joey and Angel almost in unison.

"She knew I would be waiting for her. This does not make sense at all!" indicated Joey now looking very worried.

"Okay, let's split up and check the Casino. If she is here we will find her. We meet back here at the lounge in ten minutes and be careful. I have a very strange feeling about this," said Angel before heading off into a row of slot machines. Joey and Jon-Erik did the same thing checking their watches.

They twisted and dodged around people and machines searching frantically for their companion, so much so that a tall muscular security guard stopped Joey and pulled him aside to ask him what the problem was.

Joey now almost turning white from anxiety, his heart racing from adrenaline, explained what had happened and said that he had no time to waste. His fiancée had disappeared into thin air.

Chapter 18

The thin but wiry security guard named Nick now followed emergency protocol and alerted the other numerous guards on the premises while Jon-Erik called Rollie's cell.

Rollie Sampson sleepily answered as it was now getting close to midnight and advised to let security do their thing and that they would contact the Niagara Falls local police if Tina was not found by them or the security sweep. He also told Jon-Erik to call him back with any further news and that he would drive out there if necessary.

After all, friends were more important than sleep although that was sometimes a tough sell especially at this time of night when he had been up over twenty hours.

The three now very upset and scared partyers met back at the lounge. They had come up short; no sign of Tina anywhere. It was like she was never there but the group of friends knew better. Everyone was so shocked they were now stone cold sober even after all the drinks they had throughout the course of the evening.

"Wait a minute, what if she went back to our room to freshen up? I'll go up and check, you two wait for me here," instructed Angel and was gone up the elevator in a flash. She got back to their large suite in no time flat and used her key card to open the door.

"Tina, are you in here?" There was nothing but silence in the large suite. Everything looked in order except for the large man dressed in black from head to toe; his piercing yellowish eyes and large white teeth, a stark contrast.

Mikhail sat on one of the large comfortable couches sipping Vodka on the rocks. "Not as good as in old country but will do in a pinch," indicated the executioner pointing for Angel to sit opposite him on the plush easy chair.

Even though Angel had had a number of these encounters with the Monster, she was still in shock and awe every time and this time was no exception. She willed herself to breathe calmly, slow her heart rate down and did exactly what she was told. She did not want to anger her uninvited and extremely dangerous guest, always a wise move.

Angel knew better then to ask how he had come to be here and gain access to their suite; she knew the Ninja did what he did for reasons only known to him.

"Good you are calm, only way to be. Your progress is excellent; soon you will be ready to start your training with me. Only you are worthy. Others are more skilled and ruthless but they do not have your heart. But that is not what we are here to discuss, yes?" said Mikhail.

"Tina has gone missing. We are all worried to death about her and I was hoping she had come up here to freshen up," replied Angel.

"I was here keeping an eye on you and had a little fun at the black jack tables at the same time. Even I cannot watch four people especially when they split up. I saw the commotion downstairs and knew you would come up to check," the Shape Shifter said with a low growl.

"Do you know what happened?" asked Angel.

"I can make educated guess. These people who have been intimidating your boyfriends took her to make a statement. All they have done is angered me which they will regret deeply. They are quick, organized and effective and are long gone by now," offered Mikhail.

"So what should we do?"

"Go back home, tell Security she has contacted you and decided to go home on her own. Do not involve police, they are ineffective and much like gnats. I'm sure you will have that chubby now private detective friend of yours involved and he will be fine if he stays out of my way. These people are based out of Toronto and I'm sure they will have taken her there and when *and I will* find them, they will pay," instructed the Monster.

"I will contact you soon, do not worry. You may even work with me to get your friend back, I will decide."

And before Angel could blink an eye, he was gone. Just the faintest of clicks of the door handle indicated his exit.

Angel called Jon-Erik's cell immediately and relayed what had just happened. Jon-Erik called Rollie Sampson to update him while trying to console a very distraught Joey. The two friends pulled themselves together enough to indicate to the Security guards that Tina had left on her own as she was not feeling well and was safely home in bed, apologizing for the commotion.

They then contacted the limo driver that took them there, checked out of the hotel getting a partial refund as they had to leave before even staying the night and headed back to Toronto telling the driver to put the pedal to the metal.

It was now around 4:00 am when the limo dropped them off back at Jon-Erik's and Angel's place. Everyone was bone tired and what could they do anyway at this time so Joey crashed on the couch downstairs and Angel and Jon-Erik headed upstairs too tired and upset to do anything besides fall asleep in each other's arms.

A new day would bring new hope and ideas—or so they all hoped.

Chapter *19*

Tina never saw it coming and almost did not feel it either. She had relieved herself in the plush Casino bathroom and was in the process of putting on some lipstick when she felt a tiny like pin-prick in the back of her neck and then nothing.

If she could have seen what happened next it would have gone something like this. After being injected with some sort of drug that instantly numbed her but did not knock her out, a beautiful girl put her arm around Tina's shoulder and strolled her out of the bathroom, down the hall and out a side exit into a waiting black panel truck. This occurred a scant minute before Angel got there looking for her friend and anyone that might have seen them would have sworn they saw two gorgeous drunk ladies trying to keep each other up on the way to who knows where.

Tina felt, heard, sensed and saw everything but was powerless to do anything; all her motor functions were totally impeded. The black truck with its large muscular driver and beautiful but sinister looking accomplice drove for almost two hours before coming to a stop in a seedy looking deserted warehouse area by the lake where the close group of friends lived.

Elmo unlocked the padlocked gate and Christine half guided half dragged the still very much out of it Tina into a deserted looking building, up a number of flights of stairs into a well-furnished large room which looked much too nice for its surroundings.

The building was part of an abandoned group of buildings in the Lakeshore/Evans Rd. area. If one were to follow the paper trail long enough on this structure, it would eventually lead them back to FinCo but who would have the resources and patience for that?

Since this building and other buildings in the area were not being used, no one noticed any comings and goings. All the better for Richard Rasmussin and FinCo; they had a number of these buildings within and outside of the city to support all their diabolical activities.

Tina was deposited on a large king size bed, a bottle of water left on the night table beside it. Christine and Elmo left the room and slid the massive deadbolt in place to report back to their mentor that the job had been accomplished. Good thing for them as failure had huge consequences; best not to go there.

Tina then lapsed into a dreamless sleep and slept almost to the next afternoon until she slowly awoke no worse for wear except for a slight headache and dry mouth.

She thirstily gulped down almost half the plastic water bottle left for her, thinking afterwards she should have been more careful. She felt much better however and got up to test her limbs and check out her surroundings.

It was a huge room, all steel walls with a very high ceiling. One very high window sat in the middle of the room. She was able to jump in the air and catch a ledge to pull herself up but noticed quickly the window had small spaced bars on the inside so no one could reach the actual window.

The rest of the room had a fully equipped bathroom with shower, soap, toothbrush, etc., a high ceiling fan for air circulation, one light on the ceiling which was activated by a wall switch and nothing much else. One large door seemed to be the only way in and out of the room and it was bolted solidly and would not budge.

Tina was trapped like a cat in a cage. Warm air seemed to be piped through a grill on the ceiling which again was much too high to reach even if she could find something to stand on. She finally realized the depth and despair of her dilemma and let out a long and agonizing scream that no one heard.

All she could do is sit back down on the bed, hug herself and cry. How and why did this happen to her? Who were her captors and what did they want with her? She knew Joey, Angel, Jon-Erik and Rollie would pull out all the stops to find her but could they before her captors inflicted harm?

But Tina had been toughened up by the events that occurred years ago to their group and she vowed she would not make it easy for her captors and began to practice her Tae-Kwon-Do patterns, punches and kicks.

Someone would come sooner or later for her and she would try to escape then she thought to herself while going through her paces.

The wait was not long however before the large steel door made a groaning noise and opened. Tina was ready and had already formulated a rudimentary escape plan. It almost worked.

The frightening black hooded individual that entered the room was not expecting Tina to come running straight at him and at the last mille-second stop about a foot away, pivoting around him and flying through the still open door with wings on her bare feet. She had ditched her high heels from the evening; they would be useless for speed work.

Unfortunately for her, there was back up and she ran right into a strong, muscular arm that felt like a steel cable.

She tried to free herself as she was taught by Angel by doing a double foot stomp then pivoting right to left and throwing elbow strikes to free herself. Unfortunately, that only made the large also masked muscle bound ape who carried her back into the room over his shoulder laugh as he unceremoniously dumped her back on the bed.

The other hooded character locked the door from the inside indicating she was not going to get a second chance to escape.

"Who are you people and what do you want from me?" screamed Tina jumping off the bed and looking quite menacing in her own right.

"Just a little insurance," laughed the hooded thug who stood by the muscular thug.

"But business should not all be unpleasant," chuckled her captor.

"You have not had any fun for a while. Now is your chance. I will watch to make sure you handle it right and that you do not kill her. We want her alive and well," snarled Richard Rasmussin.

"Thanks boss," said the large thug producing a long and extremely red and snake like object out of his trousers which he made even larger by whipping it into a frenzy.

When Tina saw what was about to happen she ran away from the bed screaming trying to climb the non-cooperating walls. Elmo quickly cornered her with the red, angry looking snake like thing even larger than before protruding from his pants.

He easily cornered her, blocked two quick punches and a kick attempt and grabbed the unfortunate Tina and threw her on the bed.

"Now you are going to like me, they all do when I finish with them," said Elmo Entwhistle before connecting with a solid punch to the chin knocking Tina thankfully unconscious.

The violent defilement went on and on for at least an hour before Elmo finally grunted his last grunt and zipped up.

Richard patted his protégé on the back, left a container of food and more water on the dresser and the two heartless creeps left the room sliding the deadbolt in place after them.

And the fun had just begun.

Chapter 20

Joey was frantically pacing back and forth with Angel and Jon-Erik trying to console him as best as they could. It was now around 8 am the next morning with the group hardly getting any sleep, a knock on the door interrupted their lamenting.

It was Rollie with detective Cragan in tow. Jon-Erik let them in and Angel went to the kitchen to make coffee for everyone.

"I'm getting the family involved as I should have done 5 years ago," Joey yelled out while continuing his pacing.

"We know how you feel," Rollie answered. "However, now is not the time to act irrational."

"Have any one of you been contacted at all regarding Tina?" asked detective Cragan.

"No, should we be expecting that?" answered Angel.

"At this stage we do not know what to expect. Your friend has disappeared apparently without a trace. We have no idea what happened to her if anything," stated detective Cragan.

"So what is being done to find her," Joey asked with his hands balled up into tight fists.

"Officially, Tina is not even deemed missing but her disappearance is certainly suspicious to say the least as it happened almost under all your noses. I have unofficially contacted the Niagara Falls police to have the surveillance tapes from the hotel reviewed to see if anything comes to light. Did Tina have any known enemies or had any altercations with anyone lately?" asked detective Cragan.

"Tina is a very private person and only ever spent time with me, Joey or Mindy her dog. She has not had contact with her family in years, her father died while she was young and her mother ran off to who knows where with some biker after Tina left home at 18. As far as we know, she has never heard from her since," indicated Angel.

"Angel is right; she had heard nothing from her mother for at least 12 years. She would not even know if she was still alive or what name she is using or where she has gone. Tina's last name is Locarno and her mother's name was Madeline. The last time Tina saw her mother was 12 years ago in Port Hope where she grew up. That's all we know," said Joey.

"It's a start. I'll get on the Port Hope connection immediately while Alf (detective Cragan) follows up with the Niagara police. As far as getting your family involved Joey, extra eyes and ears are always welcome in a situation such as this as long as they do not try to take the law into their own hands," said Rollie.

"You guys just sit tight in case Tina or someone tries to contact you," added Alf Cragan.

"Joey and I have to go back to the furniture store tomorrow and Angel has her first day on the job but we will have our cell phones on," said Jon-Erik and with that the two detectives left the group of stunned friends to themselves.

"I'm going home to be with Mindy and contact cousin Guido who will put the Agricolas on high alert. If anyone did snatch Tina, they will be made accountable and pain will become the normal for them. That is for certain," vowed Joey before leaving the house and heading back to his own.

Angel and Jon-Erik just sat on the couch and hugged and wondered how this could have happened to their best friend. They prayed that she was okay and would be home soon knowing that very capable individuals were out there trying to get a clue as to what happened to her— including the Shape Shifter.

Mikhail had never left Niagara Falls and had very easily disabled the individual responsible for monitoring the hotel hallways with a knock on the door and a couple of hours of sleep he had not counted on.

The Monster quickly found the security DVD from last evening, popped it in the player and scanned up to the approximate time of Tina's disappearance looking for the camera that monitored the entrance to the washrooms. He quickly picked up Tina going in and then leaving arm and arm with a woman he could not identify heading down a hallway.

In his estimation, Tina was drugged, the way she walked and was being supported by an unknown abductor. A scant 30 seconds later, he saw Angel entering the washroom and then coming out a minute later looking flustered and running back towards the Casino.

He then searched for the outside feed, synchronizing the time and quickly saw Tina being pushed into a black panel van that sped off into the night. He zoomed in on back of the van, no plates.

These kidnappers must have a device to retract the plate numbers when they feel they are being monitored. Definitely not amateurs thought the Ninja. *They will be sorry they were born when I catch up with them.*

Mikhail had no real affinity to Tina and Joey but because of their relationship to Angel, he would do what he could. Strange how things turn out; 5 years ago he was trying to eliminate the whole group of them and now he was helping them. The guard monitoring the hotel security would be awake soon; the Night Stalker exited the room as quickly and quietly as he entered and became a shadow that slithered away and out of sight.

He was heading back to Woodbridge to stake out the furniture store; they always returned to the scene of the original crime and when they did, he would be waiting.

Chapter 21

"Lady, lady. Are you alright?" was the first thing Tina heard when she returned to the world of the conscious. She shook her head and saw two younger girls in winter jogging suits, earmuffs and gloves standing over her. The bright sunlight hurt her eyes as she painfully pushed herself upward into a sitting position, feeling substantial pain in her joints and private areas.

"Where am I?" asked Tina

"You are at Colonel Samuel Smith Park on the Lakeshore," replied the taller of the two joggers.

Tina had now gotten herself into a full sitting up position and began to feel the cold even through her winter jacket. Squinting because of the sun, she saw the sparkling waters of Lake Ontario in the distance. She was sitting on a wooden park bench with the two girls still looking down on her.

"What happened to you, do you need any help?" asked the shorter perky redhead.

"I'm Mandy and this is Bailey. We were out for a jog and saw you laying there.

It's too cold to be out here and not moving."

"I don't know. Last I remember I was in Niagara Falls with my friends. I went to the washroom and next thing I woke up and you were here," said Tina rubbing her eyes and trying to clear the cobwebs.

"Do you want us to call someone, we have I-phones," asked Bailey.

Something compelled Tina to look under the bench and she noticed her brown handbag was sitting there. She reached under the bench and pulled it up towards her and did a quick inspection.

Her wallet with all her personal id, money, etc. was intact and so was her cell phone although turned off.

She pressed the on button, hearing the Telus music come on indicating the phone was booting itself back up.

"Thanks so much to both of you but I'll be fine, my phone is working and I will call my fiancée. He will be worried to death about me. Here is one of my business cards, I would be happy to buy you both dinner for your kindness and will call you once I sort this all out. Take care and be safe," said Tina.

"You too and we hope you find out what happened. We heard about these date rape drugs that are out there," and with that the two joggers kicked up their Nikes and disappeared around a bend.

Tina punched up the number of the furniture store and Jon-Erik answered promptly.

"It's Tina, I'm okay. I think I was drugged. Please put Joey on."

"Jeez Tina, you had us all worried out of our minds. So glad you are safe. I have just paged Joey; he is out back looking over a new shipment we just received. Where are you?" asked Jon-Erik anxiously

"Apparently, close to home in a park. I have no idea what happened to me or how I got here. I do not remember anything from the time I left all of you and went into the washroom at the Casino."

"Wow, listen here is Joey. He is dying to talk to you. We will hopefully see you soon. Be safe," said Jon-Erik before handing the phone to Joey.

"Honey! Are you alright? We were worried sick about you, Where are you?" yelled Joey into the receiver, his heart beating a mile a minute.

"Yes, it's so good to hear your voice. I'm in Colonel Samuel Smith Park, West of where we live sitting on a park bench. My body aches in places it should not ache. Please come and get me—hurry!" Tina replied.

"Right away hon. I'll leave Jon-Erik here to finish things up and close the shop. He will call Angel, Rollie and detective Cragan. Stay where you are, I will be there as fast as I can," said Joey running as fast as he could and jumping into the company truck.

After receiving the good news, Angel took off in her Mustang, heading West along Lakeshore Blvd. It took her maybe five minutes until she reached Kipling Ave. and the park entrance.

She parked in the designated parking area and took off at full speed into the park. It did not take her long to see Tina's back sitting on a bench facing the lake.

"Tina, oh my god are you okay?" screamed Angel scooping up her best friend into her arms and just holding her. Tears were now freely flowing from both reunited soul mates.

"I love you so much," is all Tina could muster before the stress of everything that happened to her caused her to faint right in Angel's arms.

Angel, sitting on the bench, cradled her head on her lap and watched Tina slowly return and then gave her a drink of water from a bottle of Evian she had brought with her.

"Easy now, you're fine and Joey is on his way. I was at home and much closer so I came immediately. Nothing will hurt you now and if they try, they will have to go through me and I'll take a few or all of them down....that I vow," whispered Angel quietly with a menacing growl in her voice.

"I just want to go home and shower. I feel dirty, sore and bone tired," Tina whispered just as they saw Joey's truck scream into the parking lot. He was out of his truck and at Tina's side in seconds scooping her up in his arms and showering her with kisses while Angel sat by quietly.

After the touching reunion, Joey thanked Angel for being there so fast for Tina and indicated he was taking her home to get some rest. Questions and everything else could come after Tina had rested and had some food. He carried his lady to his truck, strapped her in and took off for home with Angel following behind.

When Angel got home, Jon-Erik had just arrived as well. He told Angel that Rollie and detective Cragan were on their way.

"They will have to wait till Tina is cleaned up and has some rest. She looks like she went through some ordeal but cannot remember anything. They may have messed with her mind or something. We'll all wait here until Joey gives us the green light to come over," indicated Angel.

"Main thing is she is okay and back with us, the rest we will deal with as we need to," replied Jon-Erik pouring a glass of wine for Angel and getting himself a beer out of the fridge.

"I just wish I knew what was going on," said Angel.

"Couldn't sum it up any better," agreed Jon-Erik.

Chapter 22

When first Joey and then Jon-Erik left the furniture store in a hurry and closing the store much earlier than normal, the Monster followed a safe distance behind and quickly ascertained that Tina was safe at home.

Even he was confused with this latest turn of events. What was the reasoning behind this? Leverage of some sort perhaps or just to put a scare into them? These were not average criminals they were dealing with and had obvious sinister motives which put a nasty grin on his partially stubbled face making him look more menacing than ever.

Since the furniture store was now closed, Mikhail decided to pay a visit to some of his sources in the city to see if he could pull any information about these shakedown artists out of the woodwork.

First stop was a little unassuming Russian Bakery in the west end of the city near High Park. Mikhail parked in an alleyway behind the business, shim-mied up the fire escape and let himself in like a wisp of wind through a sliding window that he knew was never locked. He padded down the stairs into a dark hallway that led to a large room in the basement at-tended by a huge, snoring bear of a man sleeping in a chair that woke up rather abruptly as the chair was kicked out from underneath him.

"Chyort vos'mi! (Damn it!)," screamed the bulky Russian but became instantly silent when he saw what was towering over him. He got up and un-locked the door to the smoky gambling den half full of patrons, as it was early in the afternoon. The eve-ning and later would find this place full to the rafters.

Black Jack and poker tables, off track wagering and even various illegal blood sports and animal fighting piped in via the internet were all in full op-eration. In the dark corners in the back of the room were a number of booths set up with curtains where the patrons of this establishment could get any type of sex or depravity they were willing to pay for and judging by the slapping, moaning and slurp-ing sounds coming from them, business was indeed picking up.

As the Ninja walked into the room anyone in his way cut him a wide berth. No one knew him but they all knew of him and how incredibly dangerous he was.

The Shape Shifter walked up to the bar where a triple shot of Stolichnaya Vodka on ice was waiting for him. Mikhail downed the clear cold liquid in one gulp and repeated it three more times until he felt that pleasant burn in his throat and stomach.

"So Yuri, what do you know about an outfit shaking down business owners operating in and around this city?" Mikhail asked the shifty looking bartender and proprietor of this den of iniquity. Yuri was connected to everything and everyone that was doing anything shady in the city. The only one who was feared more was the Assassin.

While Yuri was preparing another triple shot he replied," I hear things in the wind and they have connections to old country that our people could only dream about. Only one message ever came and it said, *do not ever ask questions or get in their way.*

"As you know we control all the Russian action here, except them. We do not know who they are or what they are doing but their power and reach is formidable," added Yuri.

"So the old country has put the fear of god into you. Very bad for you and your business. These people have made a huge mistake by coming after those I have sworn to protect. They will feel my wrath and so will you if you do not tell me more," snarled Mikhail.

The bartender made a waving gesture and four large, muscular and menacing looking hoods surrounded Mikhail who seemed to levitate into the air knocking three of the four down with head kicks that almost separated their bulbous heads from their bodies on their way down.

The fourth one caught the monster in a crushing choke hold applying pressure like a vice. Mikhail shook himself like an angry tiger sending the goon flying over the bar smashing head first through the mirror above the bar and landing in a crumpled heap below.

The Ninja's fighting blood was now up. He grabbed Yuri with one massive paw and hoisted him in the air; the Russian bartender choked like a chicken.

"You dare go against me? I should destroy this place and everyone in it. You are all nothing but spineless cockroaches to me and I should step on you all," snarled Mikhail.

None of the four that attacked him were moving; chances are they were all dead or severely injured. No one else dared to make a move and the place had become eerily silent.

"I will give you one more chance to give me some information I can use. If I do not get it I will kill you and everyone in here. Understood?" snarled Mikhail.

"Da. The only other thing I know is they are involved in a huge financial operation. That is all I know. Do what you want with me." said Yuri.

"Stupid man. Pour me another one of those triple shots and get rid of those useless gnats on the floor. They are leaking too much blood and will make your floor slippery," Mikhail answered while releasing Yuri who could not move fast enough to pour the shot and instruct the requested cleanup.

After the monster downed the final shot he got up and seemed to disappear right in front of everyone's eyes. Even the still stunned doorman did not see him as he passed and exited out of the window he entered and left the area in his car feeling much better about the day having spent some of his energy and learning something as well.

The financial business? The punk that threatened the guys in the furniture store was some sort of financial consultant... and money was something the killer enjoyed. The blood hound was on the trail and it would be paved in green and red before he was done!

Chapter 23

Richard Rasmussin called the impromptu but severely mandatory meeting to order. Around the table were Christine Hertzog, Elmo Entwhistle and Jimmy Rudiger, Richard's inner circle.

No one spoke until Richard kicked off the festivities.

"So all of you understand the reasoning behind what we just did?"

"Yes Boss," replied Elmo with a wicked grin.

Rudiger was munching on a bag of potato chips and let out a loud belch for his response causing Richard to respond, "You only get away with what you do because of your value to me. Good job in finding the link between that punk Joey who owns the furniture store we are, shall I say, negotiating with and Tina with whom Elmo is now intimately acquainted with."

Entwhistle only chuckled when Christine said, "We followed your orders to the tee Richard but are you not concerned this could backfire on us?"

"Good point but a non-issue. This will benefit us immensely as we will have leverage on our new Productivity Consultant Team as well as the furniture store. Thanks to our benefactors, access to items such as the still experimental but highly effective memory suppression drug, Tina should not ever remember what happened to her and our large friend's appetites are now partially appeased."

"But her friends and now, I am sure, the cops know something happened and will stumble around for a bit trying to find out what. But we are going to put a stop to that quickly even as early as tomorrow and that furniture store will be ecstatic to sign on the dotted line," added Richard.

"So what's the plan Boss?" asked Elmo.

"You are going to pay that furniture store another visit after they get a voice altered telephone call. They will then be more than happy to join FinCo. If they do not, we will destroy them and their business. Non-compliance is never tolerated," said Richard putting it into financial terms.

And with a wave of his hand, the meeting was dismissed.

After everyone had left the room, Richard put his hands behind his head and started thinking about the beautiful and lethal Angel who was now in his employment. *Here was a woman he just had to have for himself. They would make a great team and tomorrow would be her first day on the job. The first day of the rest of her life.*

While Richard Rasmussin dreamed of Angels, Joey had gotten Tina home. Exhausted as she was, she jumped into the shower and scrubbed herself till her skin was raw for almost half an hour and then ran a hot bath for herself which she luxuriated in till Joey came in to check on her.

"Are you okay, hon?" is all Joey could think of saying, seeing his beautiful lady home safe again and looking even more beautiful decked out in the sudsy tub.

"Yes, but something happened to me while I was away. I am sore in places I should not be. I have bruising in spots between my legs and my breasts are sore like someone kept pulling at my nipples. I wish I could remember but everything comes up blank since the washroom in Niagara Falls."

"Maybe we should get you to your doctor for an examination and she could determine what happened to you. Main thing is you are home with me once again and safe," replied Joey kneeling beside the tub and gently kissing her forehead.

"Yes, good idea. You can call to make an appointment for me. But first I need to sleep and then I'm sure the police are waiting to speak with me. I don't know what I can tell them besides what I have told you," said Tina draining the tub and wrapping herself up in a fluffy white bathrobe.

Joey took her upstairs and tucked her into their large king size bed where she fell asleep almost instantaneously.

As soon as Joey left the room the doorbell rang downstairs. Rollie and detective Cragan were at the door.

Joey opened the door and told them that Tina had just fallen asleep but they asked to come in to find out what Tina had told Joey.

They all sat in the living room and Joey relayed what little he knew.

Cragan and Rollie were both quiet for a few minutes until Rollie broke the silence and said," Sounds to me like some sort of memory suppression was used on her."

"And possibly she was sexually violated as well," added Cragan.

"Sexually violated? It can't be. Those sons of bitches!" yelled out Joey hoping Tina did not hear upstairs.

"Relax Joey, we know nothing yet. She needs to get to a specialist who can examine her as soon as possible. I know this is stressful for both of you but we need to piece together what happened here so we can take steps to find out whom and what we are dealing with. I will arrange for one of our police medical examiners to come out and see Tina as soon as she wakes up," continued Cragan.

"She would be more comfortable if her own doctor examined her first. I will be setting up a visit with her as soon as you two leave. The doctor can then decide if anything further is necessary," Joey pointed out.

"Fine but I need to be notified of the results as soon as possible. Meanwhile, what did she tell you?" asked Cragan.

"Just that she remembers nothing after entering the washroom at the casino and feels tender and sore in places she shouldn't."

"Okay, call your doctor and get her over here as soon as Tina has rested. Time is of the essence," said detective Cragan.

"You guys know I am just a phone call away. I'll check in with you later today," added Rollie on the way out the door.

As Rollie Sampson and Cragan left, Angel and Jon-Erik came through the door.

"Normally I would ask anyone else for privacy but you two are family so come on in. She is resting now and I need to call her doctor," said Joey looking drained by everything that had gone on.

"I'll take care of that for you," said Angel. "Tina's doctor is my doctor too and I'll have her here in a few hours."

"Thanks," said Joey while Jon-Erik went to the fridge and got three Coronas out which Angel and Jon-Erik gratefully accepted.

Angel made the call and relayed Doctor Jensen would be there in about three hours, hopefully enough time for Tina to get some rest. She added that she would go to the new contract at FinCo by herself tomorrow to give Tina more time to get better.

"That's appreciated. What would we do without you guys?" said Joey hugging both Angel and Jon-Erik.

"Don't worry, we are going to find out who did this and why," Jon-Erik said with a snarl on his lips.

"And believe me, someone is going to pay for messing with my best friend," vowed Angel.

Chapter 24

Between the most southern tip of Africa and east of South America sit the Nightingale Islands, part of a larger group of Islands named Tristan Da Cunha. These Islands are un-inhabited, *at least on paper,* and administered by the United Kingdom. They consist of the Nightingale, Middle and Stoltenhoff Islands.

A number of years ago, the right palms were greased heavily in the British bureaucracy to allow the secretive and highly lethal Kirotchenko brothers Vlad and Vasily, to set up shop on Stoltenhoff Island.

The brothers ran a vast empire of human trafficking, money laundering, prostitution, drugs and weapons amongst their most notable accomplishments. Many law enforcement agencies including Interpol had tried to find and bring this loathsome duet and their organization to justice and had failed miserably because no one had ever been able to find them or trace these unsavory enterprises back to them.

It took the Kirotchenkos a little more than a year and multi-millions of illegally earned monies to build a seemingly impenetrable underground fortress on Stoltenhoff Island. This labyrinth of connected tunnels held weapon caches, massive electrical generators and computer labs equipped with the most up to date prototype monitoring.

Highly sophisticated communication and encryption technology, state of the art water filtration systems, lavish residences, kitchens and recreational facilities for the brothers and their staff were also part of the design. A helio-pad that was almost totally hidden from the air runway and landing strip completed the incredible and undetectable setup.

The brothers' empire was vast, essentially spanning the globe and had footholds anywhere where vice, corruption and illegalities thrived. If anything or anyone got in their way, they were eliminated swiftly and without any trace. Vlad and Vasily were close to actually spearheading the largest criminal organization in the world today depending what numbers one followed.

The wealth flowing into the countless offshore accounts was staggering; too large to even grasp. The people in the organization knew that one slip up and their days, even hours were numbered. Failure, disloyalty and working outside the system were not tolerated… exception being FinCo….*for now*.

Very close eyes were always kept on Richard Rasmussin and his group in Toronto. The brothers would have liked to get rid of him long ago because of his sometimes flamboyant and unorthodox methods but the truth being Richard was much too successful to take out of the picture. His profits were huge and a great way to funnel a portion of the Kirotchenko ill-gotten gains into the country.

Canada had very strict laws with checks and balances against money laundering but those who had the resources and know how could circumvent these processes. The brothers and Richard were brilliant at it and had key personnel well entrenched in the agencies that monitored this type of activity.

And of course, FinCo was a huge contributor to all the major charities and key political and special interest groups. The difference being that once the contributions were registered and on paper, they were just as efficiently retracted and returned to the coffers of FinCo and ultimately the Kirotchenkos. Those on the payoff roll were paid handsomely for their indiscretions.

When it came to FinCo and the Kirotchenko organization the less said the better for those involved. Some who had dared to cross the organization were never heard from again. Their families, relatives and friends also met the most heinous ends disappearing without a trace.

The police in the countries where this had occurred were totally at wits end as absolutely no sign of forensic or any kind of evidence at all for that matter had ever been found and those who were in the know kept their well greased mouths shut or would become part of these untraceable statistics.

The more established groups such as the Russian mob, Mafia and various Biker gangs for the most part were ignorant of the Kirotchenkos. Those who did know of them were either on the payroll which facilitated silence with some of their ill-gotten gains being ultimately and unknowingly channeled back to Kirotchenkos, or dead.

Vlad, stemming back from Vlad, the Impaler Legend which spawned countless Dracula legends and stories, was a cold blooded ruthless killer and masterful tactician. His brother Vasily was more apt to gather and channel information always ensuring the monies from their various enterprises was ever flowing and increasing.

Vlad was a large brooding man with a protruding forehead and long black hair always tied in a ponytail. Those who looked into his black eyes swore they were looking into the pits of hell itself. No one knew were Vlad got the skills he had acquired in hand to hand combat, weaponry and dispensing death and those who asked were most likely no longer able to share that information.

In contrast, Vasily was a smaller stout greybeard with green eyes that twinkled when he spoke to anyone but mistaking that as a sign of humanity or compassion would be a grave error indeed. Just like his brother he was totally devoid of emotion, just cold, calculating and vicious.

Once a week, when the supply boats came in from either Cape Town, South Africa or Sao Paulo Brazil, there was always the best cigars, vodka, caviar and women money could procure. The Kirotchenko brothers had an insatiable appetite for women and their preferences were Spanish and Negro which worked out well given the location of their fortress.

Interestingly enough, the forbidden fruit of underage girls did not tempt them as much as exotic eyes, skin tone and most of all, attitude. The more a girl had attitude, the more the Kirotchenkos were interested in destroying that attitude in the most degrading and painful ways possible.

The majority of women that set foot on Stoltenhoff were never seen again, the cold Atlantic supplying an unending watery grave with the scaly and predatory inhabitants employing their own code of silence.

Those few rare ones that did survive became part of the brothers' harem that waited on them hand and foot satisfying their every need between boat visits. The competition for the brothers' affections was fierce; you could say even life or death as every second day battle royals were staged between the now ill-fated slaves.

Those who survived lived to service and fight again, those who did not were disposed of quietly and efficiently. It was hard to image something so cruel and despicable existed in this day and age but the brothers were throwbacks from another place and time and nothing but greed, fear and intimidation satisfied them—but only temporarily until the hunger came again.

Chapter 25

After Tina awoke, she felt a little better, especially after Joey made her some herbal tea and a bowl of her favorite oatmeal with raisons. Shortly after, her doctor arrived and asked for at least half an hour of privacy with her patient. Joey, Angel and Jon-Erik waited downstairs quietly talking amongst themselves.

It seemed like hours when Dr. Jensen finally called the group back upstairs bedside. She asked Jon-Erik to contact detective Cragan indicating he would be interested to hear the results of her findings. Jon-Erik contacted Rollie Sampson as well who lived close by and was there in a matter of minutes.

Detective Cragan arrived about 15 minutes later joining everyone else who had convened in Joey's living room.

"I have given her a sedative to get at least another 8 hours of uninterrupted sleep which she desperately needs after such an ordeal," began the doctor. "After a thorough examination I have made a number of determinations. There is bruising around her pubic area and evidence of penetration both vaginally and anally although there is no seminal fluid present. Most likely her attacker used protection but was extremely rough with her," he continued.

"That son of a bitch will pay for this. No one violates my fiancée like that!" screamed Joey almost putting his fist through the door before Jon-Erik wrapped his strong arms around his best friend and calmed him down somewhat.

"I know how you all feel, believe me," said Dr. Jensen. The good news at least for Tina is that she is strong, otherwise healthy and has no recollection of what happened to her. I have taken some blood and will have it tested for presence of any substances that may induce memory loss such as Ecstasy, Xanax, Valium or other more powerful derivatives. Chances are, whatever it was has flushed through her system by now anyway but we'll do our best to find it if we can."

"Will her memory of what happened to her come back in time?" asked Rollie.

"Good question and there is no easy answer. The mind is a delicate mechanism and sometimes suppresses extremely traumatic events with or without the help of chemicals. A tiny puncture wound on the inside of her left arm was found and on her neck so she was most likely injected with something. The fact that she does not remember is a good protective mechanism for her for now but yes, her memory of those violent events could come back at any time or not at all," indicated the doctor.

"Anything else you can tell us from your examination?" asked detective Cragan.

"She has some bruising on her arms and legs. I have bagged some fingernail scrapings that you can take to your lab for processing in case Tina scratched her attackers. But since she has bathed and showered since then, the chances are slim anything remained," said Dr. Jensen handing a small plastic bag to detective Cragan.

"Not much else I can add other than Tina will be as good as new minus the memory loss once she gets sufficient rest. Your lab can test the fingernail scrapings and I will have her blood checked for whatever contaminant these perpetrators used. If our labs cannot find anything, I will turn the sample over to you as your police medical testing staff may have access to a larger database to match up to. Best thing now is to let her rest. I'm sorry I could not assist further but the main thing is Tina will be fine physically."

And with that Dr. Jensen left to return to her practice and deal with other patients.

"Well, I should be off as well with the fingernail evidence and will wait to see what the doctor comes up with as far as the blood tests go. So sorry for what happened to Tina, I will give this case my utmost attention and please keep me informed of anything that develops," said detective Cragan before leaving as well.

Rollie and the rest of the group sat down while Angel brought some snacks from the kitchen as Joey was too distraught to even function. They discussed how here they were five years later and in another threatening situation, and had no idea what they were facing.

"The difference being we are wiser and do not have the Ninja hunting for us. He may actually be an ally of ours in this case, believe it or not," said Angel.

"He still gives me the creeps but it is better to have him with us than against us," she added.

"Obviously this has something to do with the shakedown at your furniture store. Can you guys arrange for me to do some work on the floor in case that guy comes back that threatened you?" asked Rollie.

"I can do better than that. I'm sure Joey wants to stay with Tina for a few days until she is back to herself so I will need help at the shop. We can even pay you for your time if you wish," replied Jon-Erik.

"That sounds fine. I'll start tomorrow with you. As far as paying me, don't worry about that. I've got enough money saved up from other cases and my years on the police force. But you can buy me lunch, can't work on an empty stomach you know," replied the stout private detective with a twinkle in his eye.

Joey seemed to snap out of his funk and put his arms around Rollie and thanked him indicating how much he appreciated Rollie's thoughtfulness. He then hugged Jon-Erik and Angel in turn and said how lucky he and Tina were to have friends as special as them.

After they talked and munched on the snacks a bit more, Rollie left to get ready for tomorrow and

Jon-Erik and Angel left as well. Jon-Erik had to manage the whole furniture store with Rollie's help and of course the ever supportive cousin Guido. Angel had to get ready for her first day at FinCo tomorrow. With all the things that had happened in the last forty eight hours, she had almost forgotten their new consulting job which she had to begin without Tina.

She was sure that Richard Rasmussin and company would understand that Tina was under the weather so to speak. No way was she going to disclose what actually had happened to their new employer as it may make them suspicious of whom they had hired.

Little did she know. Little did she know, indeed.

Chapter 26

Another winter Monday morning began in the GTA (greater Toronto area). An additional ten centimeters of snow had fallen overnight overtop of the stuff that was already on the ground making the city and surrounding areas a navigating nightmare. The salters, sanders and snow removal vehicles had already been out and where just beginning to attack the side streets impeded by the many vehicles still parked there since they had no other options.

The weather was cold, murky and gloomy as Angel made her way to her Mustang which actually ran quite well in the winter with the addition of the high end and reliable winter tires that Jon-Erik insisted she used. She decided to stay on the Lakeshore rather than using the QEW and Gardiner which she knew would be a mess because of the Monday morning volume and the weather.

Jon-Erik had long since stored his corvette coupe for the winter and was using the van from the furniture store and swung by Rollie's place to pick him up before heading north to Woodbridge. Traffic usually was not a problem since they were going opposite of all the volume to the city but because of the nasty weather, things were a slower go for them.

Angel made her way along the Lakeshore to Yonge St. and parked her car in the underground parking lot in the BMO Tower at Yonge and Bay. The parking was a ridiculous $25 per day, something she was going to discuss with her new employers. It was now 9:15 am but considering the weather she thought she had made good time.

Jon-Erik and Rollie arrived at the Woodbridge furniture store around the same time, unlocked the doors, booted up the desk computers, turned all the showroom lights on and Rollie took a walk around to get acquainted with the store. In the meantime, Guido arrived and he and Jon-Erik made the final preparation to receive their customers which they doubted would be many in this gloomy weather, but you never knew.

While everyone else prepared for their work day, Joey sat by Tina's bedside as she opened her beautiful hazel eyes after sleeping almost around the clock.

"How do you feel Tina? I love you more than you will ever know," said Joey gently passing her a glass of cold water which she drank down in one gulp.

Tina sat up in her bed, stretched and winced at the pain she still felt in her limbs and private areas.

"Not too bad now that I am here in my bed with you. Did anyone get the number of the train that ran me over?" replied Tina with a little smile appearing on her bruised lips.

"You'll be fine, even better than fine with a little rest," replied Joey gently kissing her on the cheek. "Are you ready for some breakfast Joey style?"

"I want it all, bacon, eggs, sausage, toast, waffles and pancakes. I feel like I have not eaten properly in days. What happened to me?" replied Tina.

"Coming right up, that sounds delicious. We'll talk after we eat. Want to stay in bed for the day and just cuddle?" suggested Joey.

"That sounds heavenly. But no funny stuff yet until my legs and privates stop aching," replied Tina asking where Angel and Jon-Erik were.

Joey answered back from the kitchen over the heavenly scent of frying bacon, sausages and eggs that Jon-Erik and Rollie were looking after things at the furniture store and Angel had gone to begin their contract at FinCo.

"I'm so lucky to have all of you, especially you the love of my life," replied Tina laying back down to relax in anticipation of the terrific breakfast Joey was fixing. Life was terrific once again—at least at their house.

Angel rode up the elevator to the 42nd floor, said hello to the receptionist who did nothing but look at her watch rather annoyingly. Angel could see that corporate culture was running rampant here obviously but secretly hoping this was an isolated incident.

She swiped the access card she was given when she was hired and the door opened to a vast area full of clerical staff. The administrators had their offices around the outside of the floor with the best views of the city.

Angel walked around till she found an office marked C. Hertzog and gently knocked on the door.

"Enter," was the only answer. *Short and not so sweet* thought Angel.

When she entered the office, Angel sat down in a chair opposite Christine and the two beautiful women just looked at each other before Angel started the conversation.

"Listen, I apologize again for the other day. I should probably have pulled back a bit but your attack was intense at best."

"That is already forgotten—for now. But rest assured I will demand a rematch at the time of my choosing.

Angel again heard that challenge in her voice and replied, "Anytime, anywhere."

Once that was out of the way, Christine indicated it was time for Angel's orientation but had to throw in a quip about starting time being 9:00 am sharp.

Angel said nothing but thought her piece and could not wait for their rematch and was looking forward to putting this bitch on her proverbial butt again and the earlier the better.

Christine showed her to a small corner cubicle with a desk, chair, phone and docking station for her computer. She waited till Angel docked the computer and booted it up before passing her a manual of instructions for her to read about company policy, computer etiquette and how to log into the company's virtual private network (VPN).

"Take about an hour to acquaint yourself and, then come to a meeting in Richard's office at 11 am. to discuss your next steps. By the way, where is your partner? From what I understood Richard hired the both of you," asked Christine with a sneer on her pretty mouth.

"Tina is under the weather with a bad flu. She is on medication and should hopefully be back Wednesday or the latest Thursday. I will keep her up to date on any developments till then."

That answer seemed to put a sly looking smirk on Christine's face and with a swish of her tight mini and a click of her staccato high heels, left Angel to her own devices. She decided to use her time to introduce herself to some of the people around her cubicle instead; computer stuff could always be dealt with later.

But no one would even acknowledge her as the people around her seemed to be totally immersed in their work. *Gee, this is going to be a barrel of laughs working here but I'll have Tina here with me soon and maybe we can loosen up some of these stuffed shirts up a touch* thought Angel diving into her computer since she had a bit more time before her meeting with Richard Rasmussin.

Chapter 27

Things were slow at the furniture store as expected with the nasty weather. Jon-Erik and Guido had some time to show Rollie around. Rollie thought he would make a good salesman and since the various pieces were clearly marked, he would bring the clients to either Jon-Erik or Guido to close the sale, arrange for delivery or have any questions answered that he could not.

That worked out great for Jon-Erik and Guido as they could concentrate on replenishing the displays and receiving new shipments of various styles and colors of Lazy-Boy couches and chairs. Since Rollie was there, they ordered in pizza at lunchtime keeping their promise to ensure Rollie was well fed. Jon-Erik and Guido loved pizza as well.

What they hadn't counted on was what happened when the pizza finally arrived over an hour later. Everyone was hungry by then and were totally startled when the rather large and ominous looking delivery man with his cap pulled over his eyes threw the five dollar tip Jon-Erik gave him right back in his face.

"Listen, you were over half an hour late, you are lucky to get anything but now get out with no tip at all. We'll never order from your company again," said Jon-Erik looking quite upset.

In the meantime, the hungry Guido opened the pizza box to find nothing but a few crumbs and a tub of garlicky dipping sauce that was half gone.

"What the?" shouted Guido and before he could react further the obviously hostile delivery man shoved the empty pizza box right back into his face with so much force it knocked him backwards into the wall where he crumpled into a heap and went for an unexpected cat nap.

Jon-Erik was totally in shock and furious at the same time. His football skills had not deserted him yet and he launched himself at this large lunatic with a force out of shear desperation. He was always trained to go in low and this time it was his undoing as his huge opponent brought his thick knee up and cracked Jon-Erik in the face using his own force against him.

Just like Guido, Jon-Erik went for a totally unscheduled siesta. The sinister pizza delivery man then picked up Jon-Erik with one hand and threw a plastic water bottle that was on the counter into his bashed up face to wake him up as after all he had business to discuss with him.

All the commotion however had alerted Rollie who was in the back of the showroom to acquaint himself with some of the displays and pricing. When he saw what was happening to Jon-Erik, who was just waking up in the grasp of some huge hulk in the process of pouring water on him, Rollie sprang into action aiming his steel toed police sanctioned boot at the back of Jon-Erik's assailants knee.

Unfortunately, he never connected as an all too familiar yet almost primeval force slammed into them both knocking him across the floor right onto a 3 seater leather couch that extended its foot rest from the impact of his landing. He reached for his holstered Sig Sauer pistol that he had a permit to carry but stopped when the Monster growled, "Stay where you are you gnat. I am not after you but I will kill you quick if you make one more move. Leave this with me and do not move. Understand?" snarled the Shapeshifter who had now totally materialized into the large black ominous form that was Mikhail.

Rollie had faced the Executioner a number of times before years ago and was fortunate to escape with his life and relative health in tact. He was not about to tempt fate again and sat back to watch the show trying to clear the cobwebs.

As soon as Jon-Erik saw what was happening, he jumped behind the counter to see if Guido was alright and stayed out of the Doppelganger's way. He had also seen what Mikhail could do; the biggest mistake anyone could make was getting involved in this nightmare's business and Jon-Erik knew it. After checking on Guido who was waking up from his slumber and motioning him not to move, he peeked over the counter to watch the surreal events unfolding.

The Pizza delivery guy a.k,a Elmo Entwhistle was also flung against a large steel ceiling support beam from the force Mikhail used to separate everyone but he was up on his feet fast and pissed off as hell to say the least.

"Who the hell are you and who invited you to this little party? If I would have known we'd have this many people for lunch, I would have brought an extra pizza rather than the one I already ate before relieving the delivery boy of it," chuckled Elmo still having no clue what he was dealing with.

"So you are the punk that has been threatening my friends here? Are you also responsible for the kidnapping of Angel's friend Tina?" growled the Ninja.

"Punk? I'm just a humble business man doing my job. And right now my job is to get Mr. Surfer dude behind the counter to sign some papers and I'll be gone. As far as Tina goes, she was indeed a delectable little morsel, even better than this lousy pizza!" replied Elmo coming ever closer to Mikhail who just stood with his large arms folded across his massive chest eyeing Elmo like a leopard would his prey.

"You are just an insignificant gnat working for a larger cockroach but the fact that you defiled a friend of Angel's can't go unpunished," indicated the executioner as his gold tooth caught the reflection of one of the florescent ceiling lights making him look even more formidable.

Elmo had been inching closer and closer to Mikhail until he was near enough to throw a punch to the throat that would have disabled or crushed the larynx of anyone else but all Mikhail did was tuck his jaw into his chin and absorbed the whole punch with a wolfish grin on his face.

"Do you know how many men I have sent into the next life with my bare hands alone? Too many to count. And how many bullets I have taken and lived to talk about it. Ask the detective on the couch there. Hope he is enjoying the show and he knows not to move a muscle. I know, I talk too much, must be getting soft," said the Monster unleashing a lightning fast attack of his own consisting of a punch so quick and vicious that snapped Elmo's nose like a dry twig.

He obviously wasn't with the program, yet as Elmo snapped his broken nose back in place with a howl and then came at Mikhail with everything he had whirling and spinning like a twister throwing kicks and punches faster than the eye could follow.

Everything happened so fast it was impossible for those watching to follow with their naked eyes but the end result was Mikhail picking Elmo up over his head and smashing him to the floor with a crash. Luck was on Elmo's side as the floor was tile not concrete otherwise his super strong melon would have cracked like an egg shell as Mikhail had unceremoniously dumped him head first.

Elmo Entwhistle lay there in a crumpled heap; his hands and legs flopping around like fish trying to escape a polluted lake but his iron reserve from all the years of his own intense training plus the fact that his now damaged skull still could not comprehend what he was actually facing here.

"Stay down you fat cockroach," advised the Ninja emphasizing his words with a kick to the side that destroyed Elmo's left side kidney.

A scream of pain, fear and anger was the only answer Elmo could muster.

Mikhail picked the broken down shakedown artist and rapist up by the scruff of the neck as its mother would a kitten and deposited him in an easy chair nearby.

"Good, I see everyone is comfortable except me. This surveillance is an uncomfortable business but I am used to it. Nod if you understand me, you human piece of garbage," said Mikhail the killer elite.

Elmo was totally beaten, he had had enough. He could barely muster the nod.

"Good, you have learned what the lucky ones that still live have learned. You cannot beat what can't be beaten. You cannot hurt what can't be hurt. But you can be hurt and you can die. Understand, you insignificant gnat?" said Mikhail.

Again Elmo nodded.

"Good, now we are getting somewhere. If you do not answer the next few questions and truthfully, I will cause you more pain then even you can imagine. Nod if you understand."

Another nod was made, this one looking much more fearful however.

"Who do you work for, insect?" was the first and most important question.

Elmo shook his head before answering. "I gave an oath on my life never to disclose that. If I ever give up whom I work for, I will be killed more cruelly than even at your hand."

"Loyalty, I admire that. I was loyal to my master once and sent all those that killed him to hell. These two, pointing at Jon-Erik and Rollie know this. Now I am loyal only to myself and Angel, the blonde guy behind the counters' betrothed."

"You made the grave mistake of messing with the people Angel loves most. Now you know why you are in the mess you are in. I ask you one more time. Who employs you?"

Again, nothing from Elmo, besides a shake of his smashed anvil like head.

Then you are of no further use to me," hissed the dispatcher of men. Faster than even a video camera could capture, Mikhail produced a Shuriken (throwing star), hurled it with a force and accuracy a major league pitcher could only marvel at and embedded the metal object right in the frontal lobe of his brain, killing him instantly.

The Monster slowly walked over to the dead and beaten enforcer, retrieved his throwing star and slung him over his shoulder like the slab of rotten meat he now was.

Guido had now recovered sufficiently to pop his head up from behind the counter joining Jon-Erik with an incredulous look on his face.

But none of the three stunned witnesses could muster up anything to say and they did not move a muscle.

"You two, *addressing Rollie and Jon-Erik*, have learned well not to move. He would not divulge anything. He was trained well but not enough."

The Ninja started searching him and found nothing on him to indicate where he was from except for the same card Joey and Jon-Erik were given with a name and a number and now that number would no longer be answered. He took a roll of bills out of the dead man's wallet and pocketed them as well as his cell phone which he would examine later.

"For expenses. I will make an example of him and draw his employers to me and kill them all. They have no idea what they are dealing with. Read your newspaper tomorrow. They will see the same," said the Monster before turning and walking out of the furniture store with what was left of Elmo draped over his right shoulder.

Once the Ninja had left, everyone collected themselves the best they could. Nothing further was said as they all just wanted to go home; the store was being closed early. But they were not the only ones who were having an eventful day to say the least.

Chapter 28

A ngel oriented herself as best she could by logging into the company's private network. She found an icon allowing her access to her own email which she opened and found to be the standard Lotus Notes variety. A lot of notices about upcoming meetings, network outages past and future as well as various disaster review notices.

She wondered what these people actually knew about real disasters which she and her friends had firsthand experience in and for whatever reason seemed to be involved in another one again. It was now two minutes to 11 am so she grabbed her note book and pen and hurried off to Richard Rasmussin's posh corner office. After all, it would not look good to be late for her first meeting.

She knocked on the door and a deep voice inside asked her to come in. Richard sat behind his desk in a light pink designer shirt open at the collar flashing an expensive interlocked gold chain. His tan was darker than ever and his teeth were white to the point of being a distraction. His dark hair was trimmed but still long completing his mysterious exotic look.

Christine Hertzog had her hair styled in a shorter multi-layered bob with tastefully added blonde and darker streaks. She wore dark eyeliner which accentuated her cat like eyes and a short mini and stylish aquamarine blouse completing her captivating look.

Angel this time had her beautiful long blond hair in a ponytail; her almond shaped eyes accentuated just enough to make her look even more attractive. Her skin was tanned honey brown from regular sessions at the salon and a striking light blue pant suit along with matching hand bag completed her fetching ensemble.

"My my, isn't everyone looking good today," began Richard.

Angel replied with a quiet thank you while she and Christine were eyeing each other up and down competitively.

"Now that we have the formalities out of the way, I understand your partner is not with us this morning?" asked Richard with one dark eye brow raised.

"Yes, as I told Christine she is under the weather with the flu. She should hopefully be back with me in a few days. I will keep her up to date on developments until then," replied Angel.

"Unfortunate but I suppose these things happen. I never get sick, have no time for it actually," stated Richard.

Angel thought that was a rather insensitive statement but let it slide for now and did not reply.

Richard continued the conversation by asking if Angel had a chance to orient herself a bit.

"Computer wise yes, people wise no," replied Angel. "Everyone was too busy to talk to me."

"This is a busy company. We did not get to where we are by idle gossip. I will take you around this afternoon and personally introduce you to whom you should be speaking with. There are only a few people that fully understand the work flow around here, Christine being the most knowledgeable besides myself," indicated Richard.

The others you would be speaking with are Jimmy Rudiger and Elmo Entwhistle who are out on client visits currently," continued Richard.

Angel could not believe her ears. *Elmo Entwhistle? Wasn't that the guy's name who was threatening Jon-Erik and Joey at the furniture shop? Couldn't be…could it?,* thought Angel doing everything she could to not look as stunned as she felt.

She prided herself on her ability to remember names; this was too weird to consider but she would definitely look into it given her experiences from the past.

There was no indication on Richard's face that he had picked up on Angel's uneasiness but Christine seemed to raise her tiny eyebrows slightly.

"Listen, it's lunchtime and I have a number of meetings this afternoon. I'll leave you in Christine's more than capable hands for now and in the afternoon you will meet Jimmy and Elmo as they should both be back in the office.

"Come on, I'll show you the cafeteria. We have the best gourmet food and salads anywhere around and it's reasonably priced and subsidized for the employees," said Christine grabbing Angel's hand and leading her out of the office.

Angel, politely as she could, took her hand back and excused herself for a few minutes indicating she had some calls to make and would meet Christine there in ten minutes.

She went back to her desk and noticed her phone was vibrating off the hook indicating someone had texted her.

The texts were all from Jon-Erik asking her to call him immediately and that it was urgent. Since there was very little privacy around her desk, she went into one of the meeting rooms that was currently unoccupied, closed the door and used her cell to call Jon-Erik.

He answered on the second ring still sounding somewhat excited from the events that had transpired at the furniture store earlier that day.

He began to relay the details; Angel listening with beads of sweat appearing on her forehead which she wiped away with a tissue from her purse.

When he had finished she asked," Unbelievable, Mikhail was there and killed someone right in front of your eyes and took him away?"

"Yes, imagine how shocked we all were, even Rollie. But none of us wanted to angry this Monster even further or get in his way."

"Smart moves on your part. He seems to be fixated on my welfare now and all of yours by default. But even I do not know how he will react at any given time. I'm just thankful you are all okay," said Angel.

"Rollie will be coming over this evening to discuss these events further. So far he has not mentioned what happened to detective Cragan but I'm sure he will. We are all still shook up. How are things going on your first day in the meantime?" asked Jon-Erik.

"Listen, that guy the Ninja eliminated, what was his name?" Angel asked.

"From what I remember, Elmo something or other. Some weird English last name and he worked for some sort of Financial Institution that he was trying to get us to sign up with," Jon-Erik answered.

"It can't be. There's a guy named Elmo Entwhistle who is one of the partners in the firm here whom I'm supposed to be meeting with this afternoon when he returns from a client visit. This is just crazy," Angel stuttered.

"What?" asked Jon-Erik. "That's insane. You mean there is a possibility this guy works for the company that hired you and Tina? My god, be careful but see what you can find out without arousing suspicion. I know you can more than handle yourself but be extremely cautious because if it is the same guy they may not even know he is dead yet but the shit is going to hit the fan once they do find out and knowing how the Ninja works, that won't be long. Be extremely careful and come home to me safely," said Jon-Erik sounding extremely concerned.

"I will hon, you too and I'll call before I leave and look in on Tina and Joey for me," said Angel before ending the call.

Strange days were here again—strange days indeed.

Chapter 29

Queen's Park in Toronto, located just northwest of the downtown core, had ample green space, provincial government buildings and accommodated picnics and protests alike. It also had a number of statues of Canadian historical figures and events which drew tourists and visitors to the area throughout the four seasons.

One of those historical figures was the statue of John Graves Simcoe, the first Lieutenant Governor of Ontario. The statue depicted John Graves mounted on a high pedestal overseeing the park with a steely eye. This particular afternoon however, the honorable governor had a little more company than usual consisting of the inept and no longer threatening body of one Elmo Entwhistle.

Elmo was well tied around the right shoulder of the statue, giving it an even more bulked up look than normal. The interesting thing was no one noticed anything going about their busy day until little Mikey Millhausen kept tugging on his mother's hand in between yells of "Mom, mom."

His mother was more preoccupied with checking her look in her compact mirror. After all, she had to look her best in case some high net worth politician or businessman came along that might be interested in getting to know a sexy not yet middle aged redhead a little better.

After applying a bit more blush and lipstick, the mother decided she would take little Mikey to relieve himself since it was cold outside and nobody was taking the bait.

"No Mommy, don't need to pee. Look at the statue over there, it looks funny!" said the little nose miner.

Mom tilted her head to the left and shook her head to clear her vision. She pulled little Mikey closer to the statue to get a better look and could not believe her eyes. There was indeed a large body tied across one of the shoulders of the stern looking figure and it wasn't moving.

"Oh my god!" the mother yelled out pulling out her IPhone and calling 911.

She relayed her strange story to the operator and in less than two minutes police cars came screaming from all corners of the city converging on the area of the statue.

The shocked mother, with little Mikey in tow, was ushered to a police car to give her statement. Of course, she took the credit for the find dismissing little Mikey's pleading that he had seen the statue first.

The pending interviews would hopefully snag her a high powered date or two as the money she had bilked out her pitiful ex-husband who took up with a younger though not very well to do women, had almost run out.

To join the police, who cordoned off the area with yellow crime scene tape which of course was now attracting quite a crowd including newspaper reporters packing serious cameras and zoom lenses, a fire engine came screaming on to the scene with lights flashing and alarms blaring.

All the professionals at the site scene did nothing for the first few minutes except for staring up at the unbelievable sight until the officer in charge spoke to the firemen also looking incredulous at the strange spectacle to get a ladder up there and lighten the poor lieutenant governor's load.

This crime scene was not within Alf Cragan's jurisdiction but he heard the buzz over the police scanner and thought this may be interesting to have a look at in light of everything else that had happened so far. He gave Rollie Sampson a buzz to see if he was interested in a little trip downtown. Alf picked up Rollie within a scant 15 minutes and they headed down the QEW, Gardiner and then up Bay St. to University Ave and finally to Queen's Park.

The place was a total zoo... full of spectators, news and TV reporters and of course politicians and office workers from the parliament and surrounding office buildings that wanted to have a first-hand look at all the commotion.

Cragan finally found a parking spot in a lot just up from the crime scene and after a brisk 5 minute walk which they both enjoyed in the cold and damp temperature, arrived at the cordoned off crime scene. Cragan flashed his badge and indicated Rollie was with him and after ducking under the tape, headed over to see the Officer in charge. Lieutenant Capers was a large hulking man with short cropped dark hair, a large veiny nose, jutting chin and small beady eyes.

Detective Cragan introduced himself and his companion and gave the lieutenant a quick run-down of their case and how this situation may factor into their investigation.

Capers grunted, "Be my guest, have a look". The fireman just got him down. He weighed a ton and that's a lot coming from me."

"Be aware that this is going to be a very high profile case. The Premier and the Mayor are going to be all over this one. In all my years on the force, I have never seen or heard of anything like this. Anything relevant comes to me first, is that understood?" added the lieutenant.

The two nodded and plodded off to the area under the statue where a forensics team had already begun to do a preliminary examination of the large body now laying on an even larger tarp. Rollie took one look at the face and tried to keep his own as expressionless as possible as he nudged Cragan to step to the side.

"Cripes, that guy looks like the goon the Ninja disposed of right in front of our eyes. He was the one threatening Joey and Jon-Erik at the furniture store. I was going to tell you about it next time I saw you but wanted to keep it under wraps for now until we knew more. I guess that's now out of the question," whispered Rollie.

"You saw a guy getting killed and weren't going to tell me?" asked Alf Cragan incredulously.

"Look, this is getting totally out of hand. We need to get out of here and talk and then figure out our next steps," indicated Rollie pointing back to the car.

Detective Cragan just shook his head but he knew Rollie Sampson was beyond reproach. He went back to see lieutenant Capers, exchanged a few words and then joined up with Rollie walking back to the car.

"What the hell have you gotten me into and you have some real explaining to do," snarled Cragan as soon as they got clear of the crowd.

As soon as they got back to the car, Rollie indicated Cragan should strap in and that he was in for one hell of a tale.

"In that case, I'm going to need a large double double and an Apple Fritter. And guess what? You are buying," said Cragan, tires screeching out of the parking lot and heading to the nearest Tim Horton's near Spadina and Dundas.

"That's the least of my worries," replied Rollie with a grim look on his round face. No truer words were ever spoken.

Chapter 30

It was now later on in the afternoon. Angel had an appointment to see Jimmy Rudiger at 3:30 pm sharp in his office but Christine Hertzog stopped her on the way there and said something important had come up and that the meeting would be rescheduled.

She further indicated that Angel might as well head home and they would pick up things in the morning.

Angel shrugged, gave Christine a dazzling smile and packed up her purse and computer and headed for the elevator. Things were getting real creepy here and it was looking more and more like she and Tina would take the money and run from this contract but she needed to discuss this first with the group and hopefully Rollie.

Angel pulled out of the underground parking garage and managed to make it down to the Gardiner Express way in only 15 minutes rather than the normal half hour, building a good case for leaving earlier.

She pulled into her house just after 4:15 pm, the furniture van already in the driveway as Jon-Erik's corvette was in the garage for the winter.

Angel opened the door, hung her keys on the key hook, hung her coat up in the closet, put her handbag on the dresser in the hallway and kicked off her leather boots.

"Sit down and check this out," said Jon-Erik excitedly pointing to their 46" HD TV. A glass of Riesling white was waiting for her as she sat down and gave her lover a sexy kiss.

Jon-Erik more than returned the favor and felt himself getting aroused. Whenever he was near Angel he had felt that way ever since they met years ago and he knew that feeling would never leave him. Just the smell of her subtle but sexy perfume had him almost pole vaulting and wanting to take her right there on the couch.

But this special local TV newscast had him fascinated. Angel asked him to quickly fill her in which he did during commercials.

Angel sat there looking totally stunned before asking," Could this be the guy Mikhail disposed of this morning?"

"Good question, your guess is as good as mine. From what they say on TV, the guy had no identification, wallet or anything else on him to give a clue to his identity," replied Jon-Erik taking a sip of his beer.

"The guy was bound to a statue in Queen's Park?" asked Angel still not believing what she was seeing or hearing.

"You got it. And listen Rollie, Detective Cragan and Joey are all on their way over here. I'm just glad you are home safe," said Jon-Erik pulling his Angel close and kissing her deeply again.

"Looks like we'll have to take a rain check on this until after everyone leaves," purred Angel putting her hand down her lover's pants and rubbing his now fully stiff erection before withdrawing her hand and licking her fingers teasingly.

"That's one appointment I will not miss," answered Jon-Erik trying his best to compose himself as there was a knock on the door.

"The fun continues," said Angel as Jon-Erik went to the door and let Rollie, Detective Cragan and Joey in. In the meantime, Angel put on a fresh pot of coffee, she had a feeling they were all going to need it.

After everyone settled in with their coffees in hand, the discussion first focused on Tina, demonstrating that everyone around the table were friends and very concerned. Alf Cragan was even getting with the program as he was still relatively new to this group.

Joey reported Tina was doing much better and was up and about again fussing around the house and spending time with Mindy but she was anxious to get on with her life and her new job.

"She still does not remember what actually happened to her, which makes the fact that she was violated a lot easier on her, but certainly not on the rest of us. And who knows what she will say or do once she finds out about the latest developments at the furniture store and what happened at Queen's Park? I have not told her as she is doing so well right now but we are going to have to bring her up to speed sooner than later," Joey added.

"We'll go over as a group and gently fill her in once our discussion here ends," suggested Angel.

"Good idea, I'll leave that with all of you as she is more comfortable with all of you," indicated Alf Cragan.

"Okay, so where do we go from here?" asked Jon-Erik.

"Well, let's examine what we have here so far. We have some sort of financial extortionist bothering the guys at the furniture store. Then Tina was kidnapped, drugged, violated and strangely released without any memory as to what happened to her or why. Vandalism to your company vehicle, shots fired and then to top it all off another visit from the financial goon resulting in his death by the Ninja witnessed by Joey, Jon-Erik and myself. And finally, a guy that looks almost identical to that goon without anything identifiable on his person found strung up on the statute of one of our founding fathers with a possible tie in to the company where Tina and Angel just started working?" outlined Rollie.

Detective Cragan commented on how the summation was well put but unbelievable just the same. He further indicated how he was caught up in this mess and had not relayed this information to his superiors because he had trouble believing it himself never mind trying to explain it to someone else.

"Welcome to our world. And how do you think we feel, especially after what happened years ago… and now this?" said Angel.

"Do we know for sure the guy on the statue was the same guy the Ninja disposed of?" asked Joey.

"Not 100 percent but they sure looked the same; face, large body, etc," replied Rollie.

"So far, I have only told my superiors that there may be a link between this dead thug and the investigation I am conducting on behalf of Tina, the vandalism at the furniture store as well as the shooting at the house so I do have a bit of leeway. But I'm not going to be able to hold the wolves at bay for long. Rollie, you know how it works," said Alf Cragan.

"Okay, so let's assume there is a connection between all these events. Angel and Tina could be in danger at their workplace," suggested Jon-Erik.

"Good point. If that is the case whoever is initiating all this, knows that there is a connection between Tina, Joey, Jon-Erik and most likely Angel as well," speculated Rollie.

"But the Monster is the wild card in all this so far. No way they would know he killed him and hung him out to dry so to speak," said Joey.

"And I pray they do not think we at the furniture store had anything to do with it because if they do, they will be coming after us with a vengeance," indicated Jon-Erik looking very concerned.

"So what's the plan?" asked Angel her gorgeous face taking on a very wolfish look showing everyone in the room she was in the zone.

Detective Cragan outlined his thoughts on the situation starting with the fact that whomever was behind this would be just as shocked as they were by these developments and would most likely take some time to regroup. He was planning to go back to his office and place a couple of officers under his command in order to find out if there were other similar cases of this type of extortion out there involving a bald, bulky thug.

He and Rollie would also find out who was pried off the statue in the park and what connection if any he had to FinCo.

Cragan further suggested that Angel and Tina, when ready, continue working at FinCo as if nothing happened. It would be very difficult to tie the goon's death back to the furniture store, in light of the fact of how and where he was found.

But he did caution Jon-Erik and Joey that they may send others back to their workplace in order to find out what happened to their henchman.

Rollie volunteered to stay at the furniture store with them for a while since he knew a bit more about the business and he could keep an eye on things.

And with that Detective Cragan took his coat and headed for the door warning Angel to be extremely careful and keep him informed of anything that developed at work and to make sure that Tina was apprised of the situation.

After Cragan left, Rollie headed out the door to get some much needed food and rest as he was planning to be at the furniture store early with the guys.

That left Angel, Jon-Erik and Joey to head back to Joey's place to update Tina on the latest development and their discussion, each wondering how they would feel in her situation, as well as the pickle they were in. One of those large green German Gherkin's—no doubt!

Chapter 31

An emergency meeting was going on behind closed doors in the FinCo offices of Richard Rasmussin. Present were Jimmy Rudiger looking even more rat-like than ever, Christine Hertzog, Elmo Entwhistle and Richard himself.

"What the hell is going on?" shouted Richard directing his steely gaze at his hulking bulky protégée.

"Pretty simple boss, I hired some dumb expendable clown who looked and sounded so much like me that I could not even tell the difference to go back to the furniture store and shake these punks up. The guy was strong, fast and nasty, but of course, nothing like me or he would not have ended up the way he did," chuckled Elmo.

"So what happened to him?" snarled Richard.

"No idea boss. You know what I know. Maybe someone had a vendetta against this idiot and executed him in grand style. I doubt those punks at the furniture store or their cop friends would have had anything to do with this. No way they would have first of all been able to kill him and secondly get him up on that statue without anyone seeing them," replied Elmo.

"The news report stated that they found no id at all on this guy. Good, that means there is no link to us….unless he got to the furniture store first somehow, as you did give them your card initially with your name and number on it and our new Productivity Expert may put two and two together. But won't she be surprised when you are there healthy as a horse for your rescheduled meeting with her tomorrow," chuckled Richard.

"Will be easy to tell, boss, by her reaction. And I'm looking forward to see that tight little Tina again as well as enjoying them both sometime down the road."

"You do not go near Angel. She is reserved for me and me only. Scope out how she behaves seeing you and report back to me. And stay away from Tina for now as well; who knows what would happen if she ever regains her memory, no sense pushing it.

Our time will come soon enough my large friend, be patient. The rest of you back to work. We have a company to run and investors to bilk," directed Richard.

"Meeting adjourned and I will find out what happened to your puppet. You have exceeded my expectations once again my large friend, now keep a low profile for a while," added Richard with a sneer on his handsome face.

Richard sat back down at his desk once everyone had left his office to ponder these latest developments. There was also an increased pressure the Kirotchenko brothers were putting on him to further increase profits and flow even more ill-gotten gains through FinCo. One thing was for certain, whoever dispatched the Elmo clone was a pro through and through and he would be interested in having such talent in his organization, maybe even use him or them to replace Elmo whose methods, appetites and rebellious nature were starting to piss Richard off.

Someone like Elmo could become a huge liability for him, hell all his staff could, as after all, they only remained with him because he paid them very well and knew how extremely dangerous he was. He had a plan for them all, a retirement of sorts but much more permanent than they ever envisioned.

For the time being, he would do what Kirotchenkos wanted and make himself and FinCo even more profitable and when the time came FinCo would implode on itself similar to what happened to the World Trade Towers, a number of years ago. Richard dialed a number only known to him and started a discussion with a gravelly voice at the other end who indicated that there were few if any who had the skill to do what is being reported in the media.

The voice continued to tell Richard that they had heard of one such individual who was more legend than substance and that anyone who had ever crossed paths with him were either dead or too frightened to talk. Rumor had it, this monster had gone through Yuri's bar like a cyclone just a short time ago and disposed of a number of his staff look-ing for information.

"Yuri's place eh? I think I will pop by there and pay him a little visit," growled Richard.

"And you and I have never had this conversation," said the voice on the other end of the phone before a click signaled silence once again.

Richard called Christine in, gave her a few instruc-tions to get ready for the next day, grabbed his coat and briefcase and took his personal elevator to the parking garage where his sleek black limo waited for him. A night on the town would do him good and he was looking forward to meeting up with this so called legend.

Chapter 32

Richard Rasmussin pulled his tinted black limo into an alley close to the ramshackle looking building that contained Yuri's bar. A couple of drunk and high street punks were staggering down the alley and saw the limo and headed toward it like the shiny magnet it was.

Unfortunately for them, they did not notice what came with the vehicle as Richard had seen a hint of a glint coming out of the laneway that housed his vehicle. That reflection made him turn around and even though it was pitch black, the scene was quite visible to Richard as his vision was almost better at night than during the day.

One punk was already trying to jimmy open the driver's side door lock by using the old coat hanger trick with no avail since the vehicle was totally burglar and bullet proof.

The by now getting more upset by the second hoodlums, having figured out this ride was a hard, if not impossible, nut to crack, began to kick both sides of the car in some eerie kind of synchronization. It really began to amuse Richard, who was watching from the shadows, knowing his limo was dent and scratch proof among its other advantages.

When the larger of the two ripped out a large plank out of a neighboring fence, however, Richard thought it was time to end the fun and games. After all, who knew how long the vehicle would withstand such an onslaught. He stepped out of the shadows and snarled, "You had your fun, now run along before you both regret it!"

The smaller but more dangerous looking of the two produced a large knife even by Crocodile Dundee standards and began to brandish it in front of him in some sort of a circular pattern while advancing on Richard indicating he was intent on *carving him up like a Thanksgiving turkey*.

The larger and more stupid looking one decided to forgo any formalities, dropped the plank and produced a large and shiny handgun. He never got a chance to use it, Richard pulled a silenced weapon of his own and in one practiced and fluid motion drew it and fired a shot hitting the troublemaker square in the forehead killing him instantly.

You would think the smaller thug would get the hint but obviously not, as he advanced on Richard with large steps slicing the air with his formidable weapon. Richard chuckled and holstered his pistol, deciding to have a little bit of fun with this idiot.

As soon as the punk was in range, Richard ducked under his first swipe intended to sever his head from his body and kicked the hooligan straight in the nut sack causing him to drop his blade and hold the impacted area screaming like a banshee.

As soon as the gang banger doubled over from the kick, Richard followed it up with a front snap kick that seemed to levitate the hood straight into the air. And what goes up must definitely come down but in this case first go sideways as Richard connected with a lightning fast spinning heel kick that propelled the now unconscious assailant into the fence he had removed the plank from.

Richard reproduced his silenced hand gun, removed the silencer and pocketed it. He then pulled a handkerchief out of his pocket, wiped down the gun thoroughly and placed it in the unresponsive hand of the hood he had just toyed with.

A warped sense of humor was something that Richard always had and he so enjoyed exercising it, thinking of what would happen when the overweight slob woke up in the hands of the police with a murder charge in tow. Or even better yet, with the gun in his hand and his dead partner lying beside him with a slug from the gun in his hand lodged just above his hapless partner's nose. For sure, he would have some explaining to do to the higher ups in his gang.

Quietly humming a Russian folk tune to himself, he got into his car moving it across the street from the alley as the police would be there sooner or later and why involve himself? He had bigger fish to fry as he locked the limo and confidently went to the back entrance of Yuri's which all the insiders and players used.

The large and typically tattooed door man took one look at Richard and uttered, "Chyort vos'mi! (Oh shit!)", while moving aside and letting Richard enter. He had never laid eyes on Richard before but he knew to get out of the way of the Devil. He was one of the smart ones.

The place was in full swing as it would be at one am; gambling, drugs and prostitution never slept. Richard took a dark private booth in a quieter room adjacent to the main action; a sexy waitress with spiky black hair, legs up to infinity and breasts that could and would not be contained was at his side immediately.

He ordered a triple vodka martini, shaken not stirred, something he picked up from a James Bond movie and began to enjoy when he had the chance. The waitress asked him in a husky Russian drawl if there was anything else he wanted.

Richard told her to have Yuri join him for a drink and that his attendance was mandatory and slapped her hard on her beautiful backside steering her in the right direction. And yelled after her to be quick about it or else.

His drink and Yuri arrived about the same time. Richard slapped the waitress ample posterior again but this time stroking it afterwards making the girl almost purr like a Siamese cat.

"Bring another one of these for your boss and one for yourself as well. Your shift is over now and you are on my time," instructed Richard as the girl almost ran to the bar.

"So we meet again. What brings you here my dark friend?" asked Yuri. The sexy waitress came back with the other two drinks lightning fast and before she could settle herself in, her boss directed," Leave us for 10 minutes. We have business to discuss. See that guy in the booth across from us? He is an investment banker. See how many times you can make him come in ten minutes. Charge him no less than five hundred, he can afford it. Then clean yourself up, join us and bring Natalia with you. Our friend will want to party!"

The sexy waitress took off in a hurry, wanting to be back in ten minutes as Richard looked a lot more attractive than the short, pudgy and hairy investment banker who had breath that would melt a bulldozer; his body odor almost the worse of two evils.

The things one had to do to feed her children but the waitress knew that someday she would find a rich, caring and older gentleman to look after her and her kids; or maybe a sexy younger one, such as the tall dark stranger with her boss. She could only hope and dream.

Yuri and Richard clinked glasses and toasted each other. "Na Zdorovye," they both uttered and downed their drinks in one gulp, Yuri making the sign to another waitress for two more of the same.

Richard briefly explained the reason for his being here and what had happened at Queen's Park earlier that day.

"I saw the news, he was one of yours?" asked Yuri.

"No, but I need to find out if one of mine was targeted and who could have done something like this?" replied Richard looking more wolfish each second.

"I have no way of knowing the answers to your question but know this and you never heard it from me or from here. There is one from the old country. He comes here once in a blue moon. He killed four of my best faster than most bat an eye. He was looking for information about who is doing financial shakedowns. This man is worse than the Devil himself. He calls himself Mikhail and is the most dangerous man I have ever seen most likely the most fearsome man alive," whispered Yuri.

"I do not know your business and I do not know his. I do not wish to deal with either of you. I value my business interest and remain neutral in others affairs," added Yuri.

"Fair enough my corrupt friend. I need to meet with this Mikhail as fast as possible. I need you to set this up for me. Understood?" indicated Richard forcefully.

"I have no way to contact him but I'll put the word out through my connections. You are a reckless fool. Very few meet with him and live to tell about it. I was fortunate he did not kill me when he was here last. What's in it for me?"

"Your life!" growled Richard lifting the sizeable Yuri right off the floor and levitating him by his collar. When a couple of Yuri's goons sprang into action to aid their boss, Richard produced a handgun pointing it at Yuri's brain almost faster than the eye could see.

"One step closer and I will be your new boss. Maybe that is a good idea anyway. One more move and you will know!" snarled Richard.

"Back off, go back to your work," instructed Yuri now truly frightened.

Richard put Yuri down as soon as he saw the hired muscle retreating and put his gun away. "You see we can solve this like civilized people. If your punks ever make a move against me again, I will dispose of all of you and take over this dump and make some real money with it. You will put the word out and contact me once you know something. Understood?" Richard asked with a sly grin on his face like the cat that just ate the Canary.

"As you wish," answered Yuri thinking it was time to get out of this business while he still could but he knew these people would find him where ever he went.

"Well, bring me more Vodka and that waitress and her friend. We will enjoy them together to seal the deal," roared Richard.

Yuri called the women over, the sexy spike haired one was happy to get away from her stinky mark which disgusted her even more than she had thought. And a private party with her boss and the gorgeous dark haired stranger was just what she needed to forget about her problems.

Na Zdorovye indeed.

Chapter **33**

Things were a mass of confusion on a number of fronts. The police had no clue about who the large, bald hulk was or how he ended up on the shoulder of one of our more notable Canadian historical figures. Finger print and dental analysis brought up nothing even with the extensive search tools the police and RCMP have at their disposal. Bottom line was that if the individual was never printed nor had dental records, this was a dead end.

Detective Cragan and Rollie Sampson were still not quite ready to pass on the name of Elmo Entwhistle to the team of investigators on the case as they were determined to make some more sense of these wildly bizarre developments on their own.

Tina was feeling much better and becoming anxious to join Angel back at FinCo. She had confused feelings about the fact that she was told she was assaulted but had no memory at all of the event so to her way of thinking the best way was to jump back on the horse and join Angel at FinCo as soon as possible.

When Tina confronted the others with how she felt, their reaction was that she should stay home at least for the rest of the week and give Angel a chance to scope things out on her own at FinCo and see if she could find out anything regarding this Elmo Entwhistle character and if he was connected in any way to FinCo.

Rollie and Alf Cragan were also making some discreet inquiries of their own being careful not to ruffle any feathers or tip their hand in any way as they still had no idea what they were actually dealing with here.

While Rollie kept an eye on things at the furniture store with Jon-Erik and Joey, Cragan had instructed one of his researchers back at the precinct to find out anything she could on Elmo Entwhistle. Nothing came back on criminal and credit checks but low and behold the department of motor vehicle check spewed out one large headed, bald and rather sinister looking picture of one Elmo H. Entwhistle with an address of a mid-town Toronto condo.

The excited research officer called Alf Cragan on his cell as soon as she got the news hot off the presses. Cragan in turn called Rollie Sampson to relay that Elmo was indeed real at least as far as the DMV was concerned. The plan was for Rollie and Cragan to pay that ritzy waterfront condo complex a visit later that evening to ascertain whether or not an Elmo Entwhistle was an actual resident there and if so, to have a friendly or maybe not so friendly discussion with Mr. Entwhistle.

While Rollie and Cragan were putting their final plans in place including a couple of heavily armed ETF officers who would accompany them to the Queens Quay address just in case, the group were all at Joey and Tina's discussing these complex and downright befuddling issues.

After everyone had their say, including Mindy who would join in with a hearty bark or deep throated growl once in a while, Tina agreed she would not come to FinCo until Angel had a better opportunity to scope things out there. Under one condition however, as she felt she would go stir crazy being home alone for the rest of the week; that her and Mindy could spend some time at the furniture store daily.

Joey and Jon-Erik readily agreed as then they could all keep an eye on Tina and all look out for each other. And with that, Jon-Erik and Angel excused themselves to catch up on some much needed sex. Although Joey and Tina nuzzled and cuddled constantly comforting each other, neither felt it was the right time to take things back to the level before Tina's abduction although they both knew it wouldn't be long till things were back to normal. They were just too hot for each other.

After Jon-Erik and Angel totally wore each other out on the floor, in bed and finally in their ultra-modern European jet spray shower, they crawled into bed and just held each other until they fell asleep in each other's arms, each vowing quietly to themselves that they would ensure that no one would ever hurt them or their friends again. A nice thought to fall asleep to, even though they had no idea how they would accomplish this tall order.

Rollie, Alf Cragan and their heavily armed ETF team of two arrived at the Queens Quay condo just after midnight. Since it was a weeknight and winter at that, the streets were almost deserted. Just a few late night joggers and walkers enjoying the crisp night air with the occasional group of partiers stumbling up to the subway to catch the last train to wherever they lived in the city or the outskirts.

The no nonsense looking group attracted very little attention and entered the building lobby making a simultaneous and very annoying discovery. The building was not even occupied as yet; it was scheduled to open middle of next month according to the medium size banner sign draped over the area where half the mail boxes were inserted and the other half still missing in action.

Various scaffolds, cans of paint and other types of utensils that workers would use to put the finishing touches on a building were plainly visible from behind the large glass doors of the entrance to the Condo.

"Damn, another dead end. Does not surprise me this mysterious individual would be using a fictitious address," snarled Alf Cragan.

Rollie only nodded as Cragan dismissed the two rather disappointed looking officers and thanked them for their time.

"Any ideas?" asked Cragan.

"Not off the cuff other than you going back to your office in the morning and me joining everyone at the furniture store. Let's see what Angel comes up with at FinCo and hopefully your team will start looking into FinCo discreetly to see if there is an Elmo Entwhistle in their ranks."

"Something really stinks about all of this and my intuition tells me there is a lot more to all this than meets the eye," added Rollie.

"Your intuition worries me my rotund friend. It was almost legendary when you were on the force and it looks as if things have not changed. Get some sleep and we'll be in touch in the morning," indicated Cragan turning and walking towards his car.

Rollie decided to go for a stroll along the lakeshore as he was way too keyed up to sleep and his home was not far west of where he was. He strolled past Captain John's floating ship restaurant, taking another look as he had heard this Toronto watermark was soon to go out of business. The city was changing into an impersonal looking jumble of glass, girders and steel with a ton of cement to bind it all together.

He, like a lot of others who had grown up in or near the city when the Royal York Hotel was by far the largest building on the Toronto skyline, wished back for the simpler and more personal city he remembered from years past. As he strolled along and looked out at the dark night and shimmering water, even his keen senses failed to alert him to the set of sinister eyes that were following his every move. The Monster was restless this night as well and his new lair was also in the area.

Mikhail had watched what had happened with mild interest already having discovered that the building that was the target of these police gnats was un-occupied.

He decided to follow Rollie for a while since he had nothing better to do. Their history went back to a number of years ago when they were locked in deadly combat a number of times and only luck and cat like reflexes had saved the pudgy detective's life.

The Night Stalker would have liked nothing better than to erase this cockroach from the earth permanently but since he was a valued friend of Angel's whom he had sworn to protect, he would tag along to see if anything developed instead. Surveillance was the thing he did best besides killing and he had to be at his stealthiest for this chubby but agile detective not to notice him.

Practice makes perfect he surmised. Without a doubt.

Chapter 34

The next morning, Angel and Jon-Erik both hurriedly performed their morning ablutions, Jon-Erik having a heaping cup of Timmie's coffee ready for Angel who took a few grateful sips before flying out the door with Jon-Erik right behind her. Both headed to the QEW with Angel heading into the city whereas Jon-Erik heading up the 427 to Woodbridge and the furniture store. Another day, another dollar.

Both Angel and Jon-Erik wished they could get away for a while but with mortgage payments, car payments and various other financial obligations and feeling the need to stay close to Tina and Joey in light of recent developments, it was out of the question for now.

When Angel arrived in the little cubicle FinCo provided her and plugged in and booted up her laptop, she was surprised to find two emails from Christine

Hertzog at the top of all the other notices marked highest priority. After looking at them in more detail she was shocked to find that she had appointments with Jimmy Rudiger at 10:00 am and Elmo Entwhistle at 11:15 am sharp.

Elmo Entwhistle? she thought. *Couldn't be, could it?* So this guy was obviously very much alive. *This was going to be a very interesting day without a doubt*, Angel surmised. She decided to saunter over to the coffee machine and fix herself another cup since she barely had time for a few sips earlier this morning.

Christine Hertzog was there already pouring herself a cup of espresso and asked her how Tina was doing.

"Better every day but most likely will be here ready and raring to go Monday," replied Angel.

"Any thoughts so far on process improvement or optimization on what you have seen so far?" asked Christine.

"I have a few ideas which I will be charting but realistically speaking, I need to know much more about your internal workings before making any type of recommendations," replied Angel putting on her most corporate professional face.

"On to another subject. When do I get a chance to redeem myself after our little sparring session the other day? I have never been bested like that before and wrote that off to a lucky shot from you.

Time to put on that Angel charm as she did not really feel like going for round two at least today but she would be more than happy to oblige if pushed thought Angel to herself.

"Listen, I'm a lover first— a fighter second," purred Angel looking even more cat like and sexy than normal.

"Talk about a mood changer. I was all ready to jump back in the ring with you but now I could just as easily jump into bed with you. But either will have to wait as you have some important meetings with two of Richard's key people in a few minutes," said Christine huskily before brushing against Angel's leg and walking away.

Angel smiled to herself and thought that even though Christine was very attractive, she'd rather bed down with a cobra than someone like her and she was a one man woman after all with a little fun thrown in with Tina once in a while. That train of thought brought her back to reality and how much she would like to get her boots on who ever kidnapped Tina.

Jimmy Rudiger's office was located just across from Richard Rasmussin's and Angel knocked on the door at 10 sharp. After seemingly minutes, a higher voice that sounded like it had just been greased with an oil can, asked her to enter.

Angel had seen a quick and restless looking smaller man dart around the office here and there and was surprised to say the least when she finally saw him sitting behind his desk, stocking feet resting on the surface. A half eaten Mars bar and a can of Coke were beside him and a lit cigarette was dangling from his thin lips. He was small, greasy looking and had reddish rodent eyes that continuously darted around everywhere now focusing on her, making her a touch uncomfortable.

But Angel held her posture and composure well and sat down in one of the two guest chairs crossing her legs and pulling out a pen and steno pad.

"Ah, looks like you are prepared. Richard told me you were special and now I see why. Quite a looker, aren't you? But don't worry, you're not my type. I like 'em dark and dirty," said Jimmy with a sneer.

"I'm relieved to hear that. Now that we have the niceties out of the way, can we get down to business? I was hoping to learn a bit more on how this company operates so we can make some suggestions for improvement," indicated Angel looking a bit annoyed.

Acting like he did not even hear what Angel had said, Jimmy threw his half eaten Mars bar her way asking her if she was hungry.

Angel snatched the bar out of the air almost faster than the eye could see and placed it back beside Jimmy. "No, but thanks for the thought," replied Angel.

"Fast too. Christine mentioned you got a lucky shot in on her. Not many beside Richard, myself and Elmo have ever bested her. Keep your head up however. Christine does not handle it well when she is not on top."

"I'll keep that in mind. Can we talk about FinCo now?" asked Angel politely but secretly wishing she could wipe the smirk off the ferret like face of the individual across from her.

"If we must," replied Jimmy. "The boss asked me to co-operate so you have another half hour of my time before I hit the road seeing clients. Richard runs every aspect of FinCo with Elmo, myself and Christine, his so called executive admins."

"Everyone else is clerical, IT, accounting or customer service based. Our talent is top tier in the industry, which is why FinCo is on top or very close to it in this industry. We have a ton of high net worth, very satisfied clients all over the world and our staff is fluent in the key languages so business can be done with virtually anyone anywhere in the world," continued Rudiger while taking a sip of his coke and puffing on his cigarette rudely blowing the smoke Angel's way.

"Do you have any workflow diagrams from any of the departments," asked Angel trying to fan away a cloud of foul smelling smoke away from where she was sitting.

"And I thought this tower was a smoke free building," she added clearing her throat.

"I know nothing about workflow, that is Christine's department. Work comes in via referral, new business or existing clients that are looking to make changes or upgrade. We pride ourselves not to ever lose a client to a rival organization. Once they are with us, they stay with us and bring all their friends, business acquaintances, relatives etc. on board and the same on down the line. Can't process them fast enough," said Jimmy with a sly look on his weasely face.

"And as far as my smoking goes, that's one of my perks here for the undying devotion and dedication to FinCo. And you will not mention it again if you know what's good for you. Is that clear?" indicated Jimmy wrinkling his long nose and training his red eye slits on Angel full tilt.

Angel could only nod trying to restrain herself but her upset look was not lost on Jimmy who declared that the discussion was over and dismissed her with an abrupt wave of his hand and a majestic looking ring of smoke that hovered over his head looking like a crown.

What an arrogant sob, and how very un-executive like this guy was were Angel's thoughts as she closed the door behind her having to cough to clear her throat. Looking at her clock it was now 11:10 am, she just had 5 minutes to freshen up before meeting Elmo. She quickly freshened up and knocked on a door just down the hall from Jimmy Rudiger's office with the name plate of E. Entwhistle.

"It's open," was the deep voiced reply.

Angel stepped into a large corner office with a breathtaking view of Toronto East including the shoreline of Lake Ontario and the Beaches where she and Jon-Erik had lived a few short years ago.

"You like the view? Most do. I am hardly ever here to enjoy it. You have my attention till noon. Fire away," said the large, bald headed but impeccably dressed individual behind his solid oak desk.

"Thanks for taking the time to see me with your busy schedule," began Angel.

"No problem, always have time for the ladies, especially the good looking ones," replied Elmo laughing at his own response which made his ample belly jiggle.

"Your name is very unusual. Are you British or British descendant?" asked Angel.

"Aren't we all love? Actually I'm a distant cousin of the late but great bass player of the Who, John Alec Entwhistle known as the Ox. But I was always the real

Ox in the family if you know what I mean," replied Elmo putting on a genuine British accent.

"Really," said Angel trying to look impressed and making a mental note to ask Jon-Erik about this Who, as he was the music expert in the family. She was into Christine Aguilera, Lady Gaga, Madonna and anyone else that could make her move her sexy hips.

"Enough of the personal stuff, what else can I enlighten you about our company apart from what Jimmy covered," asked Elmo taking a sip of his cup of coffee which looked like pure black mud.

When Angel did not immediately reply, Entwhistle got up from his desk, stretched and let the most raucous wet and nasty sounding fart out that she ever heard. And the smell was no better enveloping the office like a noxious cloud.

"Got your attention, girlie? Now focus and let's get on with it," directed Elmo retaining his English accent and letting go another ripper which sounded like he split his pants, the smell mingling in with the first one causing Angel to breathe into a Kleenex she hurriedly produced.

She shook her head trying to ignore the stench which was now wafting freely throughout the office making her eyes water out of anger and disgust.

"So how do you source out new leads and retain client loyalty," asked Angel trying to take her mind off of the reeking atmosphere.

"Quite simple really, love. When we come a calling, they sign on the dotted line as we offer them something that no one else does; unparalleled opportunity, diversity and service. Once they are with us, they stay with us."

"If you want to have a look at our financials, be my guest, they are on the Internet for anyone to see. Our clients enjoy the best returns anywhere especially in this volatile economy. And our insurance products are the most comprehensive and flexible out there; our underwriters seldom refuse a client because our asset base is so strong we can handle any claims against us easily," boasted Elmo.

"Good to hear, can you arrange for me to interview a few clients to hear their experience firsthand?" asked Angel.

"Not possible. No one untrained speaks to our clients. They are busy and we do not waste their time. Check out the testimonials on our website. That is the best I can do."

The smell had finally subsided enough for Angel to breathe almost normally when Elmo indicated he had time for one more question before he had to leave.

"What in your estimation could be working better?" is all that Angel could come up with considering all that had occurred.

"Good question, love. The back office processing definitely could be expedited and made simpler but we have a ton of requirements on our paperwork from our restrictive government and regulators. That's all. If you need more, you can schedule a follow up through Christine next week. And with that the large menacing looking man left the office with a quick light step making almost no noise in the process leaving Angel very little choice but to leave right behind him.

Angel could not head back to her desk without shaking her head and trying to clear her nostrils some more while thinking to herself how these two weirdos she had just spoken with where actually part of this thriving company's executive. Something definitely stinks besides the office which she just left.

Chapter 35

Angel was frustrated as the morning had netted her absolutely nothing other than the fact that both Jimmy Rudiger and Elmo Entwhistle gave her the creeps and she was seriously considering severing her contract with Richard Rasmussin and FinCo. But she and Tina had their money and some warped sense of duty obligated her to at least hand in some sort of process improvement document.

She also felt there was some further investigating to do as far as FinCo and the quirky characters that ran it were concerned and what better way to do it than from the inside. Also, there was the unfinished business of Tina's abduction, the damage at their home and the furniture store, and the fake Elmo who Mikhail dispatched to meet his maker.

She decided to go out for a walk since it was lunch time and even in her three quarter length winter jacket, got three propositions for drinks after work by the ever horny banking types who got on and off the elevators from various floors. Angel headed up Bay St. to City Hall to clear her lungs in the cold fresh air as the stench from Elmo's office was still in her nostrils.

When she got to Queen St., she crossed over to City Hall and cruised by the different street food vendors, finally deciding on a Beer Battered Mahi Mahi Taco with fried Mahi Mahi, guacamole, chipotle aioli and coleslaw. She had every intention of sharing with the pigeons which were always close by, especially where the food vendors were.

She settled down on a bench sipping on her hot chocolate, munching on her Taco. The pigeons, having already claimed their portion, watched the skaters that were always circling around the ample ice rink. The Christmas decorations were now out and the place looked gorgeous especially after dark when the thousands of lights on the trees and surrounding area kicked in.

After finishing her scrumptious and satisfying lunch, she pulled out her cell to give Jon-Erik a call to see how things were going at the store and to update him on this morning's smelly developments but she did not get the chance as a nasty looking large hooded individual with black stubble all over his face dressed in a long coat and runners stopped in front of her and growled," Give me your cell and money bitch or I'll slice your pretty face up so whoever is giving you what I could do much betta won't recognize you. You feel me?" growled the oversized street punk.

"You are making a huge mistake, even bigger than your size. Leave now while you still can," hissed Angel now totally at the end of her rope, given everything that had happened.

But as thugs like him tend to do, they never listen, thinking they are the only bad asses on the street. This one tended to be a little more vocal than usual, flicking out a large spring loaded switch blade and calling her names that she had not ever heard.

When Angel saw the blade, she sprang into action with uncanny speed grabbing her assailant's knife hand twisting the knife away from her while coming down with a tremendous karate chop from her free hand. It not only dislodged the blade but cleanly broke her miserable opponent's wrist.

The hood screamed out in agony, as Angel used a moment of confusion to kick the knife far away from him. But the gang banger was not done yet and he launched his over 200 pounds at her like a missile. Angel did a lightning fast side step, watching, satisfied as he flew right by her onto the hard concrete.

He was up fast, and now looked really angry. A crowd of onlookers gathered to watch the festivities with no one making a move to assist the not so helpless damsel in distress. It just wouldn't do to get their Armani and Copley suits and coats dirty or get involved before their afternoon meetings.

But Angel was only focused on her attacker and when he came charging in again, she did not side step him but kicked him as hard as she could square in the punk's crotch and the scream he let out this time even scared away the feasting pigeons.

She was not done yet. As the thug bent over in obvious pain, screaming obscenities to the high heavens, Angel let go a front snap kick that knocked his jaw right into his teeth causing blood and dental work to fly in all directions over the oooh's and aaah's from their impromptu audience. She was prepared to follow that up with a spinning heel and axe kick, if required but the crook was in dream land most likely reflecting on where he was going to steal the money necessary to fix his broken mouth.

Angel's audience provided a hearty round of applause before retreating back to their offices for another round of fleecing poor constituents of their hard earned dollars via another round of tax increases or user fees. The thug was not getting up for a while and anyone who did not see the altercation would mistake him for another homeless person who had fallen asleep over one of the heat vents on the City Hall grounds.

Angel decided to high tail it out of there as she did not want to draw anymore unwanted attention to herself and headed back down to her office tower with a spring in her step. After that bit of unplanned exercise, she did not realize that a sinister pair of eyes had watched the developments with great interest and measurable pride.

Mikhail had taken in the whole scene, ready to jump in if required but Angel had accounted for herself more than handily. The Monster could not help himself as he walked directly over the prone thug's form and stepped on his face with pressure just short of killing the punk. Normally Mikhail would have killed him instantly but did not want this to come back and reflect on Angel, just in case someone did tie the body back to her.

The thug's face would need major repair but he would live to see another day. Today was indeed his lucky day although he would be very hard pressed to realize it when he woke up hours later as he dragged his destroyed face and body to St. Michaels Hospital just down the street. The Shape Shifter had indeed become more thoughtful but also more calculating and careful, but he could still snap at a moment's notice, which was very unhealthy for anyone or anything near him.

He disappeared back into the shadows from whence he came in the blink of an eye, taking the discarded knife with him so the hood would not be able to use it on anyone else or prevent some other street punk from picking it up to cause problems for someone. The Shape Shifter hated weapons and had no personal use for them but was an expert with them all, if he had to be. He preferred to use his hands, feet, uncanny speed and Ninja abilities which made him the deadliest weapon of all.

So far besides the buzz with the police and newspapers, nothing much had happened with his little Queen's Park stunt making him think that the bald overweight insect he had eliminated really did not matter much to anyone. But the message that was sent out was very clear, do not mess with Angel or her friends or the consequences would be dire.

He made himself a mental note to drop by Yuri's den of iniquity again soon to see if anything developed on that front, as Mikhail was an underground kind of guy and preferred the dark of the night for his excursions. He was also planning to look into the whole financial aspect of this, a lot further, as it looked more and more like some sort of extortion business. If the furniture store was targeted, without a doubt, they were not the only ones.

If anyone knew anything about crooked business, it was Yuri or his contacts that thrived like locusts in the dark and dank parts of the city and anywhere where illegitimate business activities flourished.

The Dispatcher of Souls slunk to his newly acquired Ford F150 black fully tinted pick up truck and headed out to his newest lair. An older house in Port Credit, right off the QEW which had a lot of land and neighbors that were few and far between so he could not readily be seen coming and going. He was renting the home from an old couple who could no longer live there and had made it plain that if anything was ever mentioned about him to anyone; it would be extremely detrimental if not fatal to their fast fading health.

In turn, he paid his rent on time in cash only which was dropped off in a plain envelope at the start of every month. He was hoping he would be able to stay there for a while as he rather liked the location and privacy of mature trees and hedges. The only thing that irked him was the constant noise of the highway making him wonder if these worker bee gnats ever went to sleep. The house came fully furnished but the Monster only ever used the kitchen and one of the bedrooms where he chose to sleep on the hard carpet by the window into which a large oak tree almost extended its branches.

Everything else in the house remained covered up with white sheets so if he had to beat a hasty retreat, he could get out of there in seconds as his duffle bag with a few belongings was always in his truck. Pity the fool that tried to steal it as it was rigged with explosives for which only he knew the bypass. If you didn't, you'd be walking around on stumps missing anything from the knee down.

Mikhail decided to head home picking up some Sushi (his favorite) on the way and getting a few hours of shuteye before visiting Yuri again, hoping he did not have to kill him before the morning came. But the Shadow man was flexible and always adapted to the situation. And the situation was becoming more and more absurd.

Chapter 36

Rollie and Alf Cragan touched base the following day to compare notes as nothing much was stirring, not even a louse. Angel and Jon-Erik had contacted Rollie late yesterday, to let him know that Angel had met Elmo Entwhistle in the flesh, stench and all. She relayed that besides the fact that he was rude and gaseous; he was very much alive and active at FinCo.

This was not a piece of news that Rollie was happy to hear. He thought that there could be a connection between this Elmo Entwhistle character, FinCo, what had happened at the furniture shop, as well as Tina's abduction and the shots fired at Jon-Erik and Angel's home. He was not tied down by the protocol the police would be working under if he was to interrogate Elmo Entwhistle and any of the FinCo executives. He knew a battery of high priced lawyers would most likely have little interest in a private detective at least at the onset paving his way for a possible interview with the stinky Mr. Entwhistle.

The other ace in the hole they had was Angel. She could do some careful snooping around at FinCo but even with the great skills Angel had as a fighter, it still made him nervous. By the look of things, the people involved were extremely dangerous, ruthless and had some formidable resources at their disposal.

He also wondered as to how many other businesses or individuals had been approached and threatened as had the furniture store. Rollie had his sources and contacts putting their noses to the pavement to sniff out if there was anything similar going on out there and the disturbing thing was absolutely nothing was coming back.

That in itself was eerie as there was always something going on in the streets but it looked as if a cone of silence has been draped over the city. But in Rollie's experience as a police officer and detective for years and now in his private practice, something wasn't right with this picture and he was becoming more and more determined to find out what it was.

He started back checking newspaper articles online to see if any type of extortion attempts had been recorded in the last few years and besides the usual gang-banger drug related disputes and shootings, not a heck of a lot of anything was going on that was relevant.

Just before he was about to give up on his research, Rollie came across an article that dealt with the mysterious deaths of Irving Morgenstein who had been a multi-millionaire investment banker and his wife Ida. He remembered hearing about this a few weeks ago, actually just before the time Tina was kidnapped and the problems at the furniture store.

What was again interesting about this was that there were absolutely no clues left at the crime scene. Even though the two events seemed to be totally separate and unrelated, the fact that Morgenstein had ties to the world of finance and the fact that this character the Ninja dispatched had a card identifying him as a Financial Advisor had to be more than just a coincidence.

When you also factor in Tina's kidnapping and the other violent events, it presented an even stronger case.

He certainly hoped so, as now they had nothing to go on since Elmo Entwhistle was very much alive as well as extremely odorous. There had to be a connection somewhere and he was planning to ferret it out and flush out the other weasels involved in this weirdness.

Rollie gave Alf Cragan a call and was actually surprised that he answered since it was now Saturday once again. Alf tried to be as much of a family man as he could on weekends, spending time with his wife Anne and their two youngsters, little Archie and Amanda who were five and four respectively and more than a handful at that age.

The Cragans were at a Chucky Cheese birthday bash for one of their kid's friends. Alf was actually glad for the interruption and excused himself so he could go outside and continue his conversation without the sound of thirty plus energized children running and climbing around the impressive apparatuses set up there to keep them entertained.

After filling in Alf Cragan on his theories, they decided to check on Angel and Tina tomorrow, to get a sense of what Angel had encountered at FinCo so far. They hatched a plan for Rollie to contact the fine folks at FinCo, under the guise of an investigation of a fictitious client claiming to have a beef with FinCo and wanting a quick, noiseless and non-lawyer resolution.

It was now time for Rollie to get some much needed rest after calling Jon-Erik and verifying that he and detective Cragan would pop by tomorrow afternoon. He had an eerie feeling right in the pit of his ample stomach that he was going to need all the rest he could get. And his gut normally never proved him wrong.

Chapter 37

Things certainly moved at a fast and furious pace even more so when the Meter was keeping time with its unrelenting cadence. Richard Rasmussin was planning a quiet weekend indoors with a couple of magnums of Bollinger champagne, Bonds favorite and a couple of high priced escorts which would even make James flinch had he known the price.

But before he could place his orders, a call came through on his special untraceable cell. The deep voice instructed him to pack an overnighter; a helicopter would be waiting for him on the helipad on top of the Toronto Trump Tower within 10 minutes. He currently resided on the 54th floor in one of the larger suites.

When he asked the thickly accented voice as to what this was all about, the answer was short and straight to the point. Urgent meeting and that he had no choice in the matter, was the only additional information he could gather before the call was disconnected.

He knew where the call came from and that he had no option but to go. He had never actually met the Kirotchenko brothers in the flesh before, now would be his opportunity.

Richard quickly got his essentials together and threw on his thickest sheepskin coat along with his beaver hat and matching boots as Stoltenhoff Island was frigid at the best of times. He wished he could have told those arrogant bastards what he really thought of them and how dare they interrupt his planned weekend of depravity but that time would come soon enough. Better to humor his nasty bene-factors for now, payback would be a bitch.

He boarded the helicopter which took off quickly and landed a short few minutes at Billy Bishop Airport on the Toronto Island. A cart and driver picked him up as soon as he left the chopper and took him to his private Bombardier Q400 turboprop chartered exclusively for him. The plane took off immediately crossing Lake Ontario and landing a scant hour and fifteen minutes with a tailwind at Newark, New Jersey.

Richard barely had time to down a couple of vodka on the rocks and munch on some goat cheese and crackers as well as call Christine Hertzog to let her know he may or may not be in Monday morn-ing depending on what transpired. When she asked where he was heading he replied, "To hell."

A cart and driver were waiting for him and drove him and his luggage to a formidable look-ing Bombardier BD700 in the same vein as what

Bill Gates used for private transportation. The plane took off immediately on its long flight to Sao Paulo Brazil without the protocol of dealing with customs, etc. Amazing what could be bridged when the right palms were greased.

Since he was the only passenger on the plane, he was lavishly entertained, wined and dined as well as any other needs taken care of by the two hot as pistols Czech flight attendants named Hana and Irena who were taking turns pleasuring him in between serving drinks and delicious food.

Richard arrived in Sao Paulo 9 hours later thinking that this was not a bad way to travel. As the plane was being refueled, it took on a cargo of subdued women and young girls with food supplies and other provisions before heading for its final destination, the Nightingales and Stoltenhoff Island.

Another five or so hours later, the plane set down on the private runway of the Kirotchenko brothers' south Atlantic Paradise. The weather outside was bitterly cold and strong almost gale force winds were blowing in off the ocean causing Richard to draw his sheepskin coat collar even tighter around his neck. After he disembarked from the plane, he and his belongings were once again taxied by a large heavy set individual in a golf cart until he stopped dead at the end of the runway.

As if by magic, the ground opened up just in front of them exposing a ramp that seemed to disappear into a hole swallowed by the ground itself. As they began their decent, an entourage of land rover type vehicles followed in behind, carting the human cargo.

The area below was well lit with even spaced lighting that was installed on both sides of the large tunnel/driveway they were now following. Richard tried to strike up a conversation with the driver of the cart he was riding in but his large chauffeur would only grunt occasionally which irked him so he said nothing further.

After about fifteen minutes of traveling along this underground tunnel, the path led abruptly upward into a large well lit antechamber. As a bonus, Richard had two formidable sub machine guns pointed at each side of his head before he could even leave the cart. But that got his blood boiling, as after all, he had consented to coming here and had made these bastards a ton of money in a relatively short time.

So in less time it took to bat an eyelash, the first machine gunner found his weapon wrapped around his large bulbous head, the second faring much worse with the gun barrel firmly implanted in between his buttocks. His screaming was further annoying Richard who kicked him square into the throat stifling the foot soldiers yelling permanently.

The stunned driver of the cart took off like a flash after seeing what had transpired but was cut down in a hail of bullets that came from a mezzanine above.

"So hard to get good help these days. How was your trip, my resourceful friend?" asked a deep, rich toned but menacing voice from above.

"Fine until I had guns pointed at my head. That was not very smart," replied Richard to the voice that still remained in the shadows.

"We are sporting men and could not resist a little fun. I wagered with my brother that these two nothing apaks (idiots) would not survive an encounter with you. So far, I half win and half lose as Mihovil there is still stirring even though you half caved his head in," replied a deeper and even more guttural speaker.

"I don't ever lose," continued the speaker filling the air with a burst of machine gun that put the first thug out of his caved-in face's misery.

"Govno (shit)!" said the first voice now stepping out of the shadows. Our wager was whether our guest would dispatch both. He did not so nobody wins."

"Garbage, they are both dead. I win and you will pay up. Four of those fresh young virgins that just came in with our friend here are mine tonight as we agreed the winner would take," said Vlad to his brother Vasily.

"Gentlemen, I am famished after my long trip and this little bit of amusement you furnished me with. I would like to freshen up, get to know those two stewardesses that entertained me a little better and enjoy some of your fine cuisine," indicated Richard looking up at the balcony where the two barrel-chested bearded Rasputins were now hysterically laughing and holding their ample stomachs.

"Fuck and feast you shall this evening... to your hearts content. Tomorrow, at the crack of dawn, we will talk business and then you will be on your way back to Canada to make us even more money. Since

the plane is on stopover tonight, we will ask the stewardesses to join us for dinner," replied Vasily.

"Your driver will show you to your quarters. Hana
and Irena will meet you there. Dinner will be served
at 8 sharp. Lateness is not tolerated," snarled Vlad.

*Arrogant bastards. Who do these knoyhs (clowns)
think they are dealing with? But he would humor them
for now and study them and learn their weaknesses
and bide his time and strike when they least expected
it. Putting these two throwbacks from another time out
of business would be his extreme pleasure. But first he
was going to humor them a bit and enjoy himself in the
process* he thought to himself as he was dropped off
at a large double door that opened via a card that the
driver gave him that he swiped across a laser sensor.

The suite was lavish, consisting of a fully stocked
bar, a huge HD TV that took up one whole wall of the
room, plush couches and chairs with real lion and tiger fur on a larger than life canopy bed. A huge hot
tub that looked as if it could hold ten or more easily
was available surrounded by walls of exquisite drap-
ery completed the stunning décor.

When Richard looked behind the curtain, he
was even surprised to see a large square ring set up
with limited seating below his quarters obviously for
some sort of combat events. Well, he was always up
for some live entertainment but first he poured himself a triple shot of Diva Vodka which he downed in
one gulp before heading over to the large shower
stall in the luxurious bathroom.

Happy to treat his body in luxury, he ran the shower piping hot before he stepped in. Before he knew it,

the two sexy stewardesses joined him and did things to his body that even surprised him. After taking care of each one in turn and then both of them together, he turned the water to ice cold to the surprised screams of his shower guests who beat a hasty retreat away from the shower back into the suite.

These women had the constitution of alley cats who do not like water thought Richard while chuckling to himself and languishing in the ice cold water. Once he was refreshed enough, he wrapped a towel around himself while watching his two still dripping wet guests do some amazing and very sexy things to each other. After pouring himself another double, he felt compelled to join them as after all three were better than two….at least in his estimation.

Chapter 38

Angel woke up on this cloudy and snowy Sunday morning as if in a dream. She found herself to her absolute delight with her beautiful legs wrapped tightly around Jon-Erik's head who was taking his work very seriously in between the occasional gasp for air.

A number of orgasms later the two lovers finally extricated themselves from each other with Jon-Erik padding downstairs to put some coffee on, pop some toast into the toaster and get the bacon and eggs ready for the frying pan that was already greased up and ready to go.

It was so nice and relaxing for the two soul mates to finally spend a morning together but after a sumptuous breakfast, the discussion quickly fell back to the cold reality of the totally insane events of the last few weeks.

"Where do we go from here?" said Jon-Erik while munching on a piece of rye toast with peanut butter.

"On the offensive. These bastards have threatened our lives, kidnapped and abused Tina and they are going to pay and pay hard. The problem is, who are they and what really is their game?" Angel replied in between sips of the delicious coffee Jon-Erik had brewed from scratch.

"Good questions honey. Maybe we will find out more this afternoon when we meet with Rollie and detective Cragan. We really should invite Tina and Joey over; Tina is feeling better every day and is chomping at the bit to do something to help.

She is a real fighter and I love her so much!" Angel continued.

"But until then, don't we have some unfinished business to attend to?" teased Jon-Erik.

"That we do. Go up and get ready for me lover, I'm just going to call Tina and ask her and Joey to come over around 4ish. Then I'm going to clean up the kitchen and get the place ready for company which should take me no more than 5 minutes as I am getting wet just thinking about what we are going to do up upstairs."

And before Jon-Erik could even finish freshening up, Angel was upstairs and guided him back to their still unmade bed pulling him firmly by his again almost bursting erection. This woman absolutely could drive him insane, she was so hot, gorgeous and he loved her more than anyone or anything he could ever imagine and before they knew it they were once again intertwined with each other in the dance of unconditional love and passion.

It was almost 3 pm when the two lovers finally came up for air and reluctantly hit the shower to get ready for their company which took a little longer than normal as they got lost into each other once again with the hot water stimulating them even more. By the time the doorbell rang, they were both dressed in comfy sweats, slippers and a glow that could not be missed a block away.

Jon-Erik ushered Tina and Joey in, a glass of white wine and a beer already waiting for them by their regular seats on the sofa along with a heaping plate of crackers, cheese and assorted meats which Angel and Jon-Erik were already diving into hungrily after their lengthy gymnastic session.

Tina was looking more like her normally beautiful and energetic self than she had in some time. The rest and downtime had done her a world of good and the fact that she still had no memory of what had actually happened to her aided her recovery tremendously. She knew that she was assaulted but could not really identify with what had happened to her because she could not recollect and it was almost like looking from the outside in.

Once she had recovered physically from her ordeal, the mental aspect was more outrage as if it actually happened to someone else, not her. And her anger was directed at those who threatened Joey and her friends at the furniture store and had shot at Angel and Jon-Erik. Tina was anxious to get back to work with Angel and help discover what was really going on and who was responsible.

This was very apparent after the four best friends hugged and exchanged some small talk about music, movies, fashion and current events. Tina broke the pleasantries by asking, "So where are we with all this crap that has been going on?"

This caused smiles to break out all around with Joey looking extremely proud of his brave dark haired beauty sitting beside him.

So the three others started bringing Tina up to date with every development that they could recall. It turned out Tina had actually missed very little as Joey had kept her abreast of developments so to speak but it was good for Tina to hear what everyone had to say. This united the group of lifelong friends more than ever. They had come a long way since the Foxy Fire days.

What had really changed for them other than the fact they were much more mature and feeling a lot less like victims, was wanting to get on the offensive, in other words be pro-active rather than re-active.

As soon as they all had caught up and were on the same page, Rollie and Alf Cragan were at the door. After more shaking of hands, and Rollie and Alf taking a sip of the strong cappuccinos Angel had put in front of them, everyone was ready to get down to business.

Alf Cragan started things off by relaying his side of things from a police point of view which ended up being very little but he did recap the investigation of the Queen's Park debacle and Tina's abduction.

As far as Tina's abduction, there was absolutely nothing new other than Alf's theory that somehow Tina was being used as leverage of some sort.

"As leverage for what? Our Furniture store signing up with some bogus financial advisor?" asked Joey angrily.

"Easy my hot blooded friend," replied Alf Cragan. "We all know you are upset as we all are over what has developed. The other part you did not give me a chance to relay is that the Furniture store extortion, Tina's abduction and the individual we thought was Elmo Entwhistle have to be all connected somehow. There is just too much coincidence not to be."

"Alf and I agree totally, everything seems to lead back to FinCo," added Rollie.

"No one has even mentioned the monstrous Mikhail in all this!" said Jon-Erik forcefully.

"Well we are at an advantage this time as opposed to what happened five years ago. This time the Ninja seems to be on our side but I caution that he is unpredictable and no one knows what he will do next. All of us besides Alf have seen his tremendous power, stealth and skills. We need to be extremely careful when it comes to him with whatever we do," offered Angel with a concerned look on her gorgeous face.

And, as if right on queue a huge, a dark and powerful shape appeared as if by magic from behind the ceiling to floor length living room curtains and sat down in the large armchair by the window.

Alf Cragan could not believe his eyes and drew his side arm but Rollie knocked it out of his hand before he could bat an eye.

"Smart move, Mr. ex detective. Does this gnat of a policeman realize you have just saved his miserable life?" hissed the Ninja.

"Alf, stay calm and do not move a muscle. You have no idea what you are dealing with here!" instructed Rollie.

"How did you get in here?" asked Cragan still sounding authoritative and defiant.

"That is my business, not yours. I have decided to join your little insignificant meeting because you are all friends of Angel's and most of you are former nemeses. You know what I am capable of. I do not trust police but have never harmed any in this country - but there is always a first time."

"Are you threatening me, I back down from no-one," yelled out Alf Cragan rising to his six foot three height.

"Some need more convincing than others," replied the monster and Alf Cragan found himself unceremoniously deposited on the ground that was luckily for him heavily carpeted, head first. This happened so quickly almost like a blur and only Angel could follow the actual sequence of events as she had seen the Ninja in action many times and had trained her eyes to follow his uncanny speed.

While Alf Cragan was trying to shake the cobwebs out of his throbbing head and getting back on his feet, Angel placed herself in between Alf and the Shapeshifter.

"Enough Mikhail, I think he gets the picture. He is not the enemy, he is trying to help," said Angel quietly.

"I see you are even more confident in your abilities. That is good, but make no mistake, if anyone in this room tries to make a move against me, you excluded as you know better, they will be eliminated without ceremony because that is what I do!"

"Do I make myself clear?" the killer added showing his large gold tooth.

"Good, you are all calm and back in your seats. A triple shot of vodka would ease my foul mood," added Mikhail while Alf Cragan was still looking extremely pissed off and rubbing the back of his head which took the brunt of his dumping.

Jon-Erik came back with a glass filled with exactly three ounces of vodka which he handed to Angel who placed it on the side table by Mikhail's chair. The Executioner downed the drink in one gulp and gestured for another. Jon-Erik came back with the rest of the bottle which Angel again placed beside the huge shape with the piercing eyes and buzz cut who had now sat back down and poured himself another triple which he knocked back with a smack of his menacing looking lips.

"Ah, not as good as the Vodka we were weaned on back in old country but goes down well just the same. I am only here as an observer and will make the occasional observation. I work alone and would only consider ever working with Angel when she is ready. I will not allow any harm to come to her especially after my former mentor Boris was disposed of. That will not happen again. I will be everywhere where she is. Do not worry, I will not invade her privacy because I know she is in love and Jon-Erik is good for her."

That made Jon-Erik smile and hold Angel's hand.

"I will never let anything happen to her either," said Jon-Erik determinedly.

"Now here is what I have to say and then I will leave you to your meeting. The people involved in this are extremely dangerous, ruthless and without conscience. Like me but I have developed some, maybe my mistake, maybe not. I am investigating in my own way and will have something soon as when you shake the tree hard enough, something will fall out. I can not protect all of you, Angel is my focus but I will do my best to keep you all informed. Be extremely careful of your next moves," instructed Mikhail and after downing another double of the Vodka, simply walked out the front door.

Alf Cragan had recovered enough to run after him but saw nothing moving on the street except an elderly lady trudging through the freshly fallen snow with her designer cockapoo who decided to stop and drop one of his tiny pellets right at the bottom of the houses walkway.

"Did you see anyone come out of this house," Alf Cragan asked the lady.

"No, just you. Don't worry, his droppings are biodegradable," chortled the old lady while waddling off.

"What the hell kind of being was that and how did he do what he did? He has totally disappeared from sight and has left no visible tracks," exclaimed Cragan still rubbing his sore head.

"He is a true Ninja. Most people never survive an encounter with him. We are all extremely fortunate.

Never ever make a move against him if you encounter him again. He was not in a confrontational mood today but that can change in a heartbeat. We have encountered him before and he seems to be fixated on me now and believe me when I say he is a better ally than enemy," indicated Angel.

"Amen to that. I have seen him take bullets that would have killed anyone ten times over; I've supplied some of those bullets and he is still walking on this earth. Whatever he is, it is so far above our skills and understanding. Normally, I do not back down from anything either but this Mikhail has made me rethink that and come up with the conclusion that *you cannot kill what can't be killed and he or it is the closest I have ever seen to that!*" Rollie said quietly.

And everyone in the room took a reflective sip of their drink knowing that death had come to visit them once again.

Chapter 39

The next morning, Richard Rasmussin awoke bright and early in his lavish guest suite on Stoltenhoff Island. He rose at 5:00 am regardless of how long he was awake the night before and the fact that no daylight ever got into the underground fortress did not change his pattern.

Richard was a creature of impulses and while he slept after his exertions with his bed mates, an epiphany of sorts came to him. A very dangerous and possibly foolish thought came to him but once he had something on his mind, action was the only course for him.

His two lovely companions were still fast asleep as he left his bed. He noticed they had curled around each other since they no longer had him to cling onto. He quietly padded to the bathroom, splashed some water on his face and brushed his teeth. Dressing without a sound into a jet black skin tight body suit which had a matching hood that all but covered his face; he checked his accessories and left the room without a sound.

The underground compound was still deathly quiet but most likely would not be for long as the activities of another day in the stronghold would soon begin. For this type of work he preferred to be barefoot, his steps making no sound as he slid down the long and sparsely lit hallway to his first destination, Vasily's quarters. Vasily was the weaker of the two and why not eliminate the easier of the two targets first.

As expected, the door to one half of the most dangerous brothers in the world was unguarded and unlocked as who on the Island would have the courage or skill to attempt what he was in the process of doing?

He pushed open the door a fraction and took a peek inside. Even though the room was pitch black, his eye sight adjusted almost instantaneously. Vasily Kirotchenko was laying on his back snoring like a chainsaw, one hand still holding a bottle while the other was cupped around the ample breast of a naked girl who looked to be very young.

Unfortunate but he never left witnesses. He moved without a sound into the room until he had the corrected angle, extracted two shurikens (throwing stars) from the pouch inside his jacket and threw them with deadly accuracy, hitting Vasily and his helpless companion in the center of the brain killing them in less time than the blink of an eye.

Richard padded over to the bedside, felt for a pulse on each body and found none. He nodded to himself satisfied, extracted the shurikens, wiped them down and pocketed them. He left the two bodies unceremoniously as he had no further use for them, planning to send a cleanup crew in later.

He had accomplished his grim task in under 5 minutes but it was only half done. He left the chamber as noiselessly as he had arrived and padded further down the hallway toward his next target. As he rounded a corner, he noticed that the more dangerous of the two brothers had posted a guard.

Isn't that always the way thought Richard as he snuck up on the dozing heavyset bearded guard who was going to be punished more severely than he ever thought as his thick neck was twisted sideways, resulting in a crackling noise louder than Richard would have liked.

Fearing the worst, he pushed the door open to the now unguarded chamber to find his concerns were not unfounded. Vlad was not in his bed. The only thing that saved him was that his trained ears picked up the faint click of the submachine gun trigger being engaged just as he had flown away from the area littered with bullets.

Richard, lithe as a cat, did a shoulder roll and came up throwing on his own at the spot where the machine gun fire was coming from. A grunt told him that he had hit pay dirt as he heard the engaged gun hit the ground. The now totally pissed off Russian crime czar was coming at him like a freight train pulling the knife out of his stomach and the throwing star out of his shoulder in mid stride.

And Richard let him come. Just before Vlad reached him, he side stepped but not before being knocked off his feet by a sweeping arm that almost decapitated him with the makeshift clothesline that the sole surviving Kirotchenko executed. What saved him was that he tucked his jaw to his chin just before he was struck. The blow would have killed a normal man but he rolled away from the brutal strike taking most of the impact with him.

But now bleeding profusely from a gaping stomach wound, Vlad was on him like a dog on a bone. Richard had underestimated his benefactor's speed and agility which was quite formidable for such a large bellied man. Vlad had Richard in a vise like grip from his large ham hock like fists and began to squeeze the life out of him while breathing oniony fumes into his face and swearing at him with the worst profanities known in the Russian language.

But whenever an underestimation took place which was rare, Richard was always quick to make the adjustment. Before the bear like Russian could finish him, Richard withdrew his knife and plunged it repeatedly into the side and neck of his adversary. And just before the life was choked out of him, Vlad released his death grip on Richard's neck and slid to the ground now bleeding out his life.

Just before Vlad closed his evil eyes for the last time he murmured in Russian, "Ya uvizhu vas v adu (I'll see you in hell)", before he expired.

"Not for a while if I can help it," croaked the newly crowned and self elected leader of the Kirotchenko empire while trying to massage some feeling back into his almost crushed larynx.

After he got a semblance of his voice and wind back, he went to his room to clean all the blood off himself, changed into some clean clothing and headed for the control center of the Island brandishing two Uzi submachine guns he found that were still fully loaded by the freshly disposed of boss' bed. He had a general meeting to call to order to let the worker bees of this now breached fortress know that there was a new czar in town as after all who would be better for the job than himself?

Chapter 40

Rollie Sampson was in a foul mood and that was never good for the objects of his displeasure. The thing was, he did not know who they were as yet but he was planning to start at the top and work his way down if he had to. And no better place to start than FinCo itself.

Since it was now the start of a new work week, he called the FinCo switchboard and asked to set up an appointment to speak to Elmo Entwhistle. He assumed the guise of an eager millionaire who was motivated to set up an investment portfolio with Elmo as the word in the circles that he ran was that Elmo was the man to see for a tangible return on his investment.

The switchboard operator told him that all upper management would be at a key meeting all morning but that Elmo should be available by mid-afternoon. So Rollie set up an appointment for 3:30 pm that afternoon which meant he would be stuck in nasty downtown commuter traffic once he finished his discussion with the questionable and dubious Mr. Entwhistle. He could never understand how a supposedly world class city such as Toronto could have such antiquated infrastructure to get in and out of the downtown core.

He usually did most of his business on the city outskirts or late evening when all the office towers and businesses had discharged their workers for the long commute home. Their trips were always fraught with perils like numerous road closings, one way streets, endless construction and had only two at all tangible ways of escape, the Gardiner Expressway west or the GO trains that headed east and west of the city.

The GO trains always had problems with people who wanted to take the easy way out by jumping in front of these fast moving juggernauts not realizing the panic and inconvenience it caused thousands of overstressed and time constrained commuters, never mind that they were on a one way trip themselves. That along with frozen switches, bad weather and scheduling problems made this a non-option to Rollie as he would rather take his chances in his vehicle.

After setting the appointment, he decided he would come across like the inexperienced investor that he actually was, someone who had come into a ton of money from a long lost aunt that remembered how cute he looked in his first pair of lederhosen.

He knew from their discussion the other day that Angel and Tina would be back in the office today and now they actually had three separate angles to approach this matter, including the research Alf Cragan and his police cronies were conducting.

Rollie would have to be extremely careful to ensure he didn't run into Angel and Tina and tip his hand in any way, hoping that whoever is behind all this had not deducted that there was a tie to Tina and Angel and the furniture store. It was risky and dangerous to say the least but since the individual the Ninja had disposed of in such a spectacular fashion was obviously not the Elmo Entwhistle he had an appointment to see, it may just work out. If not he would just have to adlib, something he had become good at with all his years in law enforcement.

While Rollie was getting himself prepped for his afternoon interview, Angel and Tina arrived at First Canadian Place a few minutes before nine after a horrid morning on the road. It had snowed again last night which made the normal rush hour traffic even harder to handle and had the ladies wondering if anyone actually understood how to drive in the winter.

The usual lustful stares and primping from the elevator co-riders were there even more so since it was Monday morning. *A lot of these up and comers must have had a rough weekend in the entertainment district trying to pick up women who were impressed by fancy clothes, buzz cuts, and promises of parties in the summer on yachts along with some white powder nights undoubtedly.* When they arrived on the 42nd floor, they noticed the whole floor was flush in excitement and everyone was whispering something to each other.

Angel led Tina to her desk which was set up right beside her in the cubicle they both shared. After they settled in, Angel took her partner around and introduced her to a few of the clerical people on the floor that she had gotten to know. She showed her the restrooms and staff room but they were not planning to spend much time there, it was nicer to go out and get some fresh air and peruse the brightly decorated downtown shops.

From all the hushed conversation, they could only pick up that something significant had happened but no one knew what it was. Only the upper echelons were privy to whatever was going on. Angel settled Tina in and began the process of filling her in on what optimization processes she had been working on, which was not a heck of a lot since she had been unable to source out little if any information so far.

Almost everything regarding FinCo and how they did business seemed to be either privileged information which only the higher management could provide and they had almost never been available. So Angel went through some Org chart data and the S.W.O.T document she had started to work on. The strengths and opportunities seemed endless, the weaknesses and threats besides the company's obvious competitors were theirs to discover and document if she could have gotten anyone to confide in her.

Angel and Tina had a session booked with Christine Hertzog around the same time Rollie was to have his discussion with Elmo Entwhistle. It was after 12 when

Angel had finished Tina's orientation and they decided to go out, get a sandwich and some fresh air.

They walked past the large boardroom where Jimmy Rudiger, Elmo and Christine were locked into a fascinating video conference. Angel and Tina would have loved to be flies on the wall but the room was totally sound proofed and they did not want to be perceived as nosy so they walked briskly by and waited for the elevator to come and take them back to fresh air and the scurrying crowds of office workers heading to and from lunch.

While the ladies trudged around the messy sidewalks looking for a place to slip in for a quick bite and a drink, the three so called FinCo executives could not even believe their ears while they listened to a far off deep and menacing voice from Stoltenhoff Island and watched Richard Rasmussin on a video screen looking even more feral and wild than they had ever seen him before.

"The Kirotchenko Empire is no longer, I have taken over the operation in its entirety so we have no one to answer to but me! And that I assure all of you is great news for those of you that continue to play ball with me. Those that do not will be disposed of quickly and painfully. Do I make myself clear?" snarled the power hungry Dictator.

"Sure as shootin, Boss. Congratulations!" said Elmo

"Onward and Upward," added the weasely Jimmy Rudiger

"Christine, what's the matter, cat got your tongue?" questioned the voice from beyond as Christine did not say anything in response immediately.

That seemed to snap her out of her silence and she replied," I'm speechless Richard. How did you do it? From what I understood, the place is a fortress."

"That it was, my martial arts challenged under-study. I went down there with the intention to listen to what those two overgrown windbags had to say and then come back and put up with more of their crap for a little longer before taking action. But then I thought to myself, why not take care of business since I was there. This place was so desolate and de-pressing I decided it needed a bit of sprucing up and now here we are," chucked Richard.

"So what happened to the brothers?" asked Jimmy.

"Same thing that happened and will continue to happen to those that oppose me. Those two over-weight Russians are furnishing the local sharks with one of their better meals along with those who were not too thrilled about what had happened, if you get my drift," indicated Richard now wearing an ear to ear grin which made him look even more dangerous and deadly than usual.

"I will be here for a few more days to wrap things up and begin an extensive expansion program, the same with FinCo. We've come a long way but I will not stop until I have put all of our competitors out of business. And the world's drug, prostitution, weapon and sex trade will all go through Stoltenhoff Island directly or indirectly before I am done,"Richard raged on.

"Shit Boss, that's great!"said Elmo
"Very cool!"added Rudiger

"Mind-blowing," added Christine but inside she was shaking. She knew that Richard Rasmussin was a power hungry psychopath but even she had had no idea to what depth he would go. She realized that her days on this earth were numbered because Richard never tolerated failure and she had failed to show up Angel in that martial arts contest Richard had set up and expected her to win.

Instead, just the opposite had happened and Christine knew that Richard now wanted to possess and dominate this Angel totally and discard her like everything else he had discarded before. She thought she had a bit more time than she did. No such luck, Richard had bumped up his timetable considerably so she knew her days were numbered.

Unless she could figure out a way to get rid of him permanently as his tendrils would reach around the world, running would not be an option. If Richard did not get her then those two idiots, Rudiger and Entwhistle would somehow screw up and bring the heat down on FinCo. In her estimation, Richard had made a bad mistake by kidnapping, drugging and letting that boorish slob Entwhistle have his way with Tina.

But maybe, just maybe these people had some high powered friends that could help get her out of this jam, judging by what had happened to the imitation Elmo. Richard now had too many irons in the fire to worry about that but Christine knew that no way in hell anyone from a furniture store would have been able to do what someone had done without being seen.

Maybe the fake Elmo had some powerful ene-mies but the whole thing seemed too co-incidental to her. Right then and there, she decided to cozy up to this Angel and Tina duo and find out if they could be of use to her in her upcoming battle to stay alive.

So she listened and contributed where she could and started hatching out a plan of her own as after all her own survival and prosperity was key for her. What else would make sense?

Chapter 41

After Angel and Tina returned back up to the office feeling refreshed but no closer to figuring out what their next steps would be, Christine Hertzog walked into their cubicle. She was looking even more attractive than they had seen her last with some slinky make up, tight blouse and a skirt that left little to the imagination. That along with her short blonde streaked pixie hair style had Angel and Tina straightening themselves out in their chairs almost instinctively.

"I'd like to get our session started; we have a lot to cover. My office in ten minutes?" asked Christine.

"Sure, that would be fine. We're just going to freshen up after the blustery walk we just had outside," replied Angel.

"Yes, it seems the drivers of Toronto don't seem to care who they splash," added Tina, pointing at her leggings which now had some unwanted salt stains on them.

Christine turned and wiggled out of their cubicle leaving the two ladies to head to the restroom to clean up.

There was no one in the room presently so they chatted freely but quietly.

"What do you think, is she going to be looking for a rematch soon?" Tina whispered.

"I hope not for her sake. I kind of got the impression she has softened up on us a bit for whatever reason. What do you think?" Angel answered in the same hush hush tone.

"Well, I do not know her as well as you do as I have been missing in action so to speak. But I'll tell you this, I am not willing to put up with any crap from anyone especially after what happened to me … whatever that was," indicated Tina.

After cleaning up and straightening themselves out, they were ready to see what they could learn from Christine as they were hired to do a job here but had a feeling this work was not what they had expected. That was already very apparent.

Angel and Tina knocked on Christine Hertzog's office; Christine opened the door and waved them in.

"Soft drinks, Tea, Coffee or mineral water? The good stuff unfortunately we are not allowed to offer although there have been exceptions," indicated Christine.

"Mineral water please," said Angel. Tina asked for the same.

Christine went to a small bar fridge in her office and pulled out two small bottles of Evian and poured them into glasses and placed them beside Angel and Tina while pouring herself a Diet Pepsi.

"I'm hooked on this stuff. It's not healthy but I can't stand the sugar in regular pop," she said while taking a sip and then settling back crossing her legs making her look even more exotic.

"So how have things been progressing with your analysis?" began Christine.

"I'm going to answer for the both of us as Tina is just back, if that is alright with you?" began Angel.

"Absolutely and how are you feeling? queried Christine. "And please feel free to join in anytime," she turned to Tina.

Tina just nodded and then the meeting began in earnest.

Angel outlined the work and research she had done so far looking at how other financial institutions ran their businesses, the hierarchy, structure and pro-cesses that they employed. How that compared to FinCo was another question entirely as Angel had been unable to find out very little above what she could observe or pick up in general email directives.

Tina picked up on the discussion and threw a question back at Christine.

"So how does FinCo differ from what Angel has laid out so far?" questioned Tina.

"Good question. You seem to have come out of your shell since you have come back," Christine remarked.

"I feel Angel has done a great job so far but we were hired as a team and now I am more than ready to do my part," said Tina.

Angel could not be more proud of her friend and loved her more than ever at this moment.

To answer Tina's question, Christine went over the organizational structure of FinCo and how Richard Rasmussin only attracted, hired and retained the absolute top talent in the industry. She continued by adding that he was not above plundering overachievers from their competitors as long as they had the attitude and skill sets FinCo was looking for.

"Isn't that unethical?" asked Angel.

"Honey, very little is unethical when you really come down to it. Our aim is to be number one with a bullet in this business and we are well on the way there. High net worth individuals flock to FinCo because our investment vehicles and funds outperform our competitors hands down and consistently. When you are a winner, everyone wants to get on the band wagon" lectured Christine.

"Fair enough. So by your own estimation, what could FinCo be doing to further improve business?" countered Angel.

"We are overworked but overpaid to compensate. Richard likes his organization lean and mean and everyone, even though they may not look it, are in excellent physical shape here," Christine relayed.

"Including Jimmy Rudiger? He does not look the picture of health and neither does Elmo Entwhistle from what we have seen so far," said Angel

"Do not let them fool you. Each is more than formidable in their own way. Even with your high skill sets you would not survive an encounter with them."

"You are entitled to your own opinion, let's hope it never comes to that," said Angel with a steely look on her gorgeous face.

"So talking about that, when are you up for a rematch?" quipped Christine but with a smile on her face.

"Anytime at all but don't we all have something better to do like what we were hired to do?" Angel retorted.

"Just kidding. I'm not anxious to get my butt kicked around the gym again. I'd rather go for a drink sometime with you two," was the response that really surprised Angel and Tina.

"Works for us," was the joint response before the conversation drifted to relationships, martial arts, the Toronto clubbing scene and other interesting girl talk.

Angel unfortunately brought the conversation back to reality by asking Christine if she had heard of what happened in Queen's Park a few weeks ago on the statue of Governor Simcoe.

Christine took her time answering and the hesitation and furtive look that now clouded her features was not lost on Angel and Tina.

She finally responded that she had and what relevance was it to this conversation.

"Well, we found out through a confidential source that the guy they found intimately intertwined with the statue was Elmo Entwhistle."

And of course we thought right away it couldn't be since Elmo is one of your executives here and obviously very much alive," Angel added.

"What type of confidential source would that be?" replied Christine now giving both ladies her full attention.

"Let's call it a friend of ours. A very reliable friend at that. The discussion centered around Elmo, an executive at FinCo as a possible tie in as how many individuals go by that name," Tina cautiously offered.

Christine looked like the cat got her tongue.

And before she could reply, Tina continued by indicating that the furniture store her fiancé and Angel's fiancé owned was repeatedly threatened by an individual named believe it or not, Elmo Entwhistle who claimed he worked for some sort of financial institution. How weird was that. She smartly omitted the shots fired, kidnapping and elimination of the obviously imitation Elmo Entwhistle by the monster named Mikhail.

Angel remained quiet but her eyes were dancing between Tina and Christine and the pride she felt for her friend had no bounds.

After a gulp of her diet pop, Christine whispered quietly…

"We have no idea if these offices are bugged. Most likely they are. Can we meet somewhere for a drink after work where we can talk a bit more freely?"

"Tina and I like the Canoe Restaurant. You know where it is of course?" asked Angel.

"I'll meet you there at 5. Please get us a comfortable booth and order me a black Russian on the rocks.

We have a lot to talk about," asked Christine before ushering the stunned ladies out.

"Black Russian? How weird is that?" said Tina to Angel on the way back to their desks. How very ironic.

Chapter 42

R ollie Sampson arrived at FinCo's reception area a
few minutes before his scheduled appointment
with Elmo Entwhistle (or at least some sort of
reasonable facsimile). The receptionist took him to
plush looking mahogany doors labeled "Entwhistle"
and gave it a knock.

"*Rolf Simpson*" to see you Mr. Entwhistle," purred
the receptionist.

"Send him in," came the answer from within.

Rollie walked into a lavishly decorated office in
the vein of the old bankers club including a large bar
fridge, old English style oil paintings of hunting and
polo playing scenes along with a breathtaking view
of the west end of the city.

"Take a seat. What can I offer you? High net worth
perspective clients are always treated royally here at
FinCo.

Rollie could not believe his eyes. This guy was almost the spitting image of the hood at the furniture store the monster had dispatched so quickly. *I must tread carefully from here on in.*

"I'll take a shot of Chivas on the rocks," said Rollie thinking that he may as well milk this for all it's worth.

"Good choice, coming right up and I think I'll join you. No sense drinking alone," indicated Elmo while pouring the liquid over large ice cubes.

"So how can I help you, Rolf?" Elmo was cutting right to the chase.

"Well, I have a portfolio that seems to be losing money every year instead of gaining and why not stuff it under the mattress if this keeps happening, right? But the load fees and taxes are outrageous to liquidate now so I was recommended by a close acquaintance to come here and see what you folks have to offer.

"Wise choice, eventually you will all come to the table. Who recommended you?"

"I was asked not to disclose his name as this individual has requested his privacy be honored. You surely understand that?," Rollie answered.

"Certainly," answered Elmo but his face did not betray his annoyance by that reply. *Once he roped this sucker in, he would quickly find out who recommended him the easy or the hard way. He truly enjoyed the hard way much better as Elmo liked to play, whether it was with a female or male. It was all in the game.*

"So how much money are we talking about here? Most of my personal clients have a net worth of over 5 million. Any less would be delegated to one of our pooled agents," indicated Elmo.

Rollie decided the best way to play this large annoying individual was to give him what he wanted to hear. "Ah, about 7.5 million split up in gold, fancy colored diamonds, mutuals, bearer bonds and various securities."

"That would certainly qualify. Whom are you invested with currently?" probed Elmo starting to lick his thin lips.

"I don't think we know each other well enough for me to tell you that. So what could you do for me that my current brokers can not?" countered Rollie.

Even Rollie was shocked as to what happened next.

"I can keep you and your family alive!" snarled Elmo now moving his bulk out of his chair and advancing on Rollie.

But Rollie always recovered fast. With a big hearty chuckle he slapped his knee and replied," You're kidding right? I can take care of that quite well myself but thanks for offering," Rollie replied with a dangerous glint in his eye which was not lost on Elmo.

"So I am only going to explain this once. We do the paperwork right here and now and all your assets are signed over to me. If you do not, your wife, kids, relatives, friends are toast. Capish, you chubby little insignificant grunt?" snarled Elmo now showing his sizeable bulk in its full glory as he covered the distance between the two of them in a blink of an eye.

Impressive Rollie thought as he produced his Smith and Wesson with even more speed than Elmo covered the distance between them finding it pointed firmly at the spot between his two beady eyes.

Just as quickly, Elmo retreated and sat back down behind his desk and took a sip of his drink. Rollie put the hand gun back into his jacket pocket where he produced it just as quickly and took a long sip himself.

"So, you are connected, biggest mistake you ever made coming here. Chances are almost certain we run whoever you are connected to and, we will find out when you leave here. You either sign the papers now or we will make life for you, your employer and everyone dear to you a living hell. With me so far?" growled Elmo.

"Oh, I'm with you alright." Rollie could not believe his good fortune thinking that he came away with a lot more than he bargained for. He now knew FinCo was definitely behind all the troubles Tina, Joey and Jon-Erik had had. *And they thought he was connected on top of everything else. How good was that?*

But first thing first, he wanted to leave this meeting on a good note at least for him.

"So you talk to your people and I'll talk to my people but make no mistake about it. You make any sudden moves against me or anyone else that is near and dear to me and I'll blow your large ass into the next world. Since you are in the business, you hopefully get my drift," said Rollie with an evil smirk on his round face which was a little redder than usual possibly from the excitement or the strong drink.

"You have no idea who or what you are actually dealing with. When you leave here and look over your shoulder, it will be too late. We don't take challenges lightly and just so you understand clearly, we are coming for you and your little peashooter will do little to help you. Just so you really understand what you are into now, I would blow you into kingdom come right now and then give your carcass a taste of what happens in our jails but the boss would say that it is not the way we do business, at least not on these premises. Do I make myself clear?" screamed Elmo now pointing an automatic weapon straight at Rollie.

"Perfectly," said Rollie picking up his coat and leaving the office as fast as his little legs could carry him, almost unable to contain his excitement. He was also extremely concerned for Angel and Tina who were still on the premises, as far as he knew. Good thing he used an alias; he hated surprises and knew these people would be after him, and fast.

How quickly even he did not know, as Elmo Entwhistle was on the phone immediately after Rollie left the room.

"Get me everything you can on a *Rolf Simpson*. This short fat guy walks in here indicated he is looking to invest 7.5 million with us and then when I give him our usual spiel he produces a hand gun and points it right between my eyes. I almost blew his ass all over my windows here but I restrained myself. I want to know who he is, where he lives, who he works for, who he associates with, who he fucks and what he eats, in short, the whole enchilada."

"And I wanted this information five minutes ago if you get my drift," Elmo added.

The voice on the other end knew his life could be on the line and started typing furiously on his keyboard and making short and precise phone calls. This Rolf Simpson and his employers were dead men walking…that much was certain!

Chapter 43

While Rollie was first on the phone to Alf Cragan and then to Jon-Erik and Joey excitedly explaining what had happened, Angel and Tina were getting ready for their after hour meeting with Christine Hertzog. As soon as they left their office tower, Angel got on her cell to call Jon-Erik who answered the phone excitedly.

"Jeez, hon we are glad you and Tina are okay. You would not believe what happened to Rollie this afternoon," relayed Jon-Erik breathlessly.

After Jon-Erik finished telling the strange story, Joey got on the line to speak to Tina. Angel overheard him saying that he loved her and for her to come home safely.

After the call ended, the ladies were heading over to the TD Tower and Canoe whispering anxiously.

"My god, what are we involved in?" asked Tina in a shaky voice.

"I have no idea but we have to play this really smart from here on in or we could all be in grave danger," replied Angel sounding no less concerned and knowing they already were rolling in the deep much more than they wanted.

"How are we going to play this with Christine?" said Tina.

"We are going to feel her out but very carefully. Let me take the lead but you help me out anytime I get flustered."

"Okay with me. Hopefully we have a few minutes to strategize before she arrives," said Tina as they arrived at Canoe a few minutes before 5, were shown to their seat and ordered two white wine and a Black Russian on the rocks for Christine.

As soon as the drinks arrived, so did Christine Hertzog unfortunately and all Angel and Tina could do was clasp hands under the table to give each other courage.

Christine arrived, smiled at Angel and Tina in turn, took off her sheepskin jacket, fluffed up her short blond hair and rubbed the cold from her hands.

Angel and Tina said nothing, watching her take a large sip from her cocktail glass.

After Christine had settled in, she seemed a lot more relaxed and as the ladies hoped, she started the conversation.

"Thanks for meeting with me. We have a lot to talk about. You are obviously much more intelligent than meets the eye. Am I right about that?"

"Depends in what context. We are good at the work we do if that is what you mean?" Angel replied.

"Let's cut to the chase. We are not on the clock now and tip toeing around like this is just a waste of all of our precious time," indicated Christine smoothing her short mini and re-crossing her gorgeous legs.

"What is the chase?" replied Tina causing Angel to smile and further squeeze her best friend's hand.

"FinCo and its executives are not what they seem. There is a much larger and infinitely more dangerous picture in play here. I, like everyone else was lured here by power and greed but after the events of the last few weeks, my days here and most likely on earth are numbered."

"You mean to tell us your life could be in danger?" asked Angel.

"How do I begin? The more I tell you the graver danger you would be in. Richard Rasmussin is one of if not the most lethal and power hungry men on earth and he has very recently acquired power and resources even beyond his wildest dreams.....or maybe not," said Christine in a near whisper.

"You already know that you both are in grave danger. You just don't know by how much ....especially you Angel. And Richard always gets what he wants.....and he wants you," she added looking even more concerned than before leaving no doubt in the minds of Angel and Tina that she was on the level.

"Wants me for what? I am engaged to be married and Jon-Erik is the love of my life," said Angel defiantly.

"He does not care about that. He only cares about what he wants and right now he is fixated on you. Once he has you, he will want someone else, with him it's the chase. Once he has had you, he will discard you like he has everyone else."

"Well, he can't have me, and if he tries he will get a very unpleasant surprise," snapped Angel almost losing her cool.

"Yes, you are a very talented martial artist but your chances against Richard are non-existent. He is a trained killer the likes of which very few have ever seen. And he now has an army behind him which stretches to every corner of the world," Christine said with a tear coming out of her eye smudging her mascara.

"Why are you telling us this?" Tina asked.

"Because when Angel beat me in the gym that day, it sealed my fate. I have no place I can hide from him and he will kill me unless I can help someone turn the tables on him. I was his love slave until he tired of me and became infatuated with Angel."

She caught her breath, took another strong sip of her drink and continued," When I saw what happened to the replacement Elmo, I knew that someone connected to you had formidable resources of their own in order to be able to do what they did."

"Will you come in and talk to our friends?" asked Angel.

"Richard's organization has eyes and ears everywhere and they see all and know all. If I am followed, and I would not even know whether I am or not, he could wipe us all out in one strike. Believe me when I say that police and the highest enforcement agencies in this country can't stand against his might. If they are not paid off, they are eliminated. Simple as that. He may even *have ears and* eyes here, nothing is as it seems," Christine said quietly. "Talking with your friends would sign all of our death warrants."

"What happened to me and why?" asked Tina looking down right scared.

"Leverage and lust and that is all I will say about that. You will most likely never remember anything which is good. I was very sorry that this happened but had no part in it," answered Christine.

"God, from what we are hearing, this is an honest to goodness nightmare. We were involved in something similar years ago and only luck, determination as well as an unbelievable adversary that through very strange circumstances has become our ally, saved our lives. He is the one who took care of the replacement Elmo as you say," said Angel carefully looking around to see if anyone was paying attention to them more than they should be.

Besides a few horny glances at the three hot ladies in the private booth, nothing seemed out of place.

"Tell me about your skilled friend," asked Christine.

"How do we know you are not just pumping us for information that your crooked boss would use against us?" asked Tina.

Angel nodded her agreement with her green eyes turning to slits showing she meant business.

"You don't. You are both going to have to trust me when I say my life is at stake here and most likely all of yours," replied Christine.

"Okay then, we need to work together. You are going to have to figure out a way to meet with our friends. They are very experienced in this sort of thing," said Angel.

"No police. If you can guarantee me that and if you are present as well, it could be possible," replied Christine.

Angel pulled out her cell and dialed Rollie's number. He answered on the third ring. Angel quickly explained the situation to him. Rollie thought about it for a minute and then suggested they meet at a local bar on the Lakeshore just east of Browns Line called Southside Johnny's tonight around 8 pm. The music didn't start till later and since it was a weeknight, they would be able to talk privately.

Christine reluctantly agreed as long as only Angel and Rollie would be there and with that took one last gulp of her drink, grabbed her coat and left the restaurant.

Angel and Tina left right after paying the bill and leaving an ample tip, keeping their eyes open for anyone even remotely suspicious but nothing or nobody looked out of place. They made their way back down to the underground parking where Angel's car was and headed back along the Lakeshore toward home. Traffic was its nasty self and the Expressway (nothing express about it) was as congested as ever. They watched the bumper to bumper action from below and wound their way around the Exhibition grounds looking for lesser traffic volume heading West toward home.

Chapter 44

The Ninja was in a more than usual foul mood. His little stunt with that trussed up overweight sack of garbage had produced no noticeable results and a dark and foreboding hush had spread over the city and surrounding areas like a pestilence. Silence reigned and the denizens of the underground scurried around like frightened rabbits. Something big had already happened but what it was no one was saying.

One option was tailing Angel to keep her safe which he was doing already. It was relatively simple for one such as him but even he would not follow her into her office unless there was no other way.

The other option he had was Yuri and the Russian Bakery. His last visit had ruffled a few feathers to say the least and the Monster hated to go to the well once too often but something big was afoot here and he was determined to find out what it was.

Yuri knew the movers and shakers of the Toronto underground and this time there would be no more Mr. Nice Guy. If Yuri did not come across with some usable information, he would breathe his last tonight. And rather than his old approach of busting up the bar and shaking a few trees to see what fell out, he had a better and more subtle at least to his methods, idea.

Yuri liked to spend a couple of hours, before things became busy at midnight, downing shots of vodka while watching videos not appropriate for general viewing, to say the least. He always had at least two or three of his attendants at the ready in case he got too excited during his screenings, which was always the case.

Mikhail had no taste or use for such depravity but he knew many others did.

It was relatively simple for the Shadow to arrive at the still quiet bakery and let himself in through the back entrance which was always unlatched for an easy escape. No one would ever want to come to such a place unannounced, no one except Mikhail. The dark shadow clung to the walls and entered the screening room beside the nightclub and gaming house without a sound or hint of his arrival.

He slunk into a filthy adjacent bathroom and waited for the activities to begin. He did not have to wait long. First Yuri arrived with a full bottle in his hand. One of his cronies came in and switched on the video equipment and next thing you knew, the screen was filled with naked flesh and lewd acts which got incrementally worse by the minute.

The technician was dismissed and in came two beautiful and young attendants who seemed to take their work very seriously judging by how quickly they got busy with each other and Yuri. One was jumping up and down on the bear like Russian's gherkin like a cat on a trampoline while the other was trying to use her tongue to keep things lubricated without getting her head crushed by her acrobatic partner.

Yuri was too engrossed to see a black shadow materialize out of the corner of the room. His lady friends had the same problem and slid to the floor noiselessly put to sleep by a special nerve grip the Shape shifter employed with lightning speed and stealth.

When Yuri opened his eyes, as his exposed privates felt a bit cold and neglected, a large powerful hand was jammed over his mouth while something else held his exposed equipment in a vice like grip while the grunting from the video was getting progressively louder.

"Vy govorite vy umrete (you speak, you die)," whispered Mikhail.

"Unless I tell you otherwise, panimayu (understand)?"

The burly Russian nodded and Mikhail took his hand away from the foul smelling mouth of his captor whose privates were being squeezed to the point of passing out.

"Good! You have learned not to cause me problems. Otherwise, you would be dead my now and that deflating organ of yours would not even be noticed among the daisies that would mark your grave."

Yuri only grunted.

"Something huge is going on out there. I hear the whispering in the shadows. What can you tell me and if I do not like what you tell me your life ends here and now?"

"If I do not tell you, I die. If I tell you, I die. But you are here now and the other is not. I will have to take my chances," said Yuri getting some of his breath back as well as his essentials.

"Wise choice. Talk," said Mikhail while taking a long pull from Yuri's bottle of Russian Standard before returning it to the cornered bar owner, who did the same.

"The mob has been taken over by an individual who is as dangerous if not more so than you. He has gained control not only locally but world wide. Word is, he has eliminated the Kirotchenko Brothers and has assumed complete control of all their enterprises globally, making him the most powerful crime lord in the world or he soon will be," whispered the Russian with real fear showing on his weathered and otherwise beaten face.

"There is no one more dangerous than me and there never will be. Be assured of that. Is this the dead man who has been shaking down people financially?"

"That, and so much more. We pay heavily to have our business exist here; or we would end up fish food in the depths of Lake Ontario. Those who refuse are never heard of again. No witnesses are ever left. I know of him but not where his headquarters are. It could be anywhere in the world!"

"Name," growled Mikhail or you will wish you were never born.

"Richard Rasmussin and that is all I know."

"And you will live to see another day my horny friend. Your girls will wake up soon. If he contacts you, tell him I am coming for him and there is no place on earth he can hide from me. No one threatens those I have sworn to protect."

And with that, the Monster seemed to disappear into thin air leaving Yuri to rub his eyes, his throat and his sore genitals while the two sleeping beauties by his feet were slowly starting to stir. He felt like he was going from the frying pan into the fire and his taste for sex and depravity had left him for now and he felt totally empty inside and took another long pull of the bottle that the Monster kindly left him. He really needed it now.

Mikhail was pleased with what he had found out. Finally a lead, Richard Rasmussin, eh? Somewhere he had heard that name before, long ago. He was deep in thought strolling back to his F10 truck when a commotion across the road snapped him out of his thoughts.

A scantily dressed woman especially for this time of the year was being physically and verbally abused by a tall skinny black man dressed in a full length coat and black hat to match. The scum ball that was most likely her pimp was yelling at her between slaps to the face and no one was around to pay attention or even assist.

The Monster would never have given them a second look but maybe Angel had rubbed off on him somewhat. He crossed the street and before the nasty pimp even noticed him, Mikhail grabbed the punk by the throat and hurled him full force right through the store front window of a boutique that had long closed for the night. The hoodlum was laying there in his own blood, down but not out as he was still moving. The store alarm was set off by the breaking of the window and by the time the hooker had recovered enough to get her wits about her, the police sirens were getting closer. Mikhail was already long gone on the way back to his new lair in Port Credit with a smile on his face and a Russian song in his heart.

Doing some good felt good to him much to his surprise. But as he headed back to his secluded home his thoughts returned to the current situation at hand. Richard Rasmussin. The name Rasmussin was familiar from his days haunting the back alleys in Moscow. But the first name was Sergei not Richard. Sergei ran a highly skilled team of killers, extortionists, pimps and drug runners out of Sointsevo, an extremely dangerous area in North West Moscow.

Fortunately for Sergei and his group, Mikhail had never crossed paths with these individuals but had heard of them. They would never have heard of him as the Ninja had always been very low key and behind the scenes even though lately he seemed to be coming out of his shell a bit more...so to speak. Maybe low key was the better way to go but the Monster always adapted depending on the situation and always trusted his instincts to do the right thing.

So Sergei had himself a brat who now had risen in the ranks. Even Mikhail did not know to what extent but one thing was certain. He was looking forward to their first and certainly their last meeting. As he pulled into his secluded driveway, he thought about the security measures he would have to take as he knew that surely they would come for him sooner or later but when they did, they would get some surprises they did not count on. A fatal surprise!

The only sad thing was, he liked this place in Port Credit even better than the house he had years ago near Old Weston Road in Toronto but he was always ready for a quick exit and this was no different.

Chapter 45

Southside Johnny's was not busy yet because it was a weeknight. A wild and brilliant blues and rock guitarist who played and looked very much like the late and great Jimmy Hendrix was booked to start his first set around ten thirty; it would get much busier as the night wore on.

Rollie and Angel strolled in just after nine taking a quick look around. No one except a perky waitress with a long dark ponytail and an infectious smile paid any attention to them.

She introduced herself as Sandy and started gushing about how fabulous this musician and his band were and asked if they were here to see him.

Rollie shook his head but indicated that since they were here, they would stay for a set. Angel ordered a diet coke and Rollie ordered a beer sitting at a secluded corner table where they could watch anyone come in or out of the club.

About fifteen minutes later, Christine Hertzog entered the pub with her short blonde hair tucked under a Toronto Raptors cap looking not at all glamorous and quite inconspicuous in a dark ski jacket and jeans. She sat down, took her jacket off and the attentive waitress was right there taking her drink order for a soda water and lime.

Angel did the short introductions and everyone took a sip of their drink before Rollie began the festivities.

"Look, first of all we need to know you are on the level. If you are trying to jerk us around in any way and believe me I have been jerked around by the best in my careers first as a beat cop, then a police detective and now as a private investigator."

"All I have is my life to lose which will happen sooner or later anyway unless I can find a way to stop Richard in his tracks because my fate was sealed when I lost to Angel in that impromptu match we had at the office," said Christine in a low voice.

Angel said with a concerned look on her face that she was sorry and had no idea that there would be repercussions such as this.

"Had I known I would lose and I have never lost, I would have figured some way around doing the match but Richard wanted to see what you had and believe me, he was impressed and so was I," replied Christine still half whispering.

"Okay, you seem sincere but I warn you, we do not take betrayal lightly," warned Rollie.

"You have no idea what you are up against and do not take that lightly. There is no more dangerous man on earth than Richard Rasmussin and he is now drunk with power and flush with success. Indications may be that he is now one of if not the most powerful crime lord on this planet," said Christine

"He has eyes and ears everywhere in every city, town and country on this earth now and they are all eager to serve him,"she added.

"Well, we have had some experience unfortunately with this sort of thing a number of years ago when we were all younger but not as wise. An Argentinean drug lord had set up shop here in the city and Angel, her friends and I got caught up right in the middle of it," indicated Rollie covering his mouth as he spoke.

"So what happened?" Christine asked.

"We are still here to talk about it and have learned a lot in the process. Tina and I both have fiancées who are knee deep with us in this mess as it all started at the furniture shop that they own and we will all fight to the death to protect our loved ones," snarled Angel.

"You do not have to convince me," replied Christine quietly.

"So where do we go from here?" asked Angel.

"We need to know as much about our enemy as we can. It is ludicrous to think we can take out his organization, they are obviously too strong and too many. But we can look at taking Richard and his close cronies here at FinCo out and I do mean out because if we do not, he most likely will not stop until he gets what he wants which is all of us especially Angel by the sound of things," said Rollie.

"And they are going to pay dearly for what they did to Tina," vowed Angel.

"I had no part in that. It was a stupid plan of Richard's and Elmo's to frighten Angel and show her a taste of their power. It was nothing personal, just business," relayed Christine.

Angel and Rollie just shook their heads as Christine continued to fill them in on Richard, FinCo, their tactics and their utter disregard for human life. All they cared about was money, greed, power and would stop at nothing to get more and more of it. She laid out how FinCo made most of their money and assets by threats, intimidation and even torture and murder.

Christine asked Rollie if he had seen something in the paper a number of weeks ago about a rich old couple on Bridle Path that had been murdered and robbed in their sleep with the police having absolutely no clues or suspects. He said that he did.

"Believe me when I say that was Richard's handy work. Anyone that refuses to play ball is eliminated and although I can never prove it, this one was his all the way. Sometimes he liked going out into the field and test his skills which have become even more formidable if he has in fact eliminated the Kirotchenko Brothers."

"The Kirotchenkos were two of the most powerful crime lords on earth and were recently never seen or heard from. Rumor has it that they operated out of a remote group of Islands in the south Atlantic. I have never been there but Richard has mentioned them here and there and with distain. No one knew that he would act so quickly and successfully as their fortress was impenetrable," Christine continued.

"Impenetrable for anyone not invited. He used the element of trust and surprise against them. Richard will be looking for those elements to be used against him. We will have to be ultra careful with our next steps. Running and hiding is not an option this time. Sounds like this guy has unbelievable resources," said Rollie.

"You were very smart to use an alias when you met with Elmo. They are already pulling out all the stops to find you," indicated Christine.

"Undoubtedly," Rollie replied. "Let them come, I do not make an easy target."

"I am going to have to think about this long and hard. These people need to pay for their actions but arresting, prosecuting and jailing them will never work. They are too strong, powerful and connected. I work with a trusted friend on the police force and will have to enlist him and his team's unofficial help with this. Everything will be hush hush and on a need to know basis only. From what I understand, Rasmussin is still not back yet so we may have a bit of time but whatever we have is precious," said Rollie.

In the meantime, it was ten thirty and a wild looking guy with dreadlocks, a smoking guitar and his tight band took the stage. Electric and amazing music filled the air; you would think Jimi Hendrix was back with much more improvisation and dexterity.

The three had to suspend their discussion until the band took their first break about an hour and a half later as the music was too loud to get a word in edge wise.

After the band stopped and before the three could continue their discussion, the guitar player sauntered over, kissed Angel and Christine's hand, introduced himself as Toney and asked them if they enjoyed the show so far.

All three nodded enthusiastically after which Toney said he would dedicate a song called "Foxy Lady" to Angel and Christine next set. And off he ambled to the bar to pour back some shots bought for him by his fans and hug the waitress that had been serving them.

"It's getting late, ladies. Let us sleep on it and we'll meet again tomorrow night at Angel's with the whole gang. Right now the best thing to do is nothing out of the ordinary. Angel and Tina will keep an eye at work although I do not think they will be there much longer. Angel and I will drive you close to your home since you cabbed it here, do not worry I can spot a tail a mile ahead." said Rollie.

And with that the three new allies paid their tab and left the bar quickly and quietly with only the guitar player looking on and wondering if these hot ladies were into Adele or Christine Aguilera instead. Oh well—life goes on.

Chapter 46

Richard Rasmussin had wrapped up his business on Stoltenhoff Island and although there was still some dissention in the ranks, the takeover was largely successful.

He was on the private plane that formerly belonged to the Kirotchenkos and was now his, along with all the trappings that came with his new stature as the most powerful crime czar in the world. At least in his estimation anyway and that was the one that counted for him.

Richard took Hana and Irena, the two hotsy totsy stewardesses, with him as they amused him for now but he knew not for much longer. Since they liked sex so much, he would probably have them working for one of the high class escort agencies in Toronto that now reported to him. One of his directives to the Stoltenhoff staff was that he needed a total inventory of their holdings and businesses throughout the world. He was planning on being pleasantly surprised.

In the meantime, being the active thinker that he was, Richard made a few quick phone calls. He wanted to send a subtle little message to one of the rival financial institutions that was always a thorn in his side mainly because their numbers were always slightly better than FinCo's no matter what they did.

The particular business was located right in the TD Tower where the Canoe Restaurant was located and to Richard's way of thinking, why not kill two or more birds with one stone?

His call was relayed to a specialized group of people who work for the Toronto Department of Public Works and were responsible for the water and water pressure that fed these Office Towers.

The supervisor for that area of town was a rough looking overweight city worker with over 25 years of service named Ernie Jones. Ernie and his team monitored the water pressure for the key areas in the financial district as well as dealing with water main breaks and issues. Today was a slow day and the boys were all on the internet watching porno clips and chowing down on submarine sandwiches when the call came in.

Even Ernie whom nothing usually bothered could not believe what he was told. He called his group together in a tiny meeting room adjacent to their monitoring center below City Hall.

"Listen guys, this is a strange one and off the books. Don't ask who authorized this; it's all off the record. And none of this comes back to us or me. Do I make myself clear?" said the supervisor.

"Sure boss, what's the deal?" asked his Foreman.

"Over-pressurize some water pipes in the TD Tower and get on it right away. These are the floors that should be impacted. And as soon as the job is done we are on an inspection call of a new construction site in mid-town to ensure we are not readily available to deal with this issue," instructed Ernie.

"This sounds crazy," said the Forman with the staff nodding their agreements.

"Don't worry; we are close to the end of the shift so when the shit hits the fan, we will all be on triple overtime. And make sure it is something you can repair pretty easily so we look like the heroes that we are. Now get on it!" instructed Ernie taking another bite of his sub and thinking how screwed up things had become. He was going to have to bump up his retirement schedule and take some of those sick days he had accrued before someone like that new anti-gravy train Mayor took them away.

It did not take long for all hell to break loose at the TD Tower. The lower financial floors, a number of designated middle and upper floors started spraying water like the fountains in the summer at City Hall. It came from the walls, bathrooms and even the ceiling sprinkler systems decided to join into the merriment.

People were getting soaked and running for the elevators and stairs in droves, ignoring the mechanical voice that told them to follow their evacuation procedures in an orderly and controlled fashion. A lot of them had neglected to take their coats and winter boots with them forgetting about the fact that they were in the middle of winter and the temperature was a frosty -10 degrees Celsius with more snow in the forecast.

A powerbroker who decided that a little private dictation was in order with the new blonde with black streaks and a rack that almost burst from her undersized blouse got more than he even bargained for.

As his bare buttocks were shaking back and forth and he was furiously pounding away at the streaky blonde who was trying her best to hang on and balance herself on the lavish bathroom counter, a jet stream of gushing water from the opposite wall gave him a rinse that he was certainly not expecting. It did not feel too bad at first and actually heightened the experience but when the gusher intensified in pressure, it knocked both of them unceremoniously into the mirror, the blonde's large breasts acting as a cushion saving them from receiving bad cuts on top of the humiliation and fear they were now feeling.

A lot of the panicked workers took off for neighboring establishments and foyers of adjacent office towers to call taxis to be taken home where dry clothes and warmth waited for them.

Building Security were beside themselves trying to guide people out of the building. Once they were satisfied the affected floors were evacuated, they began to assess the damage. The flustered building maintenance staff had never seen anything quite like this in all the time they had been on the job.

One quick thinking supervisor actually did what he was supposed to do and called the number on the wall in case of an emergency such as this. The dispatcher indicated the crew responsible for that section of town were on another job, but should be on site within the next couple of hours.

"The next couple of hours? We bloody well need help now, we are being flushed out of our own building," screamed the supervisor into the now sore ear of the dispatcher.

The arrival of Police vehicles, EMS and Fire trucks on the scene added even more drama to the existing confusion. There were surprisingly few casualties; one guy slipped on the slick floor and hyper-extended his leg and a few others sustained bumps and bruises as well as hypothermia running out into the street into the frigid weather which the onsite EMS attendants took care of.

The firemen, with the maintenance staff, found the main water shutoff for the building and stopped the flow of water but the damage had been done. Carpeting was ruined, walls had burst and a lot of computer and electronic equipment had in some cases irreparable damage.

The weasley Jimmy Rudiger was across the street watching the action first hand with a nasty grin on his ferret like face. He ducked into an alcove and called his boss direct.

"Mission accomplished boss. You should see the mayhem down here. Looks like they have evacuated the whole building and now the local news trucks are arriving in droves," reported Jimmy gleefully.

"Good," replied Richard from 25,000 feet just clearing the tip of the South American coast and flying up off the Caribbean coastline.

"Make sure the city boys get a night out in one of my upscale clubs, give them all the booze, food and women they want. Give them 5 grand each too. Those who play ball with me will be rewarded; those who do not will join their brethren in the deepest part of Lake Ontario which I understand to be more than 800 feet," indicated Richard while watching his stewardesses cover their naked bodies with strawberries and cream. He was ready to crown the whole thing with champagne and himself. But his mind was not on the action in front of him; it was on a gorgeous, gifted martial artist called Angel. *Soon she would be his.*

Chapter 47

The next day everyone was pre-occupied with the barrage of news that came from the TD Tower. Some floors had miraculously been spared but the bottom line was that the whole building had to be fully evacuated anyway while the damage was assessed and repaired. Fortunately, for most of the businesses within the tower, their main Data Processing facilities were offsite so the majority of the still traumatized and chilled to the bone staff could work from home. It was now Friday, the prognosis looked good that everything would be in full operation again Monday morning.

It was not surprising that investigators found no reason for the sudden rise in water pressure especially with the responsible crew being away on another job at the time it actually happened. The General Manager of Public Works along with the Mayor gave a brief statement indicating how sorry they were for the inconvenience, that the matter was under detailed investigation and that they anticipated that the TD Tower would once again be fully operational and open for business the following Monday morning.

Besides a few bumps, bruises and cases of hypothermia, there were relatively few health issues as a result of the flooding. The ensuing question period afterwards really yielded no new information other than accidents do happen and insurance will cover the majority of the damage. Since Ernie Jones' team were so diligently working with other maintenance and computer crews to restore service, no direct scrutiny was being focused on them, although a few insiders had their suspicions which they could not substantiate.

Angel and Tina were in the Employee Lounge at FinCo glued to a TV screen tuned to CP24 running down all the events that had transpired at the TD Tower.

"That is where Canoe is. I guess we will not be going there for a while," indicated Tina.

"They expect to have everything fixed and restored by Monday morning," replied Angel wondering whether this was another show of Richard's ever growing power and reach. She certainly would not put it past him especially after what they had heard last night.

Christine was in the office today and totally kept to herself, hardly acknowledging Angel and Tina. *Smart move if she wanted to stay healthy,* thought Angel. She had briefed Tina on the way to work this morning on what had occurred during the discussions and Tina could not believe her ears.

"You mean to tell me I was a pawn in this mad-man's delusional schemes of power?" asked Tina in the car on the way to the office.

"Looks like we all are one way or another," replied Angel.

"Rollie and the guys are not comfortable with us continuing to work here given the circumstances but quitting and running are really not options either especially with the resources this powerbroker seems to possess. It probably makes sense to continue on like we know nothing at least for now. Rollie and Alf Cragan for sure are cooking up a few surprises of their own. That is a given," added Angel.

So they agreed not to discuss anything to do with what they knew so far at FinCo and continue on with what they were paid to do….streamline and optimize.

This afternoon should be a real eye opener as they had a follow up interview with Elmo Entwhistle which Christine had scheduled for them.

"Let's go to lunch and prepare for the interview," said Tina.

"Not much to prepare for except maybe a nose plug," whispered Angel with a chuckle as they grabbed their coats and headed for the elevators.

As they went on the elevator, Richard Rasmussin was just getting off giving Angel a look that frightened her from head to toe and Angel did not frighten easily. *This guy could scare the stripes right off a Bengal Tiger* figured Angel. And that look was not wasted on Tina either as she instinctively shrunk back steadying herself on the elevator hand railing.

They went to a little café style sandwich shop just up Bay Street and were able to get a window seat that offered a bit of privacy so they could converse quietly without being heard. The waiter took their order and the two beautiful but troubled ladies just looked out at the worker bees buzzing by wishing that their lives were as dull as most of these people scurrying by.

Talking in hushed tones, they decided on a strategy of sexy politeness no matter how rude and crude Elmo would be. It was imperative that they give away nothing and maybe even pick up a few tidbits of information in the process if they could.

"I'll ask most of the questions since I have dealt with him before but do join in anytime to show you are part of the team. And try to leave emotion out of it even though you want to slug this ignorant slob over the head with a baseball bat," cautioned Angel.

"No worries, they are fortunate that I have no memory of what actually happened to me but it makes me sick to my stomach to think this Elmo character was involved in it. Just thinking about that creep actually touching me makes me crazy," said Tina.

Their sandwich order arrived although neither of them was too hungry thinking of whom they had to face when they returned to work, but the food was delicious so they did their best. The interview was scheduled for one thirty giving them enough time to get back to the office to freshen up.

They were at Elmo's office door at one thirty sharp, his distinct pitchy but menacing voice asking them to come in.

Elmo was in jovial mood watching the news on TV holding his ample belly and chuckling along with the news reporter still going on and on about the TD Center fiasco.

"Imagine that, all those people scurrying around like ants with water up their backsides. Sounds like a bad movie script that someone wrote and knowing the entertainment industry up here, this will probably make the next grade Z movie shown on the W channel. You ladies ever watch those movies?" asked Elmo still laughing.

Angel and Tina had taken their seats, crossed their legs and straightened out their hair making them look even more gorgeous and sexy.

"No, we normally don't have time to watch TV. We're busy here during the day and with our fiancées at night," replied Angel.

"Good answer, I hope you are keeping them warm at night. If you ever get bored with them, I am not hard to find…but always hard if you get my drift," replied Elmo still chuckling.

"We'll keep that in mind, now can we get down to business," replied Tina, not being able to fully hide how pissed off she really was being in the same room with this full of himself slob.

"Ah, so you are the real feisty one of this team. Okay, so how can I help you two hot honeys further?" snickered Elmo.

"I'll thank you to keep things on a business level. If you are not prepared to do that then there is no sense continuing," said Angel now upset as well.

"Ewww, you are the martial arts queen, right? I am shaking in my boots but the boss suggested I cooperate with you and cooperate I shall. So what else do you need from me?"

"Fair enough. As you know, we were brought in here to streamline and optimize this operation. We just wanted your input to some of our findings before we present them to Richard," said Angel, now totally professional.

"Let's see what you have," said Elmo as Angel and Tina took turns presenting all twenty points they had so far.

After the ladies had completed their presentation, Elmo sat up in his chair applauding loudly. "Good, concise and well researched points all. Ten of the twenty or so can be used, the rest back to the drawing board. If you come up with another ten better than the ones you already have, you should be in business. That's all on my end for now, come and see me again when you have more new information. Angel, Richard would like to see you in his office now, Tina, you can stay and entertain me some more if you like. I love them dark haired and slinky," said Elmo huskily.

"Don't hold your breath," replied Tina as they both left their seats and the room.

"The nerve of him, I can't wait for the opportunity to slap that smirk off his face," whispered Tina.

"You and me, both. I'm off to see the wizard. Wonder what he wants, just back from his trip, "replied Angel before heading back to the ladies room to freshen up for the next round.

"I'll let you know what develops on our way home. Can't wait to just kick back with a glass of wine, a movie and Jon-Erik. These interviews are stressful especially when you consider who we are talking with," she added.

These interviews were the least of their problems.

Chapter 48

*O*ften *imitated but never duplicated* was the Imitator's favorite phrase and why not as it fit him to a tee. He had plied his trade all over the world, in London, Paris, Berlin, Moscow, Tokyo, Shanghai, New York, Los Angeles and many other large and not so large urban centers worldwide.

His game was imitation and no one did it better. He did his research meticulously, had access to the most sophisticated surveillance and computer equipment known out there, technologies not yet available to the public.

He was an expert in the art of disguise including better than life facial masks, linguistics and diversion. His expertise in hand to hand combat and weaponry of all kinds was only used when needed but if he played his cards right he hardly ever had to.

His scenario was *get in while his subject was out of town on business or pleasure, siphon some funds, live high off the hog for a spell and get out before his unknowing host was back in the picture.* As a result, a number of high-powered politicians, lawyers and executives were perplexed as to why their bank accounts were a little lighter and why their wives, mistresses and escorts had a large smile on their faces with a little more bounce in their steps. The Imitator was skilled in seduction and was an insatiable lover amongst his other skill sets and he loved bedding and satisfying women that were on someone else's dime.

He had just left LA after his most recent engagement imitating one of the most influential Sports Agents in the business whose high priced clients included members of the LA Clippers, LA Kings, Miami Heat, Dallas Cowboys and even our own Toronto Maple Leafs.

It was a piece of cake for the Imitator to hack into this individual's computer system, learn his itinerary, access his accounts and virtually become that person. He never stayed long, usually no longer than 24 hours citing some last minute business he had to clear up hence the reason for his unannounced return.

He was so slick that when the agent actually did return home to his family from 10 days of hob-knobbing with power brokers, being wined and dined and getting his pipes cleaned by a number of sexy and nubile Spokes models who would do anything to get their first live gig behind a camera; no questions were asked until the missus began to wonder why her superstar was not the super stud he was in bed a few days ago.

The Imitator never miss-appropriated enough money where it would immediately become apparent but he did manage to squirrel away enough from all his ventures to live comfortably. He only ever copied individuals that matched his body type and studied his prey extensively before making his move, once he had their looks, mannerisms and speech down to a science.

His latest conquest was his greatest challenge to date but good things came to those who waited, studied and waited and studied some more. The Imitator had first heard about Richard Rasmussin about a year and a half ago as he was becoming a real mover and shaker with that FinCo outfit he ran in Toronto.

And Toronto, Canada of all places was one place that he had actually never had the opportunity to ply his trade as he could never quite find the right subject. But Richard Rasmussin was exactly the right height, weight, and even had the long dark hair the Imitator felt most comfortable wearing.

Rasmussin's Russian accent was easy to duplicate, that was a given but once he was able to hack into Richard's private computer system which had the best protection he had ever seen, even the Imitator had to take a step back and take a deep breath when he began to get a handle on what he was actually discovering.

This guy ran a criminal empire that spanned the globe and was worth billions. Dangerous was just the tip of the iceberg on describing Richard. Offshore and onshore accounts abounded everywhere and it

took the Imitator a while to find a few less conspicuous accounts that he would concentrate on. He knew
that his subject had just come back from a trip to
the Stoltenhoff Islands after his huge takeover of the
Kirotchenko Empire.

The Imitator also knew that Richard had a trip
planned to Moscow early next week to smooth things
out with a few of the old guard and that is when he
planned to strike.

This was to be his last strike and without a doubt
the best. He decided to head directly to the Grand
Cayman Islands after this last score and then live happily ever after with a little fishing charter business he
had already up and running. One of the locals was
managing it for him while he was away on business
and he was anxious to take over the operation once
his recent affairs in Toronto were wrapped up.

The thing that concerned the Imitator most of
all was the amount of private and damaging information he came across through his various imper-
sonations. He was not interested in hanging on to
anything in case black mail was an option later or
hedging a bet against his safety. The amount of dirty
dealings, corruption, money laundering, drugs, people and weapons trafficking, etc. which was out there
was truly astounding. If he measured things by what
he only saw, it would be hard to imagine how wide-
spread the problem really was.

This was to be the one last score and then out
of it forever, as even his uncanny luck and skill could
turn for the worst at any time. But with this last operation, he planned to retain some vital information

such as a cross section of bank accounts, locations and contacts just in case as he planned to live a long and healthy life and had no illusions as to how deadly this individual, his reach and organization could be.

The Imitator hated deviating from his modus operandi but in this case, it would be necessary, as his survival and prosperity was the number one concern.

The other growing concern he had from his surveillance done so far was the gorgeous hazel eyed woman that looked to be some sort of contractor working at FinCo along with an equally beautiful blonde partner. Brunettes were his thing and there was something special about this one as he could already picture her on his fishing boat with him in the Cayman's. Maybe, just maybe he could kill two birds with one stone as his planning was kicking into overdrive.

But he did not want to get ahead of himself; there was much to do before next week.

Chapter 49

Things were moving slowly for Rollie Sampson and he was not getting much assistance from his contact on the police force, Alf Cragan. The ex and current cop got together to discuss the situation and did not see much light at the end of the tunnel. They could not just go in and arrest Elmo Entwhistle for pulling a gun on Rollie as Rollie was there under false pretenses and it would be his word against Elmo's and the thug was still an executive in good standing *at least in his estimation* at FinCo.

In reality the picture here was much direr if the information Christine Hertzog provided was true; the real problem was Richard Rasmussin. Rollie was concerned at best wondering what Christine's motives really were and whether or not she was actually selling out their group to save her own skin. He just did not know at this point but did alert the whole group to that possibility.

As far as informing Alf Cragan of the meeting he and Angel had with Christine, Rollie decided to hold off figuring Alf would probably think they were raving lunatics. It was one thing to run a thriving business and be suspected of foul play on someone's unsubstantiated say so but quite another to the leader of possibly the largest criminal organization in the world.

The more Rollie thought about it, the more confused he became. He knew if you cut a head off a Hydra, there were at least another eight heads to take its place as undoubtedly with an organization of this size, there were many others groomed or being groomed to take over the reigns, if required.

When he broke it down to its simplest form, Richard Rasmussin was a direct threat to his friends and himself and that had to be dealt with otherwise there would be no accounting for what might happen next. Kidnapping, attempted murder and extortion had already happened and who knew what depths they would sink to next. Rollie thought he really had no choice in the matter; he would have to confront Richard personally.

He thought back on all of his past encounters with Mikhail, the Ninja and thanked his lucky stars that he survived them but things were a little bit different this time around; the Monster seemed to be on their side. But knowing what he knew about the unpredictable Shape Shifter, he was skeptical at best. A plan was slowly forming in his mind, one that would be extremely dangerous and difficult to execute but Rollie had never shied away from the tough stuff. He was good at it and actually liked the feeling of danger and unpredictability gave him and that was almost never good news for anyone that opposed him.

Be careful Richard, I am coming for you.

For Jon-Erik and Joey, things had settled back down to the routine of running the furniture store day to day and being with their loved ones in the evening. This particular day, Jon-Erik was in the back helping unload a new shipment and Joey was on the phone at the main counter talking to an irate customer when all hell broke loose.

Since it was early in the morning, no customers were in the store as yet as they had just opened the doors when a contingent of masked thugs burst through the front door brandishing automatic weapons.

Joey was so shocked he did not even think of calling 911, he took off like a shot to the back to warn Jon-Erik and the other staff.

As they all piled out of the back entrance, they were quickly surrounded by other lowlifes who were undoubtedly dispatched to the back in case of such of an evacuation attempt. The two scared out of their wits best friends, plus their white faced staff member were unceremoniously ushered at gun point back into the loading dock portion of the business.

The larger and most menacing of these henchmen backhanded Jon-Erik with the butt end of his weapon which he managed to block, but the force of the blow sent him sprawling. Joey sprang to his buddy's aid and received nothing but a kick which took his left leg right out from under him and sent him tumbling beside his best friend.

Both Jon-Erik and Joey knew why these people were here so they kept silent and just glared at their unwanted intruders.

"So you punks did not take our offer when it was extended before. You are both stupid and now you will be dead. But first, you will sign over your business to us. If you choose not to, you will die a very painful death and we will take your business anyway. If you sign now, we will make it quick and painless. What do you choose?" said the largest of the group brandishing his weapon menacingly.

Before either Jon-Erik or Joey could answer, two of the thugs that were guarding the back entrance dropped to the ground, their throats slit from ear to ear. Before the other three hired killers could even react by turning to look behind them, one dropped like a stone with his larynx crushed and his partner was trying unsuccessfully to dislodge a knife from his brain before his bodily functions shut him down permanently.

In a flash, Jon-Erik, Joey and their shipper/receiver scrambled behind their new shipment of furniture none too soon as the last and largest thug started filling the air with a hail of bullets that lodged themselves everywhere other than an actual human target.

With an angry and frustrated howl, the killer dropped his weapon pulling a large machete like object and began to swipe it in a lightening quick arc covering the front and back of his body. But to no avail as a cobra like strike to the wrist knocked the weapon to the ground, as a menacing and foreboding shape picked it up and examined it.

"Not the way they make them in the old country," sneered Mikhail before he nonchalantly buried the blade into the right thigh of the hood making him scream out in pain and drop to one knee.

"Who or what are you?" screamed the now lone and very much in pain extortionist.

"I am Mikhail and what I am you will never understand. You will be left alive to hobble out of here and inform your master that this will be the last time he will send anyone to this furniture store or bother my friends. Do you understand?

The hapless henchman nodded but threw a surprisingly quick knife hand strike at the throat of the Ninja. Mikhail just laughed, blocked the attempt and threw the assailant across the room finally crumpling into a heap after meeting a brick wall. The brick wall winning that altercation handily.

"You will call and get a cleanup crew in here and get rid of the mess you and your stinking friends made here. Someone, give him a phone!" the Monster directed.

After the humiliated and now badly limping thug made the call, Mikhail continued, "You instruct the one you report to who calls himself Rasmussin that this is now between me and him. These people and their ladies will be left alone. I have already killed a number of you and I will keep killing everyone that he sends my way. I will come for him and come for him soon and kill him. This is war and this is personal and there is no place on earth he can hide from me. You tell him that!" and for emphasis kicked the surviving messenger in the face and broke his nose.

"We will stay here to ensure the cleanup crew does what has been instructed. You two, close up shop and keep the shop closed until this is over and keep an eye on your ladies. I do not trust these people and they may try again as they are stubborn as we all are but my message is clear as long as this gnat delivers it. All this talking has made me thirsty, someone get me some Vodka!"

Joey did not hesitate and ran to the fridge where they kept a bottle of Smirnoff Vodka for stressful days and this was definitely one of these days—and then some. He left the bottle on a small collapsible table that was set up in the back as he had no desire to come any nearer to the Shape Shifter than he absolutely had to.

Mikhail picked up the bottle, unscrewed the cap and took a sniff, shook his head and growled, "They call this Vodka? But I am thirsty and it is better than water."

He then took a long pull almost draining half the bottle and wiped his mouth and licked his lips. Once the cleanup crew arrived, they very efficiently loaded the bodies into a large black van parked by the back entrance.

They then expertly cleaned up every drop of blood, debris and shell casings caused by the altercation without once looking at the Monster or the others in the room. Lastly, they loaded up their incapacitated comrade and disappeared as quietly as they had come.

"Very professional," remarked Mikhail who seemed to disappear as well right in front of Joey, Jon-Erik and the totally astounded shipping clerk.

"What the hell just happened here," asked Luigi the clerk.

"It's kind of like what happens when the irresistible force meets the immovable object," Jon-Erik tried to explain.

"Looks like we are closed for a while, again. I hope he wraps this up soon. Does this not remind you of what happened five years ago?" asked Joey.

"Yes, but this time Mikhail is on our side and that is a huge bonus. Luigi, here is some cash to tide you over till we open back up. You would be wise not to speak of anything you saw here today. Go visit your momma in Windsor for a while. It's always warmer down there than here."

Luigi took the envelope of cash and hightailed out of there like a flash. He was thinking he would look for a nice safe office job after this experience.

Jon-Erik and Joey made a few phone calls and then closed up the shop tight and hit the road for home hoping Angel and Tina were safe. They should be safe since they were right in the Lion's Den.

Neither one could wait to see their fiancées again and tell them of their crazy day. But first, a few drinks at Jon-Erik's were definitely in order and well earned. After that they were going to prepare something yummy for the four of them so a stopover at the grocery store and the liquor store was on the agenda first. What else could happen? Better not to ask.

Chapter 50

At around the same time all hell was breaking loose at the furniture store, a hell of a different kind was about to manifest itself at FinCo. Angel's last stop before heading home with Tina was a visit with the man himself.

That she had misgivings was an understatement; the guy just plain creeped her out. He was handsome enough but reminded her of a serpent in constant strike mode. He had been decent enough with her so far but her radar was way up every time she was even close to Richard.

She knocked on the door and was asked to come in—all she heard was a hissing sound. Angel like most people had an aversion to snakes and she was about to speak with one in the flesh.

Richard Rasmussin sat at his desk; dapper was not the word that would describe him best. Perhaps the words dashing, dangerous and mysterious were more in line with the way he appeared today.

Richard had just gotten the word from the surviving henchman as to what had occurred at the furniture store and he had to shake his head. *Why bother sending a group of idiots out to do a job when he would have done it right the first time?* he pondered.

But he had an image to upkeep and protect and it would not do if he got involved in everything. The lone messenger had already been taken care of and was most likely on his way to Chinatown in the form of those meat filled dumplings that were such a delicacy there. Little did those hungry late night snackers really know. And the Gonilac that arranged everything for Richard, his remains augmented those of the now deceased messenger.

Richard was nearing the end of his patience. If he somehow could, he would snatch Angel right from his office and take her to one of the numerous hideouts he had in Canada or anywhere in the world and have his way with her before he became bored and turned her out. That would happen soon enough. But what happened at the furniture store bothered him much more and quite frankly puzzled him.

He knew that there was someone with tremendous skills from what had happened during the previous escapade at the store. According to what was relayed back by the messenger while he still had a voice, this unique character was right off the charts and could quite possibly be a real Ninjitsu practitioner.

There were few people like that. Found in the remote mountainous regions of Tibet, Himalayas and other places that time had forgotten, skilled in this mysterious art, they were in pursuit of a higher spiritual enlightenment and not interested in criminal affairs.

There were also whispers in Moscow when his family had begun to build their power base that there was an extraordinary assassin out there with skills so finely honed that they made him almost super human. And it looked as if this Ninja had somehow aligned himself with this group of Furniture store owners and also Angel and Tina, his crackerjack Efficiency Experts.

Perhaps it was time for some strategic thinking rather than brute action as Richard considered himself one of the greatest strategists of his time. His only drawback was his impatience which usually resulted in brutally quick and concise action. He would come up with something but now the beauty and poise of Angel, as she sat down, took his breath away.

"So Angel, we meet again. I heard good things about you and Tina while I was away," began Richard.

"We have been doing our jobs if that is what you mean," replied Angel trying to remain professional and keep her composure which she certainly would not have done had she known what transpired a little while ago at the Furniture store.

"I thought we may have a working dinner one of these evenings where we can go over things in more detail and relax," purred Richard in a seductive tone.

"Our arrangement was a working arrangement between the hours of 9 to 5. I would prefer it remain that way," replied Angel politely but sternly.

"I can appreciate that although I must insist. My time during the day is limited at best which I am sure you can understand."

"My time is limited in the evening which I am sure you can appreciate," answered Angel shifting her position uncomfortably in her chair.

"Ah yes, you have a boyfriend who would not approve, no?"

"A fiancée and yes he would not approve."

"I can assure you it would be a night that you could not even imagine," Richard coaxed but his annoyed look was not lost on Angel.

"Undoubtedly but my imagination is fully focused on my fiancée," said Angel wondering what she had to do to get through to this full of himself power hungry Romeo.

"I do not take no for an answer," Richard growled with any pretense of civility now gone.

"There is always a first time," said Angel now righteously pissed as well.

"And just so we truly understand each other I am prepared to terminate our arrangement right here and now. Tina and I have done more than ample work to justify what you have paid us already!" retorted Angel with a look that would intimidate anyone except Richard who just chuckled.

"Fine, have it your own way but understand this. No one says no to me without consequences."

"Is that a threat?" Angel replied as she got up to leave.

"Take at as you wish. I am used to getting what I want and what I want is you. It will happen sooner or later and there will not be anything you can do about it," snarled Richard.

As soon as the conversation started taking this tone Angel reached into her purse to grab a tissue to dab one of her eyes at the same time activating the tiny pocket recorder she had in there and none too soon as she was getting some juicy conversation indeed.

"There is always something I can do about any-thing," indicated Angel her beautiful eyes now taking on a translucently frightening look of their own.

"Ah, you think your martial arts skills can protect you? You have no idea what I am capable of. And as far as your Ninja protector goes, he is as good as dead already. There will be no place he can hide from me or my people. It is just a matter of time."

Angel played it cool and dumb. "I am very com-fortable with my skills and would not recommend you test them. As far as this Ninja goes, I have no idea what or whom you are talking about."

She wanted to get out of there in the worst way but stayed seated, her curiosity getting the better of her and hoping to get a little more fuel for the fire on tape.

But Richard did an abrupt about face and with a dismissive gesture said, "I grow tired of this verbal sparring. You and Tina are finished here. I will not tolerate insubordination such as this. Pack up your personal belongings, do not come back and do not expect me to give you a good reference. Now leave!" snarled Richard rising to his full height and looking more like the devil himself which he was.

Angel did everything in her power not to kick this full of himself tyrant right in the head over his desk and just grabbed her purse and left the room.

She gathered up Tina, grabbed their personal things and left the premises immediately with Christine Hertzog looking concerned from her office. It never felt so good to be fired and both ladies were ecstatic they never had to come back to his office again.

But on their way home, Tina's cell rang. When she answered and heard what had transpired with Jon-Erik and Joey, Angel put the pedal to the medal to get back home and see their lovers. They were so happy that Jon-Erik and Joey were not hurt, but now even more on edge and upset. It looked like what Richard Rasmussin had said was coming true. *They really will stop at nothing.*

Chapter *51*

Just to switch it up a tad, the nightly meeting was scheduled at Joey and Tina's this evening. Jon-Erik and Joey were still shook up and the usually tanned looking Joey looked pale and disoriented. Everyone was too upset to eat but Tina and Angel got together a hasty plate of snacks with some strong coffee.

Jon-Erik had contacted Rollie Sampson as soon as they had arrived home to give him a quick overview as to what had occurred today. Rollie was flabbergasted to say the least. He knew things were escalating but even he could not believe what he heard and what had happened at the Furniture store this time around.

When Angel and Jon-Erik had finally re-united back at their house, they did nothing but hold each other for at least 5 minutes before they jumped into the shower together and tried to let the hot water wash away their pain. They were both too upset for sex but the shower made them feel better and they snuck in a quickie before they toweled off, got dressed and headed over to Joey and Tina's.

When they arrived, Rollie was already seated munching on a sausage roll and sipping on a steamy hot cup of coffee. After hugs all around, Joey and Jon-Erik began to relay their incredible tale. Rollie, Angel and Tina quietly listened uttering the occasional *Oh no* and *Oh my God*.

Then Angel added her part of this ever evolving nightmare capping it off by playing back to everyone what she was able to record in Richard's office.

"That son of a bitch," screamed Jon-Erik. "If he thinks he's going to do anything with Angel, he's got another thing coming!"

"Enough is enough after what these sick pigs did to Tina and all the trouble at our business and our home. I am calling Guido and getting the family involved which I should have done much earlier in this process," Joey shouted.

Rollie stood up and said quietly but firmly, "I totally understand how you all feel. But we need to think logically here. First of all this guy Rasmussin, even though we all know he is up in all this to his eyeballs has really done little to incriminate himself."

"The fact that he knows about Mikhail does not help things?" asked Angel looking puzzled.

"It helps us to solidify who is behind this entire fiasco, yes, but remember only we are the ones that really know about the Ninja," Rollie replied.

"And Joey, if Rasmussin has the clout and power we think he does, how do we know that he does not have your families organization in his back pocket?"

"Famiglia e per sempre," said Joey with conviction. "It means Family is Forever and our family lives by that motto. They would never sell out or die in the process."

"Fair enough but none of us have a scope on how far this madman's tendrils actually reach and do you really think their relatively small group could stand up against an organization that has worldwide reach?" Rollie asked.

"So what can we do?" asked Tina summing up how everyone else felt.

"That's a good question and I am lost for answers. Richard's reach without a doubt includes the police department and he most likely has money flowing up to the highest places in return for turning a blind eye to the indiscretions," said Rollie.

"And now we know, he is after Angel and I am not going to let anything happen to her," said Jon-Erik pulling Angel closer to him on the couch.

Before they could continue their discussion they were interrupted by a knock on the door. Mindy, the large and loyal Kangal dog, which was given to them years ago to protect them, was at the door barking in a flash. She quickly calmed down as Rollie went to the door with his revolver drawn, peeking through the top decorative glass portion of the door.

"It's Christine Hertzog. Did anyone invite her to our little meeting?" asked Rollie.

"No, but doesn't surprise me to see her. We never even got to say goodbye today after we were fired from FinCo. Glad we cashed the cheque at any rate," said Angel.

"Should we let her in?" asked Tina.

"Can't leave her standing out in the cold now can we and the fact she is here gives her a bit more credibility," said Rollie looking like he was deep in thought.

"Okay, but trust has to be earned. Let's see what she has to say at any rate," said Joey going to the door and opening it.

"I'm sorry to come unannounced but that is the only way I can come at all in light of everything that has happened. I see you are all together already discussing the day's events no doubt. Hopefully you all feel comfortable enough around me to join you," indicated Christine.

"The jury is still out on that but have a seat. A cup of strong coffee for you as well?" asked Joey.

Christine gave her coat to Joey while Tina went to the kitchen to pour another cup. Christine took the chair opposite Rollie facing everyone else on the couch.

After everyone was again seated, Christine took a long sip of the hot coffee and the conversation continued.

"So he fired you both. Does not surprise me as Richard is impatient and acts on instinct and impulse," began Christine.

"He is not the only one," a gravely and all too familiar voice uttered that came from behind the chair that Christine was sitting in along with a huge arm that snaked around her neck totally disabling her and cutting off her air supply.

"What the hell?" was all she could mutter before she lapsed into unconsciousness.

Even though everyone around the table was getting somewhat used to the Monster's unusual entrances, they were still shocked but remained calm and quiet.

"Good, you are all learning not to make any sudden moves against me as it could and would cost you your lives. I am only here to protect Angel and I tolerate the rest of you as she has chosen you as friends."

"But this one here, she is like me. Dedicated to the one she serves. But the one she serves is dedicated to your destruction so I am dedicated to his. I will kill her but first I will interrogate her," and with that Mikhail slapped their sleeping houseguest a few times and brought her back to the world of the living.

"Who are you," Christine sputtered as she struggled to sit upward and bring her breathing back to normal.

"I am what few understand. But I am here to protect Angel and your mentor is threatening her. What is his weakness?" growled the Shape shifter.

"Look, I am on all of your sides. He will kill me if he finds out I am here and knows I am talking to you," said Christine now looking truly frightened.

"Down to the basement now, all of you, if you wish to save your lives. Angel and Mr. Detective, I can probably use your help in this case although I am fine on my own."

"The rest of you go now," screamed Mikhail amongst the deep throated barking of the Kangal who had been sleeping in one of the bedrooms upstairs and was throwing her over 140 lbs. at the door trying to break it down and join her family who were now in terrible danger.

Tina and Joey bolted down into the basement closing the door behind them knowing not to obey could cost them their lives.

Then everything happened in a blur. Rollie pulled his weapon and dove behind the couch with Angel following suit. But not before seeing Mikhail snap Christine Hertzog's neck with a lightning fast twisting motion resulting in a sickening snap.

Next thing, silenced machine gun fire erupted from the back deck entrance and the side of the house entrance. All you could hear was whisking of bullets through the air, as Rollie in a crouch looking for a target. Mikhail had vanished and reappeared behind the first two fools spraying the house from the side entrance.

He grabbed each of their necks and smashed both of their heads together with such force that they broke like crushed pumpkins after Halloween.

The two other killers were now inside the house making their way silently towards the living room and before the first one knew what hit him, Rollie put three rounds expertly into his forehead killing him instantly.

The second assassin hit the floor as he heard the shots trying to roll and come up in shooting stance but a kick in the face from Angel broke his jaw and a few teeth stopping him in his tracks. But only for an instant, as the bleeding moron was up again spraying bullets at where he thought his opponents were.

Angel had shifted and was able to avoid the first volley. Now mad as hell, kicked him in the neck below the jaw, jamming his Adams apple into his wind pipe killing him with Rollie making sure by sending two more bullets. One hit him in the brain and the other taking out his left eye. He knew there was no sense shooting for the heart as these dirt bags were most likely wearing body armor. Good call.

Rollie had just enough time to push Angel behind the couch again as the next hail of bullets came flying from the front door now breached by another two gorillas in full combat fatigue.

But the Monster was not resting on his laurels as he somehow appeared below both remaining assailants, raised himself to his full height and administered two punches with his incredible hammer like fists that almost drove both of them into the floor like wooden pegs. One died immediately, and the other one almost had his head ripped off his shoulders while being thrown across the room and smashed into the closet where he remained crumpled up in a heap.

"The threat is over for now. The dead woman was not at fault but they followed her here and would have killed her anyway sooner or later. There is no mercy with these people as there is none with me. I will hunt this mad man down and kill him as he is out to harm Angel and that is his undoing,"

"Good work Angel, your skills are becoming more honed, maybe I will have you kill your tormenter yourself," snarled Mikhail before slinking into the shadows and disappearing as mysteriously as he appeared.

Tina and Joey came out the basement and everyone just sat down looking at the devastation all around them, Mindy now released, ran around the house whining in a frenzy sniffing at the dead bodies but noticeably happy nothing happened to her family.

"My God. Our home! And what do we do about the dead bodies all over the place?" sobbed Tina.

"This has gone way out of hand. The police can't help us here, the questions along with the paperwork would be endless and they would most likely try to put you all into protective custody with no idea how to really protect you," indicated Rollie.

"I will make a few calls and get these carcasses taken care of as well and get your home repaired. I still have a few friends that are loyal and discreet although who knows for how long with the payoffs and intimidation that is going on" he added.

"For the time being, you guys and Mindy are our guests," offered Angel.

"Absolutely," agreed Jon-Erik.

"They will come after us again. They will not stop until the head of the Cobra is removed at which time they will have to regroup and forget about us hopefully. We are no longer safe here however and we cannot keep banking on the Ninja bailing us out even though he has saved us repeatedly,"

"So we are on the run again. Where can we go where they cannot hunt us down again?" asked Joey looking confused and helpless.

"Leave that with me. I know a place and we pack up and leave immediately. Grab warm clothes, as much food as we can carry. We need to disappear before Richard gets wind of the fact his henchmen have failed again." Rollie instructed.

Everyone got busy, remembering what they went through just five short years ago. It was déjà vu all over again.

"Where are we going?" asked Angel.

"A trusted friend owns a place up near Parry Sound that he does not use in the winter and has given me the key to use anytime I wish. It is a large 5 bedroom home actually quite close to Lake Rosseau, if you remember. He has a ton of firewood to heat the place and he is totally isolated up there so no prying neighbors. Once you finish packing, meet me at an all-night Tim Horton's at highway 400 and 7 and we'll head up from there once we ascertain we are not being followed. Also make sure you bring as much cash as you can as these people have the resources to track ATM withdrawals. You might as well withdraw the money right here where you would be expected to," said Rollie before heading out.

"We'll borrow a van from my cousin Guido in case they have our vehicle make and plate. Here we go again….road trip," said Joey

Tina was busy packing and Angel and Jon-Erik went back to their place to pack while Joey took off to get the van from Guido. Guido always helped and asked few questions as he had helped the group in the past when they were on the run.

In no time flat, Joey was back with a dark colored Dodge Caravan that had plenty of room for everyone including the dog. They locked up their vehicles in their garages, Joey and Tina leaving their place unlocked for the expected clean up crew that Rollie had arranged for, hit a few bank machines in the area and stocked up on cash and headed up the 427 to highway 7. They bypassed the toll route 407 in case the bad guys had in roads there too and could track their progress.

At 1 am sharp, the travelers arrived at the Timmy's, loaded up on coffee and muffins and followed Rollie up the 400 towards Barrie once he swept the area and determined no one was tailing them. The group sipped on their coffees, said very little but glad they were all together and safe for the moment—hopefully.

Chapter 52

In a rage, was a mild way to describe the state Richard Rasmussin, was in. He had heard nothing from the crew he sent over to take care of his little but growing bigger problem.

He was hoping Christine would get caught in the cross-fire and if she didn't, the order was to terminate her anyway; she had outlived her usefulness long ago. But to hear nothing really infuriated him, especially in light of the fact that he had an early flight to Moscow in the morning to take care of some urgent business. There was some unrest and confusion amongst the ranks in one of the prostitution businesses his organization was involved in.

The Nachalnik (Boss) of this particular faction of his business was spending too much time testing out his ladies himself. So when it came time for them to go out and earn their keep, they were too tired or sore from his brutal trysts to satisfy their customers as enthusiastically as they should.

He tried to have this taken care of by outsourcing the problem but the Boss kept killing everybody that was sent his way to reason with him so Richard had to deal with this one himself. He admired this individual's sexual and fighting prowess but this was costing his business money and that he would not tolerate.

Reasoning with this Knoyh (Clown) would most likely not work. He would make an example of him and have his remains left out on some frozen tundra for the scavengers such as the wild boars that roamed the rural regions outside the city. Insubordination of any kind was just not tolerated in Richard's organization.

Before being chauffeured in one of his fully equipped private stretch-limo's, he called Elmo Entwhistle who was just in the process of getting to know a young and sexy oriental boy who he picked up on a late night cruise through Chinatown.

He was just about to lube himself and the object of his erection up royally when the call came in and he knew better not to answer it.

"What's up boss?" asked Elmo.

"Drop whatever or whomever you are doing and find out what the hell happened with the night assignment that I sent that crew of so-called professionals on. And get a hold of that weasely Jimmy Rudiger in whatever gambling establishment of ours he is held up in. I'm leaving for Moscow and want some answers as I have heard nothing. You follow?"

"You got it boss," said Elmo hanging up the phone and cutting a few more lines of coke for his already out of it companion.

"This will keep you till I return and you better be here if you know what's good for you," sneered Elmo. The china boy did not even pay attention. He was too busy inhaling the lines of white powder that took away his pain.

Elmo hurriedly threw on a tracksuit and his favorite full length sable coat as it was bitterly cold outside. His driver was waiting for him in front of the Four Season's Sheraton in Yorkville where the business paid for a luxury suite for him.

"Jimmy, I'm going to pick you up, you skinny slime ball. We got some business to attend to," said Elmo into his state of the art encrypted cell phone.

"This better be good, I am up 50K and on a roll," snarled Jimmy Rudiger.

"It is and quit bilking our own organization out of money," growled Elmo.

"At least it stays in the family. Take your time, I hate to be interrupted when I'm ahead," snickered Rudiger.

Talking about being ahead, after having verified that Richard Rasmussin had indeed left the country, the Imitator, leisurely strolled into the Trump Tower Hotel.

He sauntered over to reception with a confident if not downright haughty swagger in his step. The gorgeous receptionist, who looked a lot like Ivanka Trump, looked up from her computer. It was not often she saw one of their better looking and more reclusive guests, as he normally used the private elevator to his suite.

"How are you this evening Mr. Rasmussin? What can I do for you?" asked the receptionist not disguising how attracted she was to this tall, dark and handsome shaker and mover.

The Imitator liked what he saw as well. After all, his game was to imitate and that was his direct intention.

"Listen Chloe, I lent my keycard out to a friend and she was supposed to return it but hasn't and my spare is in my suite. Do you think you can help me out?" flirted the Imitator.

"Absolutely sir, here is another one and by the way, I get off in an hour," whispered the stunning girl.

"Oh, you'll get off a lot more than that I assure you. I'll have some Bollinger and Caviar chilled and ready," teased the Imitator and emphasized the whole thing by bending over the counter and sniffing her neck which almost caused Chloe to pop her cork before the champagne was even served.

The Imitator disappeared around the corner and entered the private elevator swiping the keycard and pushing the button for the 54th floor. The elevator sped smoothly to its destination, quietly and efficiently not unlike the Imitator himself. He headed for Richard Rasmussin's private suite which was on the south east side of the tower overlooking the lake and the east side of the city.

He swiped the card which opened the door to paradise. The suite was quite large, at about 3,000 square feet or more and even exceeded his high expectations. From mirrored ceilings to a bar that took up one whole side of the living room to a huge television recessed into the wall along with plush white leather furniture, was only the first impression.

Two lavish bathrooms fit for a Saudi prince with golden faucets, spectacular mirrors and lighting; one containing a enclosed shower that could hold a small party and the second a huge sunken in whirlpool tub beside which stood a bar fridge along with a mini bar.

The huge bedroom featured a spectacular wall mural of a huge white Tiger mauling a luckless victim within a lush jungle backdrop which even took the Imitator's breath away for the moment. A custom bed larger than life stood in the middle of the room with a waterfall wall on one side and a beautiful ceiling to floor fireplace.

Why would someone ever want to leave here? thought the Imitator going back to the living room while pouring himself a glass of bubbly. He got the hot tub ready and made himself comfortable for his guest who should be arriving soon. He had planned to call out for a couple of high end hookers and still would depending on how much fun he would have with Chloe, the receptionist.

He had just settled down on the lavish couch and slipped into the homeowner's comfy bathrobe when there was a knock on the door.

Looking at his watch, he realized that it was still about fifteen minutes earlier than the receptionist was expected so he looked through the peephole.

It was hotel staff with a tray of caviar and other delicacies that he ordered. Salivating at the thought of the delicious treats and deciding he was hungry enough to sample a few, he opened the door.

Bad mistake as he ended up wearing the cart and its contents. The Imitator was as quick and wily as a fox however and rolled with the impact and pushed the cart and its contents out of his way as he rose up in fighting stance still having no idea what he was dealing with. He was about to find out, however.

The Monster closed the door behind him and stood and glared at the gnat in front of him. "So you are the great Richard Rasmussin. For the pain and inconvenience you have caused Angel and her friends, these will be your last minutes on earth. Are you prepared to die, insect?" hissed Mikhail standing in the doorway with arms crossed looking more like a menacing Buddha than a hotel employee.

"Who the hell is Angel?" asked the Imitator realizing he had made a grave error here as he had no idea who this character or Angel was or who was now threatening him.

"Do not play dumb with me. You know of whom I speak. I am sworn to protect her and now you will die for your feeble attempts on her and her friends' lives."

"Listen, I do not know you or this Angel person and I am just about to have some company up here and if you do not leave now, I will help you along. I am a lover, but also a fighter so do not antagonize me further and leave while you still can," snarled the Imitator.

Worse mistake as he found himself thrown across the room landing in a heap between the spacious living room and kitchen. This time he did not get up so quickly especially with the Shape Shifter now standing over him with one of his big boots crushing his chest almost cracking his rib cage.

"There is something wrong here. You are worse than a worthless cockroach. I expected a lot more fight out of you," snarled Mikhail.

"That is because I am not who you think I am. I'm just a guy who makes his living imitating people. Who or what are you?" asked the Imitator while coughing up some blood.

"So, we were both surprised today my stupid friend," chuckled Mikhail as he settled down on the plush living room couch.

"Clean up the pushcart and gather up some of that caviar and it better be the best. And find me some good vodka, I have developed a thirst."

Who does this guy think he is ordering me around like this thought the Imitator but he quickly complied as he saw and felt what this nightmare could do and he did not want to antagonize him any further as after all the Imitator survived by his skill and wits and knew he better comply or pay the consequences.

"You are not as dumb as you look," indicated the Monster as he munched on the caviar and took a long swig of the Vodka bottle the Imitator had produced from the closest bar.

"Good caviar but not like from home and the Vodka tastes like mule piss," remarked Mikhail as he wiped his mouth.

"Sit down and join me while I decide what I am or what I am not going to do with you. You are no threat to me but make one move against me, I will rip your throat out. Get the idea?" indicated the Monster.

"Sure thing. So you are hear to kill Richard and I am here to imitate him and have some fun for a few short hours and get out of town. He obviously has some powerful enemies," said the Imitator.

"And I am the most powerful by far and it angers me that I have missed him today. Pass over the key-card you entered with. I have many ways to enter but why not use the easy way? Also the laptop and shoulder bag you have with you - Now!"

The Imitator complied as he knew he had no chance against this creature from hell itself.

"You have been co-operative but some think I have gotten soft," Mikhail hissed and before the Imitator could even fathom to respond, he keeled over due to the lightning quick punch to his solar plexus, crushing his ribcage and killing him quickly.

Always having a flair for the dramatic, the Monster carted off the dead Imitator to the deep hot tub and ran the water up to his chest. He left a simple note jammed in his mouth that stated, *I have done you a favor by getting rid of this trash and will do you another when we meet by getting rid of you—and you will never see it coming.*

Prepare yourself you insect. Simple and right to the point. As soon as Mikhail erased any hint of being there and he was preparing to exit this den of iniquity, there was a knock on the door.

He looked through the peephole and saw it was a gorgeous looking girl. It was tempting for him to play a little and have some fun but he did not want to lose his edge.

"Go away; I am tired from my trip. I will contact you when I have rested," snarled the Executioner.

"The girl looking obviously disappointed slunk away. Mikhail did the same as soon as the coast was clear armed with a keycard to his enemy's lair and a computer which could have some beneficial information on it, in the right hands. Not a bad day, he had not killed his nemesis, but he got a little closer and that worked for him as small steps or large steps were all the same to him in the grand scheme of things for one who was as stealthy as the Wolf but so much more lethal.

Chapter 53

The snow had started falling after they left the city and had intensified the further north they got. Then finally, after a long and uneventful drive except for a number of complex twists and turns, they turned onto Black Crane Lake Road. The crew in the van were happy they had Rollie's tail lights to follow otherwise they would have seen nothing but white.

They pulled into a long driveway. Rollie had a distant neighbor clear the driveway ahead of their arrival otherwise they would have never made it in there even with the excellent snow tires both vehicles had. There was at least 4 feet of snow on the ground and more of it coming down.

But the home and surrounding area was spectacular. Totally secluded with ample pine, maple and spruce trees framed the large country home, its outside walls and roof covered in snow. It was still dark outside but the snow on the ground and in the air gave the whole scene an almost ghostly translucent appearance.

Rollie unlocked the door and the group found themselves in a decent sized mud room that contained a large deep freezer as well as an area to hang coats and leave boots. He opened the door to a large, fully equipped country kitchen which looked upon a sunken in living room complete with woodstove, comfy couches and a television.

By this time everyone was exploring the place as it was deceptively large and seemed to have another surprise around every corner. Jon-Erik found an even more sunken in movie room with a huge TV and surround sound speakers along with comfortable couches to enjoy the experience.

Joey, Tina and Angel found what looked like a guest bedroom with an on suite bathroom which Joey claimed on behalf of Tina and himself. Then they discovered a set of stairs leading to four more bedrooms upstairs with another bathroom. Angel picked her and Jon-Erik's room out and Rollie took one of the remaining bedrooms far enough away so everyone had their privacy.

After that, Rollie busied himself starting up the woodstove with wood shavings, then kindling and finally a huge log. Everyone felt the place heating up very fast but Rollie also amped up the central heat thermometer a bit as the house was set just high enough so the pipes would not freeze while it sat empty.

After everyone had explored and set up their quarters, the ladies busied themselves in the kitchen throwing some chili and biscuits together found in the freezer. The guys cracked open Heinekens for them and white wine for the ladies. No one seemed to care that it was 3:30 am. The trip and all the stress of the last number of days with their more comfortable and obviously safe surroundings had them all in the mood for a party.

Even Rollie was resigned to stay at least a day until the weather calmed down a bit and the road crews had a chance to clear the highways back down to normal.

"Where the heck are we?" asked Joey between long gulps of beer and spoonsful of chili.

"We're about 20 minutes south of Parry Sound. I'll draw you guys a map of how to get there before I leave. In the winter, the town is almost dead but in the summer it is a bustling hub of the near north with a harbour gateway to believe it or not 30,000 something Islands at the northern end of Georgian Bay," said Rollie.

"What's the town have?" asked Jon-Erik.

"Oh you know, the usual grocery stores, hardware stores, Tim Horton's, McDonald's and even a few pubs and fairly good restaurants," Rollie replied.

"We'll definitely check the place out. Maybe they have some live music playing on weekends," Tina indicated.

"We're going to have to be extremely careful. If Richard's organization is as far reaching as it may be, then we could easily be spotted," Angel cautioned.

"Right you are. Crime is everywhere these days even more so in a small town such as Parry Sound.

Money is scarce up here except for a select few business owners and retirees so if anything crooked is going on, it would be very attractive to those looking to make a quick buck," said Rollie.

"I think it's best if we go out separately as couples, we would not attract as much attention as four," offered Angel.

"Or the guys hit the pub and the ladies cook dinner," chucked Joey getting a punch in the arm from Tina.

"The ladies check out the shopping and the guys roast a chicken is more like it," quipped Tina getting a kiss for her effort.

"Look, hopefully you guys won't be here that long but I would suspect at least a week. I'm going after this Richard character with or without Alf Cragan's help.

I have a few favors left to call in with some elite special team operatives in the city and who knows what the Ninja is up to? I bet he is hot on the track of Rasmussin himself," Rollie said.

"Mikhail has me really confused. On one hand I believe he is dedicated to looking out for us *or at least me* and on the other he may kill us all at any time. He's just too unpredictable to rely on but he has saved our lives a number of times already so who the hell really knows?" said Angel with a puzzled look on her gorgeous face.

"Listen, its 4:30 in the morning and I'm bushed. Care to join me my dear?" coaxed Jon-Erik.

"Thought you would never ask," Angel replied chasing her lover upstairs.

"I've about had it myself," said Rollie checking on the woodstove which was well stoked up to keep the place cozy for a while before heading to his room.

It did not take Tina and Joey long to follow suit jumping onto their bed and getting all tangled up with each other. Slipping under the covers, they were both out like lights.

Angel and Jon-Erik, however, were still too keyed up to sleep and caught up on some much needed loving first. Angel jumped on top and got busy and even though Rollie was a ways down the hall from them, they did their best to stay as quiet as possible which was really tough for Jon-Erik as he held on for dear life but loving every minute of it.

After about an hour of muffled gymnastics and seeing the beginning of daylight peeking through their window, they finally decided to sleep and sleep was instantaneous for both.

They were safe and comfortable in each other's arms and that was all that mattered…for now.

Chapter 54

Elmo Entwhistle and Jimmy Rudiger were furious and also worried as they knew their boss would not take this news very well. Not very well at all, they could even pay with their lives knowing Richard's wrath.

No sign or word from Christine Hertzog so far and no sign of the meddlesome group that looked to be a larger and larger thorn in their sides. They personally checked the houses of both Jon-Erik and Joey and both were deserted.

The one home looked like some sort of showdown occurred there but a cleanup had already been performed with exception of some stains in the carpets, holes in the walls and a broken window which had been taped up. It told a partial story.

"These people must be magicians or they are connected to some sort of organization we know nothing about as yet because no way a group of ordinary people like this get so lucky otherwise," observed Jimmy.

"The girl Angel has some martial arts skills but the rest of them are just ordinary schleps which anyone can handle easily yet they have escaped all our traps so far and are obviously still very much alive and now on the run," said Elmo.

Jimmy got on the phone and issued some stern directions," Find them and kill them all except for the blonde. She is reserved for Richard and not a hair on her pretty little head should be harmed. Put out an alert countrywide and also inform all our contacts across the border. If they are not found, heads will roll including yours.

Got it?" he directed.

A call came back to them five minutes later as they were just about to pull out of their quarries neighborhood informing them that there had been no traceable cell activity but ATM maximum cash withdrawals had been made at machines close to home.

So they were on the run and would be found sooner than later as there were eyes and ears in every large and small town as well as gas stations, train stations and airports all across North America.

What worried both Jimmy and Elmo even more was they still had no idea who was helping them. The trace on the short little guy who came to Elmo's office and threatened him came up empty; the only Rolf Simpson that they got word of was an old dairy farmer who lived on a farm that had seen better days near the town of Kincardine. They would also put the word out to find out who or what had the resources and clout to be pulling this off as all the men that had been sent out on these harassment and elimination missions were never heard of or from again either.

And to top things off, Christine Hertzog had also disappeared off the face of the earth and Elmo and Jimmy suspected that she was on the run with this miserable group of idiots, so much easier to spot and apprehend them. Christine must have known her days were numbered.

All they could do now was wait for Richard to contact them and give him the news that it would only be a matter of time before these fugitives aside from Angel were found and disposed of. Elmo dropped Jimmy back off at the Casino and then went to see about his latest boyfriend who had better be ready to show him his best side if he knew what was good for him.

Once Richard Rasmussin arrived in Moscow, he had two of his henchmen pick him up from the airport and drive him to the village of Barvikha which was only half an hour down the road. He checked into the largest luxury suite at the Barvikha Hotel and Spa and made a phone call to have some prime Russian ladies sent to his room with haste as he was horny and in a foul mood for having to make the trip out here in the first place.

The individual he was there to pay a fatal visit to, had set up shop in one of the shopping districts fine jewelry stores. The jewelry stores were used as a front to ply his drug and prostitution trade which was flourishing because of the ample tourist trade in Barvikha.

He was not so much jetlagged as bored and some good Vodka, Borscht and Kotlety along with a couple of hot blooded prostitutkis would cheer his sour mood. After a roaring drunk, feasting and exploring every orifice that his night companions would provide, he would be ready to deal with the situation he was here for. To dispatch this warlord that had set up shop in town and send a message to all those under his command that any type of insubordination was not tolerated and would have fatal consequences.

But first a call back to Toronto was in order to see what type of progress had been made. Before he could pick up his untraceable cell that worked in every corner of the world, the phone rang.

Richard picked up and listened intently for a few minutes before almost screaming back a response," I want these people found and eliminated. If the blonde gets caught in the cross-fire so be it. I prefer her alive so I can play with her a bit first but now they have become larger nuisances to me."

"I will be back in a few days and expect this to be taken care of," he added with spittle flying out of his mouth before throwing his phone into a corner of the room in a real fit of anger.

When Richard was upset he exercised to calm himself down and he pushed himself through 200 pushups, 100 on each arm. Once he had calmed down, the food and drink he had ordered was at the door as well as two tall gorgeous ladies dressed head to toe in fur as after all it was extremely cold in Moscow at this time of year.

But not in Richard's suite where a roaring fire was dancing in the fireplace, the large hot tub was ready and the fur on his luscious guests was strewn all over the plush white carpet. The ladies got busy with each other, with Richard exploring any areas that were not yet attended by the sexy ladies and for a while he forgot all about his problems and dove into his drink, food and guests with gusto and enthusiasm.

Richard slept maybe half an hour after he kicked his two insatiable guests out the door after the Russian sun became a big yellow ball in the sky but did nothing to warm up the bitterly cold new day. After getting up, he performed some lightning quick and intricate looking movements enhanced with punches and kicks that would seem to come out of nowhere to the casual observer.

He drank down two glasses of ice cold water then jumped in the shower which again was freezing cold and stayed in there until his limbs were blue from the cold. He toweled off, dressed in a designer track suit, grabbed his fur and headed downstairs to where his chauffeur along with an even larger and more menacing looking side-kick were waiting for him.

"To the Jewelry Boutiques in town. You will wait outside for me and then dispose of any bodies as I instruct. I will handle this alone. Pass me your Tokarev just in case. I probably won't need it but it never hurts to have insurance, after all I am in the financial business," Richard instructed, ensuring the gun was loaded with a full clip.

After taking the pistol, he further directed that the two behemoths in the car should not get involved under any circumstances except for cleanup and to wait for him out in the alley behind the store. This one was all his. When they got to the town square it was now mid morning and the area was filling up with tourists and business people.

The Jewelry store that the rogue pimp used as his operations base was right in the center of the business district between a high end souvenir shop and a lingerie store that by no small coincidence outfitted the pleasure ladies next door.

Richard did not believe in subtleties so he walked right in through the front door tripping off a bell that rang inside the shop letting them know a customer had arrived.

A bored looking attendant sat watching a small television behind the counter and was in the middle of painting her nails while chewing on a wad of gum that must have been massive as it kept coming out of her large red painted mouth.

"I am here to see Gregor," said Richard.

"You have appointment?" asked the girl between vigorous chews.

"Not need appointment," replied Richard getting annoyed.

"Everyone needs appointment to see Gregor," replied the girl tripping off a silent alarm and then quickly slipping out the back. But Richard was much quicker throwing the girl against a pile of wooden crates in a dingy area that looked like a stock room. In the blink of an eye he was surrounded by three large muscled but sinewy looking thugs. "Gregor is the only one who handles the girls. Now you will pay," spat the largest of the three reeking of onions and garlic.

Before the sentence was even finished, Richard came in hard and fast with a spinning back fist that knocked almost all the teeth this poor sucker had down his throat and he fell back spitting out blood and teeth.

The second thug made the mistake of head butting Richard as hard as he could while wrapping him up in an enormous bear hug which would have crushed the life out of most men.

But Richard just shrugged off the blow to the head which hurt the attacker more than himself, slipped out of the vice like grip like the slippery eel he was, turned around and with a savage ripping sound removed thug number two's penis and testicles stuffing them down the throat of the still choking first assailant who expired from the foreign equipment now obstructing his airwaves.

The first henchman was in total shock holding his profusely bleeding crotch whimpering quietly to himself. Richard would make it a point to come back and put this now misshapen piece of humanity out of his misery once his business was finished there being the fair-minded individual he wasn't.

The third thug was so shocked by what he saw that he quickly deducted this was way over his pay grade and beat a hasty retreat towards a side door of the room. It wasn't nearly quick enough however as an expertly thrown coat rack embedded itself in his neck almost removing his head from his shoulders.

Three down, one to go and since Gregor the man he was here to see still hadn't made an appearance, he was probably too preoccupied to notice deducted Richard.

Well deducted indeed as Richard was treated to quite a sight when he opened the door to the next room. All he saw was a large, white and extremely pock-marked rear end pumping furiously against an extra long set of legs that seemed to go on forever.

The crime boss had heard the alarm but was smug in thinking his associates would handle the intrusion. Big mistake.

Richard was almost in tears at the funny sight in front of him and decided the quickest way to get his new audience's attention was to plant a good swift and altogether much too hard kick where the sun didn't shine and may never again.

The kick lifted Gregor and his now shrieking paramour right off the ground, the landing being the hardest on the one on the bottom knocking her into a not so blissful state of unconsciousness.

But Gregor, considering the situation, made the best of it by extricating himself from his now right out of it lover coming up in a shoulder roll, pulling a gun of his own and filling the air with bullets emptying the whole clip—into nothing but air.

Richard had disappeared like "Puff the Magic Dragon" himself and reappeared straddling Gregor's head and executing a wrestling like maneuver sliding his body down the back of the now totally disoriented Gregor and flipping him through the air crashing into one of the brick walls.

Gregor was flopping around like a spawning Mackerel, the brick wall had definitely gotten the best of him.

Fun time was now over and Richard pulled his weapon placing 3 expert shots into the forehead of the late and obviously not so great Gregor the whoremaster.

He left the hooker alone; she probably would not remember what happened anyway. Turning around, he strode confidently out of the front door but not before putting a couple of rounds into the brain of the first thug as after all a promise was a promise even though it was only to himself.

As he walked throughout the store, it didn't look too worse for wear at least in the display area. His cleanup crew was ready to go in and dispose of the bodies and clean the place up for whomever he would deem to take over the business. There was money to be laundered, jewelry to be sold and business men to be pleased who were not happy with what their zhenschinas (women) or lack thereof were dishing out.

"Hurry it up comrades, all this activity has given me a thirst and an aching in my groin. Time is wasting!" indicated Richard now sitting back in the car and lighting himself a Sobranie and taking a good long pull of the Vodka bottle that was always in the car.

The trip was a success to his way of thinking. Now it was time to clean things up at home once and for all. But first more women, food and drink as his flight back was not till the next morning, and his personal plane was in for maintenance and refueling. Richard lived for the moment and the moment was now.

Chapter 55

Angel finally stirred around 2 in the afternoon the next day, jumping with a start out of a strange bed she did not immediately recognize. She shook her head to clear it and took a sip of water from a glass that was by her bedside.

The delicious smell of bacon and coffee assaulted her nostrils spurring her into action. She took care of her morning ablutions, jumped into a pair of jeans and a rock on t-shirt with a pair of loafers while tying her long blond hair back into a pony tail.

The downstairs area was warm with a roaring fire in the woodstove and Jon-Erik, Rollie and Joey were busying themselves in the kitchen creating a brunch fit for a queen which she definitely felt like.

"Angel, could you get Tina up, brunch is ready," shouted Joey.

"You must have really tired her out," Angel laughed and ran up over to the lower bedroom suite, opened the door and jumped on the still sleeping Tina. After rolling around with her best friend for a bit, she left Tina to get herself ready as she was getting too hungry to continue to fool around.

For the next fifteen minutes everyone was too busy refueling to talk. The guys had made biscuits, bacon, scrambled eggs, sausages, rye toast, Tim Horton's coffee from a tin and tea for Tina who hated coffee.

After brunch, the guys retired to the woodstove lounge to chat while the ladies cleaned up which was a manual operation as one thing this country home did not have was a dishwasher. After finishing the dishes, Angel and Tina joined the guys in the den and the discussion on next steps began.

"I checked the weather forecast and the roads should be fairly clear this afternoon. I'm going to be heading back in about an hour or so," Rollie said.

"And we are stuck here for how long?" asked Joey.

"You are not stuck here at all. You can go back anytime but I heavily advise against it for now after what happened," indicated Rollie now looking a touch annoyed.

"Rollie is right and he has only been trying to help us," said Jon-Erik.

"So is there a plan going forward?" asked Angel.

"When I get back to the city, we are going to mount some sort of an offensive against Richard Rasmussin. Not sure if Alf Cragan can help or not, maybe unofficially. Bottom line is, we can't use conventional channels to get him as we would be tied up in court for years. We are going to have to get creative and get rid of him without any fuss or fanfare," surmised Rollie.

"Why not just wait it out here and let the Ninja get rid of him. Chances are he is already on Mikhail's radar majorly," said Tina.

"Mikhail is unpredictable at best. He is going to go ballistic when he finds out I am not around as he seems to be fixated on me these days," Angel added.

"Good thing I guess he has saved our lives a number of times as a result. But I personally can't wait for the day when we no longer have to look over our shoulders whether it would be because of him or those who mean us harm," said Jon-Erik.

"Look, you have the untraceable cell phone, I'll be in touch and do not hesitate to call me if something comes up," instructed Rollie as he was already packing up for his trip back to the city.

"What do we do if they find us up here?" asked Tina with a worrisome look on her pretty face.

"I wish I had an answer for you besides be extremely careful. No one from this area will bother you," Rollie answered.

Just before leaving the house Rollie handed something wrapped up in an oil cloth to Jon-Erik.

"This is a Smith and Wesson 640 revolver that holds 5 rounds of ammunition. The clip is loaded, the safety is on. None of you are licensed to carry a fire arm; this is only for use in the gravest of emergencies to save your life. Put it away in a safe place close by and I pray you do not have to use it. Keep your eyes and ears open and think before you do anything. I will be in touch soon," and with that he was out the door, out of the snow covered driveway and gone.

"So here we are in a secluded country hideaway in the middle of nowhere. What's on the agenda, guys?" asked Angel with a sexy drawl.

"Hopefully some good loving, food, movies and fresh air," offered Joey.

The group high fived each other, the ladies pouring each other a glass of red wine content to stay close to the cozy fire while the guys decided to go out and explore their new surroundings.

They could not get far however as there was at least 4 or more feet of snow on the ground although the driveway and the areas around the house were cleared, anywhere else, they would be up to their thighs in it.

So they headed to the large garage adjacent to the house; Rollie had told them where to find a key.

Inside were various power and hand tools, a snow blower which they hoped they wouldn't need to use during their hopefully short stay along with a late modeled 2 seater ski-doo with key in the ignition. There were also 2 helmets on the wall along with a large canister labeled "Ski-doo fuel".

"Wow, let's take this baby for a spin. You drive, I'd probably run it into a tree or off a cliff with my luck," said Joey excitedly.

"I suggest we stay on the main road for now. We don't know the area and if this thing cuts out on us, we may be hiking hours to get home in this deep snow to boot. I'm more comfortable staying close anyway," Jon-Erik replied.

"Works for me, afterwards we can each give the ladies a guided tour. I'll tell them what we are up to, you pull the machine up to the entrance," Joey instructed.

The machine fired up first attempt which was a good sign. Jon-Erik checked the fuel gage which indicated ¾ full so no refill worries for quite a while. He pulled up to the front door and Joey hopped on behind him and off they went to explore the area. It was a gorgeous sunny day but bitterly cold and even the thick winter jackets, gloves and boots they had brought did not keep them warm for long.

They pulled out of the driveway, took the first left and marveled at how much snow was still on the main road where the city had no sign of it. They stopped admiring a frozen lake that sprung up suddenly to the right with a little parkette and play area which was totally buried in snow. A snowmobile trail seemed to start there and snake back from the direction they came from so the two adventurers decided to follow that trail which ultimately led them back to Black Crane Lake Road which they would not have known except for the sign.

Their calculations put them a bit past the house which came in sight as soon as they rounded the bend in the road. The plan was that Jon-Erik would take Angel for a spin next and then Joey would take Tina and that's exactly the way it played out. While

Angel and Jon-Erik were out, Joey decided he need-ed a good sit down in his on-suite bathroom and like a light had been suddenly been switched on, Tina made a quick 30 second phone call on the secure cell. A call which she would have no memory of mak-ing but it told the recipient all that was needed to know— their location.

Chapter 56

Richard Rasmussin was on his way back from Moscow after tying up a few more loose ends and putting the word out that what happened to Gregor would happen to anyone that crossed him. He felt the infrastructure put in place now would start paying even larger dividends real soon as the citizens of Russia loved their women, vodka, songs and other more subversive diversions that his organization was more than happy to supply to compensate for the bleak weather and way of life in this country.

His private jet pulled in Pearson Airport late Monday afternoon and since the relevant palms were always well greased, customs was a non-issue for him. His car was waiting for him which took him directly to the Toronto Trump Tower, his home. He took the private elevator up to his suite not wishing to see anyone. He needed a few hours to re-charge before getting on to the business of dealing with these meddlesome individuals that seemed to have a ton of luck and some skilled help on their side.

He swiped the card reader to his suite and he knew right away something was not right just by the smell. He could smell and sense something was not right anywhere anytime and he was taken totally by surprise when it occurred in his own private sanctuary.

He sensed no movement however but as he started looking around he noticed things were not in their usual place. In fact nothing was, it looked as if someone had lived there while he had been away as improbable as it sounded. *How the hell could someone get in here? No one had access to his apartment but himself* he tried to reason.

Richard was now on high alert but his extraordinary senses told him that there was no one in the suite with him. No one alive, that is. As he meticulously looked through his condo, he saw more signs that someone had been there. Dishes in the sink, bottles from his bar fridges that had been used and when he went into his bedroom he noticed his usually tidy bed was anything but.

He was now furious and that did not bode well for anyone near him. Thankfully, the Imitator was beyond caring as he floated belly up in Richard's large hot tub like a large bloated wilting mackerel. He was not easily noticed as the cover had been put on the tub as Mikhail knew it would make the whole thing more interesting.

He was not wrong as after searching the whole place and finding nothing other than the telltale signs that someone had been there, Richard recalled that he had left his hot tub empty and now it was full.

`Surprised was an understatement of how he felt when he took the cover off the hot tub and saw himself floating in it.

"What the bloody hell!" screamed Richard Rasmussin to no one but himself.

Nothing had ever fazed him like this before. He took a few calming breaths and willed himself to think rationally. But he was just too flabbergasted as he stared at himself deader than a duck during hunting season.

He went to his bar and poured himself a triple shot of vodka which seemed to calm him down at least for now. This was just impossible and no matter how he wrapped his mind around it, nothing made sense.

After a couple of more calming shots he started feeling a bit more focused. *This guy in his hot tub looked exactly like himself from his body structure to his hair and facial features. It stands to reason that he could have easily fooled the receptionist and asked for another key card to enter the premises. No one would be any wiser. But what happened to this impersonator of the highest order?*

Richard slipped on a pair of rubber kitchen gloves and although he was not a qualified medical examiner, he had seen a multitude of dead bodies, mostly right from his own hand.

There was no obvious indication of cause of death; it almost looked as if the dumb idiot drank himself to death. But upon closer examination judging by the discoloration of the floaters chest, it looked like his chest was crushed.

What in blue blazes would have strength and cunning enough to do that without leaving a sign as he had thoroughly checked his unit and found no sign of anyone else but his unfortunate hot tub guest?

A thought came to Richard and he began to look at his intruder's face a lot more closely and quickly noticed that his reluctant room mate wore very clever and high end facial mask along with the exact texture, length and color of his own hair. Then looking closer at his mouth, something white was lodged in it.

Richard, definitely being the non squeamish type, pried open the corpse's mouth and low and behold a piece of paper was lodged in it. Even though the paper was soggy, the message written on it was still readable and very clear.

I have done you a favor by getting rid of this trash and will do you another when we meet by getting rid of you… and you will never see it coming.

Richard Rasmussin went wild and started kicking things around his place leaping straight in the air and shattering an expensive light fixture on the ceiling like it was a porcelain doll.

Calm he said to himself. *Calm down* as he knew he was no good in this state and the way he was now was totally against all his training.

Once he was a bit more rational, he sat down and went into a state of deep meditation beside the hot tub.

Sometime later, he came out of his trance and felt like his old self again but also felt violated and extremely on edge.

Someone first of all had the gall to impersonate him, Richard Rasmussin one of the most powerful and dangerous people on earth. And then as a topper, someone else, most likely the meddlesome individual who had already disposed of a number of his people including the Elmo Entwhistle clone, gained entrance to his home and killed his double.

Just blind luck, that this all happened while he was away. He vowed right then and there that he would find and remove this individual from this earth, whoever and whatever he was. But he knew he had to be cautious and sly like a fox as this ghost had skills that he thought only he possessed.

It would be a battle of epic proportions when the two would finally meet and Richard had no doubt of the outcome. None could and had ever stood against him successfully and this killer would be no exception. He had been extremely lucky so far and his luck was going to run out and soon, if Richard had anything to do with it.

Chapter 57

One call deserved another, as Elmo Entwhistle received the second one from one of the multitude of field operatives. The fugitives were all up north ensconced in some hideaway near Parry Sound on Black Crane Lake Road. Elmo did not hesitate to call Richard who picked up on the second ring and just listened as he was still absorbed deeply in thought from the events at his suite.

"Is this information reliable?" is all he asked after receiving the information.

"It comes from Tina herself," replied Elmo

The post hypnotic suggestion to call a specific number if ever she were to leave home had its merit. Richard had forgotten about it with everything that had occurred recently but now grinned like the Russian Wolf he was.

"So we have them right where we want them, in the middle of nowhere with no place to go. Easy pickings, right? Wrong!"

"They have always found a way to escape us so far so this time things will be different. I'll handle this myself, I do not make mistakes. Stay tuned," and with that Richard disconnected the call.

Elmo Entwhistle was relieved as he had no real desire to meet up with whatever took care of his clone and the assassins sent to take care of this motley group. He knew his boss would wrap things up once and for all. He always had.

Now Richard had two problems to deal with. The first one was relatively simple and handled with one quick call which brought two burly men in maintenance outfits to his door in no time flat.

The floater in the hot tub was bagged, tagged and wrapped up in a large garbage bag which was then wound into a large but light carpet. From there, Richard activated his private elevator which took the cleanup crew and cargo in tow back down to the underground parking garage and their unmarked panel van.

The Imitator would be put on ice till spring and then would be making his last trip out to the middle of Lake Ontario on a fishing boat. His final imitation of a package encased in rope with a heavy boat anchor, which would take him to his last resting place to join the many distinguished and not so distinguished denizens of the deep eagerly awaiting his arrival.

Once his uninvited house guest was removed, Richard cleaned up his place and scrubbed and drained his hot tub as cleanliness was next to godliness for him and godliness was something he was well on the way to obtaining, at least in his estimation.

Now as he poured himself another drink, he had some detailed thinking to do. He had an empire to run and wasn't going to let these nuisances get in the way. No rash decisions however as he had some time. Knowing the group felt fairly secure for now, he would have the time to come up with a fool proof plan.

On second thought however, it came to him that Tina was to contact Elmo subconsciously again once she was home and the group would most likely feel a bit more secure if nothing happened to them up north.

So his plan was to do nothing for a while and just run his empire, his prey would come to him soon enough. But his home was compromised and that made him feel uneasy. But he had various high level accommodations in the city and another phone call would ready them for his arrival.

And all this thinking had made him randy as a rabbit so three escorts from one of his upscale business ventures were ordered to be there upon his arrival. His car was waiting for him in the underground and he was whisked off to his new digs; a large private home in the upper Royal York area where most of the neighbors were vacationing in South Beach Miami or other trendy holiday spots. And those who remained behind were too old and rich to pay attention to who was coming or going in their exclusive neighborhood.

For every action there is an opposite and in some situations not so equal reaction and this case was no exception. Even though communication in Richard's organization was at a high level and need to know basis only, some things always filtered through the cracks.

One such crack ended up depositing its information in the ear of Bosco Barzinski, a mid-level thug who contracted his services to Richard Rasmussin via Elmo Entwhistle. Elmo, was always looking to score additional points with Richard and Bosco in turn had no problem moving up a few rungs of the ladder of corruption.

And Bosco just happened to have some connections up in Parry Sound to people who would have no problem slitting their own grandmother's throat as long as they got paid well for the effort.

So with one phone call the deal was sealed. A group of four motley but motivated individuals were dispatched to Black Crane Lake Road to take care of these four meddlesome individuals. They were told to arm themselves to the teeth and be extremely careful as their quarry so far seemed to have luck and skill on their side and that they also might have some extremely skilled help.

The leader of this crew, by the name of Clyde, was a burly 270 lbs. of muscle and when he heard they were essentially hired to take out two men and two women and possibly another more skilled protector, he licked his chops and downed another long necked Bud in one gulp.

His men were not over skilled but what they lacked in technique, they more than made for in enthusiasm. Their modus operandi was always the same, get in quick, do the job and get out without leaving a trace. However, the fact that there were two women who apparently were real lookers involved here plus the location for this hit was totally in the middle of nowhere, gave Clyde the idea that they may be able to have a bit of fun with the ladies once their male companions were disposed of.

Clyde and his crew did not want to waste any time as jobs like this only came along once in a blue moon and their wallets were all getting a bit long in the tooth. Their wives and girlfriends were always bitching and moaning about the lifestyles they should be providing for them.

Clyde was the leader with Joe and Billy who were both weaned in the North Country and hunted and fished like experts by the time they became teenagers. Joe was tall, skinny with scraggly long hair and a thick beard but moved as stealthy and quiet as a panther. Billy was a mountain boy all the way and was happiest when he was outdoors; he did well in any kind of weather.

With his short blond hair, freckles and dimples when he smiled, he could fit in almost anywhere but he was a dangerous scrapper and marksman and could lose his temper at the drop of a hat.

The fourth member of this odd lot was an older guy they called Norris who always wore a green John Deere hat which almost totally covered his eyes. A good thing too as anyone that looked into his eyes saw nothing but evil and malevolence. Norris was not as agile as the other three but was more practiced at being a stone cold killer than the rest of them. And he did so enjoy his work.

The plan was for the four of them to arrive in two separate vehicles. Norris had an older Jeep Cherokee which could get through any type of weather easily and Clyde drove a Dodge Ram truck that could hold all the gear they needed. A trusty 30 odd 6 hunting rifle along with pistols and bowie knives all around should be more than adequate to get the job done.

Everyone was all dressed in warm snow mobile gear which worked well with the 2 skidoos loaded on the back of Clyde's truck that the team of killers would double up on to get in and out of their destination. No one would give two snowmobiles a second listen or look in that area as most would have turned in by then or would be watching a program on Satellite TV in the depth of night.

The team was all packed up and ready to go as the clock struck one a.m. It was a bitterly cold snowy night and the visibility was almost non-existent except for those who knew where they were going. They arrived at the mouth of Black Crane Lake Road about half an hour later, unloaded the machines and their gear, fired them up and headed towards the secluded home.

They parked their machines under a group of pines which almost rendered them invisible and trudged down the road on foot so their targets could not hear them approaching.

To their distain, the lights were on and there was movement in the kitchen. Joe was sent in to scout while the other three huddled in the pitch black behind the shelter of the garage. Joe came back a scant few minutes later with a full report.

"Two hotties in the kitchen, a blonde and a brunette fixing snacks. Two average size guys in the den drinking beer. And a large dog the size of a small horse lying by the fireplace. That's going to be a problem," whispered Joe.

"Shit, no one said nothing about a dog, especially a large one," said Billy.

"No problem. Norris will pop the dog right through the front window at which time we'll make our grand entrance and join the party. Let's git er done, there's money to be made and some hot ladies, food and drink in there waiting for us," instructed Clyde with a wave of his hand.

Let the games begin.

Chapter 58

"Something is up with Mindy," whispered Joey as the big Kangal got up from his spot by the woodstove and began to pace back and forth emitting a low growl. At the same moment, Jon-Erik noticed an ominous looking shadow skirting by the front window.

"Shit, there is somebody out there," yelled Jon-Erik. "Everyone get behind something, now!"

And none too soon as a gun blast shattered the front window and hit the spot where Mindy was seconds ago.

Tina ran for one of the bedrooms trying to take the dog with her. But the large Kangal had other ideas and headed for the front door barking furiously. By the sounds of things the intruder or intruders had already breached the mud room and were now trying to bash in the front door.

The door had a regular lock and dead bolt and was as solid as they come and did not budge under the smashing and banging from the now even more upset attackers. Since they could not get in the front door and that seemed to be the only access to the home, Clyde directed Joe and Billy to smash a window and come at them that way.

The windows much to their dismay however were at least 8 feet off the ground and they would need a ladder to climb up and break them.

"Damn, this place is a fortress. Looks like we are going in the front window, which looks to be the only option," snarled Joe after they trudged back to tell Clyde and Norris.

While the four bumbling assassins outside were regrouping, Jon-Erik was on the phone calling Rollie who answered on the second ring and told the group to call 911 immediately. He also told them to use the revolver he had left with them if their lives were in danger which by all indications was certainly true and that he would be heading back up there pronto.

"How many of them are there?" screamed Angel.

"No idea," replied Joey feeling like he was going to pee his pants any second.

Tina had locked herself in the upper bedroom, not up for another dangerous confrontation. She was hyperventilating and had a splitting headache to boot. Joey tried to go in to comfort her but she was sobbing uncontrollably and did not react to him.

Angel was huddled with Jon-Erik behind the kitchen table, the revolver ready and safety off. The 911 operator, after having taken down their information and trying to get them to stay on the line, indicated it would be at least an hour due to the distance away as well as the bad weather before someone could get there but they would make every effort. The other bit of advice they were given was stay out of sight and do not confront the intruders.

Not the comforting information they were looking for at this time, that was for sure. Everything had gone still quiet again outside with nothing stirring, not even the four louses.

"I'm not going to be a sitting duck in here, I'm going out after them," whispered Angel pulling on her snow suit, fur hat and boots. "Are you coming or staying behind?" she whispered to Jon-Erik.

"Damn babe, I should stay here with the gun in case they crash the window or the door. We are on our own for a while and we are going to stay alive at all costs. I know you will be careful…but be careful," Jon-Erik said giving Angel a quick kiss and hug.

Angel decided her best bet was to slip out of the lower bedroom window at the back of the house but even that window was at least 8 feet off the ground but she had to chance it. When she took a peek out, all seemed to be still but she did note all the footprints around the back window indicating that their nemesis had already scoped the back of the house out and found it to difficult to breach.

She quickly removed the screen, opened the window and hang-dropped like a cat to the cold and snowy ground. She quickly shimmied along the side of the house and carefully took a glance around the corner where there was some illumination coming from the outside garage light. She heard voices coming from inside the garage; that must be where they were holed up.

The cold and icy snow was nipping at her face and even though she had been outside only for a minute, she hastily covered her face with a scarf she had the sense to wear under her snowsuit.

She had to get them to come out and see how many there actually were before she decided on what to do next. An idea came to her. She packed four snowballs till they turned to hard ice and whipped the first two at the garage door with all the strength she possessed at the same time darting behind one side of the garage.

Bingo, two goons in full snow gear and armed with rifles shot out of the garage like cannons looking around. Another two joined them and the four looked around puzzled as they saw and heard nothing.

The one who looked like the leader whispered something quickly and the best case scenario for Angel occurred.

Clyde sent his henchmen in all directions in some sort of search pattern; Norris back to the front of the house with Joe circling the garage and Billy the house. Thankfully, there was a huge tree behind the garage which gave Angel the cover she needed.

And when Joe snuck by her tree hideaway, Angel pounced like an angry lioness jumping on his back, muffling his mouth with one hand while locking the other in a guillotine choke around his throat cutting off his airway. He struggled for a few furtive seconds but Angel hung on for dear life and squeezed like no tomorrow which would not be if she failed.

Normally, if a person was choked this way they could be revived providing the hold was only applied for a short interval but Angel hung on until Joe did not breathe again. She dragged him behind the tree and quickly covered him up with snow smoothing out the area with a pine branch.

With Joe on ice permanently, she now had his rifle as well which stacked things a little more their way. But she was only planning to use it if she had no other choice as a shot was loud and would draw the other killers quickly.

The whole Joe operation had only taken a couple of minutes if that and her next best bet was to go for the guy who was circling the house from the back. Again, luckily for her, there were a group of thick pines running along the length of the house behind it, most likely planted as a shield for those nasty northern winds and snow gusts.

Angel slowly made her way along the outside of those pines until she positioned herself right behind ingrate number two who was looking up at the open window at the back scratching his head under his toque.

At that moment, Angel came flying through the air and cracked the assassin over the head with the rifle making a sound like a ripe melon smashing into bits and pieces.

The killer went down in a heap; Angel not knowing whether he was alive or dead, she took no chances and kicked him in the head full force with her heavy snow boot.

She felt for a pulse and found none so she repeated what she did before dragging the body behind the pines and covering him with snow and then erasing all relevant tracks.

Two down and two to go. Luck had been with her so far and she deep breathed to calm herself. But things did not go so well from here on as Norris decided enough is enough and smashed the front window and followed up shoulder rolling into the den and almost knocking over the woodstove which he avoided at the last minute.

This caused Jon-Erik to open up with his pistol on the prone form on the floor. Unfortunately because Norris was moving so fast, he only clipped him on his side opening up a flesh wound.

The noise now brought the leader Clyde out in the open as well yelling for Joe and Billy to go in after Norris. No answer from either which made him nervous but they had come too far to back out now.

The only thing that Clyde could do now is follow Norris in but cautiously since he heard shots. Hopefully, Norris had gotten everyone inside but he had to be careful in case some of the meddlesome group had stayed alive.

With all the shots and commotion, Joey came back into the picture once he made sure Tina and the dog were safe and behind closed doors. As he was coming back into the den an incredulous sight greeted him.

One thug was laying on the floor behind the woodstove trying to get a bead on Jon-Erik who was hiding behind the kitchen island. He ducked behind the couch as he saw another one enter through the broken living room window brandishing a weapon.

He could think of nothing else to do but stay put since he had no weapon but the two goons now inside their house certainly did.

Before Clyde could even properly assess the situation inside, Angel came hurdling through the window scissoring her strong legs around Clyde's neck and then executed a roll snapping her now powerless victim like a twig. He shook twice and lay still.

Angel came up in a shoulder roll with the rifle she had confiscated from the recently departed Joe and screamed, "Drop your rifle now or I'll shoot!" at the prone form of a hurt and now totally outnumbered Norris.

Norris was acting on pure instinct now as he pointed his rifle at the voice to his right. Unfortunately, not a very good instinct as Jon-Erik popped up behind from the island and pumped two quick rounds at the cretin who was threatening his fiancée.

At the same time, Angel also fired and needless to say Norris *luckily no relation to Chuck* was on his way to join his accomplices in hell.

"Are there any more?" screamed Joey hysterically behind the couch.

"No, it's over. They are all down and out," replied Angel beginning to hyperventilate from the stress of the last few minutes.

Jon-Erik ran to Angel and showered her with kisses while Joey ran up to tell Tina the coast was clear. Tina came out in tears and shaking with Mindy at her side growling and sniffing at the two dead bodies on the floor in their den.

"Listen up! The OPP are on their way here and could be here any minute. They are not going to understand what happened. We have to get these bodies out of here now and clean up," instructed Angel still operating on full adrenaline.

"There is a sled in the garage. I'll get it so we can haul these carcasses out of here," said Joey getting with the program quickly and wanting to do his part.

Whipping his jacket and boots on, he disappeared out the door while Angel and Jon-Erik dragged Clyde and Norris outside. Tina was cowering on the couch still right out of it; the stress of everything had rendered her almost immobile.

The cleanup took scant minutes before the group of three convened back in the den, the woodstove still giving off warmth which was even more needed with the busted window.

"Joey, stow all the rifles in that cubbyhole under the stairs along with this handgun," said Jon-Erik in between holding and kissing Angel who was shaking and crying as she was coming down from her adrenaline rush and the realization of what had just happened hit her hard.

Unfortunately, a flood of lights where now coming up the driveway. The cavalry had arrived although too late and no one was looking forward to the interrogation they were now going to be facing.

"Let me do the talking. Joey and Angel, you can add stuff if they speak to you direct but the jist of it has to be that they shot out the window and then took off as we started yelling and screaming and must have scared them away. Are we all on the same page?" asked Jon-Erik.

Everyone nodded beside Tina who was still not coherent. Joey took her back to the bedroom while Jon-Erik and Angel greeted their fashionably late guests.

Four large Ontario Provincial Policemen burst into the room, two with handguns drawn and the other two with semi-automatic weapons of some sort. They were in full body armor and well outfitted against the cold.

"Is anyone hurt or armed in here," asked the first officer through the door.

"No, we are all fine but pretty shook up," answered Jon-Erik.

"How many of them were there?" the second cop asked.

"No idea," Jon-Erik replied.

"Where did they go?", the baton going back to the first cop.

"No idea, we never saw them," Jon-Erik continued to reply.

"Okay, my name is Detective Sergeant Grimsby and these are Constables York, Jones and Alphonso. We need to know what happened here and please start at the beginning. Is there anyone else here besides you three?"

"My fiancée, Tina. She is too shook up to speak and trying to get some rest." said Joey.

"Alright let's start from the beginning," said Sergeant Grimsby pulling out a notepad. "Jones, Alphonso and York, please secure the area."

"Well, we were sitting around the fire having a drink and talking and the ladies were making snacks when we heard what we thought were shots and then the front window smashed to bits," relayed Jon-Erik.

"How many shots?" asked Grimsby.

"Sounded like four but could have been more," indicated Angel sipping from a glass of water.

"Do you four live here or is this someone else's place?"

"We are up here on a little winter vacation, snowmobiling and all that. The house belongs to a friend of a friend." Jon-Erik answered.

"So you do not know who owns this place?"

"Our friend Rollie would know, we wouldn't."

"Rollie who?"

"Rolland Sampson, former metro Toronto detective now in private practice."

"Where does he live?"

"Near the lakeshore in Toronto's west end in the area we all live. Rollie is on his way here now. He is the first person we called as he is our best friend and more experienced in these matters than we are."

The three other Police Constables returned indicating there was no one in the vicinity of the house or property, just a lot of foot prints around the perimeter of the house meaning the place was cased.

"Did any of you see who did this?" continued Grimsby.

"Just some dark shapes outside the window. Too dark to make anything out," Jon-Erik responded.

"Anybody wish you four any harm that you know of?"

Thankfully before that question had to be answered Rollie Sampson came bursting in taking in the crazy scene in one glance.

He showed his id and private detective license to the officers and indicated to Sergeant Grimsby that this group had been through a lot and that they were exhausted as it was now almost five am.

"Do you know of anyone that would want to cause this group any harm?" Grimsby asked Rollie directly.

"Not to my knowledge," lied Rollie but sounding very convincing. "No one besides me would have known they were out here in the middle of nowhere."

"Who owns this place? Could this assault have been meant for them?"

"No way, it belongs to the father of a cop I used to work with in Metro. He's 85 years old now and not too mobile anymore. He has given me access to this place for the last 5 years or so and I thought the gang here might enjoy a vacation in the great white north."

"Look, I'll come in and give you a full statement after we get some sleep and we have to plastic up this window as too much cold air is getting in for the woodstove and the electric heat to handle," said Rollie.

"Fair enough and bring the group's spokesman there with you. However, I will need to have all of your names and addresses before we go. I assume you are armed and will take responsibility for this crew until we speak at the station. Here is a card with my name and station address. I expect to see you tomorrow afternoon around 2 pm."

"Looks like you all were very lucky tonight. We will discuss further tomorrow until then get some rest," and the four officers left the building so to speak.

After the officers had left and they saw their headlights in the distance, Rollie gave everyone in turn a hug and went to the fridge and got himself a beer.

"How the hell could this have happened?" asked Rollie to no one in particular knowing he would not like the answer if it were to be supplied anyway. No, he certainly would not.

Chapter 59

It wasn't till about noon the following morning that everyone was up. Angel, Jon-Erik and Rollie where sitting in the kitchen over coffee and sweet rolls, Joey still tucked in with Tina sleeping the sleep of the exhausted.

After Rollie had heard the whole story from Angel and Jon-Erik, who still seemed wired from last night's events, he just sat back sipping on his coffee before finally speaking.

"No words to describe," is all he finally could muster.

But then he mustered in spite of himself and said," You have four dead bodies on ice out there?" shaking his head back and fourth slowly not even believing what he had just said.

"That about sums it up," replied Angel.

"How do you feel about what happened?" asked Rollie.

"I'm numb, totally numb," Angel mumbled.

"Can't add much to that," added Jon-Erik.

"You guys have gone through so much and I can't forgive myself for leaving you out here alone. I obviously underestimated these people; that will never happen again."

"So what the hell do we do now?' asked Jon-Erik again to no one in particular.

"Should we stay or should we go?" hummed Angel trying to inject a bit of levity into the situation.

"The first thing we need to do is get our story straight and then dispose of these bodies somehow. Who knows who these people were and if they have relatives or loved ones that will miss them but we can not worry about that now," Rollie surmised.

"Jon-Erik and I have to go to the police station in town for two. Joey and Angel, you will have to do the dirty work. My suggestion is we bag the corpses and then you sled them out deep into the forest with the snowmobiles, find a clearing, douse them with gasoline and light them up," he added.

"We still have at least 2 months of deep winter left out here and by the time the spring thaw occurs there will no trace of them remaining," Jon-Erik deduced.

Jon-Erik went to get Joey who was ready to do something since Tina was still fast asleep and three men went out to see to their grisly task sparing Angel the indignity. A short time later, the sled was wrapped up and bundled tight and ready to go.

While Rollie and Jon-Erik got ready to go see Detective Sergeant Grimsby, Joey waited on the fired up snowmobile while Angel dressed herself against the bitter cold. When Angel was ready with a gas can in tow with lighters and matches, the strange looking procession slowly wound their way across the open fields into the deep woods beyond.

Rollie and Jon-Erik started to lock the place up tight, praying Tina would be safe until Joey and Angel returned, hopefully, as quickly as possible. Angel had the other key so they could get back in when they returned.

After a careful fifteen minute ride with their horrific cargo in tow, Joey and Angel came into a clearing in the midst of a dense patch of forest that they had to maneuver very carefully through. Joey dug a pit out with a shovel he brought, essentially clearing the snow on all sides until a crevice of sorts had been fashioned.

The two then trudged through the high snow depositing their freight into the pit one by one. Then Angel liberally doused the four bagged bundles with gasoline while Joey shoveled out a little track leading out of the pit which Angel also gave a good soaking.

Last act in this macabre play was to light the track and watch the fireworks. The gasoline trail ignited immediately and quickly snaked its way into the pit where the four assassins lit up with a combustible whoosh. A good thing Angel and Joey were well out of the line of fire as the eruption of heat and flame was massive. The smell coming from the charnel pit was enough to make the two almost gag as they got on the snowmobile and headed carefully towards the house.

Luckily, there was sizeable snowfall on the way this evening which would erase all tracks of what had occurred and hopefully no one would ever be the wiser. When they got back to the house, Angel spent another half hour eradicating all signs of anything that could look suspicious, while Joey went to look in on Tina who was finally showing signs of life.

Rollie and Jon-Erik arrived at the O.P.P. station just outside of Parry Sound. They went to the desk and indicated they were there to see Sergeant Grimsby.

Grimsby came right out and led them into a sparsely furnished room most likely used for interrogations.

"Can I offer you both some coffee?" asked Grimsby.

"I'll take mine black," said Jon-Erik.

"Regular for me," Rollie added.

Grimsby returned with their coffees as well as one for himself.

"Do you mind if I record our conversation?" asked the officer.

Rollie and Jon-Erik both chimed in, "No problem."

"Let's start with names and addresses for all concerned," began Grimsby.

After Jon-Erik supplied their group's information, Rollie gave his.

"Okay, so your story was that the four of you were up here on vacation sponsored by Rollie here when someone shot out your front window. That right so far?" asked Grimsby.

"Correct," said Jon-Erik.

"And what happened then?"

"The dog started barking and the ladies began to scream and we all hit the deck."

"Who made the 911 call?"

"My fiancée Angel did after I called Rollie."

"Why call Rollie first?"

"Just instinct. He is a dear friend and had put us up in this house."

"How many people did you see outside?" prodded Grimsby.

"Possibly one or two. It was too dark to see anything but shapes and things happened so quickly," answered Jon-Erik.

"Was anyone hurt?"

"Luckily not although we were all shook up."

"What happened next?"

"Tina, Joey's fiancée locked herself up in the bedroom and the rest of us sought cover and stayed still."

"And then?" Grimsby continued.

"We saw and heard nothing further. We thought the dog and the screaming might have scared them off. And then your team arrived and Rollie right afterwards."

"How long have you known this group?" this question directed at Rollie.

"Over five years."

"How did you get to know them?"

"I was involved in a case where these four were targets of a ruthless South American drug lord," Rollie answered knowing this would raise an eyebrow; lying about this would only make things worse understanding very well how this game was played.

"I remember something about a case where the O.P.P supplied some resources to help out around that time. Was that the same case?"

"Most likely a part of it but that situation was satisfactorily resolved years ago," indicated Rollie.

"Any relevance to what has happened here?"

"Not to our knowledge. To my way of thinking this was some sort of random invasion or robbery attempt," answered Rollie.

"You know, I tend to agree with you. Our guys did find two snowmobiles hidden in a dense group of pines just down the road from your house. Any thoughts on that?"

"Were they stickered?" asked Rollie.

"Good question but expected from a former cop and my guys tell me you were one of the best," said Grimsby.

Rollie just nodded humbly.

"No they weren't but that is to be expected if someone is using these machines for illegal purposes," the O.P.P. Sergeant added.

"Looks like we are at a standstill here. We have taken the snowmobiles to be printed and searched but chances are the perps were wearing gloves unless they were totally crazy with the cold out there. Otherwise, I have no option right now as to go along with your theory the unsubs (unknown subjects) were scared off. There are many people who are up to mischief out here due to the unemployment situation and random break-ins do occur, but never with people in the house and actively awake. That part puzzles me.

METER OF CORRUPTION 393

Also that they left their snow machines if in fact they were theirs," summarized Grimsby.

"Not much we can add to that," said Jon-Erik.

"Are you planning to stay up here?" asked Grimsby.

"Yes, we've got a snow storm coming in. I doubt they will be back; the group did the right thing and scared them off. Tomorrow we will see," said Rollie.

"Here is my direct number. Call me immediately if anything else occurs. I will do the same if we find out anything further. Thanks for coming in," and with that they shook hands all around, Rollie and Jon-Erik gladly leaving the station.

They stopped at a McDonalds in town getting big Macs and fries takeout for everyone before heading back to the house on Black Crane Lake Road.

"Shit, we knew nothing about their snowmobiles," said Jon-Erik on the drive back.

"No way, you could have but that will give the police cause to keep this case active. Undoubtedly, they will try to trace the machines to someone and most likely four people will garner missing person reports sooner than later. Hopefully, later than sooner."

"Let's get back to see how Angel and Joey did. They most likely have cleared things up. What an awful thing to have to do," said Jon-Erik.

"And once you take someone's life, it always stays with you no matter what the circumstances. Your lives will never be the same," Rollie indicated.

"Our lives have never been the same since Angel and I met. But we are still alive, in love and are determined to remain that way."

"Amen to that," replied Rollie. "Amen to that."

Chapter **60**

Elmo Entwhistle was getting concerned. The job these four underlings were hired to do in Parry Sound should have been a piece of cake; yet not a word from anyone and nothing even in the news out that way. *What the hell was going on up there?*

He figured he was safe either way as Richard knew nothing about what he had set in motion, however Richard had eyes and ears everywhere and that made him a touch unsettled. If his plan succeeded, he would have looked even better in his boss' eyes and if it didn't, none would be the wiser.

But Elmo could not help thinking that these people lead beyond a charmed life as everything that was ever sent their way was never seen or heard from again, including his very own clone. Maybe the best thing to do was let Richard handle it himself as Richard had never been known to fail at anything he ever did.

Time to forget about this and get on with what he was truly good at, bilking rich and unwilling successful people out of their hard earned money and having his way with young girls and boys as after all he was an equal opportunity deviant.

The next victim on the list was a secluded and senile elderly statesman who had made a fortune in the used car business by selling dressed up old clunkers to people who thought they were getting a good deal until things started stalling, seizing up or down right falling apart.

Murgatroyd "Muzzy" Marten had to cease his cheating and illegal ways and retire ungracefully as Carfax reports, Safety Checks and other measures were implemented to protect the potential buyer. But the damage had been done, Muzzy amassed himself a tidy sum of over 10 million dollars some of which the tightwad kept with a local bank and the rest socked away in a wall safe at his modest three story home in the Toronto Beaches which had increased in value to over a million dollars as most of the homes in that area had— whether they were really worth it or not.

Elmo's plan was simple; to pay Muzzy a visit and make him an offer he could not refuse as the counter offer would be the death of him literally.

Elmo waited till dark as why tempt fate being recognized. He pulled up to the snow covered street after 10pm on a weeknight and since the home was almost at the bottom of the street, he could see the waves of Lake Ontario angrily crashing against the shore. He parked his vehicle far enough away in a cull de sac so it would not be associated with a visit to the house in question.

The area was deserted as it was a work and school night and bitterly cold. From what Elmo had found out so far, Muzzy lived all alone; Mrs. Muzzy having gone on to greener pastures a few years ago and there were no children as the Martens were too pre-occupied with spending all their ill-gotten gains gambling in Casinos and betting on the ponies.

When Muzzy's significant other shed her mortal coil, there was a full investigation into her death as the Used Car Magnate had a 1.5 million dollar term life insurance policy out on the love of his life. Although she seemed to be in good health, she was getting on in years.

The reason for her death was finally diagnosed as a massive coronary which seemed unusual since Mrs. Muzzy still jogged along the Beaches boardwalk regularly and had just passed her annual physical with flying colors.

But after a lengthy investigation, the monies were finally signed over to Muzzy who truth be told liked wealth much better than he did his cranky battle-axe of a wife who refused to have sex with him for the last number of years now because she claimed his overhang was too large and his penis was much too small.

Nothing that a tiny injection, using a syringe filled only with air between the toes, wouldn't cure. And it did—with Muzzy's latest windfall serving as a brand new account opening in the Grand Cayman Islands which was on his bucket list to visit.

All that now mattered very little as Muzzy rested in his ample walk in closet which was one of the larger rooms in his Beach mansion with his bull like neck snapped like a twig. The Highway man had come calling and even the poet Alfred Noyes who wrote this famous poem would not have envisioned this nightmare that had decided to pay a visit this cold and snowy night.

Mikhail, the monster was angry and upset beyond belief and with good reason. Angel and her group had disappeared without a trace and even one as talented and deadly as he could not be in two places at once. While he was trying to track down Richard Rasmussin and his minions, those he had sworn to protect had disappeared without a trace.

Obviously, that meddling ex-detective Rolland Sampson had something to do with it but in token the group was most likely safe in his hands. Little did he know.

The Ninja knew he could track them down sooner than later but first he had some unfinished business with one of Richard's lieutenants, Elmo Entwhistle. He had easily disposed of this trickster's clone and now the plan was to get rid of the real thing but not before finding out the easy way or the hard way where Richard Rasmussin was hanging his hat these days.

Mikhail knew Richard was a formidable opponent but he was certain what the outcome would be for him as it had always been for all that stood against him. Death, just the degree of suffering yet to be determined.

It had not been easy to track Elmo as he covered his spoor well and used the cover of night and various vehicles to his advantage. But once the Hunter of the night set his sights on something or someone, there was no escape.

Imagine the surprise on Elmo's face after he rang the doorbell expecting to see a bearded out of shape ex-used car salesman but instead coming neck to huge and steely mitt with the Shape Shifter himself.

The Monster, dispensing with the introductions, decided the direct way was most effective and ushered his now more than reluctant guest inside by grabbing him by his huge neck almost choking the life out of him with a grip of iron that left gaping imprints between Elmo's large head and shoulder blades.

Elmo was then tossed like a sack of garbage across the small and narrow kitchen landing on Muzzy's kitchen table; the impact shattering it into pieces. Wooden splinters flew everywhere, a few embedding themselves into Elmo's sizeable rear end to make things even worse.

But Elmo Entwhistle was no stranger to pain or combat especially in the business he was in. Showing surprising agility for a man his size and having taken no time to deduce that closing with this apparition was not the most intelligent path to follow, he shoulder rolled to the chair underneath which a loaded, silenced revolver was hidden for just an emergency as this.

But the Night Stalker had already anticipated such a move and was on Elmo's back before he could even reach for the gun hammering him with a vicious two handed blow directly on both ears which would have knocked most men into another universe.

But it did have the desired effect as Elmo sat stunned trying to shake the cobwebs out of his aching head and trying to will his ears to stop ringing.

Mikhail calmly sat down in the other chair first taking care to pick up the gun, remove all the bullets and then tossed it aside into another corner of the room.

Since Elmo was still doing his hugging the floor thing, the Ninja calmly lifted the extortionist into the air and deposited him into the other chair where he would stay if he knew what was good for him.

"Bring me a bottle of Vodka and a glass. Heaven will not help you if you have none," directed Mikhail.

Elmo, still in groggy land but knowing enough to know better, complied.

The Monster poured a generous triple shot and gave the glass to Elmo before taking a long drawn out pull from the bottle, repeating this action three or four times before wiping his dripping jaws with his sleeve.

"Does everyone drink this cheap rot gut here which would not even qualify for mother's milk in old country?"

"Vodka is Vodka. Hard to tell the difference," Elmo replied having composed himself enough to half-heartedly answer.

"Where is your boss?" came the next question direct and to the point.

"Who is asking?"

"I am Mikhail. I am asking and I better get a good answer. The alternative will not go well for you. That you can believe."

"Well Mikhail, my boss just does not see anyone. And if he does not want to see you, he'd just as soon kill you."

"He can and will try but he will fail as they all do. I am not in the mood for games. Where is he?"

"I will be killed if I tell you."

"You will be killed if you do not. Your call to make."

"So I am between a rock and a hard place seemingly. I guess it had to come to this sooner or later," said Elmo with a little more strength.

"Decide now or die!" snarled the Shape shifter.

"He is in one of his homes in the west end of the City. He had to leave Trump Tower as his apartment was compromised."

"By me and just pure dumb luck that someone impersonating him rather than he himself was there. But I sent him a message which he will not forget."

"You should leave and forget you ever saw me. Richard will burn the whole planet down to find and kill you. I can give you a few hours head start. After that all bets are off," said Elmo.

"Address, now!" spat the Horror. "Or I will rip you to pieces right here and throw your remains into the lake where the larger fish always appreciate a good meal.

Seeing he had no choice, Elmo scribbled an address onto a piece of paper; a number just off the South Kingsway. The Ninja had no way to verify until he actually went there but concluded this oversized cockroach was probably telling the truth.

"Where are the people that own this home?" asked the Monster with his gold tooth catching some overhead ceiling light reflection.

"Dead in the walk-in closet upstairs,"

"So not only are you an extortionist gnat and rapist, you are a cowardly killer,"

"All just part of the job," answered Elmo launching himself at full speed right into the sitting Mikhail before his sentence was finished.

What happened next was truly uncanny. The Monster seemed to levitate right into the air and all Elmo connected with was the other chair. And then Mikhail descended as he had ascended wrapping his huge legs tightly around the head of Elmo Entwhistle and squeezing with a power that only an Anaconda wish it had.

And quickly, Elmo realized he was done for and could not even draw his last breath thinking the unthinkable before he left this world; *that this monster was even more formidable than his boss Richard.* And then he thought nothing more at all.

Mikhail, who was always looking to make a statement while leaving no trace of himself, noticed the kitchen had an old gas stove. How antiquated but advantageous for him. He ensured all windows were shut tightly, turned on the oven full blast along with all four burners after having disabled the pilot lights.

He then made an unceremonious exit out of the back kitchen door but not before striking a match, lighting the whole book and then tossing it into the house. The massive explosion shattered this quiet night in the Beaches as this semi attached home burst into a huge caldron of flame and smoke. Mikhail was long gone in his vehicle heading back to his lair in Port Credit.

By the time they sifted through the rubble, they might find the dental remains of the two dead men in the house sometime in the future but no connection to him as usual would be found. He briefly thought about tenants in the adjacent home being affected and then just as quickly lost that thought as after all it would be just collateral damage.

Chapter 61

They all sat in the kitchen on Black Crane Lake Road sipping on steaming hot coffee and listlessly munching on toast with peanut butter and jam. The snow was coming down heavily now in wave after wave which did little to cheer their sour mood.

Jon-Erik had his strong arms gently around Angel as she broke out into sobs in between sips of her coffee. Joey had a still very sleepy looking Tina nestled against his shoulder; Rollie picking up the palatable tension in the room while feeling totally frustrated with the whole situation.

No matter how it was broken down, four people had been killed and Angel and Jon-Erik would never be the same again. But they did what they had to do to save their own and their best friends' lives and for that they could and should be very proud according to Rollie's way of thinking.

Now it was time to discuss the next moves. Rollie was in a bind as he could not readily protect the group and go after Richard Rasmussin. The only thing that made any sense to him was that the four friends split up again as they would not be such an easy target. And the other thing of great concern was how Richard's henchmen had found the group so quickly.

No one should know where they had gone and yet somehow someone did.

"Okay, listen up. A few observations. We can't stay here as they may send others after us once they discover that this attempt failed," Rollie remarked.

"So where do we go from here?" asked Joey with a forlorn look on his face.

"It will not be we. Having you all together is much too dangerous. Your skills saved you this time but even your skills and terrific luck can't be depended on forever," replied Rollie.

"So we should split up again?" questioned Jon-Erik thinking that history may repeat itself from five years ago.

"Do you have somewhere to go as individual couples where no one would expect you to be?" Rollie continued.

"Tina and I will go see cousin Guido. He can stow us away somewhere where no one will find us. Come to think of it, we should have relied more on Guido years ago and now," indicated Joey.

"Not a good idea. Isn't Guido looking after the furniture store right now? How fast do you think they could get to him" questioned Rollie.

"Guido is well connected and protected at all times. He has people watching his back and helping him with the store and they are all family or very close to the family. And these guys do not play nice and they will have our backs." said Joey.

"And on top of that now, I will get them involved in helping us stamp out this menace once and for all. Look at all the crap we went through years ago when I was told not to involve the family. We are way beyond that now and need all the help we can get and obviously this is much too large to entrust the cops with," Joey added.

Rollie had no response to that and wearily nodded his head.

"Angel and Jon-Erik?" he asked.

"Truthfully, we are better off with you. We have proven ourselves a number of times that we can handle ourselves and you are going to need some help to get this guy," said Angel snapping out of her depressed mood.

"Can't argue with that logic either. We should be okay up here for another day or so until this weather breaks and it will hopefully be a few days till Rasmussin and his organization find out things did not go as planned up here. We are on the road as soon as the snow eases up and that will give me a chance to plan our next moves."

"Make sure there is no sign left anywhere of what occurred here and let's get some more plastic sheeting on the outside and inside of that broken front window as no one will come out here to fix it until the weather gets better," Rollie added.

Tina said nothing during this discussion and just stared at everyone with vacant looking eyes. The group knew this was not the Tina they knew and loved, and figured the stress of everything that had happened was too much for her. That was certainly partially true but the drugs as well as the hypnotic suggestions that were given to her during her earlier kidnapping ordeal were still wreaking havoc within her system. Plus everything else was just too much for Tina who had a fairly fragile disposition in the first place.

Joey hoped that spending time with the family and feeling safe once again would turn her around and all he could do for now was to put Tina back to bed and roll up his sleeves to help his friends with the final inspection and cleanup.

They may as well hunker down as the Canadian winter was mercilessly dumping another 50 cm of snow onto the already beleaguered countryside, but assisting in eradicating all signs of their struggle and ensuing brush fire.

After another thorough inspection of the outside grounds and areas where the struggles occurred, everyone was satisfied no traces remained. And if any did, the weather would cover it up. While Rollie and Joey worked on the final patch up of the house's front window, Angel and Jon-Erik took another ride out to the site where they had set the fire. Absolutely nothing remained, as a ton of fresh clean snow covered the memory of what had happened such a short time ago.

When they returned, Joey was grilling steaks on the large barbeque outside which was protected from the elements by an overhang that could house one car and the grill. While Joey and Rollie were busy with the steak, baked potatoes and vegetables, Angel went inside to see how Tina was doing. Jon-Erik fired up the heavy duty snow blower and began to clear the front walkway and then the driveway to the road.

They would probably have to clear it again in the morning before they left as the snow just kept on coming with no signs of abating.

Rollie was not comfortable with the idea of Jon-Erik and Angel attaching themselves to him not because they were not capable; they had certainly proven themselves in spades. He was just more comfortable working alone and liked to come and go as he pleased, and with everything that had transpired so far, he was just not confident in his ability to protect them at this stage.

The food was now ready and the table was set. Angel came out arm in arm with Tina who looked a little more refreshed and actually hungry.

The group dug in and enjoyed the feast with beer and wine flowing freely. After the meal, Joey revealed a mouthwatering apple pie topped with slices of cheddar cheese and even though everyone was full from the meal, dessert was quickly devoured.

After dinner was finished and the dishes were cleaned up, everyone sat with their drinks around the woodstove which was stoked with wood to the brim giving off wonderful warmth as the temperature was plummeting to -20 degrees and getting colder.

"How the hell can people live up here all year round?" asked Jon-Erik trying to break the ice.

"The people up here will take this any day over the pollution, noise and overcrowding of the cities. They are a proud hardy breed, who love all the seasons alike," said Rollie.

"Yeah, nine months of winter with a dash of rain and thunderstorms thrown in for a changeup," chuckled Joey succeeding in lightening the mood.

"When it is beautiful up here, it's spectacular. Why do you think so many people make the commute from the city each weekend in the summer and sometimes even in the winter to ski and snowmobile?"

"Fair enough Rollie, so we are out of here first light. Tina and I will head straight to Guido's who will safely tuck us away somewhere. What are the rest of you doing?" asked Joey.

"Rollie?" asked Angel.

"I move better and am more comfortable on my own. No offense Angel and Jon-Erik. Have you thought of anywhere you can go where you would be relatively safe?"

"There is a place on Queen St. in the Beaches that rents furnished apartments on a weekly basis very close to where my apartment was years ago. It caters to business people and people who are visiting the area for a short time. The owner is a friend and he always keeps a unit free in case of emergencies and this is definitely one," replied Jon-Erik.

"And Angel and I know the area well and the unit has a good view of the street so we can see most comings and goings. Makes the best sense for us right now."

"Good, I'm turning in as I have a long day tomorrow," Rollie said with a yawn holding his even larger belly after that meal while Joey threw a big hunk of left over steak Mindy's way who wolfed the meat down with one gulp looking for more.

"I'll second that emotion, Tina and I have some sleep and other things to catch up on," scooping his fiancée up in his arms heading for their room with the large Kangal in tow leaving Angel and Jon-Erik cuddling by the fire.

"God, four people. Why did this have to happen?" asked Angel the tears coming again.

"God had nothing to do with this. It was the greed and corruption of people, plain and simple. We have to thank God that we all are still alive, without him we would not be here to talk about it," whispered Jon-Erik.

"Sounds like you have found religion. Well, let's head back to our room and I'll show you something that definitely will put a tear or two in your eye as well. I am wired as hell and I know only one way to take the edge off and I promise you it will be more than a religious experience."

And with that, she pulled an anything but reluctant Jon-Erik via his quickly stiffening erection to their room where she was all over him, and he lost himself into his gorgeous but insatiable Angel. He was totally intoxicated by her and lost count of how many times they orgasmed and finally fell asleep. Jon-Erik was still tightly wedged inside the love of his life and for this short time, they both felt safe, totally secure and happy, not caring about what was lurking around the corner. Lurking and waiting.

Chapter 62

The Reporter worked for one of the three large city Newspapers. All the Papers were biased these days and supported those who were most in line with their views and of course greased the right palms, as after all, it was a matter of survival. Especially with the onslaught of electronic media such as blogging, Facebook, Twitter and many others were knocking on the door of the multitude of computers and hand held devices out there.

To the Reporter's amusement, everyone fancied themselves an expert on what was going on in regards to criminality, politics and anything else that happened to flash across their screens.

He had been working as a reporter for many years and had won many awards for getting the scoop on rival news sources, breaking stories and being un-corruptible, as truthful as one could be in that business.

Of course as a result, he had more enemies than friends spanning the police force, local and provincial government. As far as he was concerned, some of the more than well connected movers and shakers of this great city were determined to mold it into their own ideals rather than the majority of the hard working peoples' ideals.

One of the major stories that really made him chuckle was the current plight the city's new Mayor was currently going through; constantly facing a nonstop barrage of media heat while he in fact was actually trying to do some good for a city that had been abused by corrupt and self-serving politicians for a long time.

He actually felt empathy for this beleaguered elected official but would not go near this one with a ten foot pole as there was enough coverage on this story already and any voice of reason would be drowned out by the hungry wolf pack mentality of the media looking for blood.

The Reporter received more than his share of flack from his editor and other higher ups for not offering up a stitch on this media frenzy. He had come across something much more intriguing to him and held them off with promises he was working on something much bigger which would take time to uncover.

The fact that everyone was knee deep in the Mayor's story gave him the leeway to pursue something that had puzzled him for a long time. What frustrated him was that he was making very little progress and every time he thought a door was opening to him, five more would close loudly in his face.

Ever since FinCo had made such a dramatic rise in the financial market, the Reporter had his suspicions. Most major banks and financial institutions spent years, even decades rising to their dominating positions of wealth and influence whereas FinCo had essentially come from obscurity to prominence in a few short years, which was unheard of.

Because the media was so wrapped up in the city's mayoral scandal, which had been going on for the last year and a half or so, no one paid much attention to financial news especially with the stock market leveling out since the crash of 2008. To the Reporter, however, something stank to high heaven here and it wasn't the Soya plant on the Lakeshore.

A number of things did not quite add up and would only be noticeable to someone attempting to connect the dots and that was the Reporter's specialty having broken some major stories this way. The first thing that puzzled him was how little information he could dig up about Richard Rasmussin, the president and CEO of FinCo. Other than the fact he had credentials that showed him to be a Harvard graduate and had some impressive financial designations, the guy was a total mystery.

Even Harvard would not divulge any information about Richard other than he was a graduate from there and he detected more than a touch of nervousness even at the mention of his name.

As a matter of fact, every inquiry about Richard ended up netting very little other than the usual upstanding corporate citizen spin and how active he was supporting local charities. The Reporter had repeatedly attempted to interview people at FinCo about Richard right up to his executive staff but the response was always the same; Richard and his staff did not give interviews.

Secondly, the Reporter always had his ear to the ground when it came to the city's crime beat and he sensed something big had happened lately, almost like a realignment of some sort but nobody was talking. Normally, someone always had something to say which made this so abnormal.

Thirdly, the story about a dead guy found wrapped around a prominent historical statue a number of weeks ago should have been huge but very quickly fizzled out. When the Reporter checked with his insiders all he could get was that it was under investigation and nothing else.

Finally, a news story just broke out of northern Ontario where four individuals with ties to crime in the area had disappeared off the face of the earth. As the story goes, these people were suspects in a blotched home invasion near Parry Sound and then vanished without a trace. Interviews with next of kin, friends and relatives had produced nothing other than the fact that no one had been seen again since the night of the alleged crime.

The O.P.P. had traced the two abandoned snowmobiles to a Norris Allen and a Clyde Smith of Parry Sound. That led them to two other individuals that these two malcontents associated with and the thing in common was that all four had just vanished. A couple of them still lived at home and the other two were shacked up with their girlfriends and no one close to them had any idea what had happened to them.

The police executed search warrants of their homes and work places but besides some stashed away money and small quantities of marijuana, nothing turned up. The stories were all the same, the four had gone out late the last night they were seen to help some friends who were stuck in a ditch outside of town due to the weather. This, of course, was proven false when the friends in question were tracked down and verified having been at the local watering hole in town making nuisances of themselves as usual.

The very thin thread that connected this weird story to FinCo and Richard Rasmussin was that it ended up by overturning stone after stone. The Reporter had found out that two of the four people that were at the house where the invasion had taken place were former contractors working for FinCo and Richard Rasmussin.

And now, it turned out that the two ladies along with their fiancées had also disappeared and had not turned up back to their Toronto West End Lakeshore homes.

Further digging led to even more bizarre information which made the Reporter think he was definitely on to something huge, but was not even close to understanding what it was. Sketchy information about a kidnapping and unharmed recovery as well as a damaged home from gunshots was uncovered after a lot of prodding of his sources within the Toronto police.

After much more detailed research, the reporter uncovered that these four individuals were involved in a complicated crime syndicate story that spanned all the way to South America a number of years ago and miraculously emerged unscathed. And here again, 5 years later, the same four seemed to be knee deep in another pile of steaming manure.

He wondered if this was just an un-lucky coincidence or did these people just have a knack for it? And what if there was any relation to what was happening now to the events of a number of years ago?

The Reporter knew he had connected dots that the police for whatever reason had failed to and was undecided on the next steps to take. If he submitted what he had, he could have gotten offers to write romance fiction for one of these publishing houses that churned this kind of stuff to fill the shelves at the local Walmart and Target stores, however, his career as a crime beat reporter would be cut short due to total lack of concrete evidence.

He would have to do much more research before he brought anything to his editor, that was for certain. But the Reporter was on the trail of something and the funky smell of it was wafting across his nostrils as he loved the hunt and the chase. This was why he loved his profession so much and few did it better.

Chapter 63

Richard Rasmussin was vicious, cruel and nothing fazed him but something was definitely wrong within his vast empire. First Christine Hertzog was nowhere to be found. That was no great loss to Richard, she had outlived her usefulness and Richard had planned to get rid of her sooner than later anyway. The fact that she knew what she knew and still could be out there somewhere, and no one including his inner circle had any information whatsoever, plagued him. He would ratchet up the pressure, someone had to know something.

To top things off, his right hand man, Elmo Entwhistle, was now on the missing list. His slimy sidekick, Jimmy Rudiger had no clue as to Elmo's whereabouts and could only speculate that the big sicko was shacked up with one of his younger love interests' somewhere but he was not answering his phone calls, the phone just going to voice mail.

Richard and Jimmy sat in Richard's spacious office overlooking a cold and dreary looking Lake Ontario and Richard was fuming to say the least.

"What the hell is going on Jimmy? I need some answers and need them yesterday?"

"Boss, we have eyes and ears everywhere and nothing is coming in. I have just found out that Elmo was on a recruitment run last night. One of our admins is forwarding the information to us as we speak," Jimmy said looking at his cell phone.

Jimmy studied his phone display looking like he had seen a ghost which managed to upset Richard even more.

"Out with it. What has happened?"

"Apparently Elmo was seeing some rich skinflint named Marten in the Beaches area of the city last night. Turns out this guy's whole house was leveled by some sort of explosion. Nothing left and so far no sign of any survivors. Cops, fire and ambulance are still all over the place with their fingers up their backsides."

"What else?" snarled Richard.

"Some more stuff coming in. Apparently our people have just found Elmo's vehicle parked on a side street locked and empty."

"Get someone to tow it out there before the city does and it is traced back to us somehow, now!" screamed Richard. Jimmy had never seen his boss so upset before and issued the orders immediately.

Richard got on his own phone and barked a few orders and immediately promoted two individuals from the ranks to take Elmo's and Christine's place.

He had to keep things running at least for now and there were a pool of up and comers just waiting for the opportunity to impress him and right now he was anything but impressed.

"Get into every hole and crevice of this damn city, province and country and find out what the hell is going on," Richard directed looking like a demon possessed.

After Jimmy had barked some more instructions into his cell, Richard poured them each a stiff triple shot of Vodka before beginning to review what they did know.

"Christine and Elmo have disappeared; someone sent us a message via Elmo's twin, someone else impersonated me and was killed in my condo. What the hell is going on?" questioned Richard in between pouring himself more Vodka.

"Not to mention that Angel and Tina and their boyfriends have pulled the old vanishing act," said Jimmy.

"Who is running the furniture store right now?" asked Richard.

"From what we have found out, a group of Italian goombas are part of Tina's boyfriend's family. These guys are armed and look like they can handle themselves, to say the least."

"And these clowns are not part of our organization?"

"Most organized crime is but there are still pockets out there such as this. The Italians are a proud people and do not look kindly upon someone messing with family."

"Make a note to get this rectified and teach these schmucks a lesson they will never forget. But first, we have bigger fish to fry. There is obviously some group of very lucky or extremely skillful individuals looking to discredit us who work outside the law, the same as we do."

"There must be some sort of tie in to these people and with Angel and Tina too. We have come up empty there, so far," Jimmy indicated.

"And finally, this unknown ultra-skillful killer is operating with his own agenda. He obviously has me in his sights judging by what happened with Elmo's clone and my condo. Only a person with incredible skill could have pulled that off and I have no doubt this ghost is knee deep in all of this. I will figure out a way to draw him out and I will show him hell like even one such as him would not imagine," growled Richard.

"How about the guy impersonating you?" asked Jimmy.

"I think that was an isolated incident and no relationship to everything else that has occurred. And that stalking Assassin actually did me a favor as that impersonating bastard had somehow gained access to a few of our accounts and had begun siphoning money into his own But our systems people caught it and reversed the transactions before any damage was done. As a matter of fact, we drained that insect's accounts on top of that, he will no longer be needing the money," chuckled Richard.

"Good one boss, so what are our next steps?"

"I fear Christine and Elmo have been erased. I am going to take steps to sell off FinCo. A lot of our competitors are like wolves at the door and we can use the proceeds to shore up our underground inter-ests locally and internationally. FinCo was really just a front to launder money for the Kirotchenkos and never really my cup of Vodka."

Jimmy looked concerned with this latest news.

"Don't worry my loyal weasely friend. I will take you and a few loyal members of our team with me, the rest that know anything will join their brethren in the cold depth of the lake. It will take them years to figure out the scams we were running and by that time it will be too late, and nothing will be traceable back to us. What do you say?"

"Sounds great, boss. One more thing, word is some reporter is nosing around. What do we do about him?"

"As soon as our shares are on the open market, give him the exclusive and let him know that the ex-ecutives of FinCo are retiring out to their yacht on the Spanish Riviera. One of the few places we don't have one, as yet, but will soon. And don't worry, Tina will lead us to wherever these ingrates are hiding out and I will finish them off once and for all if I have to do the job myself, no mistakes. They will not know what hit them my slimy brother from another mother!"

And with that the meeting was adjourned. There was much to do, Richard and Jimmy wasting no time getting at the task at hand. As soon as a price per share had been determined, FinCo was put up for sale and of course a bidding war erupted. The Reporter was fed the exclusive which he had to submit for print otherwise his paper would have been scooped by one of the other papers or financial publications.

He, however, thought this was more suspicious than ever, given the facts that he had gathered up so far.

He asked to get an interview with Richard Rasmussin and the word came back that Richard was already out of the country and would not give interviews. The same was asked of Jimmy Rudiger who also respectfully declined as there were not enough hours in the day as he had to wrap up a business and tie up all the knots.

Since it was one of the prerequisites to be single to work for FinCo, in any sort of higher capacity, no one would miss them. Easy to round up the shocked staff that had been given their walking papers with generous settlements that were worth nothing more than the paper the figures were written on.

They were quietly and quickly dispatched by people in Richard's underground, and shipped out by freighter to the middle of the freezing cold Lake Ontario where they were wrapped up, weighted down and slung overboard to meet the many that had previously shared their fate.

The bodies most likely would never be found due to the immense depth and murky bottom of the lake. But if they ever were, Richard and his cronies planned to be far, far away on some isolated tropical isle as Stoltenhoff just did not have the climate Richard liked.

Things were moving quickly and according to plan allowing Richard to retreat to his secluded west end home and Jimmy had a date with a poker table in Niagara Falls. Richard expected a call from Tina at any time since she had changed locations and that was the key to the drugs and hypnotic suggestions given to her.

Of course, all this wheeling and dealing had made him horny as hell as he made the call for two of the best girls in his many stables.

They were oriental and had tricks up their sleeve that would bring dead men back to life. Some highest quality opium, champagne, the finest beluga caviar with a number of bottles of Stolichnaya would round out this party. Richard felt in control again and that was the only way that was acceptable for him.

Chapter 64

Mikhail was anxious, concerned and majorly upset and angry at the same time. He still had no idea where Angel was, so tracking her was his highest priority. He sat cross legged in his Port Credit hideaway and focused his immense energy on one target, to pinpoint where she was. This was a talent that the Shape Shifter had acquired with years of meditation and constant practice tuning in on the life force or chi of an individual to eventually pinpoint their current location.

After about an hour of being immersed in this trance like state, the Monster stood up, stretched his arm and leg muscles and pumped out 500 pushups and sit-ups with cat like agility and ferocious strength.

He had discovered what he was after. Angel was safe and sound in an apartment in the East End Beaches area. Her lover must have gone back to the area he felt safest in and knew best. How ironic was it that he was just there a short while ago dispatching one of Richard Rasmussin's key cronies. At that time however, he had no sense that Angel was in the area. She most likely was not there earlier.

The Shaker of Souls got into his tinted Ford truck and headed to the Beaches which was now just a short drive away. It was nearing dusk and all the commuters were tucked away in their under spaced and overpriced domiciles. The apartment that came to him in his vision was right on the main street, the second floor facing the street. His climbing acrobatics would not be of much use to him now as Queen Street was still fairly busy with people scurrying about and doing last minute errands before settling in for the night.

It was cold and unpleasantly damp outside and the threat of more snow hung in the air. Mikhail decided the best approach here was the direct approach so he buzzed the apartment in question. "Who is it?" questioned a male voice suspiciously.

"One you should not leave out in the cold if you know what is good for you. And you know I can find other more inventive and drastic ways to enter," Mikhail answered.

The reply was the buzz of the entrance opening. The Killer glid noiselessly up the stairs to an open door at the top and entered the small furnished unit with both of his massive arms folded and no expression on his wolfish face, his gold tooth catching a reflection from the street light below.

Jon-Erik sat on the couch, remained motionless; having learned his lessons well from previous encounters with this demon in human form. Angel closed the door behind him and took her place be-side her man but not before going to the small bar and pouring them each a shot of Vodka, a triple for their mysterious and deadly house guest.

"You are indeed both learning well," Mikhail said as he downed the glass with one gulp licking his lips and gesturing for a refill.

This time Jon-Erik got up, took the glass from the Monster and filled it with more Vodka before return-ing it to him. He could taste and smell his own fear as he did this. So could Mikhail while he downed his second triple shot.

As Jon-Erik got up to refill him again, Mikhail ac-cepted the glass before gesturing him to take his seat beside Angel.

"I thank you for your hospitality and do not wish to cause you further stress. You most likely have had enough already."

"How did you find us?" asked Angel.

"How is not important. Just know that I am always close but even one such as I cannot be in two places at the same time. And that is where I lost track of you. I sense you both have been through trauma. What has happened?"

Angel took a sip of her own drink to calm her-self before answering," Rollie set us up in a hideaway up north. But they found us straight away and four thugs tried to kill us. They did not succeed. Jon-Erik and I, with a lot of luck on our side, were able to kill all of them before they could do any harm to us."

The Monster flexed his facial muscles before answering," You have admirable survival skills and I sense they are becoming stronger and more developed daily."

"Killing is horrible nonetheless," said Angel almost ready to tear up again but she wanted to remain strong especially in his presence.

"We differ on that, which you already know. They are tracking you somehow. Most likely, via your friend Tina since she was taken by them. The fact that you split up is good for you, bad for her and her man."

"How?" asked Jon-Erik.

"That I do not know but my guess is via some drug or hypnotic suggestion or a combination of both. She needs to be watched, she does not even know what she is doing most likely."

"Damn, my best friend is a puppet for them?" asked Angel.

"Exactly, but she will lead us right to the one I will destroy. He is as deadly and as dangerous as they come, except for me of course. I will draw him out and play with him like a cat with a toy before I send him to hell."

"Stay away from Tina and you will remain safe. I will contact you again when the trap is set. I have already eliminated one of his lieutenants, the slug they called Elmo Entwhistle. The real one this time," Mikhail snarled as he turned to leave.

"I may give you your first lesson in the elimination of a gnat, when you are ready Angel. I will be in touch." And with that the large predator disappeared without a sound from whence he came, the door closing softly behind him.

"That guy scares the living you know what out of me!" exclaimed Jon-Erik.

"You and me both but thankfully, he is on our side this time around, although that could change any-time, knowing what we know about him," said Angel.

"I don't think so. He will protect you to the end just as he did several years ago. And now, he will re-main closer since he lost track of you once," reasoned Jon-Erik.

"Stress like this always makes me wet baby," Angel purred and was all over her lover in an instant as Jon-Erik once again got fully lost in his Angel.

Chapter 65

The first call Jon-Erik made was to Rollie, who was in a meeting with Detective Alf Cragan. He very quickly relayed where they were and what had just happened. Rollie was stunned to say the least and went to a private room to continue the conversation telling Cragan he would fill him in afterwards.

"So you think they have been tracking you guys via Tina? It certainly would account for a lot," said Rollie.

"Yes, but it looks to us like Tina and Joey are in terrible danger," replied Jon-Erik.

"Here is the thing. I'm not sure if we can protect the two of them more than their family can," speculated Rollie.

Jon-Erik put their secure phone on speaker enabling Angel to join the conversation.

"When it comes to protecting one of their own, Joey's family are no slouches, and they will have them somewhere that is not easy to breach," continued Jon-Erik.

"We are going to have to alert Joey to the fact that Tina could be the reason why we have been so easily found by this never ending group of assassins they are sending our way," added Angel.

"Absolutely, but we need to think this thing through carefully. It may be our opportunity to trap this bastard once and for all, and if we can cut the head off the snake hopefully the body will die as well."

"And Mikhail is now tuned in to this and wants Richard Rasmussin even more than we do," said Angel.

"Ideally that would be the preferable scenario all around but we cannot afford to be complacent. And we have no idea whether this psycho will take things in his own hands this time or farm out the work again to the never ending parade of thugs and lowlifes this guy most likely has at his disposal."

"Agreed, so what are the next steps?" asked Jon-Erik.

"First, we need to warn Joey. Leave that with me. Secondly, we are going to stake out from a safe distance where Tina and Joey are once we find that out. Nothing against Guido and the family but the more eyes and ears are out there, the better," advised Rollie.

"So what do you expect us to do, just sit tight and wait for things to happen?" asked Angel with obvious frustration in her voice.

"That's what I would suggest for now but obviously I can't force you to do anything. Whatever you do....stay safe. As Mikhail indicated, the fact that you have split up is safer for you two right now so keep that in mind. I will call you after I finish my meeting with Alf Cragan and speak with Joey. Rollie over and out for now."

"It's so damn frustrating not being able to do anything to help our friends," said Angel shaking her head making her long blond ponytail flip back and forth driving Jon-Erik crazy as usual.

And before they knew it they were back in their small bedroom tearing their clothes off one another and giving as good as they were getting. After that, they jumped in the shower needing a second shower to clean up after the stuff they were up to during the first one.

Even though their sexual energy had been temporarily satisfied, they were still antsy and not happy being cooped up in such a small unit such as this apartment. They decided to get bundled up and go for a long walk along Queen St. and then loop down to the Beach and then back to their apartment.

It was now quite late in the evening and besides a few late visitors to the 24 hour Timmy's and a few insomniacs, the street was quiet. Another round of snow had begun to fall making everything look white and clean. They walked hand in hand taking in the clean fresh air and the now pristine scenery.

"I just can't sit by and do nothing," said Angel.

"I hear you but what can we do?" replied Jon-Erik.

"Not sure as yet but we'll think of something. We always have," Angel said gripping Jon-Erik's hand tighter and quickening their pace considerably.

The two walked as far west as Woodbine Ave. and headed south past the large monumental Olympic pool that sat deserted for most of the year until they hit the boardwalk. They were just in the process of turning back east toward their temporary lodgings when Jon-Erik's phone rang.

They went under the shelter of the huge pool overhang to get out of the now thickening snow to take the phone call. It was Rollie who informed them of what he had found out so far.

Joey and Tina were at least for now safely stowed away in one of cousin Guido's relative's homes, very close to the home near Highland Creek park where the group stayed a number of years ago. This house was also on a secluded street with very few neighbors. As a matter of fact, the few homes in that area were owned by family members or relatives thereof.

This little community had eyes and ears everywhere, making it difficult if not nearly impossible to get near this secluded spot east of the Scarborough bluffs.

"That's great but what about the situation with Tina?" asked Angel after Jon-Erik handed her the phone.

"Tina is doing very well. She misses her home and you guys but otherwise seems to be very reassured by how Joey's family is treating her."

"How did Joey react when you mentioned to him about the suspicion that Tina may be the beacon leading Richard Rasmussin and his cohorts to them?"

"He was surprised to say the least but indicated he would keep a closer eye on Tina from now on."

"The other thing he said was if Mikhail's theory is correct, the damage could have already been done.

There are a number of phone extensions in this home and he hadn`t been watching Tina every minute until this was mentioned just now."

"So you are saying the bad guys may already know where they are?" questioned Angel.

"It's a possibility. The other thing that Joey said was let them come. And when they do we will have a reception planned for these bottom feeding murderers; they will not be expecting in their wildest dreams."

"I told Joey to be careful what they wish for and under no circumstances underestimate this Rasmussin. He has sent his henchmen to do his dirty work and that has not worked out well for him so far. This time he may look to handle things himself," added Rollie.

"We need to contact Mikhail and let him know where they are. Maybe with him out there Richard will get a surprise he did not bargain for."

"Can you contact him?" questioned Rollie.

"He seems to know when and where to find us. Knowing him, he will be waiting at our door when we get back to our apartment. We'll let you know. Over and out for now," said Angel ending the call.

And before Jon-Erik could even fully put the phone away, a large shadow separated itself from the dark recesses of the nooks and crannies of the Swimming Pool structure, the glimmer of the huge gold tooth from the boardwalk light giving the Shape Shifter away.

"As I have said over and over, I am always nearby. Where are they hiding out?" snarled Mikhail.

Angel and Jon-Erik knew better than to hold anything back from this nightmare walking the earth and calmly gave him the information asked for.

"So what will you do?" asked Angel, knowing that simpler was better with this dangerous denizen of the shadows.

"I am torn between guarding you and eliminating this gnat that is behind all the threats directed against you. You are safe for now but your friends are the magnets that will draw him in. And when he comes, I will be waiting and rip the flesh off his bones and feed the neighborhood wildlife with his entrails." spat out the Monster before melting back into the shadows from whence he came.

Even though Angel and Jon-Erik had had many encounters with Mikhail; the earlier ones bad, the most recent better but still massively chilling and nerve-wracking to say the least, they both still marveled how he seemed to appear and disappear at will.

"Wow hon, I wonder if someday he would ever teach me. Only the good parts of his skills, of course not the evil side of things."

"I think the good and the evil come part in parcel, you would have to taste the dark side to learn his skills and I hope you never have to. I love the Angel that I know now."

"Baby, I have already tasted the dark side and so have you. Years ago and again with what we are going through now. It's kill or be killed and we've seen killing and now participated first hand. And even though we are revolted by it, we would do it again to save each other's and our friends' lives," whispered Angel knowing she was speaking for her lover as well.

Jon-Erik said nothing but hugged her tighter as they wound their way back to their apartment on a cold, snowy winter's night both feeling that this was indeed the calm before the real storm began.

Chapter **66**

Richard Rasmussin was in a state to say the least. All the perversity, debauchery and riches in the world did not slake his thirst for revenge. Somehow four simple, insect like, insignificant people had given him more trouble than he had ever had to deal with before and he had dealt with more than most could ever dream of.

But Richard was also a realist and knew that behind every dark cloud (if he himself was not behind it) was a silver lining. FinCo had become a huge headache for him and that problem was now almost just another dark memory. The final stages of dissolving the company were almost complete and now Richard truly had squirreled away more money than God, at least in his estimation.

His multitude of criminal enterprises were flourishing and gobbling up those who had not on their own accord joined him as yet like a virus chewing up an unprotected computer hard disk.

And for every cell that was taken down somewhere in the world, a bunch of newer, more aggressive and ruthless cells took their place. Richard's succession planning was a thing of sinister brilliance and beauty. But these four individuals, with some obviously skillful and damned lucky assistance, had managed to evade him for much too long.

His training and background signaled to him just to leave these flies on the wall alone and concentrate on traveling the world in search of the finest pleasures and possessions that were his for the taking but Richard hated unfinished business and it wormed him to his core.

As he sat, in his soon to be, former new residence in the city's west end pondering his next move, the call he had been waiting for came in.

"Boss, its Jimmy. We just heard from Tina." Anyone that worked with Richard was straight to the point and direct. If they were not, their time on this earth would not be long, simple as that.

"And?" questioned Richard.

"We have the address where they have her stashed away. That's all she gave us as the post hypnotic instructed. We do not know as yet who is with her and how many are guarding her."

"About time. I will handle this personally from here on in. No more mistakes and no more casualties. The only casualties that will be invoked are the ones that I will set in motion. Wrap up things with FinCo and then stand by. We should be in a position to blow this popsicle stand of a town soon. I tire of the constantly bickering political landscape here and the more bribes I send their way, the more they expect."

"Good luck Boss," said Jimmy Rudiger, the last and the most cockroach like to remain of Richard's crew in Toronto, who fully intended to remain that way and reap the rewards of what laid ahead.

Richard had no idea where this obscure address in the extreme east end of Scarborough was but he was not a fool to go in halfcocked. He would go in fully loaded and then some. He put out a few exploratory phone calls and when the responses came in shortly thereafter, as those in his organization knew to delay was to sign your own death sentence, was not anywhere near pleased.

That address along with a lot of other homes in at that area belong to the pesky and elusive Agricola family who thus far had avoided doing business with Richard's organization by staying strong and steadfast as well as claiming safety in numbers.

There were over one hundred family members active in a variety of legal and not so legal business ventures in the greater Toronto area and they protected each other zealously to say the least. To this point, Richard had decided to stay away from this group as they kept totally to themselves and meddled in no one's affairs but their own.

As it turned out in this case, however, Joey the fiancé of their own homing beacon Tina, unbeknownst to herself, was a member of this now more than ever annoying clan.

Richard sat back and weighed his options as he always did unless he got too keyed up and threw caution into the wind and went on impulse alone. That had served him well before but these people had caused him enough aggravation to this point.

His options were very simple really; he could go in there gangbusters and take out as many family members as he could in the course of reaching his targets and eliminating them once and for all. It could even be staged to look like a large gang war which kind of appealed to him being the sadist that he was but he had no desire to lose any more of his soldiers as they were required to staff his many local ventures.

The next possibility open to him was to go in there using his honed Ninja skills and eliminate the four fugitives right under their protectors' noses. What bothered him, however, was the fact that their mysterious benefactor possessed some uncanny skills which rivaled or even surpassed his own.

His highly tuned senses smelled a trap and his intuition was seldom wrong. He would test his skills against this Ninjitzu practitioner but at a time, place and circumstance of his choosing. Knowing your surroundings was always a huge advantage and Richard always ensured all the cards were stacked in his favor.

With that thought in mind, a plan was forming in his twisted but highly logical mind. He had to eliminate this Ninja killer from the equation and then he could toy with his prey like the shark in shallow water that he was.

In order to eliminate this enigma, he had to draw him out and Richard now had a fool proof plan to do just that and his adrenaline kicked into high gear just at the thought of this inevitable confrontation. It also kicked his other appetites into high gear barking a few commands in Russian to the two gorgeous naked ladies sprawled out in all their glory on his huge sectional sofa.

On cue the ladies started doing things to each other that most people would only dream of doing or having done to them and once Richard was fully aroused, he jumped into their midst and took them and took them again and again until they screamed for mercy exhausted, raw and sore. And then he took them once again to drive home the point that he was their master and they were there to please him as they definitely would not like the alternative. No one ever did.

Chapter 67

Surveillance was a bitch under the best circumstances and it had descended on the quiet and already protected to the hilt suburb of the West End of Scarborough where the Agricola family resided with a vengeance. Everyone in the family who lived in the surrounding area was now on high alert and even the German shepherd, Rottweiler and Pit bull dogs that most of the family employed were more on edge pacing in their back yards and sniffing the air nervously.

Pit bulls were an illegal breed of dog in Ontario due to their aggression and fighting skills but since the Agricola family pretty well owned this whole remote area everyone backed each other up and the authorities were none the wiser.

Rollie Sampson was just on the cusp of completing a long and frustrating discussion with Detective Alf Cragan which was partially rewarding but mostly unfruitful and downright frustrating. Rollie had laid everything out on the table with the exception of what had really happened near Parry Sound.

Even though Cragan was somewhat sympathetic to the ongoing plight of Rollie's friends and from what Rollie had ascertained, the main problem was there was not a shred of proof to implicate Richard Rasmussin.

Yes, it would be convenient to implicate Richard for the kidnapping of Tina, the gun violence at the homes and business of the four companions as well as the attack up north but the proof was in the pudding and the pudding was nowhere in sight.

Alf Cragan indicated he could really not get involved until some sort of hard evidence came to light although he did find it personally suspicious that Richard Rasmussin seemed to be wrapping up his financial interests in Toronto rather abruptly.

Of course, there was no law against dissolving a company unless laws were broken but no one was saying a thing or implicating anyone. So Rollie was left to his own devices and those devices pointed him to the entrance of the tight knit community nestled by Lake Ontario and flanked by over 100 feet of the steep and rocky Scarborough bluffs.

After discussions with Guido and Joey Agricola, it was mutually decided that Rollie would station his car in a driveway of one of the family members that lived just outside of the complex and he would work in tandem with the family to ensure a 24 hour seven day a week watch was executed on whom entered and exited the complex. A quick wave of the hand from the residents of the community coming and going was the signal to those on watch.

Mail delivery was not an issue since the community mail boxes were all located outside the complex so no mail delivery people had need to enter. But other delivery, courier, repair and utility drivers had to be able to enter and exit at will since it was not a gated community. As a result, they were meticulously scrutinized.

But the Agricola clan was Italian and Italians loved their pizza and even though most members of the family were encouraged to order by phone and pick up, a few still opted for the convenience of delivery after a hard working day or the beginning of a weekend.

And the pizza of choice was always Frizolli's Village Pizza, just a short distance away. But for this next delivery, Frizolli's would have a new driver, one not familiar with the area. Old Franco Frizolli knew better than to argue with one that looked like the devil himself come to visit an old pizza maker in human form.

The uniform, hair tied in a ponytail under the delivery cap and a cheap pair of sunglasses helped round out the disguise for Richard Rasmussin. And he did not have long to wait until the first call came from an address within the compound. There were delivery calls to other areas that Frizolli's served but Richard was only interested in one location; the other driver was told to go to the local watering hole for a few cold ones and not ask any questions if he knew what was good for him. He did what he was told, the alternative was not very attractive and he could picture himself shot through the brainstem and then flung over the bluffs like a sack of garbage.

Richard used the GPS in the disgusting looking vehicle at least by his standards to find the location of the delivery which just happened to be one street away from the address that housed Joey and Tina according to his Intel. He hated the smell of the extra-large loaded pie which reminded him of the sewage in the allies of mother Russia and made him wonder how people chose to eat such slop not even fit for wild boars that preferred their food alive and kicking.

The best approach was always the most direct for Richard but since he was on a scouting mission, he decided to do a drive around just to see what he could see. And what he saw surprised him to say the least. The area was definitely family oriented but his heightened senses felt eyes on him every turn he made. To get a better feel, he actually spoke to a few of the people in the area pretending he was lost since he was a new driver.

Even though the people were polite they eyed him suspiciously with darting eyes and cautious body language. Before actually delivering the pizza, he decided to have a look at the address that Tina had given him. Unfortunately, he could only do a quick drive by or else he would arouse suspicion. He had a feeling that they had this area locked up tighter than a drum and anything or anyone that seemed even remotely out of place would be closely scrutinized at best.

Richard slowed down to a dull crawl when he turned onto the street in question and kicked his detail recall abilities in high gear. *Ordinary enough looking bungalow, decent size front yard with porch and a nicely manicured and landscaped front lawn.* What really caught Richard's roving eye was that the home looked to be backing right onto the bluffs themselves which most likely made them feel safe from any assaults coming at them from the back.

His highly developed vision also picked up Tina's silhouette behind the sheer curtains so Richard knew his Intel was sound. What he did not know was whether or not Angel and her pesky fiancée were there too. He had no choice but to continue to drive by and make the turn onto the next street and complete his delivery and then taking this clunky delivery vehicle back to a still shaken Frizolli, who swore on his mother's grave that he would say nothing to anyone about his extremely temporary driver.

Good for him, as Richard would just as easily have killed old Franco on the spot, or so he told him. In reality, killing this old geezer would have resulted in more questions and a police presence in the area which was just not worth the aggravation at this stage. His plan was to go in quietly and eliminate this pesky group of meddlers while not even disturbing the constant breezes coming off the lake. Now he knew how he would accomplish it if he could only get the smell from that lousy pizza out of his nostrils.

He would be back and tonight was the night. They would receive a visit from the Night Caller shortly and one they would take to their graves. Besides the normal suspicious glances thrown the pizza driver's way, the hungry eyes of a lone Wolf on the prowl noticed something in the bearing of this pizza driver that was far beyond ordinary.

The Monster knew tonight would be the night and he would be beyond ready. And beyond was where he intended to send this crafty killer. Straight to hell with no ticket back and no mercy. The thought of that put an evil grin on his face as he sat unseen in a clump of thick bushes in a neighboring parkette that was deserted due to the snow and cold weather. The cold snow and blowing wind was mild in comparison to what he experienced in the old country and it just sharpened his already on edge senses.

He licked his lips in anticipation and produced a pocket flask full of vodka and took a healthy swig and then repeated himself, the strong liquid warming his insides making him even more dangerous and alert than normal. Let him come.

Chapter 68

Night descended on the little West Hill hamlet that housed the Agricola clan and it was a bitterly cold one. Even the Monster was becoming a tad uncomfortable in his parkette roost but he was in that place where his breathing had slowed down to next to nothing and all his senses were on high alert and overdrive.

Joey and Tina had settled into a movie and cousin Guido decided to take Mindy's brother Maxi, an even larger male Kangal dog out for a romp in the snow. And like the calm before an approaching storm, Richard slunk his way across the snowy and icy bluffs as surefooted as a Tibetan mountain goat. The going was slow, however, and he was glad that the latter portion of his hastily devised plan would call for him to leave much more comfortably than he came.

Unfortunately, for the Shape Shifter his observation perch only allowed him a sightline to the side of the house where Tina and Joey were stashed and he could not readily leave his post without being seen. Once it was pitch black he would use the shadows to get a closer look.

Richard finally arrived at the back of the safe house. He sniffed the air and listened carefully and flattened himself against the back of the house as he heard Guido and the large dog come back in from their walk. But even Maxi's well developed senses could not pick up the danger out back as the dog was still stoked and happy from the walk with his master.

This would be definitely even more difficult than Richard imagined with the dog now in the house but he had come too far to turn back now. First thing was first and that was to get into the house without being seen or heard.

Easy enough for one of his talents to pick the lock on the back door and slither inside like the black mamba snake that he was. The first obstacle was the dog who just happened to trot into the kitchen for a munch after its invigorating walk. Maxi did not know what hit him when the potent poison from the blow dart entered the blood stream causing the dog just to lay down and go to sleep permanently.

When Guido went to see how Maxi was progressing with his dinner, he was gagged and restrained faster than the eye could see. The only reason cousin Guido was still breathing, he was needed for the bold escape plan ahead.

Two down - two to go and Richard was not even breathing hard as yet. He never did. His plan for Joey was quick and decisive. A step behind, snapping his neck like a rotten branch and before Tina could even comprehend what was happening; her fiancée was lying lifeless on the couch.

Just as she readied herself to emit a bloodcurdling scream, she was quickly gagged and restrained with extra strong duct tape. Only things still functional were her screaming brain and her legs. Now, for the easy part. Richard's earlier scouting mission had shown him that the house had an adjoined garage which could be entered from the house.

He quickly pushed both Tina and Guido into the garage, grabbed the car keys off the conveniently located hook and stuffed Tina in the trunk. So far he was on schedule, this whole operation taking about three minutes, give or take, a few seconds.

Next part was crucial and he whispered some quick but concise instructions to Guido. *Do as you are told to do or die* — simple as that. Guido also still totally stunned by what was occurring could only nod.

Richard removed Guido's gag, removed his restraints and climbed into the passenger seat beside him. Guido engaged the garage door opener and drove off into the night no one giving him a second glance except Mikhail thinking he was going out to fetch a last minute errand. A huge mistake, but even the Monster had no inkling as to what had just happened under his nose as the TV in the house was still playing the movie Tina and Joey had begun to watch.

But a deep instinct told him he should have a closer look. And when he peeked into the front window from the shadows of the oncoming night, he knew he had been duped as he saw Joey's lifeless body slouched over on the couch.

Like a flash of lightning, he entered the house through the back door which Richard had left unlocked in case he had to make an unscheduled exit and saw the dead dog on the kitchen floor near his bowl.

If it could not get any worse, Rollie, Angel and Jon-Erik came bursting through the front door scant moments later looking like the cavalry that had arrived too late. Mikhail was sitting cross legged on the floor and Angel held her companions back knowing very well that this was not the time to pressure the Ninja as if any time was. His face told the story that he had been beaten to the punch.

When Angel and Jon-Erik saw Joey's lifeless body on the couch, it was Rollie's turn to hold his friends back as he knew this was now a crime scene and there was no way to even begin to cover this one up.

"No one touch anything," ordered Rollie.

While Jon-Erik held Angel who was choking back her tears and Mikhail stayed in his state of apparent meditation, Rollie put on a pair of rubber gloves he always carried with him through force of habit and checked Joey's body.

He found no pulse and discovered his neck was hanging down without support from his head. "He is gone, his neck has been broken," said Rollie. "What happened here?" his icy stare directed squarely at the grounded Executioner.

"Address me with the respect I deserve or I will finish the job I should have years ago," growled Mikhail slowly raising himself to his full height and size.

"I was too late," the Executioner added.

"What did you see," asked Angel regaining some of her composure.

"I had the house under surveillance and saw the garage open and a car drive away. Something about the look on the driver's face told me something was not right. The back door was unlocked and now you see what I saw."

Rollie toned his questioning down considerably not wanting to antagonize the Shape Shifter any further as all he had tried to do was help out.

"Is there anyone else in the house?" asked Rollie.

"No one I can sense alive or dead."

"So it looks as if Guido and Tina are gone, most likely abducted in that car," speculated Rollie.

"I will find him and end all his nine lives, this I vow!" growled Mikhail.

"What are we going to do now?" sobbed Jon-Erik also choking back tears for his fallen best friend.

Rollie did not immediately answer but went into the kitchen to check on the also lifeless dog, immediately noticed the dart protruding from the animal's neck.

"Looks as if he was poisoned; the blow dart is still imbedded. The perp obviously did not have time to remove it."

"The perp is Richard Rasmussen and there is no place on earth he can hide," screamed Angel with a fury that amazed Jon-Erik and Mikhail in different degrees and made them both proud.

"I'm going to call this in with a 911 call. But you all need to be long gone from here when the police arrive as all hell is going to break loose," indicated Rollie.

"Even you have not seen the hell that this Richard Rasmussen will," snarled the Executioner.

"Mikhail, can you take Angel and Jon-Erik somewhere safe?" asked Rollie.

"Yes, I will take them to my lair. They will contact you after you wrap this up. It looks like we will work together against this powerful enemy from now on as he will not stop until he eliminates all of you."

With a gesture for Angel and Jon-Erik to follow him out the back entrance, Mikhail made his exit totally unspectacularly; when you consider his usual antics. There was nothing more to say. Angel and Jon-Erik followed him into the cold night noticing how quickly and carefully he eliminated their footprints in the snow.

This left Rollie to place the call knowing this whole area would be crawling with police in a matter of minutes; no way was this going to be swept under the rug. Joey deserved more than that.

Rollie Sampson placed his first call to Alf Cragan quickly apprised him of the situation. Alf thanked him for the heads up and that he would square it with his superiors to be on site under the guise that this was related to other cases he had been working on, which could not be closer to the truth.

His next call was the 911 call where he advised the operator he was a private detective visiting friends and came upon a deceased male and dog. He was asked to remain on the scene; police and ambulance were on their way.

He took his gloves off and put them back in his pocket and sat in a chair holding his head and wondering how the hell things had gotten to this. Why did someone else have to die to fuel this madman's ambition? And he could not tell the police his suspicions as again there was no proof direct or indirect that Richard Rasmussen was involved in this travesty.

And where had this psycho taken Tina and Guido and what would be his next move? He was so tired and wished he could lay his head down for a while to clear it and refresh his thoughts but no time for that now as the police and ambulance sirens pierced the still night causing the neighbors to wake up and realize that their worst fears had become true. War had come to their family and neighborhood.

Chapter **69**

A convoy of ambulances, police vehicles and even a fire truck for good measure descended on this east end hamlet. Detective Alf Cragan arrived shortly after and spoke briefly with the commanding officer on the scene. The area was expertly cordoned off with yellow and black crime scene tape giving the neighborhood an eerie surreal look.

Now residents had come out onto their porches, some still in their pajamas, others wrapped up in their winter coats. There would be many questions asked, some awkward especially since the neighborhood was either directly related to the people affected by this crime or more indirectly related in business.

While crime scene techs scoured the scene for evidence, Rollie haplessly began to field questions from Detective Samuels, a tall man with short gray hair and a general military look about him with Officer

Stinson who was shorter and a bit stocky not unlike Rollie himself.

"How did you happen to be here?" was the first question from Samuels.

"Joey and Tina were friends and we spoke earlier on the phone and they asked me to stop by and chat."

"Any reason for that?"

"None other than a friend visiting friends."

"How long have you known these people?" prodded Samuels.

"Approximately six years or so."

"Good crisp answers, I like that," said Samuels. "Our records indicate you were a Detective in Toronto and Mississauga until fairly recently. Why did you leave the force?"

"It was time to hang out my shingle so to speak and go into business for myself."

"Were you on a case connected to this visit?" asked the detective.

"Just visiting friends," repeated Rollie with Alf Cragan looking on but keeping a straight face and giving nothing away.

"How did you get into the house?" asked officer Stinson.

"I forced the front door sensing something was wrong."

"It was locked?"

"Yes."

"Are you aware the back door was unlocked?"

"No, once I saw the body on the couch and the dead dog and ascertained they were both dead, I called 911."

"Did you touch anything in the house?"

"I checked for signs for a life and found none. I touched nothing else and wore gloves in that process."

"We understand you were a highly decorated detective and officer. Your old habits have not deserted you obviously," said Samuels with Rollie detecting a touch of sarcasm in that last question.

"I know my way around a crime scene, yes."

"Who are the deceased?"

"Joey Agricola and I believe the home owner's dog."

"The deceased is not the home owner?" questioned officer Stinson.

"Not to my knowledge."

"Where is the home owner?"

"I have no idea."

"Who is the home owner?" asked Samuels.

"As far as I know Joey's cousin Guido owns the house,"

"Was there anyone else you were expecting to see tonight that is not here now?" continued Samuels.

"Yes, Joey's fiancée Tina."

"Any idea where she would be?"

"None the slightest."

"Could the homeowner have run off with the girl leaving this mess behind?" asked officer Stinson.

Rollie had to restrain himself from decking the arrogant officer. "Guido was Joey's cousin and he loved Joey and Tina like the family they were."

"Hey, no harm done. We did not understand the relationship fully here. Thanks for clarifying it for us," said Samuels who quickly picked up that the junior officer was on dangerous ground with Rollie.

"So to sum things up, you showed up here around 10 pm to see your friends, and busted the front lock after no one answered the door. Correct so far?" questioned Samuels.

"Yes."

"Why did you break the front lock?"

"I heard voices and music from the TV but no one answered the door so I became concerned."

"Do you always bust doors down when you do not get an answer?"

"Not lately but I have been known to in the past."

This broke the tension somewhat even eliciting a chuckle from both policemen.

"And what is this guy doing here out of his jurisdiction?" queried Samuels referring to Alf Cragan.

"I can speak for myself. I have been working on a case involving the once again missing Tina. She was kidnapped earlier this year and then released. We have not yet found the perpetrators." said Alf Cragan.

"And you were working with him?" the question directed at Rollie.

"Just helping out a friend unofficially. As I said before, Tina and Joey were friends as well."

"You sure have a lot of friends and I'm not sure if having you as a friend is the safest thing in the world but be that as it may. So this Tina and Cousin Guido are both missing and the fiancée and the house pet are dead," stated detective Samuels.

"Any idea what kind of car this Guido drives?"

"None," replied Rollie.

"No problem, we'll get the info from the neighbors. Put out an all-points bulletin on the car and the inhabitants as soon as we know the make of the car and plate number," directing his remarks at officer Stinson.

"In the spirit of co-operation we will share information with you as well as the fact that your Precinct commander golfs with ours," indicated Samuels.

"As far as you go, we cannot stop you from conducting your own investigation but stay out of our way, x-cop or not. And do not leave the city without checking with us or detective Cragan over there first, but you know the drill right?"

"Sampson, go home and get some sleep, you look like the wreck of the Hesperus. See you at 10:00 am tomorrow at the station where I'm sure we'll have more questions to throw your way. Cragan, you can hang tough with us or hit the road but we expect to see you same time same station tomorrow as I have a feeling we have much more interesting stuff to go over. Something really stinks and I intend to find out where these people have disappeared to and who killed the person and animal in this house," motioned Samuels.

Alf Cragan indicated he could use some sleep himself and left with Rollie.

"Follow me to the local all-night Timmies, my friend. We've got some talking to do," said Cragan getting into his car.

Another night and it was going to be a long one.

Chapter 70

Richard Rasmussin had his private jet touchdown on a secluded runway, part of Norman Manley airport in close proximity to Kingston, Jamaica. His pilot had already radioed ahead for the necessary clearance which was essentially the mention of Richard's name. The airport customs officials and local law enforcement were always very well compensated to let Richard and any guests come and go as they pleased and word had quickly spread that this individual was extremely powerful and connected. To what extent they did not know and did not wish to know in fear of retribution.

Key members of the dreaded Jamaican Posses based in Kingston had been made available to Richard, two of which pulled up in a large tinted black panel van with two more Rastas riding shotgun in the back. A groggy trussed up Tina and Guido were unceremoniously loaded into the back on top of a pile of blankets while Richard and the weasely Jimmy Rudiger climbed into the secondary set of seats.

The van left the airport under the cover of night and sped toward the road that would take them to the dense tropical forests and altitude associated with the Blue Mountain area of the island. Once off the main road, the vehicle executed a number of twists and turns that seemingly rocketed the van into the middle of nowhere. The only sounds that could be heard was the throaty hum of the van's engine and the call of various tropical species of birds that were not happy with the intrusion.

After an about 2 hour climb and quick changes in altitude popping everyone's ears repeatedly, the vehicle came to a sudden stop. Except for a mobile spotlight which swept across the area in short intervals, everything was pitch black surrounding the van.

The prisoners were removed from the van, each one slung across the shoulder of one of the Rastas with the other two, Richard and Jimmy falling in behind. Around the corner of a lush group of trees and jungle vegetation, sat a sprawling massive bungalow overlooking a steep chasm that emptied out into a large valley deep below surrounded by even higher mountains and jungle all around. But since it was still night, nothing could be seen except for the lights coming from the villa.

Tina and Guido were roughly deposited onto two medium size beds in a room decorated appropriately in Rainforest motif. Their gags and bindings were removed along with some stern instructions from Richard.

"Escape is futile and will cost you your lives. We are in the middle of nowhere and if my men do not get you, the poisonous snakes will. A guard will be stationed outside your room and he is armed and on orders to shoot first and ask questions later. With me so far?" asked Richard.

Both Tina and Guido nodded still trying to shake off the cobwebs of the injections they were given before the flight.

"Food will be brought to you soon and then we all need some rest. In the morning, I will give you a tour of my Island home. You are my guests and your treatment will depend on how you conduct yourselves. See you in the morning," and with that Richard turned and left the room.

Two drop dead gorgeous brown skinned ladies were waiting for Richard, a larger but equally beautiful lady for Jimmy who had always favored the larger ladies. Each turned in to their lavish suites stocked with the best liquors and spicy Island tidbits both knowing that sleep was the last thing their horny companions were interested in.

Sleep was also the least on the minds of Guido and Tina although they were exhausted from their ordeal and still trying to shake the effects of the drugs they were given.

"Where are we?" asked Tina to no one in particular.

"Dammed if I know," replied Guido who was up and exploring their room.

Water and some mango and pineapple fruit was left out for them which Guido examined and dug into after finding nothing suspicious. Tina also drank some water and then sat back down holding her head between her hands.

"This guy is extremely dangerous and ruthless. He has most likely captured us to use as bait to lure Angel and even Mikhail here. But where is here?" lamented Tina.

For the time being, daylight was slowly pushing the dark of night back into the abyss and the two reluctant house guests could see their predicament out of their window.

"Breathtaking," is all Tina could muster.

"Agreed but this is not anywhere near home. My guess is we are on a tropical island somewhere," said Guido.

"We have to get out of here and get help. Whatever Richard has in mind for us will not end well that is for certain," whispered Tina.

Guido examined the window and it opened quite easily. But what caught his eye was the heavily armed guard just rounding the corner of the building.

"They have the house and area patrolled. Let's see if we can spot a pattern in their patrol and maybe we can slip by," offered Guido.

"And then what do we do? We have no idea where we are or how to get to anywhere," Tina lamented.

"My father taught me well. There has to be a road out of here and we follow that in the cover of the forest. Maybe we'll get lucky and pick up a ride once we get far enough away from here but we have to do something and do it fast," replied Guido.

So they took turns watching out the window and it looked as if the guard was circling the place around every ten minutes. So when the guard passed by their window again, they made their move quickly opening the window and climbing out.

They had each stuffed their pockets with fruit and each carried a bottle of water as they had no idea how long they would be out there before they would make it to safety or be re-captured. The latter was not an option as it would surely result in their death.

Guido pointed towards the rainforest and they quickly sprinted across the clearing into the cover of the underbrush. Guido's plan was to skirt the house using the jungle as cover until they found the road out and then follow it. His idea was quite good since there was just enough vegetation to keep them from being seen and they found the road quickly.

Each still had their wrist watch on, Guido's having a built in compass which would not help them much here but at least gave them something to check periodically. They knew they had to move fast because it would not be long until it was discovered they had escaped and then all hell would surely break loose.

As soon as they cleared the first bend in the narrow jungle path, Guido decided their best bet was to trek down the open road and jump back into the underbrush at the first noise. This served them well for the first half hour as they made great time at least in their estimation until they heard the noise of an approaching vehicle and dove into the jungle.

A land rover type of car passed them… thankfully from the direction in which they were going, not from where they were coming.

"We have luck on our side. These bastards must be sleeping it off thinking there is no way we would attempt escape. Let's keep moving," said Guido.

They noticed that the path they were following seemed to take them further and further downhill which made them feel somewhat better in hopes there could be civilization below.

Suddenly they arrived at a fork in the road and they had to decide whether or not to follow the path they were on or take a right hand turn.

"Let's see where this leads," said Guido pointing to tire tracks on the even narrower passage.

The two fugitives followed this path for about 10 minutes until a small thatch roof cabin came into view with what looked like a small jeep parked beside it.

"Okay, here is what we do. If the door to the vehicle is open we put it in neutral and push as far away from the cabin as we can. Then I will hotwire it and we are off. Got it?" asked Guido.

"You can do that?" questioned Tina.

"All tricks of the trade. Okay, you get to the passenger side and I'll go to the driver's side. We're in luck, the door is open."

Guido grabbed the wheel and shoved the shifter into neutral. "Now push, I'll steer."

The vehicle was quietly moved from its parking spot. As soon as Guido felt they were far enough away, he motioned for Tina to stop pushing and crawled underneath the steering column and felt for the ignition wires. He quickly found them and freed them up. He then cut them with a small pocket knife he kept in a small pouch in his jeans which thankfully was not found as his captors were obviously so sure of themselves they had not even searched him. Or maybe they had and missed this little gem.

He then expertly joined them up the correct way and the engine sprang to life. He also noticed the gas gauge indicated three quarters full which again went in their favor.

He quickly made it back to the original road, turned right and continued down the path they were first following. Everything they had done had taken about an hour so far and each made a silent prayer that their escape had not been discovered as yet. They needed to get to a safe place and call Rollie, Angel and Jon-Erik for help.

And luck continued to be on their side. They made it down to the lowlands after about another hour without running into anyone threatening and saw the outskirts of a large city.

"Any idea what this place is?" asked Guido.

"No, but it looks like someplace I would like to visit in better circumstances," replied Tina. "Should we go there and look for help?"

"If this is indeed a tropical Island maybe they have some resorts nearby. If we can latch on to a couple of people from there maybe they can help us. A better bet than going into the city as who knows where this maniac has ears and eyes,"

"Good thinking. Luck has been on our side, let's hope it continues," said Tina. And, miraculously it did as they all of a sudden saw a sign indicating Morgan's Harbour Resort and Hotel. They decided to pull over by the entrance and after about ten minutes or so a couple looking to be in their early thirties pulled in.

Guido hailed them over and they stopped right away apparently glad to hear someone else speak the English they were used to.

"Are you guys okay?" said the cute redhead sitting beside her tall dark haired boyfriend.

"Listen, we need help. My name is Guido and this is Tina. We are from Toronto Canada and were transported here against our will. First of all we need to know where we are."

"You're kidding right? Just like a scene out of a movie. I'm Gail and this is James. We are from Guelph Ontario just down the road from you. What can we do to help?"

Tina broke down in tears of joy while Guido quickly explained what had happened to them leaving out the fact that their kidnapper was known to them as well as a lot of other juicier details.

"You guys are in Jamaica. We are on a resort near Kingston. We wanted to be as close to the city as possible but there sure are some dangerous types lurking around so we have only taken day trips so far," explained James.

"We thank you so much for your kindness and will reward you handsomely if you help us get back home. First thing, we need to ditch this vehicle somewhere where it will not be found for a while. Any ideas?" asked Guido.

"This is so exciting. I feel like I am in a James Bond movie," said Gail.

"You got the James Bond part right but shouldn't we go to the authorities?"

"We do not know who we can or cannot trust. The people who abducted us may have far reaching tentacles," said Guido.

"Okay look, there is a shopping market area close by. Follow us and just leave the vehicle there. The way things work in this country, it will not be there long hopefully. And then you can come back to our hotel to freshen up and we'll contact your friends back home. How does that sound?" asked Gail.

"Heavenly. You guys are awesome. Thank you so much," said Tina.

After ditching the vehicle, James and Gail took their new found friends back to their resort and room. They had a lot to talk about but first things first—call home.

Chapter 71

Richard Rasmussin woke up just after 9 am on a glorious Jamaican morning. The sun was shining brightly and the multitudes of tropical birds were singing their own special songs. Jimmy Rudiger still had not stirred; *his large companion must have really worn him out* thought Richard.

He decided to look in on his house guests, the stationed guard still sitting in his chair across from the room that held his reluctant captives. The guard drawled in his patois dialect that he was tired and wanted someone to relieve him. Richard opened the door and totally lost it. The room was empty.

He uttered a blood curdling scream and ripped the room apart searching every nook and cranny. Nothing. In the meantime, the commotion had brought Jimmy running still in his boxer shorts which would have been funny at any other time.

Richard grabbed the guard and threw him against the wall and as he crumpled in a heap, he said he had heard nothing and did not abandon his post. Jimmy rallied all the guards and servants; nobody had seen or heard anything.

After taking his rage out on a couple of helpless staff members that ended up taking an unexpected free fall off the huge cliff adjacent to the house, Richard and Jimmy again searched the room and noticed food and water was missing and that the window was open slightly.

"These people are either more stupid or gutsy than I thought. They actually took their chances in the jungle. They could not have gotten far since the cliffs are not negotiable. They must have backtracked along the road which would be their only option."

"Get out and find them now and alert everyone that works for us on the Island that these people need to be captured and returned to me immediately," Richard directed looking even more dangerous than the crocodiles that frequent certain areas of the Rainforest.

"Listen boss, this may actually work to our advantage. Even if they manage to somehow get away and contact their friends at home, they will have to come home with both of their passports otherwise they would never get out of the country."

"Good thinking my weasley friend and then we will have them all where we want them and believe me, they will not escape again as they will all take that one way ride over the cliff that no one has ever returned from. Make sure everyone on this Island with eyes and ears is on alert for these two and their friends who may come for them. Issue detailed descriptions of each person so there is no mistake," added Richard.

While the new Warlord of Jamaica and a good chunk of the rest of the world and his slimy sidekick barked out orders, Guido and Tina were feeling much better after each had a much needed shower. James had ordered up room service being careful not to order too much to not raise undue suspicion.

As soon as they had eaten, Guido made the call on James' cell phone and connected with Rollie on the third ring.

He quickly explained where they were and what had happened to them and asked about Joey. Rollie skirted the issue and told them the priority was to get them back home safely. Tina grabbed the phone and asked again about Joey, Rollie could do nothing but tell her the truth, with a very heavy heart.

Tina broke down and started crying and the tears kept coming even though Guido held her and tried to keep her calm. James and Gail could only stand by and empathize, what else could they do?

The conversation ended after Guido told Rollie exactly where they were and indicated that their helpful benefactors were in Jamaica only two more days. Something had to be done before then else Guido and Tina would surely be discovered by some set of paid off eyes around the nearest corner.

While the distraught Tina and Guido did their best to rest after their ordeal and grieve their fiancé's and cousin's loss, Rollie contacted Angel and Jon-Erik laying things out as he clearly saw them. They had to get in and out of Jamaica fast and pick up their friends by skirting the authorities and any prying eyes. He had no idea how to do that especially in this short time frame.

Angel and Jon-Erik had done their best to make themselves comfortable at Mikhail's secluded hide-out but the lack of furniture and the loss of their best friend Joey did not make that easy. After Rollie's frantic call, Angel went to find Mikhail but the Monster found them instead pulling one of his famous appearances seemingly out of the even darker shadows of this hideaway.

Angel quickly relayed what Rollie had told them while Jon-Erik stayed quiet, and keeping his distance as he did not want to ruffle this Shape Shifter's feathers.

"Is Richard Rasmussin still there?" is all that Mikhail asked after Angel finished her incredulous story.

"As far as we know, yes. But time is of the essence. We need to get Tina and Guido out of there. My god, Tina has been through so much. She needs me now more than ever," replied Angel.

"I care not for Tina or anyone else. My mission on this earth now is to protect you but this Rasmussin is a gnat that must be stamped out once and for all," growled Mikhail picking up his untraceable phone, putting a finger to his lips before Angel or Jon-Erik could say anything.

The Monster placed a call to a remote region in the wilds of South America to cash in on a favor with a pilot named Joseph. He had worked with Mikhail a number of years ago to stop an evil drug lord named Miguel Alvarez who had actually let him live.

Joseph answered immediately and the two exchanged hushed words before the Ninja turned his wolfish gaze back to his two houseguests.

"A plane will meet us at the Billy Bishop Airport on the Toronto Island at midnight. I have worked with the pilot before and he is totally trustworthy. I worked with him years ago when we destroyed Miguel Alvarez's empire."

"He will go to Jamaica and we will pick up your friends there. He has connections here and everywhere, that are strong and allow him to fly under the radar. And I will go and kill Richard Rasmussin once and for all."

"Not without me you won't. This bastard has attacked and kidnapped people I love repeatedly and now has killed Tina's fiancée. I'm going with you!" said Angel with a steely determination in her voice.

"And what about me?" asked Jon-Erik. "Am I just chopped liver? Joey was my best friend too."

The Ninja paused for a minute before replying. "Angel, you are ready to come on a mission with me and have earned it. I will feel better having you with me and under my protection." And he continued, "As far as you are concerned *referring to Jon-Erik*, you are a gnat but Angel loves you. You will stay behind with that chubby pesky detective friend of yours and wait for us all to return safely. This is not negotiable. Understood?"

"This is not fair. I belong at Angel's side," muttered Jon-Erik still keeping his distance however.

"Fair is what I say it is. When we leave here, we will drop you off at the harbour front. You can then contact your detective friend. Enough talking, we must make preparations." instructed the Executioner before turning his massive back and walking out of the room as a normal person would. You could never predict what he was going to do.

"Honey, listen. He is right. I know you can hold your own but the lighter we travel the better chance we have for success. We will bring them home safely. I trust him although he still scares the living crap out of me."

With that, Angel jumped into Jon-Erik's arms and gave him one of the most passionate kisses he ever got and he had a few from Angel to compare against. Then she turned about and went after their dangerous benefactor leaving Jon-Erik just sitting there partially stunned but realizing they were probably right and there was nothing he could do about it anyway.

Dark clothing that was light and breathable with sturdy hiking shoes was the order of the day and Mikhail who was prepared for everything already had a bag ready for Angel. She quickly went through everything and all was sized and perfect for their mission. The Ninja emerged with a small bag of his own and gestured for Angel and Jon-Erik to head for the door which Mikhail did not even bother locking. If anyone did come, nothing would be found linking the home to him as after all he was the invisible man and had every intention of staying that way.

They were on their way to a dangerous and unknown adventure and Angel's adrenaline and anticipation was off the charts. She took some deep calming breaths; the Monster looking at her like a proud father. Their mission loomed dark and dangerous ahead. Bring their friends back home safely and once and for all eliminate their tormentor. No small task.

Chapter 72

Richard Rasmussin was furious but also concerned about the resolve, skills and tenacity his foes had shown so far. He had struck quickly, concisely and what did he have to show for it? One casualty on their side inflicted by himself and numerous losses on his end including key members of his inner circle which he would have eliminated himself sooner than later, truth be told.

But the idea forming in his mind now was so diabolical and incomprehensible it even made him shudder for a second. He picked up his phone and made two calls. The first was to arrange for him and his faithful sidekick Jimmy Rudiger to be picked up by one of his larger yachts on a secluded beach close to Kingston harbour.

The boat took them up and around the Jamaican Island, between Cuba and the Dominican Republic, skirted the Bahamas and along the east coast of

the US and landed in a secluded and totally off limits beach; off limits to anyone except for those who
worked, with the highest security clearances, on the
mysterious and controversial ridden Plum Island.

The Island was joined to the state of Massachusetts,
USA via a causeway that spanned the Plum Island
River and even though people lived and visited the
Island regularly, the area known as Building 257 near
Fort Terry was guarded more carefully than Fort Knox
via land, sea and air.

Originally or so the story goes, this area was designated as an animal disease research and control
center but unknown to even the US government *except for those of course that were made an offer they
could not refuse*, Richard Rasmussin's slimy tendrils
now had taken over this facility and things were
much worse than ever imagined.

Richard's plan was to confront his enemy on his
terms and this confrontation would ensure him vic-
tory without a doubt. If Richard was a betting man
(which he was), he was betting the whole kit and ca-
boodle on himself as the black limo took him and his
slimy sidekick Jimmy on their journey of destiny.

Instructions were left with those guarding his
Jamaican compound to kill anyone that came near
and also eliminate the fugitives immediately if they
were found.

"Boss, you are an absolute genius. If they are as
stupid as we know they are and come after you to
the place we are heading to, they will wish they were
never born," snickered Jimmy the Weasel.

"They will come and I will send them to hell and not even break a sweat," replied Richard as they reached their waterfront destination and boarded the large, spacious and luxurious yacht.

While they were on their way to Fort Terry, Plum Island, and the Monster and Angel boarded their under the radar flight to Jamaica with the reliable Joseph at the controls, Rollie Sampson picked up Jon-Erik at the Toronto Harbour front. The two friends sat down at a Tim Horton's on Queens Quay and the tiredness and frustration showed on their faces.

They were both visibly upset at how things had developed and the fact they were shut out of the action but both knew better than to challenge Mikhail. All they could think of doing for now was to go back to Guido's home and comfort the family and let them know all was being done that could be done without actually going into details which would have made everyone more uneasy than they already were.

They planned to assist the best they could with Joey's funeral arrangements which would not occur until Tina was either safely back; the alternative being unthinkable.

In the end, all Rollie and Jon-Erik could do was sleep on it and meet up the next day and head back up to West Hill. Rollie was also being pressured more and more by Alf Cragan whose trained sniffer told him that something stank to high heaven and dead fish season had long since passed in the Toronto area. Alf was being squeezed by his brass and also the Reporter who had latched on to him to try to get the lowdown of what was actually going on. Wouldn't they all like to know?

Whilst Rollie was tossing in a fitful sleep semblance and Jon-Erik paced nervously around in his confining Beach rental, the Executioner and Angel boarded a private plane piloted by the Monster's acquaintance Joseph. Mikhail had no friends; they would be just liabilities as he could not afford to let anyone get too close to him. Angel was different as she gave him a purpose in life and Joseph could be trusted standing side by side against a drug dealing, bottom feeding Warlord, years ago.

Mikhail and Joseph caught up on things while they were in the air, Angel finding out by listening that Joseph was instrumental in helping wipe out Miguel Alvarez's power base who was a thorn in all their sides until the Ninja dispatched him to a hell that he had not even anticipated.

The flight to Jamaica's Norman Manley Airport lasted approximately four hours and Joseph taxied down on a prearranged seldom used runway. It was now mid-morning in Jamaica and the heat was stifling in comparison to back home.

Two very grim looking individuals dressed in Airport Security garb came to speak to Joseph who told Mikhail and Angel to stay on board the airplane. After a couple of minutes discussion and some money exchanging hands, the not so official looking officials turned the other way and marched towards one of the large Hangars.

Joseph indicated they had five minutes to clear the area and that a car was waiting for them to take them to the hotel where Guido and Tina were held up. He was going with them; they would need a guide and he knew Jamaica well from his past dealings on behalf of the late Kingpin Miguel Alvarez.

A few glaring eyes glanced their way, some doing a double take seeing the large man glide like his feet never touched the floor, but no one made a move to stop them. Joseph still retained a lot of clout and respect in this country from his past work here.

The driver of the car had already been briefed and he took them without uttering a word to their destination. Joseph rode up front with him, Angel and the Monster in the back. The airport was only a short distance from Morgan's Harbour Resort and the decision was made for Angel to go in and get her friends as she would arouse the least suspicion.

When the door opened to the room, Tina was in tears as she fell into the arms of her best friend. After calming her down somewhat, Angel hugged Guido and greeted James and Gail and told them that if they ever needed anything she and her friends would be there in a flash. She also tried to pay them for their kindness, which was flatly refused.

She quickly laid out the plan. Tina and Guido would be driven back to the plane and smuggled aboard in a covered baggage cart and would wait there till they were joined by the rest. There was food aboard so they could make themselves comfortable. Angel indicated that she, Mikhail and Joseph would be driven close to Richard Rasmussin's hideaway where they could hopefully finish things once and for all.

And with that Angel herded the couple of frightened fugitives quickly into the car leaving James and
Gail to wonder whether this was a dream so they
pinched themselves. They ended up doing a lot more
than that as stress can bring on passion and passion
could only mildly describe what these two now once
again safe lovers did to each other.

Chapter 73

After Tina and Guido were stowed safely aboard the airplane, Joseph, Angel and the Monster set off on their quest to bring an end to the reign of terror of Richard Rasmussin. They had gotten fairly concise directions from Guido and since it was now turning dusk, they headed up the secluded Blue Mountain pass. They each wore combat fatigues and heavy boots which Joseph outfitted them with as well as an HK VP70 semi-automatic handgun with enough ammo to do sufficient damage.

Angel and Mikhail refused the pistol but Mikhail insisted that Angel keep hers just in case since they had no idea what they would be facing in the jungle. Joseph was a small man with a dark, swarthy complexion but he was strongly built as well as being a master in hand to hand combat and all types of weaponry.

When the three avengers finally arrived at the fork in the road that lead to Richard's mountain fortress, they decided to hide their vehicle in the jungle and set off on foot. Mikhail led the way sliding along the path like a Cobra, silently and deadly with Joseph behind him and Angel at the back, some of the jungle sounds making her skin crawl.

Suddenly, the Ninja stopped dead in his tracks sniffing the air. Something was not right. He motioned for Angel and Joseph to stop and throw themselves into the jungle. And not a second too soon, as a large jeep came tearing around the bend, which would have mowed them down had they not sprang out of the way.

But now, the jig was up as the four Posse members in the vehicle saw the flurry of activity and came to a screeching stop, machine guns peppering the underbrush where Angel and Joseph had taken cover. As far as the Monster, he disappeared into the thin mountain air and then reappeared just as quickly through the roof opening on top of the jeep into the midst of the shocked horde of hired killers.

Things went quickly downhill from there for the stunned Rastas as two were unceremoniously ejected from the vehicle with their throats slashed from ear to ear. The third one's nose was pushed through his skull and down his throat making breathing impossible while he joined his two brethren on the cool and damp path. The fourth member of this doomed group was younger and more agile and decided discretion was the better part of valor and in the commotion was able to escape the vehicle and dove head first into the forest and high tailed it out of there in the opposite direction.

Good plan if it was not for the fact that Joseph who had worked with the Shape Shifter before and rather than concentrating on the havoc that he had raised, saw the dreadlocked henchman disappear into the underbrush but not before putting two well-placed slugs into the buttocks of the fleeing hireling.

As the man laid screaming and writhing on the lush forest ground, Joseph put another two rounds into his forehead ending his pain once and for all. Angel was astounded how quickly her two companions neutralized this threat even though she had seen Mikhail in action many times before. Now her mind flashed back to the four killers she and Jon-Erik had to send to the next world. A tear ran down her cheek as she missed her lover so much and prayed he was safe.

"How close are we to the compound?" asked Mikhail quietly even for him.

"From what I understood from Guido not more than half a mile or so," answered Joseph.

"They would have heard the shots and will be ready for us. This is why I hate using guns unless they are silenced," said the Monster.

"Point well taken my large friend but what would we have done without that Rocket Launcher in Argentina?" questioned Joseph smiling.

Angel said nothing but took a long sip from her canteen. The heat was still stifling even though night had now fallen once again.

"They now know we are coming and will be ready for us. But we are ready for them," grinned the Ninja his gold tooth gleaming in the moonlight. This is where he was at his best. A foe or foes to eliminate.

"But now we move through the jungle; no more surprises."

The Killer led the way once again moving without a sound like the quiet jungle cat that he was until again he stopped dead in his tracks motioning the others to do the same.

"Shine your flashlight down here," whispered Mikhail to Angel.

Sure enough, a tiny gossamer like thread that looked like it was spun by a large spider of some sort appeared just in front of where the Ninja stood.

Joseph squatted to have a look. "A tripwire of some sort. Primitive but most likely effective. What would you suggest?" directing his gaze to the Shape Shifter.

"We give them what they want," motioning his companions to take a long berth around the trap and once they were all clear, the Ninja picked up a branch and threw it at the tripwire with deadly accuracy.

A machine gun opened up instantaneously and peppered the area where they were just standing with bullets until the magazine was empty.

They had to hit the ground to avoid some of the stray bullets that sprayed the area.

"Effective. Even if they miss us they know we are approaching. Now there is no doubt," said Joseph.

"The only doubt remaining is when they will all die and it will be sooner than later," snarled Mikhail. He pointed to deeper into the jungle indicating they could not possibly have booby-trapped the whole area.

But this group was obviously more resourceful than anticipated when the ground suddenly opened up and swallowed Mikhail whole. Angel shone her flashlight into the deep dark pit in which the Monster had sunk into miraculously evading a number of huge wooden spikes that would have impaled any normal man.

Now being in Jamaica one would expect that, if a poisonous snake was used, the native Lance Head snake would be the snake of choice. But not so for Richard Rasmussin's minions who imported their poisonous killers from Australia, the deadliest of the deadly, the Inland Taipan Snake who slithered out from a hole in the ground to greet their new guest.

The Ninja stood perfectly still in the middle of the spiked pit and with a movement too fast for the naked eye to see, extracted one of the spikes meant for him out of the ground and speared the first snake through the head impaling it into the pit.

Angel and Joseph could only look on with awe as that blurry movement was repeated until all the snakes were impaled and dead except one slithering towards its even more deadly prey. As the snake struck lightning fast at Mikhail's calf, the Monster plucked the snake out of the air like a fly and held it behind the head where it was unable to inject its deadly poison into its captor.

He then flicked out his hand, catching the serpent with a blow that did not kill it but put it to sleep for about an hour or so. The Ninja then extracted a black bag from his pocket which he always kept for situations such as this and put the snake inside, tying off the top.

He then literally levitated himself into the air and out of the deathtrap.

"You were doing this for fun?" asked Angel incredulously.

"That and to learn. Nobody would have survived that and now I know what to look for with other traps. I do not know what type of snake this is but it may turn out to be useful later. It is always good to see how far your enemy will go," said the Ninja with a chuckle before motioning them deeper into the forest.

Angel and Joseph just followed along shaking their heads again realizing they were aligned with the most dangerous human being on earth. Was he really human or something else entirely, which they both suspected and would not say. The wolfish grin on the face of the Master of Mayhem told them that he most likely could read minds as well.

That and a whole lot more thought Mikhail projecting directly into Angel's brain which made her stop and do a double take realizing she was linked for the rest of her life to this extra— ordinary creature. He nodded his agreement as they trudged quietly towards their targets.

Chapter 74

The luxury yacht arrived at its mysterious and sinister destination in the afternoon of the next day and they were instantaneously surrounded by four sleek unmarked boats complete with machine gun turrets and armed to the teeth guards.

The high speed whirling noise coming down on top of them indicated a helicopter was above them. Richard was pleased; the security was as tight as ever.

As soon as it was verified who was on the yacht, the guard boats formed a two sided escort and the Helicopter turned and went back to its base. Only Richard and Jimmy Rudiger had the clearance to be able to come aboard land near the area of Building 257. The pilot of the yacht was told and only told once to get his boat out of the area as fast as his 1300 horse power V12 engine could take him. He hightailed it back to Jamaica without further prodding as the hair on the back of his neck was standing up being so close to this forbidden and downright spooky island.

Once they were on dry land, a totally tinted Humvee picked them up and drove Richard and Jimmy to their quarters. Most of the research scientists and armed personal stayed in their own barracks but Richard and Jimmy were quartered in the luxury guest house which was equipped with state of the art communication, pools and exercise rooms, plush furniture and the finest chef created and overseen foods.

Tomorrow they would get down to business but today was all about dining and relaxing. Richard had ordered some severe modifications to make this gloomy hell-hole a little more palatable; at least when he was there entertaining perspective clients.

Correction, confirmed clients— individuals that were given the sales pitch from Plum Island and did not want to do business, were never heard from or seen again, as after all, who would admit to going there in the first place?

But first a little tour of Building 257 was in order which Jimmy tried his best to skip but now being second in command by attrition, he had no choice in the matter.

There was room after room all equipped with the highest tech lab equipment, electronics, computers and surveillance equipment in the command center. The scientists who worked there all signed up for the chance to make ground breaking discoveries and worked with the finest equipment, tools and test subjects money could buy.

What they did not bargain for, however, was once they were on the Island, they were never getting off again. Their payment was their lives as after all there was nothing to spend your money on in this god forsaken place. Escape attempts or any insubordination were offences punishable by instant death, if fortunate. If not, a long painful torturous ordeal awaited them as test subjects before a grisly death finally awaited them.

It was always nice to get one or two test subjects fresh from the Island once in a while rather than having to go to the mainland and raid the slums, ghettos and transient communities monthly for their fill of human guinea pigs. The same area was never hit twice and since the people taken were missed by no-one, this little enterprise on the Island was flourishing.

Clients were flown in by Helicopter from New York City and Boston. They were usually representatives of some seedy third world dictatorships wanting to instill even more fear and unrest in their populous. Nothing a little germ or genetic warfare could not take care of. But it was the biggies that really interested Richard, especially Al Qaeda who had commissioned the locusts of Plum Island via Richard Rasmussin to create a weapon so sinister and deadly none dare even speak of it with the exception of the head scientist of the Island and his talented but ruthless researchers that were heading PROJECT UBERTIER.

Ubertier was the German translation for Super-Animal, a creation so fast, strong, tenacious but controllable that could eliminate hundreds of humans in a very short time frame depending where the beast was unleashed.

The prototype was mastered by a simple hand held control device that worked with the neutrons implanted in its vicious and blood thirsty brain. It was kept in a large tungsten steel enclosure in the bowels of Building 257 and could only be viewed through tightly strung together steel bars with an outer layer of impenetrable Plexiglas.

Today, Richard had a very special demonstration arranged with Herr Werner Zeigler, the mastermind on Plum Island behind PROJECT UBERTIER. The final prototype was ready for a live test. It so far had surpassed all expectations but never had been tested with a human specimen before. All test animals from small field mice to large, ferocious bears, jungle cats and even a majestic African Lion were ripped apart and devoured until only the bones remained by the Ubertier in a matter of moments.

Werner Zeigler was one of the last Nazi Scientists not yet dead or jailed, as he was still fairly young during World War 2. He learned quickly from his older counterparts and developed a taste for the grotesque and macabre early in his life, becoming one of the most feared scientists revered by Hitler himself.

After the end of the war, Werner went underground and settled in Ushuaia, Argentina which is the southernmost city in the world and since the climate was quite severe there, no one ever came to look for him there or even wanted to.

He had set himself up a little test lab, of course, funded by the government to continue his research and experimentation of creating the ultimate weapon, das Ubertier and things were going very well for him until an ultra-secretive faction of the American government found him and made him an offer he could not refuse; to head the research facility on Plum Island.

Werner's budget and resources were un-limited and things got even better for him when Richard Rasmussin positioned himself to be in charge of this facility, as it protected him and other radical government officials even more since Richard had taken responsibility.

What the government did not know was Richard had a much more diabolical agenda of his own. Unlike the government who had their favorites, he just sold to the highest bidder and this one was going to cost a pretty penny. With Richard, it was not about the money itself any more as he was a billionaire already; it was about greed and sadistic power which he could never get enough of.

Every once in a while, even with the best and tightest precautions, one or two of the earlier test Ubertier creatures would get away and try to swim to the mainland and usually drowned along the way as Werner's creatures were created for land and not sea.

In July 2008, something the press named the "Montauk Monster" washed ashore in Montauk, Long Island onto one of their more isolated beaches. The official word was that this was a raccoon that lost its fur as it was in the water too long but anyone in the know knew that this was something else entirely and suspicion was that it came from Plum Island.

But as all newsworthy items tend to do, the story quickly lost steam and fizzled out and no one actually knew what was going on in Building 257 except for a select few for whom head scientist Werner Zeigler had set up today's demonstration for.

And it was going to be a doozy— that he promised.

Chapter 75

Rollie Sampson was fit to be tied. He was frustrated as hell, as on one hand, he had Alf Cragan breathing down his neck. He was being pressured from his higher ups for results as now the cops that were investigating the death of Joey Agricola and the disappearance of Guido and Tina had nothing but dead ends. And since the police had nothing whatsoever to go on, they focused their attention on detective Alf Cragan who in turn had to put pressure on Rollie.

As a result, Rollie agreed to meet with detective Alf Cragan bringing along Jon-Erik, who was just as upset with the death of his best friend, and with Angel being in a dangerous foreign country working with a loose cannon and extremely unpredictable character such as the Ninja.

They met in a little neighborhood coffee shop on Lakeshore Blvd. west of Toronto. Since it was just after dinner, the place was not as busy as it would be later; with neighborhood people coming in for their fixes of cappuccinos, lattes and other designer delicacies. Rollie and Jon-Erik ordered regular coffees and Cragan went for a cappuccino with a raspberry scone.

While sipping on their drinks, Alf Cragan broke the ice and that was putting it mildly.

"What the hell is going on here Rollie? And spare me the bullshit; I am in no mood for it."

Rollie and Alf Cragan always had a healthy respect for each other and that was in danger of being dissolved right here and now as Rollie had zero tolerance for being spoken to like that.

"What do you want me to tell you, Alf? You are talking as if we had something to do with these bizarre events."

The look on Rollie's face told Cragan that he might have overstepped his bounds here and toned down his approach somewhat.

"Look, give me something. On the record or off the record…but preferably on," said Cragan.

"On the record, you know what we know. Joey Agricola is dead and his fiancée Tina and Joey's cousin Guido are missing.

"Do you have any clue where they are?"

"Officially or Unofficially?"

"Both!"

"Okay, here is the official version once again," and Rollie laid out everything that had happened at Guido's home.

"I am aware of all that. Do you think Guido and Tina had anything to do with Joey's murder?" said Alf Cragan looking annoyed to say the least.

"Absolutely not. Guido was Joey's cousin and they loved each other and were family. Tina was Joey's fiancée and they were also deeply in love. And you can put that down as being official," replied Rollie.

"Joey was also my best friend and my fiancée Angel was best friends with Tina. No way that they had any part in this," Jon-Erik spoke up.

"Okay, so where are they and where is your fiancée Angel?" questioned Alf Cragan.

"Officially or unofficially?" was Rollie's comeback.

"Anyway you wish," indicated Alf Cragan shaking his head.

"Okay, here is what we know unofficially and if you ask me if we have any proof of any of this, we do not." said Rollie and began to outline the whole incredible story from Angel and Tina being hired by FinCo, to Tina's first kidnapping, the threats and attacks at the Furniture store and their homes, the numerous interventions of the Ninja and finally Joey's murder and Tina and Guido's abduction to Jamaica.

What Rollie left out was the attacks and disposal of the bodies near Parry Sound. No way would that story have flown and again there was no evidence to support that it had ever happened. It really had no relevance to the situation other than to emphasize the lengths Richard Rasmussin would go to.

While Alf Cragan just shook his head and ordered a large double double coffee, Rollie finished off his sordid tale ending with the Ninja and Angel going to Jamaica to free their kidnapped friends and bring them home.

"And how the hell do they expect to accomplish all this, given the fact that whether I actually believe your incredible story, it sounds more like something that James Patterson would come up with in one of his numerous thrillers he publishes yearly?"

Rollie then made Alf Cragan intimately aware of what type of a person or better yet thing, Mikhail the Ninja actually was and the battles they were involved in years ago.

"This story is sounding more ridiculous the more you go into it. But I know you, Rollie, you are a straight shooter, and a great cop and detective. If this was anyone else telling me this, I would laugh in their faces." Alf Cragan chortled.

"Everything Rollie has mentioned is true and then some. For some reason, this Monster has attached himself to Angel and so far he has kept his word and kept her safe. But this Richard Rasmussin, he is rich beyond belief and more dangerous than we can even comprehend. Because of the danger he represents to Angel, Mikhail has taken this personally. And I have no doubt that Mikhail is the only one on this earth who can actually eliminate this evil although I would love the opportunity to ram my fist down his throat a number of times," said Jon-Erik.

"And that is my two cents worth, take it or leave it, from someone whose love and future is in the hands of a real Monster," he added.

"My god, we don't even have jurisdiction in Jamaica. This is totally insane and I could never go to my superiors with a story like this. They would have me committed," said Alf Cragan still shaking his head.

"My suggestion to you is to go back to your brass and tell them you are doing everything you can to find Tina and Guido and once they are back, we will have to concoct some sort of story to appease everyone. Besides that, we are all in a waiting game. But I agree with Jon-Erik, if anyone can bring them back it is Mikhail and Angel."

"Keep me informed, …unofficially," and with that Alf Cragan stomped out into the cold dark winter night vowing to down more than a few shots of his favorite whiskey.

Rollie and Jon-Erik parted ways, promising to inform each other immediately if anything came up. Neither one of them prayed much but they both said a silent prayer for their friends and loved ones and yes… even one for the Ninja who held the balance of a number of lives in his large and highly skilled hands.

Chapter 76

No further annoying booby traps were encountered by the stealthy three avengers that were creeping through the jungle now approaching Richard Rasmussin's Blue Mountain hideout. The Ninja gave the signal for Angel and Joseph to lay low behind a large tree trunk that was surrounded by high grasses and other tropical vegetation. They could see the outline of the compound, as the first signs of a new day were showing on the horizon.

Even though it was still dark out, the trio had no illusions that their quarry would not be ready for them and were anxious for some real action, but the Monster was on a scouting mission and Angel and Joseph knew better than to question him.

Mikhail got the lay of the land quite quickly noticing that the large house was flanked on either side by jungle and protected by a large and deep precipice in the back of the fortress.

His incredible vision, sense of smell, hearing and extra-ordinarily developed sixth sense told him the area was teeming with hidden snipers and danger, as he surveyed the area expertly hidden in the dense foliage of a large Cotton Mango tree bordering the underbrush. Some were hidden in bushes, trees not counting the ones patrolling the house regularly and whoever was inside, he could not readily ascertain from his perch. The enemy now numbered one less since the Executioner hated to share his perch with anyone.

The dead dreadlocked man was tied up to one of the larger upper branches of the tree by his hands and feet, his broken neck hardly able to support his face which had that look of utter astonishment on it that most had after being dispatched by the Monster. This one heard nothing but the snapping of his own neck, as the Ninja appeared behind him without a sound and sent him to meet his maker.

Mikhail retraced his steps until he appeared hovering over the spot where Angel and Joseph were hidden. They never heard or sensed a thing.

"Good thing I am not the enemy or you both would have been eliminated. I can handle this easily on my own but would not want to have all the fun."

And then he laid out a very rudimentary plan. Normally, the Monster detested plans; he just went with his instincts but this time since he had two partners with him he decided for a little more structure to his mayhem.

First, he would eliminate all threats hidden in trees and bushes in the area and all he asked for was fifteen minutes. Then Angel and Joseph would be free to take care of the guards who were circling the outside of the stronghold while the Ninja dropped in on those inside, giving them their last and final unexpected surprise.

"So synchronize your watches to 15 minutes from now and remember the guards circling are heavily armed. How you take care of them is up to you. I'll be busy inside and I trust you both to be quiet and quick," and with that Mikhail disappeared as he appeared, without a sound.

Angel and Joseph checked their watches and weapons and decided that they would stick together, one backing up the other when the time came. For now, the Ninja was well into his deadly mission eliminating guard after guard with precision and speed as only he could. The bodies were unceremoniously flung over the edge of the escarpment; the killer not having to eliminate them but only removing their tongues so no one could hear them scream in flight.

As a result, Mikhail was well ahead of schedule with five minutes to spare so he had a chance to scout around the barracks where the guards and staff were quartered and decided to try his direct approach by opening the door and walking straight in like he owned the place - which he did.

Four Rastas were so absorbed in smoking Ganja and drinking Red Stripe beer they did not at first notice the Monster standing there. But when they did, it was already too late as one was in his death throes choking on a beer bottle, the second had his throat slit from ear to ear and their two brethren did not fare much better.

The third tried to spring back from the table where they were all sitting but was grabbed by the neck and smashed into the floor so hard his brains were crushed like a ripe melon. The fourth one was much larger and more agile than his three now dead companions and was able to grab his machine gun and start riddling the room with bullets while screaming, "Die Diable".

But the "Diable" was a long way from dead as he had already done one of his famous disappearing acts into the room's shadows. And when the large Rasta had emptied his magazine and tried to load a new one, the Monster reappeared behind him and stuffed the whole magazine down his throat which resulted in a gurgling exit from this planet.

Unfortunately, the shooting had alerted the hired help in the main house as well as the guards circling the perimeter and they came out guns a blazing. So much so that they expertly shot three of their own before they even realized what had happened.

Angel and Joseph were in position and jumped out of the bushes behind two of the shooters still spraying the area. Joseph clubbed one with his pistol handle and then put four rounds into his head and body for good measure.

At the same instant, Angel put the other one in a guillotine choke from the back and wrapped her strong legs around his middle and squeezed the life out of him like an Anaconda. Good thing for her as she hit the ground with her dead prey, a hail of bullets went over her head from another henchman that came flying out of the main house.

To his surprise, however, he found himself driven like a nail into the ground by two large and heavy boots from above. As a result of his broken back and two dislocated shoulders, he became still, forever.

Finally, the shooting and all noise stopped. The Ninja cautiously sniffed the air and then made a sign to Angel and Joseph that the coast was clear. He pointed to the bodies strewn about the area and then to the deep drop off behind the house. Cleanup was a bitch but someone had to do it and everyone grabbed an arm or a leg until all of Richard's minions were flying through the air and smashing into bits and pieces upon the craggy rocks hundreds of feet below.

"The bastard is not here obviously," snarled Angel the fighting lust still upon her.

"The coward has escaped once again but there is no place on earth he can hide from me. But let's take a look around in case he left us any clue as to his whereabouts," said Mikhail.

And they did not have to look too far for what they were after. The answer sat right on the first table they saw as they entered the main house. The note simply said,

The fact that you are reading this note means you have killed all my men and most likely found your friends. Admirable skills. But if you want to kill me and I know you do then come to Building 257, Plum Island in Massachusetts USA two days from now at midnight. I will be waiting and make sure you arrive safely. We have a lot to talk about. Love Richard.

"Plum Island, where the hell is that?" asked Angel.

"Does not matter. Joseph will get me there," replied the Ninja.

"Will get us there. I want to see that toad squirm before we kill him. But first, let's destroy this place and get Tina and Guido home safely," said Angel.

"Well spoken," said Mikhail who was already busy dousing the inside and outside of Richard's Jamaican hideaway and supporting buildings with cans of gasoline he found in the tool shed.

"Nothing will be found but cinders," said Joseph lighting a match and then igniting the whole book before throwing it at Casa Rasmussin. The whole place; tool sheds and sleeping quarters went up in a giant phalanx of flames. Richard would not be able to come back to this spot again, there would be nothing left of it.

And with that, the three avengers headed back down the trail to retrieve their vehicle and get Tina and Guido out of this beautiful but dangerous country and back home where they belonged. Angel, still grieving over Joey, vowed that Richard Rasmussin would pay the ultimate price. But they still had miles to go before she could sleep.

Chapter 77

Six hours later, the tired but ecstatic travelers arrived at Guido's home in West Hill. Angel had called Jon-Erik on route and had told them they were all fine. Even Tina had held up reasonably well except for the occasional wracking sob for her fiancée who would never be coming back. The police had so far finished their investigation and Joey was resting at the neighborhood funeral home. Arrangements for the funeral had not been made yet as Tina and Guido had been missing. The police had found absolutely nothing; no hair, fingerprints, fiber, blood or anything else that would be a clue as to who the killer was. Only traces of the people who were at the house at the time, hence the cops were really anxious to find Guido and Tina as all roads led back to them.

Jon-Erik and Rollie stormed in a few minutes later after the weary travelers arrived. Angel flew into Jon-Erik's arms and as soon as they kissed passionately

Angel ran over to Tina hugging her and not letting go.

Mikhail and Joseph stood by and watched the proceedings, with the Monster actually showing a touch of a grin on his wolfish face. It was kind of gratifying to see the love these gnats had for each other. But the tender moments did not last long and everyone was quickly brought up to speed.

Rollie quickly filled everyone in on the story he had concocted to get the police off the backs of Guido and Tina. *Guido had been restless and needed a breath of fresh air and Tina decided to join him. They were gone less than ten minutes, came back and found Joey and the dog dead. Fearing for their lives, they fled on foot to one of the relatives homes that they knew were out of town for a week and hunkered down there; Guido knowing where the key was. They had decided not to tell anyone where they were until they knew the coast was clear and the police had wrapped up their activities. That is why they were back now.*

Even though the story was flimsy, Rollie called Alf Cragan to come and bring in Tina and Guido for questioning.

In the meantime, Joseph told the group his concerns regarding Plum Island. This place had more security than the Whitehouse. Flying in or going in by boat would be impossible.

"Then I will go in posing as a tourist and trek in on foot. Nothing that is man-made can stop me," growled the Monster.

"We will go in on foot. I am sure this is largely about me. I intend to end this once and for all and avenge my best friend's fiancée," said Angel with a fierce look of determination.

"Joseph will fly us down to Boston's Logan Airport tomorrow and wait for us there. You and I will end this then but we need to be prepared for the worst. We will let them catch us and take us into their midst and then destroy them all. Get some rest and we will pick you up tomorrow at your house," Mikhail directed to Angel.

Before she could answer the Shape Shifter and Joseph disappeared without a sound. Joseph was learning from the Ninja. How scary was that?

Angel and Jon-Erik followed suit after each hugging Tina once more and telling them all not to worry plus thanking Guido for his bravery and looking after Tina.

"After all she is family," said Guido but Angel and Jon-Erik were already gone anxious to spend a few hours together before she would leave again and hopefully for the last time. They decided to go back to their west end home. Neither one had seen it for far too long, and they both knew that neither would get any sleep tonight; just a ton of urgent, needy, passionate animal sex during which Jon-Erik planned to let the love of his life know that he was going with her and arguing the point was not an option. Even waiting with Joseph was better than being far away from his Angel again.

A short time later, detective Alf Cragan arrived and after indicating he was happy to see them safe, briefed them on a few enhancements to their story.

"Even though I do not fully believe what is going on here, the police will believe your story. Just make sure you have your story straight and only answer the questions as they are asked. It will look like someone had a vendetta against your family, a professional hit man was sent and the dog got in the way. You both would have also been killed if you would have remained in the house. Got it?" asked Cragan.

Both nodded that they did and then were escorted out to Alf's car to 43rd Division for interrogation and hopefully to be released back into Alf's custody and then at least two days of sleep. How could they sleep thinking about what Angel was about to embark upon - but they had faith in the skills of the Ninja. What other choice did they have?

Rollie was the last to leave and went home for some much needed shut eye. He wanted nothing more than to accompany Angel and the Ninja on their crazy dangerous mission and put a few well-placed bullets into this madman's skull but he knew trying to argue with the Monster would be futile and that there was no love lost between the two of them. So he planned to busy himself with flushing out some of Richard's connections right here in town and letting them know the Meter of Corruption at least in this town was ticking to an end.

Chapter 78

Head scientist, Herr Werner Zeigler had finished his preparations. A few dignitaries and representatives from a number of subversive foreign regimes and groups were on Plum Island in Building 257 with checkbooks in hand. If they liked what they saw, millions would exchange hands now with triple as much to come when the final products were delivered. Dignitaries and representatives of shady, devious overseas powers were lead into an Amphi-Theater of sorts. A viewing area was set high up in the room supported by thick impenetrable glass opening up the view below to a closed in space surrounded by the toughest tungsten steel money could buy. Two heavily enforced steel doors could be seen at either side of the room, the floor made of solid cement. There was nothing else in the room but that was about to abruptly change.

The viewers including Richard Rasmussin and Jimmy Rudiger were in place ready for the show to begin and Werner was not one to keep his soon to be captivated audience waiting. One of Zeigler's assistants hit a remote switch activating a mechanism which opened one of the two doors to the room below.

The first thing that hit everyone was the smell. Musky, wild and powerful was the first assault on the senses. After everyone's nostrils became accustomed, the smell got even more pronounced. Something between truckloads of crushed worms and a farmer fertilizing a field with a stiff breeze blowing was the best way to describe it and Werner had to turn on two large overhead fans which did next to nothing to contain the stench.

"What the hell have you got down there?" asked one of the foreigners in his broken English. "It smells like the millions of unwashed armpits of my countrymen."

"You will see soon enough," answered Werner and as if on cue something began to emerge from the now open passageway. All everyone in the room could do was gasp in between holding their noses, some using handkerchiefs to curb the obscene odor. The Ubertier shambled out into the room letting out its version of a part growl part scream causing everyone in the room except Werner and Richard to shrink back a step or two.

It was huge, larger than a Lion with incredibly developed front and back legs that were bunched up with obscenely large and powerful looking muscles.

The torso was covered in a thick brown maze of fur/ hair combination and was long, thick and incredibly strong looking. It had a small stumpy tail similar to a boxer and a huge angry looking red phallus hanging half way to the ground. The most fascinating and also frightening thing about this creature that looked to be conceived from the bowels of hell itself, was its head.

The best way to describe it would be something you would get if you combined a human being with a Lion and a Shark. Some of the features were feline, others definitely human especially the large but beady green eyes that glowed with an unearthly intelligence. The nose and jaws protruded outward and the fangs of the creature looked like a combination of a Great White Shark and a prehistoric Saber Tooth Tiger.

An even more bloodcurdling shriek followed after which the creature began to tear around the enclosure with a speed and agility never seen before by human eyes. Its leaps took it almost to the ceiling of the room which was at least thirty feet up in the air causing the audience to take another step back after which Werner assured them they were perfectly safe.

"This Ubertier is the culmination of a lifetime of my work and with the support of Richard Rasmussin here, we are now in the stages of creating hundreds of these magnificent specimens. Each one will be engineered to obey the master or masters it has been assigned to and carry out instructions without fail. They will understand any language they are programmed for, are ten times faster than any Cheetah on earth and have the strength of a whole pride of Lions."

"They will be programmed to evade and destroy any man made or mechanical threat against them and one hundred of these Ubertier could destroy a city within a matter of hours. Nothing can contain them but the strongest alloys and they can evade bullets even from a machine gun with ease," Werner continued.

As Werner spoke the Ubertier leaped right to the ceiling in one bound and actually adhered itself somehow crawling along in an insane upside down shuffle.

"This creature can adapt itself to any environment on land or sea. It is a strong swimmer and can hold its breath up to twenty minutes underwater and woe to the Shark that tries to make a meal of our creature down there," boasted the German.

"Can it be harmed or killed?" asked one of the Middle Eastern buyers.

"Perhaps with a rocket launcher or a missile of some sort but the Ubertier would evade it easily even if it was a heat seeker," Werner answered.

"But you came here to see the Ubertier in action and we do not want to deprive you of that," Werner said making a signal for Richard to flip another switch causing the floor to disappear right from under Jimmy Rudiger whose weasely body was now on a one way slide for a personal get acquainted session with the Ubertier.

"Nooooo boss!" was all the captive screamed and now extremely focused audience heard.

Jimmy Rudiger was unceremoniously dumped to the bottom of the chute which lead to the opening of the door to the arena and a slavering Ubertier more than ready for Act 2 of this grizzly drama.

And even before the startled Jimmy could fully lift his head to scream at his stone cold boss again, the creature was upon him with an uncanny speed and ferociousness.

Blood, spittle and guts were flying in all directions as the abberation made a crimson mess of his prey which was in seconds reduced to a bloody unrecognizable pulp.

And adding to the ultimate indignity, the creature did things too hideous to detail to the lifeless husk that was Jimmy Rudiger before taking its exit without a bow, back into the tunnel from which it appeared, the thick door closing behind the creature.

Everyone was too stunned from what they had seen to say anything, except Richard.

"Ubertier got your tongues? I expect a minimum hundred per order from each one of you. They will be delivered to the location of your choice within a year from now but all money is required up front. Yes, the deal has changed and if you decide you want to back out now, the Ubertier is always happy to entertain more of you. So the faster I see your checkbooks the faster you can be on your way back to your corrupt regimes," instructed a gloating Richard.

Everyone was furiously writing to save their miserable lives thinking regardless of how many virgins they were promised in the next life, none were ready for a brutal death such as this.

Richard Rasmussin rubbed his hands in glee. He was becoming the richest and most powerful person on earth and the one coming to stop him was in for the surprise of his life when he would meet the mis-creation for the first and final time.

And Angel would sit at his side and watch this Ninja being humbled and ripped into pieces right in front of her eyes. And then he would do all the things he imagined to her before giving his Ubertier anoth-er tidy and delectable morsel to prey upon.

Yes he thought to himself puffing up his chest with pride *he had all the bases covered and had never even played that stupid American game.*

Chapter **79**

The flight to Boston's Logon Airport was quick and uneventful. Joseph had connections everywhere and Beantown was no exception. Mikhail was pissed to say the least that Jon-Erik had been so insistent to go with them but he could not help but admire this gnat's tenacity. Joseph had a six seat Dodge Caravan waiting for them.

The trip up the I95 to the Plum Island turnpike took just over an hour and another half hour or so on the Island. As they arrived at the large fenced off area guarded by two guard towers manned with sentries complete with formidable looking automatic weapons, they were quickly surrounded. The only one not surprised by how quickly their mini-van was surrounded by heavily armed guards was the Monster whose grin looked like he was ready for a luncheon of sentries.

"We are here to see Richard Rasmussin," snarled the Ninja at everyone and no-one in particular.

"Only you and the blonde. The others need to go back wherever they came from or they will be shot on sight," replied the guard seemingly in charge.

"Before you or your unskilled hirelings could ever squeeze the trigger, I could kill all of you," replied the Ninja with a snarl that had the guards shrink back a few steps.

"But we will comply to make things simple. On my way back, I will make sure to give you all more pain then even your feeble brains could comprehend," added the Shape Shifter.

The guards said nothing further before putting Mikhail and Angel into handcuffs and leading them away into one of the Range Rovers that had pulled up.

"We'll wait for you at the Arbor View which we passed a while back," shouted Jon-Erik. "I love you Angel—and be safe."

All Angel could do was blow back a kiss before being taken through the gates with the huge steel doors closing behind them. Joseph and Jon-Erik were escorted back to the main road before the guard detail left them to their own devices.

"Do not worry my young friend, Mikhail will bring her back for you and I pity to think what he has in store for them all. He is unstoppable," said Joseph before heading down the road to check into their quarters to wait. Jon-Erik wished he shared Joseph's optimism but what other choice did he have?

Angel and Mikhail were on their way through a maze of buildings, roads and barracks that rivaled any top notch military compound in North America, maybe even the world. Then they stopped at an even more heavily guarded checkpoint where the drivers of the vehicle and passengers were thoroughly checked for identification as Mikhail growled at the head interrogator making his buzz cut stand even further away from his otherwise melon of a head.

After passing this checkpoint and a few more twists and turns in the road, the vehicle pulled up to a massive complex which was as vast as the eye could see. The grounds around it were just barely up-kept to the minimum to ensure walking paths were kept clear and vegetation did not creep into the building structure. The Land Rover's cargo was unloaded and two huge guards came to guide the visitors to their destination.

Another thorough body search later, with Angel almost ready to show one of these guards what a snap kick to the jaw would look like, their handcuffs were removed and each were guided to rooms where they were asked to wait for further instructions.

Each room was equipped with a large queen size bed, fresh clothes made to measure with ample shower facilities, plates of fresh looking food and other libations. Richard had thought of everything, including a couple of chilled bottles of Stolichnaya Vodka in each room of which the Killer downed half before wiping his chin.

The gnat has some class which will not do him much good when I am done with him thought the Monster before taking another lusty pull of the bottle.

Angel, in the meantime, tried to prepare herself physically and mentally for the upcoming

confrontation ahead but since the food looked delicious and smelled fresh, what harm would it do to
fortify herself a bit first.

Once they had eaten and showered and changed
into the new comfortable dark blue martial arts GI's
that were set out for them, the same two guards that
led them there came to get them.

"Richard is waiting for you in the Amphi-Theatre.
Please follow us and no funny business. There are
weapons trained on your every step and although
Richard wishes to entertain you, he has given orders
to shoot on sight if you try anything."

Angel nodded and Mikhail showed no emotion
whatsoever while being led through doorways and
passageways before standing in the grand viewing
area that the late Jimmy Rudiger had become so intimately acquainted just a few days ago.

"Sit down my friends and do not look so tense,"
spoke a voice with a hint of an accent and as smooth
as silk. Angel did not even have to turn around to
know it was her hated ex-boss talking to them.

"Welcome to my humble research facility. I trust
your trip was enjoyable?" asked Richard still remaining cordial and polite.

"We finally meet. Only curiosity is keeping me
from ripping you and this facility of yours' apart," spat
the Ninja but did not move a muscle.

"There is lots of time for that my large and impatient countryman. You and Angel have been excellent adversaries and have caused myself and my
organization a lot of casualties. Very impressive what
you did in Jamaica, Toronto and Parry Sound. I have

underestimated you but all roads have led you to here."

"What are you planning to do you sick bastard? Set up some sort of combat situation for us down there?" asked Angel looking even more ferocious and gorgeous than even Richard had seen before.

"Patience, my lethal beauty. I would like to introduce you to Herr Werner Zeigler, the head scientist of my humble facility here in Building 257."

The pale gaunt German entered the room and took a seat next to his benefactor.

"Ein Vergnugen zie kennen zu lernen (pleased to meet you)," said the Researcher.

"Richard has bestowed a huge honor on both of you. You will be the first non-buyers to see our new creation which will revolutionize the way man wages war against each other!"

And before even the nimble Ninja could react, a section of the floor where Mikhail sat swallowed him up. He came up easily after his tumble into the large enclosed room below checking out his new surroundings with an appraising eye and noticeably calm demeanor.

Like a coiled spring, Angel launched herself at her hated adversary who shook her off as if she was water from a shower.

"You want to play. And I will play with you but for now we will wait and watch the show I have arranged for both of you. Unfortunately, your skillful friend here is a key part of this demonstration and you have the extreme privilege to watch as my Ubertier destroys what could up to now not be destroyed."

"Release the beast," instructed Richard.

"If my creature passes this final test and destroys our friend, he will be ready for cloning and mass production. Let the fun begin."

The Monster stood perfectly still in the middle of the large enclosed room sniffing the air and he knew what assaulted his nostrils now was not human. The other door in the room opened and nothing happened for a second or two until a flash of color streaked into the battleground. But even the blood-thirsty and highly on edge creation hesitated just for a moment, as its finely tuned senses told it this was not the usual offal it was used to tearing limb from limb. This was something that made it sit back on its large muscular haunches and study this powerful looking human now also fully focused on it before making a move.

"Good, it has sensed that this opponent is extra-ordinary and is studying him before attacking. We have never had the opportunity to see it do this until now," exclaimed the German, rubbing his hands with glee.

Angel was too transfixed by the sight below her to make any more sudden moves. She just sat there rooted to her chair watching a creation from the bowels of hell itself creeping ever so slowly up to her protector. And as if on cue, knowing this was its starring role, the Ubertier moved with incredible speed diagonally along one of the outer walls before launching itself onto the spot where the Ninja stood.

Never having seen this type of speed and ag-gression before, Mikhail could only launch himself straight up in the air to avoid the deadly teeth and talons that seemed to be flailing at thin air.

The Ninja was ready for the next attack and connected with a hammer fist so hard it would have knocked anyone or anything's head clean off. But the Ubertier rolled with the punch and slashed with a talon so fast and powerful that part of Mikhail's uniform was ripped right off his body as his mid-section ripped open exposing the tender organs underneath.

The Monster never thought the day would come where anything could best him but now the blood-lust was upon him prepared to give his own life to end this shambling thing's existence. Angel could only gasp and scream, "Mikhail!" before the creature attacked again, this time even faster and more viciously than before.

The Shape Shifters entrails were leaking onto the floor and only his iron will and incredible strength kept him from passing out. The Ubertier smelled Mikhail's blood and came in for another decapitating blow. But the beast had underestimated the mortally wounded Ninja, who pivoted to the side at the last second sustaining another massive shoulder blow from the colorful devil beast that stank like a backed up sewer and with all the strength left in his rapidly dwindling body, wrapped himself around the large neck of this Abattoir and squeezed with all his rapidly ebbing power. Richard and Herr Werner were screaming at the beast to shake his prey off and finish him and all Angel could do was hold her head and watch the incredible sight.

Chapter 80

But the Ubertier was too busy fighting for its miserable genetically given life to listen to two fools screaming at the top of their lungs from above. The Monster felt his own life flow out of him but cinched in his vice grip on the thing's neck, tighter and tighter. At first the beast was climbing the walls and smashing itself repeatedly into the enclosure and ceiling but there was no shaking off what squeezed the last gasp out of it.

The Ubertier was built to withstand assaults of all kinds but still needed air to breathe. And as it was getting none and witling away at its last air reserves, it slowed down its wild thrashings and it came down to two totally spent forms in the middle of the combat room attached to each other in one final dance of death.

When the Ubertier finally drew its last breath, the dying Mikhail extricated himself from the motionless hulk below and with a final reserve of pure will and strength, grabbed the head of the misshapen monstrosity ripping it right off its body and throwing it with all his might at the spot where Richard Rasmussin sat, not believing his own eyes as to what had just transpired.

Angel could not even look; the whole scene was just too nightmarish to comprehend. And then, with one more final defiant hand movement, the Ninja died in his own blood.

With Herr Werner, Richard and Angel all still in a trance from what just occurred below, Angel was the first one to react and it was a fatal reaction for the German who lacked the skills Richard did.

A swift and deadly kick to the throat saw the German expiring, chewing on his' own Adam's apple. And then, Angel turned her deadly stare to her tormentor.

She attacked with a banshee like scream throwing a whirlwind of kicks, punches, scratches and anything else she could muster at her hated opponent who deflected everything she threw at him with relative ease.

"So it has finally come to me and you. Your Ninja protector is dead but so is my head scientist and my Ubertier. But I have others who can carry on where he left off and I have learned much about improving our prototype even more," said Richard, after Angel had finally exhausted herself and tried to gather herself for a next attack.

But before she could spring, she felt a sharp ping in her neck and then it all went black.

"Now I will have my way with you and expose you to depravity beyond your comprehension. And then you will serve as the guinea pig that you are for our next version of the Ubertier."

With that sentiment, Richard removed the poison dart from Angel's beautiful neck and carried her off to his private chambers in the compound. Everything seemed to melt into a sea of hurt and pain for Angel after that, as she sometimes could feel the abuse and indignities heaped upon her by her cruel and sadistic captor and other times the drugs that he administered to her regularly numbed or heightened the experiences in various degrees.

When she thought she was at the end of her will, Richard unleashed a new torrent of demeaning games and atrocities and this was repeated over and over again until she could only escape to that place in her mind where there was no more pain and hurt until he came for her again and again and again.

Joseph and Jon-Erik waited at their Arbor View Guesthouse for two days and heard and saw nothing from Mikhail or Angel. They went back to the gates on the third day and were told that Richard Rasmussin would not see them again and to leave the Island because their friends were both dead.

"I swear to God I will raise an army to storm this place and bring my Angel back home!" screamed Jon-Erik at the guards who looked as if they could not care less.

Joseph tried to calm down Jon-Erik as best as he could, telling him that this place was virtually impenetrable; it was a US government protected facility and even with the shadowy resources at his command, they would not have a chance.

"We are going to have to bide our time and get Richard when he is away from this stronghold. Sooner or later, he will make a mistake and then we will have him. But now, we have to leave and be patient. I'm sorry for your loss," said Joseph before turning his vehicle around to leave this hellish Island.

After Richard Rasmussin had finally finished abusing Angel, he began to nurse her back to health for her final confrontation with the next and hopefully final phase of his Ubertier. Six months had passed and the Amphi-Theatre was once again prepped with a healthy but resigned Angel sitting in the center of the killing room awaiting her fate.

A yellow, brown and green flash of teeth, fur and talons bore down upon her as she prepared to give up her life fighting; she let out one bloodcurdling war cry like scream for the ones she lost and for herself. And then from the darkness that enveloped her, everything became a beautiful white brilliant light.

Chapter *81*

The scream coming from their bedroom now bringing in the shining light of a brand new sunny day did not seem to end, causing Jon-Erik to vault the stairs of their beautiful Lakeshore home three at a time.

He burst into the room seeing the love of his life, his fiancée the beautiful Angel sitting up in their bed bathed in sweat and screaming like he had never heard her before.

She had had some nightmares in the past, most likely due to the events of five years ago but nothing ever like this. He had decided to let her sleep as she had tossed fitfully from side to side last night and talking a lot in her sleep. *Something must be really bothering her*. He had hoped her favorite bacon, egg and pancake breakfast would cheer her up on this gorgeous sunny and cold Saturday morning.

"Angel, wake up honey, you are here in bed with me. It's a beautiful day and you are safe. Wake up honey, please," Jon-Erik pleaded.

His holding her seemed to slowly bring her back. Angel was shaking like a leaf, bathed in sweat staring straight ahead and saying, "It's coming for me!"

"What's coming for you honey, you were having a bad dream and you are safe at home with me in your own bed."

"The Ubertier!" yelled Angel.

"What the hell is an Ubertier? It sounds German."

Her eyes began to focus as she looked upon the one and only true love of her life.

"Jon-Erik!"

"Yes, hon, I am here and so are you!"

"Where am I?"

"At home honey, safe in your bed."

"At our home?"

"Yes, at our home!"

"And Tina, Guido, Joey?" asked Angel now beginning to focus more.

"They are all fine hon. It's Saturday today and we have a date to go downtown to see the new Ripley's Aquarium in a couple of hours," said Jon-Erik still mopping her brow with a damp cloth.

"You mean this was all a dream?"

"Yes and it must have been a doozy!"

"And Mikhail and the furniture shop, Rollie and oh god— poor Tina!"

"Everything is fine honey. Tina is great and so much in love with Joey. Things are going great at the shop. Rollie is keeping busy with his private eye business. As far as Mikhail goes, we have not seen him for a while but I'm sure he's just fine as well."

"Oh thank god. You wouldn't believe what I dreamt. Did I dream it? I did, I just pinched myself and it hurt!"

"Baby you don't know how much I need you," cooed Angel pulling Jon-Erik on top of her. And for the next hour they forgot about breakfast, dreams and everything else but each other.

After they were finally spent, showered and downstairs for a burnt breakfast, Angel indicated she had a tale to tell everyone tonight after they got home from the Aquarium.

"Can't wait to hear it. Should be an amazing story," said Jon-Erik in between bites.

"It is and you can bet on one thing," replied Angel.

"What's that?"

"No how, no way, are Tina and I going to that interview at FinCo next week."

"Your call honey, I'm sure I'll understand more when you tell your story tonight. Right now we have to rush to pick up Joey and Tina, we're already late."

And as the two lovebirds locked up the house and sprinted down their snowy stairs to hop into their car and pick up their two best friends, a concerned pair of hooded eyes followed their path from the shade of the side of the house.

Little do you know my talented apprentice, little do you know!

Author bio

Wolf Schimanski is a man of many interests and talents. He is trained in full-contact martial arts, enjoys a variety of sports, and is an accomplished guitarist and musician. Professionally, Schimanski has worked for many years in the information technology, management, and financial planning industries.

An avid reader turned breakthrough author, Schimanski brings his own unique spin to the action thriller genre, and has thus far released two exceptionally gripping, fast-paced works of fiction—*Meter of Deception* and *Meter of Corruption*.

Schimanski lives with his wife, Terri, near Mt. Forest, Ontario, Canada, where he is currently working on his third novel, the final installment in the Meter trilogy.

Made in the USA
Charleston, SC
18 October 2015